美国亚裔文学研究丛书
总主编　郭英剑

An Anthology of Chinese American Literature

美国华裔文学作品选

主编　郭英剑　付军岭　刘向辉

本研究受中国人民大学科学研究基金资助，系 2017 年度重大规划项目“美国亚裔文学研究”（编号：17XNLG10）阶段性成果。

中国人民大学出版社
·北京·

美国亚裔文学研究丛书
编委会

总 序

美国亚裔文学的历史、现状与未来

郭英剑

一、何为“美国亚裔文学”？

“美国亚裔文学”（Asian American Literature），简言之，是指由美国社会中的亚裔群体作家所创作的文学作品的总称。也有人称之为“亚裔美国文学”。在我国台湾学术界，更多地称为“亚美文学”。

然而，“美国亚裔文学”这个由两个核心词汇——“美国亚裔”和“文学”——所组成的术语，远没有她看上去那么简单。说她极其复杂，一点也不为过。因此，要想对“美国亚裔文学”有基本的了解，就需要从其中的两个关键词入手。

首先，“美国亚裔”中的“亚裔”，是指具有亚裔血统的美国人，但其所指并非一个单一的族裔，其组成包括了美国来自亚洲各国（或者与亚洲各国有关联）的人员群体及其后裔，比如美国华裔（Chinese Americans）、日裔（Japanese Americans）、菲律宾裔（Filipino Americans）、韩裔（Korean Americans）、越南裔（Vietnamese Americans）、印度裔（Indian Americans）、泰国裔（Thai Americans）等等。

根据联合国的统计，亚洲总计有48个国家。除此之外，还有我国的台湾地区，以及香港、澳门特别行政区。因此，所谓“美国亚裔”自然包括在美国的所有这48个亚洲国家以及我国台湾、香港、澳门社会群体的后裔，或者有其血统的人员。由此所涉及的各国（以及地区）迥异的语言、不同的文化、独特的人生体验，以及群体交叉所产生的多样性，包括亚洲各国由于战争交恶所带给后裔及其有关人员的深刻影响，就构成了“美国亚裔”这一群体具有的极端的复杂性。在美国统计局的定义中，美国亚裔细分为“东亚”（East

Asia)、“东南亚”(Southeast Asia)和南亚(South Asia)。[1] 当然,也正由于其复杂性,到现在为止有些亚洲国家在美国的后裔或者移民,尚未形成一个相对固定的族裔群体。

其次,文学主要由作家创作,由于“美国亚裔”群体的复杂性,自然导致“美国亚裔”的“作家”群体同样处于极其复杂的状态,但也因此使这一群体的概念具有相当大的包容性。凡是身在美国的亚裔后裔、具有亚洲血统或者后来移民美国的亚裔作家,都可以称之为“美国亚裔作家”。

由于亚裔群体的语言众多,加上一些移民作家的母语并非英语,因此,“美国亚裔文学”一般指的是美国亚裔作家使用英语所创作的文学作品。但由于历史的原因,学术界也把最早进入美国时,亚裔用本国语言所创作的文学作品,无论是口头还是文字作品——比如 19 世纪中期,华人进入美国时遭到拘禁时所创作的诗句,也都纳入“美国亚裔文学”的范畴之内。同时,随着全球化时代的到来,各国之间的文学与文化交流日益加强,加之移民日渐增加,因此,也将部分发表时为亚洲各国语言,但后来被翻译成英语的文学作品,也同样纳入“美国亚裔文学”的范畴。

最后,“美国亚裔”的划分,除了语言、历史、文化之外,还有一个地理因素需要考虑。随着时间的推移与学术界研究【特别是离散研究(Diaspora Studies)】的进一步深化,“美国亚裔”中的“美国”(America),也不单单指 the United States 了。我们知道,由于全球化时代所带来的人口流动性的极度增加,国与国之间的界限有时候变得模糊起来,人们的身份也变得日益具有多样性和流动性。比如,由于经济全球化的原因,美国已不单单是一个地理概念上的美国。经济与文化的构成,造就了可口可乐、麦当劳等商业品牌,它们都已经变成了流动的美国的概念。这样的美国不断在“侵入”其他国家,并对其不断产生巨大的影响。当然,一个作家的流动性,也无形中扩大了“美国”的概念。比如,一个亚洲作家可能移民到美国,一个美国亚裔作家也可能移民到其他国家。这样的流动性拓展了“美国亚裔”的定义与范畴。

为此,“美国亚裔文学”这一概念,有时候也包括一些身在美洲地区,但与美国有关联的作家用英语创作的作品,或者被翻译成英语的文学作品,也会被纳入这一范畴之内。

应该指出的是,由于“亚裔”群体进入美国的时间早晚不同,加上“亚裔”群体的复杂性,那么,每一个“亚裔”群体,都有其独有的美国族裔特征,比如华裔与日裔有所不同,印度裔与日裔也有所不同。如此一来,正如一些学者所认为的那样,各个族裔的特征最好应该分开来叙述和加以研究。[2]

---

1 参见:Karen R. Humes, Nicholas A. Jones, Roberto R. Ramirez (March 2011). “Overview of Race and Hispanic Origin: 2010” (PDF). United States Census Bureau. U.S. Department of Commerce.

2 参见:Chin, Frank, et al. “Preface” to *Aiiieeeee! An Anthology of Asian American Writers*. Edited by Frank Chin, Jeffery Paul Chan, Lawson Fusao Inada, and Shawn Wong. A Mentor Book. 1991. p.xi.

二、为何要研究"美国亚裔文学"？

虽然上文中提出，"美国亚裔"是个复杂而多元的群体，"美国亚裔文学"包含了极具多样化的亚裔群体作家，我们还是要把"美国亚裔文学"当做一个整体来进行研究。理由有三：

首先，"美国亚裔文学"与"美国亚裔作家"（Asian American Writers）最早出现时，即是作为一个统一的概念而提出。1974 年，赵健秀（Frank Chin）等学者出版了《哎咿！美国亚裔作家选集》。[3] 作为首部划时代"美国亚裔作家"的文学作品选集，该书通过发现和挖掘此前 50 年中被遗忘的华裔、日裔与菲律宾裔中的重要作家，选取其代表性作品，进而提出要建立作为独立的研究领域的"美国亚裔文学"（Asian American Literature）。[4]

其次，在亚裔崛起的过程中，无论是亚裔的无心之为，还是美国主流社会与其他族裔的有意为之，亚裔都是作为一个整体被安置在一起的。因此，亚裔文学也是作为一个整体而存在的。近年来，我国的"美国华裔文学"研究成为美国文学研究学界的一个热点。但在美国，虽然有"美国华裔文学"（Chinese American Literature）的说法，但真正作为学科存在的，则是"美国亚裔文学"（Asian American Literature），甚至更多的则是"美国亚裔研究"（Asian American Studies）。

再次，1970 年代之后，"美国亚裔文学"的发展在美国学术界逐渐成为研究的热点，引发了研究者的广泛关注。为此，旧金山州立大学、加州大学系统的伯克利分校、洛杉矶分校以及斯坦福大学率先设置了"美国亚裔研究系"（Department of Asian American Studies）或者"亚裔研究中心"，成为早期美国亚裔研究的重镇。随后包括宾夕法尼亚大学、哥伦比亚大学、布朗大学、哈佛大学、耶鲁大学等常青藤盟校在内的众多美国高校也都陆续增添了"美国亚裔研究"（Asian American Studies）专业，开设了丰富多彩的亚裔文学与亚裔研究方面的课程，教学与研究成果丰富多彩。在我国台湾地区，包括台湾"中央研究院"、台湾师范大学等在内的研究机构与高校，大都开设有亚裔文学与亚裔研究方面的课程，召开过众多的国际会议，研究成果丰富。

那么，我们需要提出的一个问题是：在中国语境下，研究"美国亚裔文学"的意义与价值究竟何在？我的看法如下：

第一，"美国亚裔文学"是"美国文学"的重要组成部分。不研究亚裔文学或者忽视甚至贬低亚裔文学，学术界对于美国文学的研究就是不完整的。如上文所说，亚裔文学的

---

3 Chin, Frank; Chan, Jeffery Paul; Inada, Lawson Fusao; Wong, Shawn. *Aiiieeeee! An Anthology of Asian-American Writers*. Howard University Press, 1974.

4 参见：Chin, Frank, et al. "Preface" to *Aiiieeeee! An Anthology of Asian American Writers*. Edited by Frank Chin, Jeffery Paul Chan, Lawson Fusao Inada, and Shawn Wong. A Mentor Book. 1991. pp.xi-xxii.

真正兴起是在20世纪六七十年代。美国六七十年代特殊的时代背景极大地促进了亚裔文学发展，自此，亚裔文学作品层出不穷，包括小说、戏剧、传记、短篇小说、诗歌等各种文学形式。在当下的美国，亚裔文学及其研究与亚裔的整体生存状态息息相关。种族、历史、人口以及政治诉求等因素促使被总称为“亚裔”的各个少数族裔联合发声，以期在美国政治领域和主流社会达到最大的影响力与辐射度。对此，学术界不能视而不见。

第二，我国现有的“美国华裔文学”研究，无法替代更不能取代“美国亚裔文学”研究。自从1980年代开始译介美国亚裔文学以来，我国国内的研究就主要集中在华裔文学领域，研究对象也仅为少数知名华裔作家及长篇小说创作领域。相较于当代国外亚裔文学研究的全面与广博，国内对于亚裔中其他族裔作家的作品关注太少。即使是那些亚裔文学的经典之作，如菲律宾裔作家卡洛斯·布洛桑（Carlos Bulosan）的《美国在我心中》（*America Is in the Heart*, 1946），日裔女作家山本久枝（Hisaye Yamamoto）的《第十七音节及其他故事》（*Seventeen Syllables and Other Stories*, 1949）、日裔约翰·冈田（John Okada）的《不—不仔》（*NO-NO Boy*, 1959），以及如今在美国文学界如日中天的青年印度裔作家裘帕·拉希莉（Jhumpa Lahiri）的作品，专题研究均十分少见。即便是像华裔作家任璧莲（Gish Jen）这样已经受到学者很大关注和研究的作家，其长篇小说之外体裁的作品同样没有得到足够的重视，更遑论国内学术界对亚裔文学在诗歌、戏剧方面的研究了。换句话说，我国学术界对于整个“美国亚裔文学”的研究来说还很匮乏，属于亟待开发的领域。实际上，在我看来，不研究“美国亚裔文学”，也无法真正理解“美国华裔文学”。

第三，在中国“一带一路”倡议与中国文化走出去的今天，作为美国文学研究的新型增长点，大力开展“美国亚裔文学”研究，特别是研究中国的亚洲周边国家如韩国、日本、印度等国在美国移民状况的文学表现，以及与华裔在美国的文学再现，使之与美国和世界其他国家以及我国台湾地区的“美国亚裔文学”保持同步发展，具有较大的理论意义与学术价值。

三、“美国亚裔文学”及其研究：历史与现状

从历史上看，来自亚洲国家的移民进入美国，可以追溯到17世纪。但真正开始较大规模的移民则是到了19世纪中后期。然而，亚裔一开始进入美国，就遭到了来自美国社会与官方的阻力与法律限制。从1880年代到1940年代这长达半个多世纪的岁月中，为了保护美国本土而出台的一系列移民法，都将亚洲各国人排除在外，禁止他们当中的大部分人进入美国大陆地区。直到20世纪40至60年代移民法有所改革时，这种状况才有所改观。其中的改革措施之一就是取消了国家配额。如此一来，亚洲移民人数才开始大规模上

升。根据2010年的美国国家统计局分析显示，亚裔是美国社会移民人数增长最快的少数族裔。[5]

“美国亚裔”实际是个新兴词汇。这个词汇的创立与诞生时间在1960年代后期。在此之前，亚洲人或者具有亚洲血统者通常被称为Oriental（东方人）、Asiatic（亚洲人）和Mongoloid（蒙古人、黄种人）。[6] 是美国历史学家市冈裕次（Yuji Ichioka）在1960年代末期，开创性地开始使用Asian American这个术语，[7] 从此，这一词汇开始被人们普遍接受和广泛使用。

与此同时，“美国亚裔文学”在随后的1970年代作为一个文学类别开始出现并逐步产生影响。1974年，有两部著作几乎同时出版，都以美国亚裔命名。一部是《美国亚裔传统：散文与诗歌选集》，[8] 另外一部则是前面提到过的《哎咿！美国亚裔作家选集》。[9] 这两部著作，将过去长期被人遗忘的亚裔文学带到了聚光灯下，让人们仿佛看到了一种新的文学形式。其后，新的亚裔作家不断涌现，文学作品层出不穷。

最初亚裔文学的主要主题与主要内容为种族（race）、身份（identity）、亚洲文化传统、亚洲与美国或者西方国家之间的文化冲突，当然也少不了性别（sexuality）、社会性别（gender）、性别歧视、社会歧视等。后来，随着移民作家的大规模出现，离散文学的兴起，亚裔文学也开始关注移民、语言、家国、全球化、劳工、战争、帝国主义、殖民主义等问题。

如果说，上述1974年的两部著作代表着亚裔文学进入美国文学的世界版图之中，那么，1982年著名美国亚裔研究专家金惠经（Elaine Kim）的《美国亚裔文学的创作及其社会语境》[10] 的出版，作为第一部学术著作，则代表着美国亚裔文学研究正式登上美国学术界的舞台。自此以后，不仅亚裔文学创作兴盛起来，亚裔文学研究也逐渐成为热点，成果不断推陈出新。

同时，人们对于如何界定“美国亚裔文学”等众多问题进行了深入的探讨，进一

---

5 参见：Wikipedia 依据“U.S. Census Show Asians Are Fastest Growing Racial Group” (NPR.org) 所得出的数据统计。https://en.wikipedia.org/wiki/Asian_Americans。

6 Mio, Jeffrey Scott, ed. (1999). *Key Words in Multicultural Interventions: A Dictionary*. ABC-Clio ebook. Greenwood Publishing Group. p.20.

7 K. Connie Kang, “Yuji Ichioka, 66; Led Way in Studying Lives of Asian Americans,” *Los Angeles Times*, September 7, 2002. Reproduced at ucla.edu by the Asian American Studies Center.

8 Wand, David Hsin-fu, ed. *Asian American Heritage: An Anthology of Prose and Poetry*. New York: Pocket Books, 1974.

9 Chin, Frank; Chan, Jeffery Paul; Inada, Lawson Fusao; Wong, Shawn. *Aiiieeeee! An Anthology of Asian-American Writers*. Howard University Press, 1974.

10 Kim, Elaine. *Asian American Literature: An Introduction to the Writings and Their Social Context*. Philadelphia: Temple University Press, 1982.

步推动了这一学科向前发展。相关问题包括：究竟谁可以说自己是美国亚裔（an Asian America）？这里的 America 是不是就是单指“美国”（the United States）？是否可以包括“美洲”（Americas）？如果亚裔作家所写的内容与亚裔无关，能否算是“亚裔文学”？如果不是亚裔作家，但所写内容与亚裔有关，能否算在“亚裔文学”之内？

总体上看，早期的亚裔文学研究专注于美国身份的建构，即界定亚裔文学的范畴，以及争取其在美国文化与美国文学中应得的席位，是 20 世纪七八十年代亚裔民权运动的前沿阵地。早期学者如赵健秀、徐忠雄（Shawn Wong）等为领军人物。随后出现的金惠经、张敬珏（King-Kok Cheung）、骆里山（Lisa Lowe）等人均成为了亚裔文学研究领域的权威学者，他 / 她们的著作影响并造就了第二代美国亚裔文学研究者。90 年代之后的亚裔文学研究逐渐淡化了早期研究中对于意识形态的侧重，开始向传统的学科分支、研究方法以及研究理论靠拢，研究视角多集中在学术马克思主义（academic Marxism）、后结构主义、后殖民、女权主义以及心理分析等。

进入 21 世纪以来，“美国亚裔文学”研究开始向多元化、全球化与跨学科方向发展。随着亚裔文学作品爆炸式的增长，来自阿富汗、印度、巴基斯坦、越南等族裔作家的作品开始受到关注，极大丰富与拓展了亚裔文学研究的领域。当代“美国亚裔文学”研究的视角与方法也不断创新，战争研究、帝国研究、跨国研究、视觉文化理论、空间理论、身体研究、环境理论等层出不穷。新的理论与常规性研究交叉进行，不但开创了新的研究领域，而且对于经典问题（例如身份建构）的研究提供了新的解读方式与方法。

四、作为课题的“美国亚裔文学”研究及其丛书

“美国亚裔文学”研究，是由我担任课题负责人的 2017 年度中国人民大学科学研究基金重大规划项目。“美国亚裔文学”研究丛书，即是该项课题的结题成果。这是国内第一套较为完整的“美国亚裔文学”方面的系列丛书，由文学史、文学作品选、文学评论集、学术论著等所组成，由我担任该丛书的总主编。

“美国亚裔文学”研究在 2017 年 4 月立项。随后，该丛书的论证计划，得到了国内外专家的一致认可。2017 年 5 月 27 日，中国人民大学科学研究基金重大规划项目“美国亚裔文学研究”开题报告会暨“美国亚裔文学研究高端论坛”在中国人民大学隆重召开。参加此次会议的专家学者全部为美国亚裔文学研究领域中的顶尖学者，包括美国加州大学洛杉矶分校的张敬珏教授、南京大学海外教育学院前院长程爱民教授、南京大学海外教育学院院长赵文书教授、北京语言大学应用外语学院院长陆薇教授、北京外国语大学潘志明教授、解放军外国语学院石平萍教授等。在此次会议上，我向与会专家介绍了该项目的基本

情况、未来研究方向与预计出版成果。与会专家对该项目的设立给予高度评价，强调在当今时代加强“美国亚裔文学”研究的必要性，针对该项目的预计研究及其成果，也提出了一些很好的建议。

根据计划，这套丛书将包括文学史2部:《美国亚裔文学史》和《美国华裔文学史》；文学选集2部:《美国亚裔文学作品选》和《美国华裔文学作品选》；批评文选2部:《美国亚裔文学评论集》和《美国华裔文学评论集》；访谈录1部:《美国亚裔作家访谈录》；美国学术论著2部（中译本）：*Articulate Silences* 和 *Chinese American Literature Without Borders*。同时，还计划出版若干学术专著和国际会议的论文集等。

根据我的基本设想，《美国亚裔文学史》和《美国华裔文学史》的撰写，将力图体现研究者对美国亚裔文学的研究进入到了较为深入的阶段。由于文学史是建立在研究者对该研究领域发展变化的总体认识上，涉及文学流派、创作方式、文学与社会变化关系、作家间的关联等各方面的问题，我们试图通过对亚裔文学发展进行总结和评价，旨在为当前亚裔文学和华裔文学的研究和推广做出一定贡献。

《美国亚裔文学作品选》和《美国华裔文学作品选》，除了记录、介绍等基本功能，还将在一定程度发挥形成民族认同、促进意识形态整合等功能。作品选编是民族共同体想象性构建的重要途径，也是作为文学经典得以确立和修正的最基本方式之一。因此，这样的作品选编，也会对美国亚裔文学的研究起到重要的促进作用。

《美国亚裔文学评论集》和《美国华裔文学评论集》，将主要选编美国、中国以及世界上最有学术价值的学术论文，虽然有些可能因为版权问题而不得不舍弃，但我们努力使之成为中国学术界研究“美国亚裔文学”和“美国华裔文学”的重要参考书目。

《美国亚裔作家访谈录》、美国学者的著作汉译、中国学者的美国亚裔文学学术专著等，我们将力图促使中美两国学者之间的学术对话，特别是希望中国的“美国亚裔文学”研究，既在中国的美国文学研究界，也在美国和世界上的美国文学研究界发出中国学者的声音。“一带一路”倡议的实施，使得文学研究的关注发生了转变，从过分关注西方话语，到逐步转向关注中国（亚洲）话语，我们的美国亚裔（华裔）文学研究，正是从全球化视角切入，思考美国亚裔（华裔）文学的世界性。

那么，我们为什么要对“美国亚裔文学”进行深入研究，并要编辑、撰写和翻译这套丛书呢?

首先，虽然“美国亚裔文学”在国外已有较大的影响，学术界也对此具有相当规模的研究，但在国内学术界，出于对“美国华裔文学”的偏爱与关注，“美国亚裔文学”相对还是一个较为陌生的领域。因此本课题首次以“亚裔”集体的形式标示亚裔文学的存在，旨在介绍“美国亚裔文学”，推介具有族裔特色和代表性的作家作品。

其次，选择“美国亚裔文学”为研究对象，其中也有对“美国华裔文学”的研究，希望能够体现我们对全球化视野中华裔文学的关注，也体现试图融合亚裔、深入亚裔文学研究的学术自觉。同时，在多元化多种族的美国社会语境中，我们力主打破国内长久以来专注“美国华裔文学”研究的固有模式，转而关注包括华裔作家在内的亚裔作家所具有的世界性眼光。

最后，顺应美国亚裔文学发展的趋势，对美国亚裔文学的研究不仅是文学研究界的关注热点，也是我国外语与文学教育的关注焦点。我们希望为高校未来“美国亚裔文学”的课程教学，提供一套高水平的参考丛书。

五、“美国亚裔文学”及其研究的未来

如前所述，“美国亚裔文学”在20世纪70年代逐渐崛起后，使得亚裔文学从沉默走向了发声。到21世纪，亚裔文学呈现出多元化的发展特征，更重要的是，许多新生代作家开始崭露头角。单就这些新的亚裔作家群体，就有许多值得我们关注的话题。

2018年6月23日，“2018美国亚裔文学高端论坛——跨界：21世纪的美国亚裔文学”在中国人民大学隆重召开。参加会议的专家学者将近150人。演讲嘉宾除了国内的美国亚裔文学研究领域中的著名专家学者外，还包括了我国台湾“中央研究院”的特聘教授、欧美研究所前所长李有成先生；我国台湾“中央研究院”特聘教授、欧美研究所前所长、华人世界著名的美国亚裔研究学者单德兴先生；我国台湾“中央研究院”副研究员、现在中央美术学院的访问教授王智明先生等。

在此次会议上，我提出来：今天，为什么要研究美国亚裔文学？我们要研究什么？

正如我们在会议通知上所说，美国亚裔文学在一百多年的风雨沧桑中历经“沉默”、“觉醒”、走向“发声”，见证了美国亚裔族群的沉浮兴衰。21世纪以来，美国亚裔文学在全球冷战思维升温和战火硝烟不断的时空背景下，不囿于狭隘的种族主义藩篱，以“众声合奏”与“兼容并蓄”之势构筑出一道跨洋、跨国、跨种族、跨语言、跨文化、跨媒介、跨学科的文学景观，呈现出鲜明的世界主义意识。为此，我们拟定了一些主要议题。包括：1. 美国亚裔文学中的跨洋书写；2. 美国亚裔文学中的跨国书写；3. 美国亚裔文学中的跨种族书写；4. 美国亚裔文学中的跨语言书写；5. 美国亚裔文学中的跨文化书写；6. 美国亚裔文学的翻译跨界研究；7. 美国亚裔文学的跨媒介研究；8. 美国亚裔文学的跨学科研究等。

事实上，21世纪以来，亚裔群体、亚裔所面临的问题、亚裔研究都发生了巨大的变化。从过去较为单纯的亚裔走向了跨越太平洋（transpacific）；从过去的彰显美国身份（claiming

America）到今天的批评美国身份（critiquing America）；过去单一的 America，现在变成了复数的 Americas，这些变化都值得引起我们的高度重视。由此所引发的诸多问题，也需要我们认真对待。比如：如何在“21 世纪”这个特殊的时间区间内去理解“美国亚裔文学”这一概念？有关“美国亚裔文学”的概念构建，是否本身就存在着作家的身份焦虑与书写的界限？如何把握“美国亚裔文学”的整体性与区域性？“亚裔”身份是否是作家在表达过程中去主动拥抱的归属之地？等等。

展望未来，随着新生代作家的迭出，“美国亚裔文学”将会呈现出更加生机勃勃的生命力，“美国亚裔文学”研究也将迎来更加光明的前途。

2018 年 8 月 28 日定稿于哈佛大学

专家推荐语

“美国亚裔文学研究丛书”包括美国亚裔文学史、美国亚裔文学作品选读、美国亚裔文学评论集、美国亚裔文学研究专著等，具有基础性、综合性、前沿性的特点。从研究范围看，将美国华裔文学研究拓展到美国亚裔文学，呈现出一幅更为完整的美国少数族裔文学版图。从研究深度看，论著作者均为美国亚裔文学研究领域著名专家，学术积累丰厚，研究水平一流。作为中国人民大学科学研究基金重大规划项目的研究成果，“美国亚裔文学研究丛书”为我们开展美国亚裔文学教学、研究、翻译提供了亟需的学术资源，有助于促进我们国家对美国文学全面深入的研究。

——王守仁，中国外国文学学会副会长、南京大学人文社会科学资深教授

This series is a groundbreaking work not just for the Asian American literary field, but for literature on the whole. As the first series of books about Asian American literature in China, it will undoubtedly inspire an unprecedented scholarly movement and bring greater and deserved awareness to issues including—but by no means limited to—gender, sexuality, and race as depicted through the lens and narratives of Asians and Asian Americans, perspectives too little seen and heard until now.

—Henry Louis Gates, Jr., Alphonse Fletcher University Professor and Director of the Hutchins Center for African and African American Research at Harvard University

Chinese American literature, for the past hundred years or so, has always straddled at least two cultures: the American and the Chinese. This ambitious and impressive series edited by Prof. Yingjian Guo brings the complex world of Chinese American writers to a broader Chinese-language readership. Such scholarship will help broaden, for Chinese scholars and students, the horizons of literary discourse and the range of appreciation for the Chinese American experience. Asian American literature, when read in a comparative light, reveals aspects of an American and Chinese American cultural terrain which spans politics, law, culture, and more. This collection will be useful for those in China, the Chinese diaspora, as well as the Americas to understand the rich linguistic, generational, political, and gendered diversity within Chinese American literature.

—RussellC. Leong, Editor of UCLA's *Amerasia Journal* (1977-2010); Author of *Phoenix Eyes and Other Stories* (The American Book Award), and; Current Editor of CUNY FORUM, for the City University of New York

美国亚裔文学研究的第一本专书 1982 年于美国出版，中文世界有关美国华裔文学的学术研究也始于 1980 年代，在接近“不惑之年”之际，实有必要盘点以往的研究成果，了解当前的学科生态，并策划未来的研究发展。郭英剑教授担任总主编的“美国亚裔文学研究丛书”，经过审慎规划，是中文世界有关此领域的第一套具规模、有系统的出版品，内容涵盖文学作品、文学评论、学术专书、文学史与访谈录等，多方位、具深度地提供有关美国亚裔文学与研究的代表作品，值得高度肯定。

——单德兴，台湾“中央研究院”欧美研究所前所长、特聘研究员

“美国亚裔文学研究丛书”涵盖面甚广，有文学创作，有文学史，有学术论著，有文学评论等，属单一领域的多元呈现，为近年来大陆出版界所少见，颇能反映大陆学术教育界在美国亚裔文学研究方面的具体成就。

——李有成，台湾“中央研究院”欧美研究所前所长、特聘研究员

“美国亚裔文学研究丛书”内容涵括文学史著作、文学作品选读、文学批评选集、学术论著，为国内第一套全面性介绍亚裔美国文学的丛书，中文学术著作之外亦有英文著作译本，具有推广文学以及搜集研究资料的双重功能，对于华语世界的亚裔美国文学研究极其重要。

——冯品佳，台湾交通大学前教务长、特聘教授

前言

“美国亚裔文学”研究，是由中国人民大学“杰出学者”特聘教授郭英剑先生担任课题负责人的2017年度中国人民大学科学研究基金重大规划项目。“美国亚裔文学研究丛书”是该项课题的结题成果，由郭英剑教授担任该套丛书的总主编。这是国内第一套较为完整的“美国亚裔文学”方面的系列丛书，由文学史、文学作品选、文学评论集、学术论著等组成。

所谓“美国华裔文学”，是指具有中国血统的美国人（即华裔）用英语创作的文学作品。这里的华裔不仅指在美国出生的本土华人，也包括在美国本土以外出生后来到美国的移民作家（包括成年之后的移民者），如裘小龙、哈·金、李翊云等。“美国华裔文学”的题材不仅仅局限于反映华裔在美国的经历，也可以是关于中国乃至世界的故事。

“美国华裔文学”无疑是“美国亚裔文学”的杰出代表，它们在短时间内取得了引人注目的成绩，成为美国少数族裔文学中的佼佼者。现在，“美国华裔文学”已经成为观察美国社会过去与现在的平台之一，使人们了解这个国家在短短历史中所发生的许多重大变化，同时作为观照，也促使我们进行自我文化反思。

中国人到美国的移民史可以追溯到19世纪中叶。今天我们能够看到的最早的华裔作家，包括19世纪后期的容闳（Yung Wing）和李恩富（Yan Phou Lee）。但华裔文学的第一位重要作家，还是非黄玉雪（Jade Snow Wong）莫属。她在1950年出版的《华女阿五》（*Fifth Chinese Daughter*）是华裔文学早期的代表作。

“美国华裔文学”在第二次世界大战之后得到了长足的发展，取得了突飞猛进的成就。其标志性事件是1976年出版的汤亭亭的《女勇士》，被誉为是华裔乃至亚裔作品中的经典之作。1970年代正是美国社会多元文化风起云涌的时代。在这样大的背景下，一批华裔作家登上了历史的舞台。这个时期的代表人物包括汤亭亭、谭恩美、赵健秀和任璧莲等。后来，包括哈·金、李翊云在内的移民作家的加入，更是壮大了美国华裔作家的队伍。

虽然“美国华裔文学”属于“美国亚裔文学”的一部分，虽然“华裔文学”在美国并不是作为一个学科存在的，然而，作为中国学者，面对众多的华裔作家及其众多的优秀文学作品，我们认为还是应该将“华裔文学”单独列出来，编写这部《美国华裔文学作品选》，从而让人们看到更多的华裔作家的风采及其更多的优秀作品。

《美国华裔文学作品选》以历史为发展脉络，精选了近30位美国华裔作家的作品，并以作家的出生年代为顺序进行编目排列。

该作品选力图反映美国华裔文学一百多年间的发展历程和变化，深刻反映抗争、身份认同与文化冲突所构成的华裔文学传统的重要议题。该作品选努力求“新”，体现更大的兼容性。我们选取了多位新生代作家（如60后谢耀、姜峯楠、张纯如，70后李翊云、刘宇昆，80后伍绮诗、黄颐铭、林韬等），以彰显华裔文学最近几十年的发展与繁荣，同时也表明华裔文学生机勃勃，后继有人。并且，对于老一代作家，不仅选其经典之作，也特意选取他们晚近的“新”作品，反映他们老骥伏枥、笔耕不辍的精神，这种精神成为华裔文学向前发展的动力。

《美国华裔文学作品选》力图体现华裔文学的新发展、新现象。为此，我们努力扩大了所选华裔文学作品的体裁范围。虽然该作品选仍然以长篇小说、短篇小说、诗歌、戏剧几大体裁为主，但就小说而言，我们还选取了侦探小说、科幻奇幻小说、儿童文学等门类，以反映华裔文学发展的整体概貌。

当然，令人遗憾的是，任何一部选集都会因为篇幅问题而难以做到面面俱到，《美国华裔文学作品选》也是如此，依旧有许多优秀的作家没有收录其中。但通过这些入选作品，大家可以按图索骥去进入更大的美国华裔文学的海洋之中。

无论如何，我们都希望《美国华裔文学作品选》能够成为中国学术界研究“美国亚裔文学”，特别是“美国华裔文学”的重要参考书目。

编　者

2018年8月28日

目录

1

(Yung Wing, 1828—1912)
容闳

作者简介

容闳（Yung Wing, 1828—1912），广东香山（今属珠海）人，著名教育家、外交家、社会活动家。1854 年毕业于耶鲁学院（耶鲁大学前身），成为首位受过完整美国教育并取得学位的中国人。1855 年回国后，曾在广州美国公使馆、香港高等审判庭、上海海关等处任职。在其不懈努力下，1872 年成功派遣首批 30 名中国幼童官费赴美留学，从而开启了中国近代留学教育的先河。1875 年被清政府任命为驻美国副公使。1876 年，耶鲁大学为表彰容闳对中美文化交流做出的贡献，授予他荣誉法学博士学位。晚年支持革命。

《西学东渐记》（*My Life in China and America*, 1909）是容闳晚年用英文撰写的一部自传体回忆录，记述了他的早期教育、赴美留学后的中学与大学生活以及归国后谋业经商、参加洋务运动和维新变法运动等种种经历，饱含着他对祖国前途命运的忧心思考与展望。痛感于故国的落后与黑暗，他自始至终强烈提倡改造中国，并为实现中国进步做出了巨大努力。1872 至 1875 年间，他先后组织了四批共 120 名中国学生赴美留学。由于保守派的掣肘与抵制，1881 年清政府撤销幼童出洋肄业局并召回留学生，致使教育计划半途而废。但是这批留美学生后来大多成为中国各个领域的骨干力量，分别在外交界、海关、军界担任重要职务，成为当时中国现代化启蒙运动的生力军。容闳为中国近代留学事业做出了卓越贡献，被誉为“中国留学生之父”。

《中国派遣留学生》（“The Chinese Educational Mission”）选自《西学东渐记》第 17 章，讲述了容闳最终得以成功派遣赴美留学生的经历。多年的夙愿终于变成现实，令他异常兴奋。他与刑部翰林陈兰彬共同主持幼童出洋肄业局。筹建留学生预备学校、规定留学生的名额、筹划留学生在国外所需经费、规定留学年限等相关事宜一一落实。1872年7月赴美为首批留学幼童安排衣食住行和就读学校。8月11日，30名中国幼童横渡太平洋前往美国留学，开创了中国历史的一个新纪元。

作品选读

My Life in China and America

Chapter 17 The Chinese Educational Mission

Taking advantage of their presence, I seized the opportunity to press my educational scheme upon the attention of Ting Yih Chang and urged him to present the subject to the Board of Commissioners of which Tsang Kwoh Fan was president. I knew Ting sympathized with me in the scheme, and I knew, too, that Tsang Kwoh Fan had been well informed of it three years before through Governor Ting. Governor Ting took up the matter in dead earnest and held many private interviews with Tsang Kwoh Fan as well as with the other members of the Commission. One evening, returning to his headquarters very late, he came to my room and awakened me and told me that Viceroy Tsang and the other Commissioners unanimously decided to sign their names conjointly in a memorial to the government to adopt my four propositions. This piece of news was too much to allow me to sleep any more that night; while lying on my bed, as wakeful as an owl, I felt as though I were treading on clouds and walking in air. Two days after this stirring piece of news, the memorial was jointly signed with Viceroy Tsang Kwoh Fan's name heading the list, and was on its way to Peking by pony express. Meanwhile, before the Board of Commissioners disbanded and Viceroy Tsang took his departure for Nanking, it was decided that Chin Lan Pin, a member of the Hanlin College, who had served twenty years as a clerk in the Board of Punishment, should be recommended by Ting to co-operate with me in charge of the Chinese Educational Commission. The ground upon which Chin Lan Pin was recommended as a co-commissioner was that he was a Han Lin and a regularly educated Chinese, and the enterprise would not be so likely to meet with the opposition it might have if I were to attempt to carry it out alone, because the scheme in principle and significance was against the Chinese theory of national education, and it would not have taken much to create a reaction to defeat the plan on account of the intense conservatism of the government. The wisdom and shrewd policy of such a move appealed to me at once, and I accepted the suggestion with pleasure and alacrity. So Chin Lan Pin was written to and came to Tientsin. The next day, after a farewell dinner had been accorded to the Board of Commissioners before it broke up, Governor Ting introduced me to Chin Lan Pin, whom I had never met before and who was to be my associate in the educational scheme. He evidently was pleased to quit Peking, where he had been cooped up in the Board of Punishment for twenty years as a clerk. He had never filled a government position in any other capacity in his life, nor did he show any practical experience in the world of business and hard facts. In his habits he was very retiring, but very scholarly. In disposition he was kindly and pleasant, but very timid and afraid of responsibilities of even a feather's weight.

In the winter of 1870, Tsang Kwoh Fan, after having settled the Tientsin imbroglio, returned to Nanking, his headquarters as the viceroy of the two Kiangs. There he received the imperial rescript sanctioning his joint memorial on the four proposals submitted through Ting Yih Chang for adoption by the government. He notified me on the subject. It was a glorious piece of news, and the Chinese educational project thus became a veritable historical fact, marking a new era in the annals of China. Tsang invited me to repair to Nanking, and during that visit the most important points connected with the mission were settled, viz.: the establishment of a preparatory school; the number of students to be selected to be sent abroad; where the money was to come from to support the students while there; the number of years they were to be allowed to remain there for their education.

The educational commission was to consist of two commissioners, Chin Lan Pin and myself. Chin Lan Pin's duty was to see that the students should keep up their knowledge of Chinese while in America; my duty was to look after their foreign education and to find suitable homes for them. Chin Lan Pin and myself were to look after their expenses conjointly. Two Chinese teachers were provided to keep up their studies in Chinese, and an interpreter was provided for the Commission. Yeh Shu Tung and Yung Yune Foo were the Chinese teachers and Tsang Lai Sun was the interpreter. Such was the composition of Chinese Educational Commission.

As to the character and selection of the students: the whole number to be sent abroad for education was one hundred and twenty; they were to be divided into four installments of thirty members each, one installment to be sent each year for four successive years at about the same time. The candidates to be selected were not to be younger than twelve or older than fifteen years of age. They were to show respectable parentage or responsible and respectable guardians.

They were required to pass a medical examination, and an examination in their Chinese studies according to regulation—reading and writing in Chinese—also to pass an English examination if a candidate had been in an English school. All successful candidates were required to repair every day to the preparatory school, where teachers were provided to continue with their Chinese studies, and to begin the study of English or to continue with their English studies, for at least one year before they were to embark for the United States.

Parents and guardians were required to sign a paper which stated that without recourse, they were perfectly willing to let their sons or protégés go abroad to be educated for a period of fifteen years, from the time they began their studies in the United States until they had finished, and that during the fifteen years, the government was not to be responsible for death or for any accident that might happen to any student.

The government guaranteed to pay all their expenses while they were being educated. It was to provide every installment with a Chinese teacher to accompany it to the United States, and to give each installment of students a suitable outfit. Such were the requirements and the organization of the student corps.

Immediately upon my return to Shanghai from Nanking after my long interview with the Viceroy, my first step was to have a preparatory school established in Shanghai for the accommodation of at least thirty students, which was the full complement for the first installment. Liu Kai Sing, who was with the Viceroy for a number of years as his first secretary in the Department of Memorials, was appointed superintendent of the preparatory school in Shanghai. In him, I found an able coadjutor as well as a staunch friend who took a deep interest in the educational scheme. He it was who prepared all the four installments of students to come to this country.

Thus the China end of the scheme was set afloat in the summer of 1871. To make up the full complement of the first installment of students, I had to take a trip down to Hong Kong to visit the English government schools to select from them a few bright candidates who had had some instruction both in English and Chinese studies. As the people in the northern part of China did not know that such an educational scheme had been projected by the government, there being no Chinese newspapers published at the time to spread the news among the people, we had, at first, few applications for entrance into the preparatory school. All the applications came from the Canton people, especially from the district of Heang Shan. This accounts for the fact that nine-tenths of the one hundred and twenty government students were from the south.

In the winter of 1871, a few months after the preparatory school had begun operations, China suffered an irreparable loss by the death of Viceroy Tsang Kwoh Fan, who died in Nanking at the ripe age of seventy-one years. Had his life been spared even a year longer, he would have seen the first installment of thirty students started for the United States—the first fruit of his own planting. But founders of all great and good works are not permitted by the nature and order of things to live beyond their ordained limitations to witness the successful developments of their own labor in this world; but the consequences of human action and human character, when once their die is cast, will reach to eternity. Sufficient for Tsang Kwoh Fan that he had completed his share in the educational line well. He did a great and glorious work for China and posterity, and those who were privileged to reap the benefit of his labor will find ample reason to bless him as China's great benefactor. Tsang, as a statesman, a patriot, and as a man, towered above his contemporaries even as Mount Everest rises above the surrounding heights of the Himalaya range, forever resting in undisturbed calmness and crowned with the purity of everlasting snow. Before he breathed his last, I was told that it was his wish that his successor and protégé, Li Hung Chang, be requested to take up his mantle and carry on the work of the Chinese Educational Commission.

Li Hung Chang was of an altogether different make-up from his distinguished predecessor and patron. He was of an excitable and nervous temperament, capricious and impulsive, susceptible to flattery and praise, or, as the Chinese laconically put it, he was fond of wearing tall hats. His outward manners were brusque, but he was inwardly kind-hearted. As a statesman he was far inferior to Tsang; as a patriot and politician, his character could not stand a moment before the searchlight of cold and impartial history. It was under such a man that the Chinese Educational Commission was launched forth.

In the latter part of the summer of 1872 the first installment of Chinese students, thirty in number, were ready to start on the passage across the Pacific to the United States. In order that they might have homes to go to on their arrival, it devolved upon me to precede them by one month, leaving Chin Lan Pin, the two Chinese teachers and their interpreter to come on a mail later. After reaching New York by the Baltimore and Ohio, via Washington, I went as far as New Haven on my way to Springfield, Mass., where I intended to meet the students and other members of the commission on their way to the East by the Boston and Albany Railroad. At New Haven, the first person I called upon to announce my mission was Prof. James Hadley. He was indeed glad to see me, and was delighted to know that I had come back with such a mission in my hands. After making my wants known to him, he immediately recommended me to call upon Mr. B. G. Northrop, which I did, Mr. Northrop was then Commissioner of Education for Connecticut. I told him my business and asked his advice. He strongly recommended me to distribute and locate the students in New England families, either by twos or fours to each family, where they could be cared for and at the same time instructed, till they were able to join classes in graded schools. This advice I followed at once. I went on to Springfield, Mass., which city I considered was the most central point from which to distribute the students in New England; for this reason I chose Springfield for my headquarters. This enabled me to be very near my friends, Dr. A. S. McClean and his worthy wife, both of whom had been my steadfast friends since 1854.

But through the advice of Dr. B. G. Northrop and other friends, I made my permanent headquarters in the city of Hartford, Conn., and for nearly two years our headquarters were located on Sumner Street. I did not abandon Springfield, but made it the center of distribution and location of the students as long as they continued to come over, which was for three successive years, ending in 1875.

In 1874, Li Hung Chang, at the recommendation of the commission, authorized me to put up a handsome, substantial building on Collins Street as the permanent headquarters of the Chinese Educational Commission in the United States. In January, 1875, we moved into our new headquarters, which was a large, double three-story house spacious enough to accommodate the Commissioners, teachers and seventy-five students at one time. It was provided with a schoolroom where Chinese was exclusively taught; a dining room, a double kitchen, dormitories and bath rooms. The motive which led me to build permanent headquarters of our own was to have the educational mission as deeply rooted in the United States as possible, so as not to give the Chinese government any chance of retrograding in this movement. Such was my proposal, but that was not God's disposal as subsequent events plainly proved.

2

(Yan Phou Lee, 1861—1938)
李恩富

作者简介

李恩富（Yan Phou Lee, 1861—1938），广东香山（今属中山）人，是第二批30名留美幼童之一。1880年考入耶鲁学院（今耶鲁大学）攻读法律。1881年清政府解散出洋肄业局，他被迫回国，后设法返美完成学业。在校期间，积极参加耶鲁的文艺社团，多次在演讲、辩论中表现出惊人的语言才华。1887年以优异成绩从耶鲁毕业。同年出版英文自传《我在中国的童年》（*When I Was a Boy in China*），这是华裔作者第一次在美国出书。后来辗转于美国多个城市，从事过农业、商务、法庭译员、新闻等工作。

当时美国社会中充斥着对中国的种种偏见，为此李恩富经常发表演讲介绍中国社会的风俗礼仪，在报纸上撰文为华人辩护，为在美华工争取权利。《我在中国的童年》对中国传统文化进行了富有文学趣味的书写，涉及中国的哲学观念、学校教育、文学传统、宗教信仰、家庭伦理、节日庆典、饮食文化、休闲娱乐等各个方面，重塑了正面的华人形象，对修正美国人对中国的种族偏见和种族歧视有着重要意义。1889年，李恩富在《北美评论》（*North American Review*）发表了著名文章《中国人必须留下》（"The Chinese Must Stay"），对美国《排华法案》进行抨击。

《女孩子们》（"Girls of My Acquaintance"）选自《我在中国的童年》第5章。许多美国人是通过报纸和别人的旅行见闻来了解中国的，以讹传讹的情况时有发生。中国人很注重血缘关系和宗族观念，家族成员间的相互扶持与帮助十分普遍。女孩子并没有一出生就被扼杀在襁褓中。虽然中国有重男轻女的习俗，但大部分家庭生了女孩也会举行庆祝仪式。

通过这些描写，可以看出作者在努力消除美国人对华人的误解，消除因种族、文化差异而形成的鸿沟。《中国人必须留下》选自同名文章。作者陈述了华工遭受的不平等待遇，呼吁美国政府不要违背其尊崇自由、平等的立国原则，驳斥了反对华人的流行观念。

作品选读

When I Was a Boy in China

Chapter V Girls of My Acquaintance (Excerpt)

I STILL continually find false ideas in America concerning Chinese customs, manners, and institutions. Small blame to the people at large, who have no means of learning the truth except through newspapers or accounts of travellers who do not understand what they see in passing through our country. From the time of Sir John Mandeville, travellers (with a few noble exceptions) have vied with each other in relating the most wonderful stories about our ancient empire. Accordingly, what I tell in this series of article about Chinese customs, manners and institutions may often contradict general belief.

There is far less of truth told about the "fair section" of the Chinese people than of the sterner sex, because far less is known. What I myself propose to tell is chiefly derived from daily observation of the female members of my family and those of my kindred. Very distant relatives are recognized in China; a man prides himself upon the large number of his connections as well as upon the influence his family exert in the community on account of wealth or position. A "poor relation" there is treated with much more consideration and affection than in this country. Generosity towards that class of unfortunates is so common, and its practice is so strenuously insisted upon, in the moral code of the Chinese, that it almost ceases to be an individual virtue — it is a national virtue.

Of the numerous cousins, aunts and other fair relatives that fell to my earthly lot several lived in the same house with us, under the superintendence of my grandmother, as I have before said; there were two aunts who were then too young to marry, two aunts by marriage, and three young cousins in the house. Then on the same street dwelt about thirty or forty families, all related to us by blood, whose female members it was my privilege, as a relative and as a youngster, to see often. I assure you they comprised among them girls of all sorts of tempers and characters. The gentle, refined and modest stood side by side with the rough, uncultured and forward. There were good-looking ones, and there were homely ones.

Let me add that these girls had not been "killed during their infancy." I am indignant that there should be a popular belief in America that Chinese girls at their birth are generally put to death because they are not wanted by their parents. Nothing can be further from the truth. In a country like China, where women do not appear in public life, it must follow that sons are more to be desired, for the very good reasons that family honor and glory depend on them and ancestral worship necessitates either the birth or adoption of sons to perpetuate it. I venture to say that in proportion to population and distribution of wealth that infanticide is as rare in China as it is in this country. Extremely poor people, finding it hard to keep even themselves alive, often prefer to "make way" with their babies rather than see them slowly starve to death. With them, girl-babies are more often sacrificed because boys are readily adopted by rich and childless persons, while the female infants rarely can be thus provided for. But let it be understood that there are established in every goodsized town infant hospitals in which these waifs are kept and brought up with care by means of funds furnished by good people. The same ceremonies of christening are observed with girl babies, and though relatives may growl, they nevertheless bring the customary presents of cloth, jewelry and pigs' feet.

In spite of the restraint all Chinese children are subject to, we little boys and girls used to have good times together. Among the boys were two brothers of mine and a whole troop of cousins of whom five were about my age. We used to play cat's-cradle, puss-in-the-corner, jack-straws and jack-stones, the girls (all the way from four to eight years of age) taking as much interest in the games as we did. Of course at any time when the gentlemen of the family were present, we used to sit as quiet as mice and as demure as monks and nuns.

In those games which depend on dexterity and activity, we boys were winners; but when it came to games demanding skill, patience, quick wit and delicacy of touch, we were distanced by the girls.

Many a quarrel did we have as points of dispute came up; and often one of our set would not speak to another, or would even cut the whole of us for days together on account of some unfair play. Those little tiffs seemed to be of momentous importance then. But the boy whose heart swells with indignation at that which offends his sense of justice is likely to grow up a true man after all.

But our chief amusement and delight was to hear stories; especially those about fairies and ghosts. Oh! the blood-curdling stories that we were privileged to hear. They were enough to set anybody's teeth a-chattering and to stand his hair on end. They were always told in a low, sepulchral tone of voice, and the lamps were turned down, which very much heightened the artistic effect. We were also entertained with healthful anecdotes, such as scraps of history or biographical sketches of China's great men and famous women. But when we coaxed "real hard," we could generally get someone to tell us stories of goblins, imps that haunted the forests, spectres that dwelt in old coffins, and witches and fairies that were good to those who pleased them. After listening to a glowing account of their antics and deeds, good or mischievous, it was useless to attempt making me go to bed alone or without a light. Even when someone accompanied me with a light, I never felt safe until I had covered my head with the bedclothes. That superstitious dread haunts me yet, especially when walking alone in the dark. I think it is impossible that I shall ever outgrow it.

The Chinese Must Stay

(Excerpt)

No Nation can afford to let go its high ideals. The founders of the American Republic asserted the principle that all men are created equal, and made this fair land a refuge for the whole world. Its manifest destiny, therefore, is to be the teacher and leader of nations in liberty. Its supremacy should be maintained by good faith and righteous dealing, and not by the display of selfishness and greed....

How far this Republic has departed from its high ideal and reversed its traditionary policy may be seen in the laws passed against the Chinese.

Chinese immigrants never claimed to be any better than farmers, traders, and artisans. If, on the one hand, they are not princes and nobles, on the other hand, they are not coolies and slaves. They all came voluntarily, as their consular papers certified, and their purpose in leaving their home and friends was to get honest work. They were told that they could obtain higher wages in America than elsewhere, and that Americans were friendly to the Chinese and invited them to come. In this they were confirmed by certain provisions of the treaties made between China and the United States, by which rights and privileges were mutually guaranteed to the citizens of either country residing in the other. No one can deny that the United States made all the advances, and that China came forth from her seclusion because she trusted in American honor and good faith.

So long as the Chinese served their purposes and did not come into collision with the hoodlum element afterwards imported to California, the people of that State had nothing to complain of regarding them. Why should they, when, at one time, half the revenue of the State was raised out of the Chinese miners? But the time came when wages fell with the cost of living. The loafers became strong enough to have their votes sought after. Their wants were attended to. Their complaints became the motive power of political activity. So many took up the cry against the Chinese that it was declared that no party could succeed on the Pacific coast which did not adopt the hoodlums' cause as its own....

It has been urged:

I. That the influx of Chinese is a standing menace to Republican institutions upon the Pacific coast and the existence there of Christian civilization.

That is what I call a severe reflection on Republican institutions and Christian civilization. Republican institutions have withstood the strain of 13,000,000 of the lower classes of Europe, among whom may be found Anarchists, Socialists, Communists, Nihilists, political assassins, and cut-throats; but they cannot endure the assaults of a few hundred thousands of the most peaceable and most easily-governed people in the world!...

IV. That the Chinese have displaced white laborers by low wages and cheap living, and that their presence discourages and retards white immigration to the Pacific States.

This charge displays so little regard for truth and the principles of political economy that it seems like folly to attempt an answer. But please to remember that it was by the application of Chinese "cheap labor" to the building of railroads, the reclamation of swamp-lands, to mining, fruit-culture, and manufacturing, that an immense vista of employment was opened up for Caucasians, and that millions now are enabled to live in comfort and luxury where formerly adventurers and desperadoes disputed with wild beasts and wilder men for the possession of the land. Even when the Chinaman's work is menial (and he does it because he must live, and is too honest to steal and too proud to go to the almshouse), he is employed because of the scarcity of such laborers.... You may as well run down machinery as to sneer at Chinese cheap labor.

Machines live on nothing at all; they have displaced millions of laborers; why not do away with machines?....

V. That the Chinese do not desire to become citizens of this country.

Why should they? Where is the inducement? [Yan Phou Lee recited the laws discriminating against Chinese to argue they have not been encouraged to become citizens.]... Are you sure that the Chinese have no desire for the franchise? Some years ago, a number of those living in California, thinking that the reason why they were persecuted was because it was believed they cared nothing for American citizenship, made application for papers of naturalization. Their persecutors were alarmed and applied to Congress for assistance, and the California Constitution was amended so as to exclude them....

VII. The Chinese neither will have intercourse with Caucasians nor will assimilate with them.

Yes, just think of it! As soon as the ship comes into harbor, a committee of the citizens gets on board to present the Chinaman with the freedom of the city (valued at $5). A big crowd gathers at the wharf to receive him with shouts of joy (and showers of stones). The aristocrats of the place flock to his hotel to pay their respects (and to take away things to remember him by). He is so feted and caressed by Caucasian society that it is a wonder his head is not turned (or twisted off)....

Such are the charges made against the Chinese. Such were the reasons for legislating against them;—and they still have their influence, as is shown by the utterances of labor organs; by the unreasoning prejudice against the Chinese which finds lodgment in the minds of the people; and by the periodical outbreaks and outrages perpetuated against them without arousing the public conscience.

3

(Edith Maude Eaton, 1865—1914)

伊迪丝·莫德·伊顿

作者简介

伊迪丝·莫德·伊顿（Edith Maude Eaton, 1865—1914），笔名水仙花（Sui Sin Far），出生在英国，经过在中国、欧洲、加拿大和牙买加等地的逗留或生活，她最终在美国定居，安度了晚年。她一生创作颇丰，被认为是“最早的美国亚裔作家之一”。

她的主要作品有：自传体回忆录《一个欧亚混血儿的心理档案》（*Leaves from the Mental Portfolio of an Eurasian*, 1909）；短篇小说《中国以实玛利》（*A Chinese Ishmael*, 1899）、《秋扇》（*An Autumn Fan*, 1910）、《爱之鸟》（*The Bird of Love*, 1910）、《中国稻田里的爱情故事》（*A Love Story from the Rice Fields of China*, 1911）等；短篇小说集《春香夫人与其他故事》（*Mrs. Spring Fragrance and Other Writings*, 1912）。

伊顿的所有作品中，短篇小说集《春香夫人与其他故事》是她最为经典、最具有代表性的作品，被誉为“最早的一部在美国出版的，由华人和白人混血作家创作的小说”。这部短篇小说集由“春香夫人”（*Mrs. Spring Fragrance*）和“中国儿童故事”（*Tales of Chinese Children*）两个故事集组成。这些故事主要描写了华裔家庭的喜怒哀乐以及中西文化之间的矛盾冲突，淋漓尽致地再现了华裔移民在两种文化夹缝中的困惑与挣扎。

《春香夫人》（“Mrs. Spring Fragrance”）与《在自由的国度》（“In the Land of the Free”）选自短篇小说集《春香夫人》。《春香夫人》虽然在一定程度上塑造了华裔被“同化”的形象，但却开创性地对华裔的“正面”形象进行关注，颠覆了西方世界固有的“东方主义”观念。《在自由的国度》的题目出自美国国歌《星条旗永不落》，故事却通过描绘一个华裔家庭悲剧，对美国的立国之本进行辛辣讽刺。这两个故事共同表达了华裔移民对“美国梦”的追求以及中西文化之间的不相容性。

作品选读

Mrs. Spring Fragrance
(Excerpt)

Mr. SPRING FRAGRANCE was walking to business with Mr. Chin Yuen. As they walked they talked.

"Yes," said Mr. Chin Yuen, "the old order is passing away, and the new order is taking its place, even with us who are Chinese. I have finally consented to give my daughter in marriage to young Kai Tzu."

Mr. Spring Fragrance expressed surprise. He had understood that the marriage between his neighbor's daughter and the San Francisco school-teacher's son was all arranged.

"So' twas," answered Mr. Chin Yuen; "but it seems the young renegade, without consultation or advice, has placed his affections upon some untrustworthy female, and is so under her influence that he refuses to fulfil his parents' promise to me for him."

"So!" said Mr. Spring Fragrance. The shadow on his brow deepened.

"But," said Mr. Chin Yuen, with affable resignation, "it is all ordained by Heaven. Our daughter, as the wife of Kai Tzu, for whom she has long had a loving feeling, will not now be compelled to dwell with a mother-in-law and where her own mother is not. For that, we are thankful, as she is our only one and the conditions of life in this Western country are not as in China. Moreover, Kai Tzu, though not so much of a scholar as the teacher's son, has a keen eye for business and that, in America, is certainly much more desirable than scholarship. What do you think?"

"Eh! What!" exclaimed Mr. Spring Fragrance. The latter part of his companion's remarks had been lost upon him.

That day the shadow which had been following Mr. Spring Fragrance ever since he had heard his wife quote, "'Tis better to have loved," etc., became so heavy and deep that he quite lost himself within it.

At home in the evening he fed the cat, the bird, and the flowers. Then, seating himself in a carved black chair—a present from his wife on his last birthday—he took out his pipe and smoked. The cat jumped into his lap. He stroked it softly and tenderly. It had been much fondled by Mrs. Spring Fragrance, and Mr. Spring Fragrance was under the impression that it missed her. "Poor thing!" said he. "I suppose you want her back!" When he arose to go to bed he placed the animal carefully on the floor, and thus apostrophized it:

"O Wise and Silent One, your mistress returns to you, but her heart she leaves behind her, with the Tommies in San Francisco."

The Wise and Silent One made no reply. He was not a jealous cat.

Mr. Spring Fragrance slept not that night; the next morning he ate not. Three days and three nights without sleep and food went by.

There was a springlike freshness in the air on the day that Mrs. Spring Fragrance came home. The skies overhead were as blue as Puget Sound stretching its gleaming length toward the mighty Pacific, and all the beautiful green world seemed to be throbbing with springing life.

Mrs. Spring Fragrance was never so radiant.

"Oh," she cried light-heartedly, "is it not lovely to see the sun shining so clear, and everything so bright to welcome me?"

Mr. Spring Fragrance made no response. It was the morning after the fourth sleepless night.

Mrs. Spring Fragrance noticed his silence, also his grave face.

"Everything—everyone is glad to see me but you," she declared, half seriously, half jestingly.

Mr. Spring Fragrance set down her valise. They had just entered the house.

"If my wife is glad to see me," he quietly replied, "I also am glad to see her!"

Summoning their servant boy, he bade him look after Mrs. Spring Fragrance's comfort.

"I must be at the store in half an hour," said he, looking at his watch. "There is some very important business requiring attention."

"What is the business?" inquired Mrs. Spring Fragrance, her lip quivering with disappointment.

"I cannot just explain to you," answered her husband.

Mrs. Spring Fragrance looked up into his face with honest and earnest eyes. There was something in his manner, in the tone of her husband's voice, which touched her.

"Yen," said she, "you do not look well. You are not well. What is it?"

Something arose in Mr. Spring Fragrance's throat which prevented him from replying.

"O darling one! O sweetest one!" cried a girl's joyous voice. Laura Chin Yuen ran into the room and threw her arms around Mrs. Spring Fragrance's neck.

"I spied you from the window," said Laura, "and I couldn't rest until I told you. We are to be married next week, Kai Tzu and I. And all through you, all through you—the sweetest jade jewel in the world!"

Mr. Spring Fragrance passed out of the room.

"So the son of the Government teacher and little Happy Love are already married," Laura went on, relieving Mrs. Spring Fragrance of her cloak, her hat, and her folding fan.

Mr. Spring Fragrance paused upon the doorstep.

"Sit down, Little Sister, and I will tell you all about it," said Mrs. Spring Fragrance, forgetting her husband for a moment.

When Laura Chin Yuen had danced away, Mr. Spring Fragrance came in and hung up his hat.

"You got back very soon," said Mrs. Spring Fragrance, covertly wiping away the tears which had begun to fall as soon as she thought herself alone.

"I did not go," answered Mr. Spring Fragrance. "I have been listening to you and Laura."

"But if the business is very important, do not you think you should attend to it?" anxiously queried Mrs. Spring Fragrance.

"It is not important to me now," returned Mr. Spring Fragrance. "I would prefer to hear again about Ah Oi and Man You and Laura and Kai Tzu."

"How lovely of you to say that!" exclaimed Mrs. Spring Fragrance, who was easily made happy. And she began to chat away to her husband in the friendliest and wifeliest fashion possible. When she had finished she asked him if he were not glad to hear that those who loved as did the young lovers whose secrets she had been keeping, were to be united; and he replied that indeed he was; that he would like every man to be as happy with a wife as he himself had ever been and ever would be.

"You did not always talk like that," said Mrs. Spring Fragrance slyly. "You must have been reading my American poetry books!"

"American poetry!" ejaculated Mr. Spring Fragrance almost fiercely, "American poetry is detestable, abhorrable!",

"Why! why!" exclaimed Mrs. Spring Fragrance, more and more surprised.

But the only explanation which Mr. Spring Fragrance vouchsafed was a jadestone pendant.

In the Land of the Free

III

(Excerpt)

THE winter rains were over: the spring had come to California, flushing the hills with green and causing an everchanging pageant of flowers to pass over them. But there was no spring in Lae Choo's heart, for the Little One remained away from her arms. He was being kept in a mission. White women were caring for him, and though for one full moon he had pined for his mother and refused to be comforted he was now apparently happy and contented. Five moons or five months had gone by since the day he had passed with Lae Choo through the Golden Gate; but the great Government at Washington still delayed sending the answer which would return him to his parents.

Hom Hing was disconsolately rolling up and down the balls in his abacus box when a keen-faced young man stepped into his store.

"What news?" asked the Chinese merchant.

"This!" The young man brought forth a typewritten letter. Hom Hing read the words:

"Re Chinese child, alleged to be the son of Hom Hing, Chinese merchant, doing business at 425 Clay street, San Francisco.

"Same will have attention as soon as possible."

Hom Hing returned the letter, and without a word continued his manipulation of the counting machine.

"Have you anything to say?" asked the young man.

"Nothing. They have sent the same letter fifteen times before. Have you not yourself showed it to me?"

"True!" The young man eyed the Chinese merchant furtively. He had a proposition to make and he was pondering whether or not the time was opportune.

"How is your wife?" he inquired solicitously—and diplomatically.

Hom Hing shook his head mournfully.

She seems less every day," he replied. "Her food she takes only when I bid her and her tears fall continually. She finds no pleasure in dress or flowers and cares not to see her friends. Her eyes stare all night. I think before another moon she will pass into the land of spirits."

"No! " exclaimed the young man, genuinely startled.

"If the boy not come home I lose my wife sure," continued Hom Hing with bitter sadness.

"It's not right," cried the young man indignantly. Then he made his proposition.

The Chinese father's eyes brightened exceedingly.

"Will I like you to go to Washington and make them give you the paper to restore my son?" cried he. "How can you ask when you know my heart's desire?"

"Then, said the young fellow, "I will start next week. I am anxious to see this thing through if only for the sake of your wife's peace of mind."

"I will call her. To hear what you think to do will make her glad," said Hom Hing.

He called a message to Lae Choo upstairs through a tube in the wall.

In a few moments she appeared, listless, wan, and hollow-eyed; but when her husband told her the young lawyer's suggestion she became as one electrified; her form straightened, her eyes glistened; the color flushed to her cheeks.

"Oh," she cried, turning to James Clancy, "You are a hundred man good!"

The young man felt somewhat embarrassed; his eyes shifted a little under the intense gaze of the Chinese mother.

"Well, we must get your boy for you, " he responded. "Of course" —turning to Hom Hing— "it will cost a little money. You can't get fellows to hurry the Government for you without gold in your pocket."

Hom Hing stared blankly for a moment. Then: "How much do you want, Mr. Clancy?" he asked quietly.

"Well, I will need at least five hundred to start with."

Hom Hing cleared his throat.

"I think I told to you the time I last paid you for writing letters for me and seeing the Custom boss here that nearly all I had was gone!"

"Oh, well then we won't talk about it, old fellow. It won't harm the boy to slay where he is, and your wife may get over it all right."

"What that you say?" quavered Lae Choo.

James Clancy looked out of the window.

"He says," explained Hom Hing in English, "that to get our boy we have to have much money."

4

(*Island: Poetry and History of Chinese Immigrants on Angel Island*,1910—1940)

《埃仑诗集》无名氏集体作者

作者简介

1910至1940年间，大约有17.5万名主要自广东珠三角一带申请入境美国的华人移民曾被留置关押在位于旧金山湾的天使岛（Angel Island），等候移民官甄别其入境资格。华人移民在拘留所木屋留下了大量的旧体诗文题壁之作。遗憾的是这些诗作并没有明确的作者，只能从墙上看到"台邑李镜波题""玉清氏作台山溏溪""台山　南村李海题""石宁题""未已处孟夏谷题""亚程"等。当然，是否就是作者本人，仍无从审定。少数作者则冠以姓氏、地名或年月，如"香山人题""香山许生勉客题""台山余题""阮题""香山许生自慰题""香山题"。

1980年，天使岛移民后裔麦礼谦（Him Mark Lai）、林小琴（Genny Lim）、杨碧芳（Judy Yung）等三人将这些文字整理、校订、编译成中英双语文本《埃仑诗集》(*Island: Poetry and History of Chinese Immigrants on Angel Island,* 1910—1940)出版，成为迄今"天使岛诗歌"研究最重要的文本。从内容上看，这些诗歌可以分为思乡情怀、壮志未酬、忧国忧民、无奈苦闷、满腔仇恨、囚居生活和典故、神话传说及历史人物故事等类别。作为美国华裔文学的早期文本，也是北美华文文学的拓荒性文本，埃仑诗歌堪称一群早期"新移民"碰撞在与中国现实迥然不同且遭受排斥的西方语境里之困厄灵魂的悲歌。本章节选的五首无题诗歌均是早期华裔移民灵魂悲歌的生动再现。

作品选读

Island: Poetry and History of Chinese Immigrants on Angel Island, 1910–1940

Poem 1

Imprisoned in this wooden building, I am always sad and bored.
I remember since I left my native village, it has been several full moons.
The family at home is leaning on the door, urgently looking for letters.
Whom can I count on to tell them I am well?

困囚木屋常愁闷;
忆别家乡月几圆。
家人倚望音书切;
凭谁传语报平安?

Poem 2

On a long voyage I travelled across the sea.
Feeding on wind and sleeping on dew, I tasted hardships.
Even though Su Wu was detained among the barbarians, he would one day return home.
When he encountered a snow storm, Wengong sighed, thinking of bygone years.
In days of old, heroes underwent many ordeals.
I am, in the end, a man whose goal is unfulfilled
Let this be an expression of the torment which fills my belly.
Leave this as a memento to encourage fellow souls.

梯航远涉历重洋,
风餐露宿苦自赏。
苏武沦胡归有日,
文公遇雪叹当年。
自古英雄多磨折,
到底男儿志未伸。

满腹苦衷聊代表，
留为纪念励同魂。

Poem 3

I lean on the railing and lift my head to look at the cloudy sky.
All the mountains and rivers are dark.
Eastern Mongolia is lost and the date of her return is uncertain.
The recovery of the Central Plains depends on the youth.
Only the tongue of Changshan can slay the villainous.
To kill the bandit we must wave the whip of Zu Di.
I am ashamed to be curled up like a worm on Island.
I grieve for my native land but what else can I say?

凭栏翘首望云天，
一片山河尽黯然。
东蒙失陷归无日，
中原恢复赖青年。
诛奸惟有常山舌，
杀贼须扬祖逖鞭。
忆我埃仑如蜷伏，
伤心故国复何言。

Poem 4

Crude Poem Inspired by the Landscape

The ocean encircles a lone peak.
Rough terrain surrounds this prison.
There are few birds flying over the cold hills.
The wild goose messenger cannot find its way.
I have been detained and obstacles have been put my way for half a year.
Melancholy and hate gather on my face.
Now that I must return to my country,
I have toiled like the *jingwei* bird in vain.

感景拙咏

沧海园孤峰，
崎岖困牢笼。
鸟疏寒山致，

鸿使莫寻踪。
留难经半载，
愁恨积满容。
今将归国去，
空劳精卫功。

Poem 5

When a newcomer arrives in America,
He will surely be seized and put in the wooden building.
Like a major criminal,
I have already been here one autumn.
The Americans refused me admission;
I have been barred and deported back.
Alongside the ship, the waves are huge.
Returning to the motherland is truly distressing.
We Chinese of a weak nation,
Sigh bitterly at the lack of freedom.
The day our nation becomes strong,
I swear we will cut off the barbarians' heads.

新客到美洲；
必逮入木楼。
俨如大犯样；
在此经一秋。
美国人不准；
批消拨回头。
船中波浪大；
回国实堪忧。
国弱我华人；
苦叹不自由。
我国豪强日；
誓斩胡人头。

5

(Louis Chu, 1915—1970)
雷霆超

作者简介

雷霆超（Louis Chu, 1915—1970），广东台山人。九岁时随家人移居美国新泽西州。1940 年毕业于纽约大学，获得社会学硕士学位。第二次世界大战期间曾在驻扎于中国云南的美国通讯兵团服役。他是纽约市颇受欢迎的电台主持人和社会福利工作者，在华人社区十分活跃。自 1952 年起的十年间主持过一档每天（周末除外）90 分钟的《中华节日》电台节目，有新闻、访谈、广告，还播放中国音乐，很受洗衣工人和餐馆工人喜爱。1961 年发表长篇小说《吃碗茶》（*Eat a Bowl of Tea*）。

《吃碗茶》是美国华裔文学中的开创性作品，不过当年出版后并未受到多大关注。1970 年代初赵健秀等一批美国亚裔学者重新发现此书并编入他们的《哎咿！美国亚裔作家选集》，称赞它是真实描写唐人街生活的"第一部美国华裔小说"。故事背景设在第二次世界大战后的纽约唐人街，围绕宾来和美爱的婚姻展开。19 世纪后期美国反华浪潮十分猖獗。1882 年美国国会通过《排华法案》，除了少数豁免阶层外，禁止华人移民美国，直到 1943 年该法案才宣告废除。在此期间，已婚华人无法与中国的妻儿团聚。由于华人女性数量稀少，造成华人社区男女比例严重失衡，形成了唐人街畸形的单身汉群体。第二次世界大战之后至小说出版的年代，美国移民法已有所松动。到 1961 年《吃碗茶》出版时，华人社区的面貌已大为改观。《吃碗茶》忠实描述了变化前夕的纽约华人单身汉社会，以现实主义笔触对其优点和缺点进行了刻画，并在文字上再现了唐人街华人生动的语言。年轻一代女性美爱的到来，为唐人街带来了改变，虽然不尽完美，但仍然带来了希望之光。

下面选文选自《吃碗茶》第 2 章。故事场景是在王华基开的麻将室里。华人受到种族歧视性法规的限制，无法参与美国主流的经济、文化生活，大多靠经营餐馆、洗衣店、麻将室为生。他们的生活圈也局限在这些地方，下班后去看看戏、看场电影或聚在麻将室赌几个小钱。麻将室里也是人们传播流言蜚语的地方。阿桑是一位中年单身汉，模样也好看，很有女人缘，风流韵事不断，为后文他勾引美爱埋下了伏笔。

作品选读

Eat a Bowl of Tea

Ⅱ

(Excerpt)

One Saturday several months before the wedding, the day had broken humid and muggy. Heavy rain had splashed the side-walks of New York intermittently during the night. The month of May had just ended. Chong Loo, the rent collector, hobbled down the flight of stairs to the Money Come club house in the basement at 87 Mott Street in New York's Chinatown.

"No money!" Wang Wah Gay, the proprietor, greeted the agent as he came through the door. "Wow your mother. No money today. You come back."

"All right, uncle, all right," said Chong Loo. "I'll be back on the fifteenth." He started to leave. Then he stopped abruptly, with one hand on the door knob. When he turned his head, he gave the impression of having a stiff neck; his whole body swung with it. "Did you see the pugilist master at the Sun Young Theater last night?" he grinned, showing his new set of teeth. The last time he had come around he had not a single tooth.

"Wow your mother," said Ah Song, a hanger-on at the club house. "Go sell your ass."

"Did you hear about the fight last night between a Lao Lim and a Lao Ying in front of the Lotus Tea Shop? This Lao Lim accused Lao Ying of taking his wife out."

"Wow your mother. Why don't you go and die?" said Ah Song, looking up from his newspaper, the Chinese COMPASS, at the mah-jong table.

"Later on the police came and separated the two men," Chong Loo continued. "Heh heh.

Women nowadays are not to be trusted."

If the rent collector weren't so old, people might mistake him for a student, with his ever-present brief case. His head was big at the top and tapered off almost to a point at the chin. He had no hair on the dome, but sparsely-scattered long black hair mixed with grey on the circumference.

"Remember a year ago some Lao Tsuey ran down to South Carolina with Lao Ning's wife? She's the niece of the president of the Bank of Kwai Chow," Chong Loo persisted. "Have you heard the latest about…?"

"Wow your mother," said Ah Song, this time a little louder than before.

Across from Ah Song, sitting on the couch, the proprietor, Wang Wah Gay, smiled his agreement. "You many-mouthed bird, go sell your ass."

"Heh heh. See you on the fifteenth, Mr. Wang."

His stooped shoulders and large head and brief case disappeared out the door and he began mounting the steep steps that led to the sidewalk. Wah Gay, from his half-reclining position on the sofa, could follow his exit until the rent collector's unpressed pants gradually ascended out of sight.

"Wow his mother," exclaimed Wah Gay, stretching himself. "He never fails to show up on the first of the month. You don't have to look at the calendar. When he arrives, you know it's the first." He crossed his legs and flicked the ash from his cigar on the tray.

"Chong Loo is all right," said Ah Song. He turned another page of the Chinese COMPASS. The circle of light from the overhanging lamp played on the newspaper. "Wow your mother. That's his job. It's his responsibility to show up on the first of every month to collect rent. Maybe he is a many-mouthed bird but he works for a living."

Ah Song let the newspaper drop flat on the table. Usually he read with glasses, but today he had been looking at the big letters in the advertisements. "Wow your mother, Wah Gay, do you think he's like you, never worked in your life?"

They both chuckled. "You dead boy," said Wah Gay. "You're still young yet. Why don't *you* go to work?"

"Who, me? I've worked more than you ever hope to work, you sonavabitch." Ah Song was a youthful-looking man in his mid-forties, with just a touch of grey at the temples. His neatly combed black hair had the effect of a crew-cut. A white handkerchief always adorned his breast pocket. Even on the hottest days he would never roll up his shirt sleeves or be caught without a necktie.

"When did *you* ever work?" replied Wah Gay. "I've known you for almost twenty years." He pointed a finger at Ah Song. "You sonavabitch, if you ever worked at all, you must have worked when you were a mere boy. Ever since I've known you, you haven't done a single day's work."

"Shut up your mouth. Do I have to tell you when I go to work?"

The basement club house was cool. Compared to the heat and humidity of the street, it was a refreshing paradise. The sudden intensity of the early summer heat had caught everyone unprepared. A few days before, it had been so damp and chilly and windy that Wah Gay had to turn on the gas heater.

The door creaked open.

"Nice and cool here," said the newcomer. He turned and made sure the door closed tight.

"Thought you went to the race track," said Wah Gay.

"I overslept," replied the man. "Might just as well. On a day like this." He looked around the room. "Where is everybody? Still early, huh?" He walked over to an easy chair in the corner and sat down. He took out a cigar and lit it. "you know, on a day like this, I think this is the best place in the city. Nice and cool, with natural air conditioning."

Lee Gong was slight of build, with silvery black hair. He continued puffing on the Admiration which had been given him at a banquet the night before. He and Wah Gay had come over to America from China on the *President Madison* together and had shared the confined quarters of Ellis Island as two teen-age immigrants many springs ago.

In his early days in the United States, Lee Gong worked in various laundries in New York. Later he, himself, owned one in the Bronx. In 1928, he went back to China. He remained there only long enough to marry. Then he returned to the Golden Mountain, leaving his wife in China. He received the news of the birth of his daughter, Mei Oi, several months after he had returned to the United States.

Some ten years later, he sold his laundry. With the proceeds from the sale of the laundry plus his small savings, he had planned to spend the late evening of his life in the rural quiet of Sunwei. The Sino-Japanese War had prevented him from realizing this long-cherished goal. The unsettled conditions of subsequent years in the Far East, which saw Mao Tse-tung grab control of the Central Government of China from Chiang Kaishek, had weighed heavily in his decision not to return to Sunwei. While there were intermittent periods of peaceful travel in China for those who wanted it, Lee Gong could not bring himself to see anything permanently stable for a retired *Gimshunhock* in China. So reluctantly he remained in New York.

"Ah Song, my boy," said Lee Gong from his easy chair, "You have good results lately?"

"What good results? I haven't been to the tracks for a whole week. No luck and no money."

"Ah Song is a smart boy," said Wah Gay. "He wouldn't go to the races unless he's lucky, heh heh."

"You go to hell." Ah Song folded his paper, got up and stretched his arms. He yawned. Yawning was a habit with him, almost as natural as breathing. "It's so hot you don't want to move."

"You just moved, you sonovabitch," said Wah Gay.

Ah Song ignored the remark and started toward the door.

"Where are you going to die?" Wah Gay called after him. "Be smart. Go get someone down here and start a little game. Where can you go in this hot weather?"

"To the race tracks!" Ah Song slammed the door behind him.

Lee Gong went over to the mah-jong table and sat in the chair that Ah Song had just vacated. He picked up the paper. "That sonovabitch Ah Song eats good, dresses good, and he never works!"

"He's got what you'd call *Life of the Peach Blossoms*," chuckled Wah Gay. "The women like him. He's a beautiful boy."

"Maybe he was born under the right stars. "

"Three years ago he went to Canada and I've heard he married a rich widow from Vancouver and she bought him a car and gave him money."

"What has happened to the widow now?" Lee Gong asked, surprised that Ah Song was ever married. As far as he knew, Ah Song was living the life of a bachelor in New York.

"Nobody knows," the club house proprietor shook his head. "You know Ah Song's type. He never tells you anything. I heard he had some trouble with the police out in Portland when they caught him without proper registration for his car two years ago."

"I've never heard of that," said Lee Gong. "But you don't have to go back that far. Just a year ago he was mixed up with that Lao Woo's wife. Someone saw him and Woo's wife together around Times Square on a Saturday night. Soon the news got back to the husband, who took the matter up with the elders of the Woo Association. The chairman of the Woo Association sent a representative to see Ah Song…"

"What happened?"

"Ah Song was squeezed for $1,000. "

"Did he pay?"

"Of course."

The afternoon was unusually quiet at the club house, and the two friends found this light talk helped pass the time away.

"This generation of girls is not what it used to be," lamented Wah Gay. "In nine cases out of ten, if the girl were good and honest, no trouble would come to her." Wah Gay got up and started pacing the floor. "You look at this generation of *jook sing* boys and *jook sing* girls. They have no respect for elder people. H'mn, they would call you by name. They would call you Lao Lee even though you are almost twice as old as their old man."

"Regardless what anybody might say," put in Lee Gong. The words seemed to flow out of his mouth effortlessly. "Girls born in China are better. They are courteous and modest. Not like these *jook sings* born in New York. They can tell good from bad." He paused. The newspaper remained unread on the table. "Summer is coming. You'll see them running out on the streets almost naked. You could almost see their underpants."

They both chuckled.

The afternoon moved slowly. Even the sidewalk outside was deserted on this hot, sticky day. The perennial voices of children playing, the roar of their roller-skates against the pavement, were missing. An occasional rumble of passing trucks could be heard in the quiet retreat of the Money Come club house.

6

(Jade Snow Wong, 1922—2006)

黄玉雪

作者简介

黄玉雪（Jade Snow Wong, 1922—2006），出生于美国加利福尼亚州旧金山，在兄妹中排行第五。1942年毕业于奥克兰的米尔斯女子学院。大学期间对陶瓷艺术产生了兴趣，战后在唐人街开了间陶瓷作坊，获得成功。与丈夫创办旅行社，多次组织旅行团到亚洲国家观光。1972年在尼克松总统访华一个月后，她和丈夫成功获得来华签证，《不是华人异乡客》（*No Chinese Stranger*, 1975）一书记述了这次经历。此后他们多次带团来中国游览，目睹了中国的巨大变化。她常被视为美国亚裔妇女成功的化身，获得多项荣誉。汤亭亭称赞黄玉雪是“美国华裔文学之母”。

《华女阿五》（*Fifth Chinese Daughter*）是黄玉雪的自传，1950年在美国出版后引起读者与评论界的极大兴趣，立即成为畅销书。美国国务院组织出版了本书的日语、汉语、孟加拉语、泰语、缅甸语等亚洲国家或地区语言的译本；1953年，又资助黄玉雪到日本、印度、菲律宾、缅甸等许多亚洲国家作巡回演讲，意在宣传在美国民主制度下，即使出身贫寒家庭的孩子通过努力奋斗也能取得成功。《华女阿五》以第三人称叙事讲述黄玉雪24岁以前对其生活产生影响的人生重要片段。这位第二代华裔女子凭着坚强的意志和内在力量，战胜一切艰难困苦，克服来自华裔社区和白人社会的双重偏见，最终获得成功。这本书不仅描写了唐人街华人家庭的日常生活，也展现了父女之间的冲突。从更广泛的意义上说，这是老一代移民与土生土长的美国华裔之间思想观念上的冲突。

《些许自由》（“A Measure of Freedom”）选自《华女阿五》第15章。在黄玉雪的成长过程中父母对她管教极为严格。有一次她要和男孩子出去看电影，遭到父亲斥责，她据理力争，用父母自己的话进行反驳，赢得了胜利。这也为她赢得了一定程度的自由，此后她出去约会再也没有受到父母的盘问。这也预示着他们容许她将来可以努力追求自己的生活方式。

作品选读

Fifth Chinese Daughter

15. A Measure of Freedom
(Excerpt)

Of her college courses, Latin was the easiest. This was a surprise, for everyone had told her of its horrors. It was much more logical than French, almost mathematical in its orderliness and precision, and actually a snap after nine years of Chinese.

Chemistry, true to the instructor's promise, was difficult, although the classes were anything but dull. It turned out that he was a very nice person with a keen sense of humor and a gift for enlivening his lectures with stories of his own college days. There were only two girls in a class of more than fifty men—a tense blonde girl from Germany, who always ranked first; and Jade Snow, who usually took second place.

But if Latin was the easiest course and chemistry the most difficult, sociology was the most stimulating. Jade Snow had chosen it without thought, simply to meet a requirement; but that casual decision completely revolutionized her thinking, shattering her Wong-constructed conception of the order of things. This was the way it happened:

After several uneventful weeks during which the class explored the historical origins of the family and examined such terms as "norms," "mores," "folkways," there came a day when the instructor stood before them to discuss the relationship of parents and children. It was a day like many others, with the students listening in varying attitudes of interest or indifference. The instructor was speaking casually of ideas to be accepted as standard. Then suddenly upon Jade Snow's astounded ears there fell this statement:

"There was a period in our American history when parents had children for economic reasons, to put them to work as soon as possible, especially to have them help on the farm. But now we no longer regard children in this way. Today we recognize that children are individuals, and that parents can no longer demand their unquestioning obedience. Parents should do their best to understand their children, because young people also have their rights."

The instructor went on talking, but Jade Snow heard no more, for her mind was echoing and re-echoing this startling thought. "Parents can no longer demand unquestioning obedience from their children. They should do their best to understand. Children also have their rights." For the rest of that day, while she was doing her chores at the Simpsons', while she was standing in the streetcar going home, she was busy translating the idea into terms of her own experience.

"My parents demand unquestioning obedience. Older Brother demands unquestioning obedience. By what right? I am an individual besides being a Chinese daughter. I have rights too."

Could it be that Daddy and Mama, although they were living in San Francisco in the year 1938, actually had not left the Chinese world of thirty years ago? Could it be that they were forgetting that Jade Snow would soon become a woman in a new America, not a woman in old China? In short, was it possible that Daddy and Mama could be wrong?

For days Jade Snow gave thought to little but her devastating discovery that her parents might be subject to error. As it was her habit always to act after reaching a conclusion, she wondered what to do about it. Should she tell Daddy and Mama that they needed to change their ways? One moment she thought she should, the next she thought not. At last she decided to overcome her fear in the interests of education and better understanding. She would at least try to open their minds to modern truths. If she succeeded, good! If not, she was prepared to suffer the consequences.

In this spirit of patient martyrdom she waited for an opportunity to speak.

It came, surprisingly, one Saturday. Ordinarily that was a busy day at the Simpsons', a time for entertaining, so that Jade Snow was not free until too late to go anywhere even had she had a place to go. But on this particular Saturday the Simpsons were away for the weekend, and by three in the afternoon Jade Snow was ready to leave the apartment with unplanned hours ahead of her. She didn't want to spend these rare hours of freedom in any usual way. And she didn't want to spend them alone.

"Shall I call Joe?" she wondered. She had never telephoned to a boy before and she debated whether it would be too forward. But she felt too happy and carefree to worry much, and she was confident that Joe would not misunderstand.

Even before reporting to Mama that she was home, she ran downstairs to the telephone booth and gave the operator Joe's number. His mother answered and then went to call him while Jade Snow waited in embarrassment.

"Joe." She was suddenly tongue-tied, "Joe, I'm already home."

That wasn't at all what she wanted to say. What did she want to say?

"Hello! Hello!" Joe boomed back. "What's the matter with you? Are you all right? "

"Oh, yes, I'm fine. Only, only…well, I'm through working for the day." That was really all she had to say, but now it sounded rather pointless.

"Isn't that wonderful? It must have been unexpected." That was what was nice and different about Joe. He always seemed to know without a lot of words. But because his teasing was never far behind his understanding he added quickly, "I suppose you're going to study and go to bed early."

Jade Snow was still not used to teasing and didn't know how to take it. With an effort she swallowed her shyness and disappointment. "I thought we might go for a walk…that is, if you have nothing else to do…if you would care to…if.…"

Joe laughed. "I'll go you one better. Suppose I take you to a movie. I'll even get all dressed up for you, and you get dressed up too."

Jade Snow was delighted. Her first movie with Joe! What a wonderful day. In happy anticipation she put on her long silk stockings, lipstick, and the nearest thing to a suit she owned—a hand-me-down jacket and a brown skirt she had made herself. Then with a bright ribbon tying back her long black hair she was ready.

Daddy didn't miss a detail of the preparations as she dashed from room to room. He waited until she was finished before he demanded, "Jade Snow, where are you going?"

"I am going out into the street," she answered.

"Did you ask my permission to go out into the street?"

"No, Daddy. "

"Do you have your mother's permission to go out into the street?"

"No, Daddy."

A sudden silence from the kitchen indicated that Mama was listening.

Daddy went on: "Where and when did you learn to be so daring as to leave this house without permission of your parents? You did not learn it under my roof."

It was all very familiar. Jade Snow waited, knowing that Daddy had not finished. In a moment he came to the point.

"And with whom are you going out into the street?"

It took all the courage Jade Snow could muster, remembering her new thinking, to say nothing. It was certain that if she told Daddy that she was going out with a boy whom he did not know, without a chaperone, he would be convinced that she would lose her maidenly purity before the evening was over.

"Very well," Daddy said sharply. "If you will not tell me, I forbid you to go! You are now too old to whip. "

That was the moment.

Suppressing all anger, and in a manner that would have done credit to her sociology instructor addressing his freshman class, Jade Snow carefully turned on her mentally rehearsed speech.

"That is something you should think more about. Yes, I am too old to whip. I am too old to be treated as a child. I can now think for myself, and you and Mama should not demand unquestioning obedience from me. You should understand me. There was a time in America when parents raised children to make them work, but now the foreigners regard them as individuals with rights of their own. I have worked too, but now I am an individual besides being your fifth daughter."

It was almost certain that Daddy blinked, but after the briefest pause he gathered himself together.

"Where," he demanded, "did you learn such an unfilial theory?"

Mama had come quietly into the room and slipped into a chair to listen.

"From my teacher," Jade Snow answered triumphantly, "who you taught me is supreme after you, and whose judgment I am not to question ."

Daddy was feeling pushed. Thoroughly aroused, he shouted:

"A little learning has gone to your head! How can you permit a foreigner's theory to put aside the practical experience of the Chinese, who for thousands of years have preserved a most superior family pattern? Confucius had already presented an organized philosophy of manners and conduct when the foreigners were unappreciatively persecuting Christ. Who brought you up? Who clothed you, fed you, sheltered you, nursed you? Do you think you were born aged sixteen? You owe honor to us before you satisfy your personal whims."

Daddy thundered on, while Jade Snow kept silent.

"What would happen to the order of this household if each of you four children started to behave like individuals? Would we have one peaceful moment if your personal desires came before your duty? How could we maintain our self-respect if we, your parents, did not know where you were at night and with whom you were keeping company?"

With difficulty Jade Snow kept herself from being swayed by fear and the old familiar arguments. "You can be bad in the daytime as well as at night," she said defensively. "What could happen after eleven that couldn't happen before?"

Daddy was growing more excited. "Do I have to justify my judgment to you? I do not want a daughter of mine to be known as one who walks the streets at night. Have you no thought for our reputations if not for your own? If you start going out with boys, no good man will want to ask you to be his wife. You just do not know as well as we do what is good for you."

Mama fanned Daddy's wrath, "Never having been a mother, you cannot know how much grief it is to bring up a daughter. Of course we will not permit you to run the risk of corrupting your purity before marriage."

"Oh, Mama!" Jade Snow retorted. "This is America, not China. Don't you think I have any judgment? How can you think I would go out with just any man?"

"Men!" Daddy roared. "You don't know a thing about them. I tell you, you can't trust any of them."

Now it was Jade Snow who felt pushed. She delivered the balance of her declaration of independence:

"Both of you should understand that I am growing up to be a woman in a society greatly different from the one you knew in China. You expect me to work my way through college—which would not have been possible in China. You expect me to exercise judgment in choosing my employers and my jobs and in spending my own money in the American world. Then why can't I choose my friends? Of course independence is not safe. But safety isn't the only consideration. You must give me the freedom to find some answers for myself."

Mama found her tongue first. "You think you are too good for us because you have a little foreign book knowledge."

"You will learn the error of your ways after it is too late," Daddy added darkly.

By this Jade Snow knew that her parents had conceded defeat. Hoping to soften the blow, she tried to explain: "If I am to earn my living, I must learn how to get along with many kinds of people, with foreigners as well as Chinese. I intend to start finding out about them now. You must have confidence that I shall remain true to the spirit of your teachings. I shall bring back to you the new knowledge of whatever I learn."

Daddy and Mama did not accept this offer graciously. "It is as useless for you to tell me such ideas as 'The wind blows across a deaf ear.' You have lost your sense of balance, " Daddy told her bluntly. “You are shameless. Your skin is yellow. Your features are forever Chinese. We are content with our proven ways. Do not try to force foreign ideas into my home. Go. You will one day tell us sorrowfully that you have been mistaken.”

7
(Frank Chin, 1940—)
赵健秀

作者简介

赵健秀（Frank Chin, 1940— ），出生于美国加利福尼亚州柏克莱，被称为美国亚裔文学的奠基人。曾参加爱荷华大学作家坊学习文学创作；1965 年毕业于加州大学圣塔芭芭拉分校。1970 年代初于旧金山创办“美国亚裔戏剧创作坊”。首部剧作《鸡笼里的中国佬》（*The Chickencoop Chinaman*）于 1972 年在美国天地剧院（American Place Theater）上演，是纽约上演的第一部美国亚裔作家创作的剧本。主要作品还有剧本《龙年》（*The Year of the Dragon*，1974）、长篇小说《唐老亚》（*Donald Duk*，1991）和《甘加丁之路》（*Gunga Din Highway*，1994）。并与华裔作家陈耀光、徐忠雄和日裔作家稻田房雄合编了影响深远的《哎咿！美国亚裔作家选集》（*AIIIEEEEE! An Anthology of Asian-American Writers*，1974）和《大哎咿！美国华裔与日裔文学选集》（*THE BIG AIIIEEEEE! An Anthology of Chinese American and Japanese American Literature*, 1991）。

赵健秀力图塑造全新的华人男子汉形象、建立华裔文学中的英雄主义传统。《鸡笼里的中国佬》重塑了美国华裔族群的整体形象。受到种族歧视的长期影响，华裔在美国社会中一直是唯唯诺诺的鸡仔形象，然而此剧颠覆了这样的刻板面孔，塑造了具有反抗精神的华裔新形象。《唐老亚》描写了唐人街上十二岁男孩儿唐纳·德从蔑视甚至仇视中国文化到初步认识中国文化的抗争性并从中汲取力量的转变。通过阅读和亲友的讲述，小主人公了解到华工不仅参与修建美国铁路而且是最具竞争精神的群体，这有力反驳了华裔逆来顺受的种族主义观点。他最终在家庭和自己的华裔身份中找到了民族自豪感。

第一篇《在谦次住所》(“Kenji's apartment”)选自《鸡笼里的中国佬》第2幕第4场。剧中人物之间的矛盾冲突在这里集中爆发出来，他们相互指责对方的逃避行为。谭伦对汤姆粗鲁无礼让谦次大为恼火。受到谦次的责备后，谭伦宣布将拍摄一部真正的职业拳击片，里面不会掺杂什么冒牌老爹，这说明他已从失望中醒悟过来。第二篇选自《唐老亚》第17章。唐纳·德和他的白人朋友阿诺德一起到图书馆查阅历史文献寻找真实历史的证据，重新发现了华人的历史，揭露了白人的谎言，得以在课堂上当众指出老师的错误，驳斥了中国人无进取精神的谬论。

作品选读

The Chickencoop Chinaman

Act Two　Scene 4: Kenji's apartment

(Excerpt)

LEE: Tam just met me today, and he knows me better than you ever did, Tommy.

TOM: Oh, I see it. Lee does this all the time, brother. Games! She's put you through your paces and you don't care. Well, don't be blinded by her white beauty. You're not going to allow a white girl set you against a brother, are you? It's not worth it. I'm tellin you. I was married to Lee, can you dig it?

TAM: I don't see no white girl here. And I'm not hustling none of your ex-wives no matter what color.

LEE: Thanks a lot.

TAM: I'm not bragging, mindya. You're not the only woman I'm not hustling.

TOM: Now who's playing the fool?

TAM: Did I say you were playing the fool? I thought I called you straight out, "fool," fool!

TOM: I'm not prejudiced against Chinese like you. Just between you and me, brother, you have problems.

LEE: Oh, Tom the intellectual!

TAM: You Chinese? You don't talk like a Chinese.

TOM: Listen, you ever looked at yourself? You're willowy.

TAM: What're ya talkin about?

TOM: I'm telling you, for your own good, your peace of mind…

TAM: What? You got trouble with the language, Tom? What?

TOM: ... you better be Chinese because Americans are hungup about homosexuality.

TAM: Huh? Lee, I think his mind just snapped!

TOM: It's true.

TAM: What're ya talking about. What's bein Chinese gotta do with "homosexuality"?

TOM: In American eyes we don't appear as he-men types.

TAM: Oh, we look like queers!

TOM: Yeah.

TAM: But if we read up on Chinese culture, building walls, writin with a brush, talk enough about gunpowder, paper money, Chairman Mao we can fool folks into thinking we're the way we are not because we're queer but because we're Chinese! "Willowy" huh? Me, I'm not going to go round sayin, "I'm not queer, boss, I'm Chinese!" (POPCORN *laughs.*) No wonder she says you're not a man.

TOM: You're prejudiced against Chinese.

TAM: I said Lee says you're not a man!

TOM: You're prejudiced against Chinese!

TAM: Foreigners don't bother me, but ornamental Orientals like you make me sick.

TOM (*interrupting*): I don't know what you're trying to prove, brother. But you'd better face facts. You and me... we're both Chinese. Now maybe you don't like being Chinese and you're trying to prove you're something else. I used to be like that. I wondered why we didn't speak up more, then I saw we don't have to. We used to be kicked around, but that's history, brother. Today we have good jobs, good pay, and we're lucky. Americans are proud to say we send more of our kids to college than any other race. We're accepted. We worked hard for it. I've made my peace.

TAM: You sold your baby to be accepted by whites? Now you're at peace? That's too moochie shi-yet!

TOM: I didn't sell my baby.

TAM: Oh?

TOM: My mother didn't like Lee.

TAM: Oh. Why?

TOM: Why? Because she wasn't Chinese.

TAM: Your mother's not Chinese?

TOM: No, *Lee's* not Chinese!

TAM: Tom, you're beautiful. You wanted to be "accepted" by whites so much, you created one to accept you. You didn't know Lee's got a bucket of Chinese blood in her? At least a bucket?

TOM: She's white. Hey, I know! I was married to her. I know Chinese from white.

TAM: Gotcha scared, huh, Tom? How about that funny red in her hair, huh? Peroxide? She just peroxided her hair, Tom. You! Your whole soul, man, has been all washed out, treated, your nerves all taped up and packed away like mummies in the monster movies, man...

KENJI: Tam!

TAM (*speaking through*): doin the wicked work of nutty priests. Man, when they dig you up, they're gonna find petrified Cheerios, gobs of Aunt Jemima pancakes, a shiny can of Chun King chopped phooey.

TOM: You're going to call me white. Well, I could call you black!

TAM: Oh, did I turn Tom's feeings? Look at her. Go on up and get a good look, fella, and you tell me who's prejudiced against Chinese. You wanted a white girl so bad, so bad, you turned her white with your magic eyes. You got that anti-Chinaman vision.

TOM: We're wonderful, I can call you "Chinaman" and insult you.

TAM: Do you want to insult me?

TOM: I can call you "Chinese American" and insult you, "Americanized Chinese" and insult you. "Chinese" and insult you, "American" "Chink" "Jap" "Japanese" "White" and insult you, "Black" and insult you. You're angry. I used to be angry like you. I understand, brother. But try to see me.

TAM: What is this talk? *You* should be angry man, pissed off! about this family and Lee foolin you to come out here... not this, this smalltalk.

TOM: Let's not lose our heads...

TAM: Let's lose our heads! Let's panic, fly off the handle, go off half cocked. Let's act like animals!

KENJI (*taking* TAM *aside violently*): Tam, man, you're making trouble...

LEE: What're you doing? I want to hear.

TAM: Lee's terrific... putting us all through the hoops, man. The ringmaster!

KENJI: Keep Lee outa your mouth. What're you jumpin all over Tom for? He's a guest in my house.

TAM: What's all this "my house" trash, man? Look, I've eased all the tensions here. Lee's not barking up pregnancy tales. Tom's not pissed off about anything personal. There's no situation! Just a dull party, with smalltalk, man.

KENJI: Why do you talk so god damned much? I used to think it was funny, brave, man, the way you ripped everybody up with your tongue, showin 'em up for clowns and bullshit. Your tongue was fast and flashy with the sounds, man, savin your ass from this and that trouble, making people laugh, man, shooin in the girls ... I used to know why you were mean and talkin all the time. I don't anymore, and you're still talkin the same crazy talk.

TAM: You were my silent pardner. We used to run together.

KENJI: It's not fun anymore. I never was the runner you were, never as crazy or ... I don't even know why I admired you. You're vicious now. Vicious! Really ... all over everybody, calling names...

TAM: Is... think... I've lost my head. I've ... I must be crazy, huh?

(LEE *laughs*.)

KENJI: I told you it's not funny, now, man. Nobody wants it anymore. You're too old to be badmouthing everything, everything like you do. Nobody's gonna run with that, man.

TAM: Yeah, I'm a loner.

KENJI: You wanta be a loner, you're a loner. You're a mean rogue, somewhere, out there, ya know what I mean?

TAM: Like a mad elephant, blowin his nose alone in the dark.

KENJI: It isn't funny.

LEE: It is funny.

KENJI: I'm tellin ya this. I loved you, man. And if you make a crack about that to Tom I'll take your face off!

TOM: Can't we...

KENJI (*to* TOM): Now you be careful o' your mouth!

LEE: Sit down, Kenji, you're scaring me!

TOM: ...Can't we be friends ... act like friends at least?

TAM: We should be friends, you know that? Easy, Kenji, I raised my hand before opening my mouth, huh? I know we should be friends. I know that. But I don't want to be your friend.

KENJI: Who you talkin to?

TAM: You have to ask?

KENJI: Who you talkin to?

TAM: Who you got?... (TAM *and* KENJI *stare down.*)Why couldn't we have just slapped hands and trotted out old radio shows, dead hit tunes and movies? I don't want to be your friend. I'm tired of you, man. Just one look, and I'm tired of you. I'm tired of everything...

KENJI: Tired of talking?

TAM: Really... really tired of talking, especially talking. But everytime I stop it's so goddamned awful!

POPCORN: I never been alone with so many Chinese before. Ever! Uh. I never seen so many before without bein in a Chinese restaurant, you know what I mean? I don't mean you be foreigners ha! I know you're American ... I been listenin, but it's late... (*Low nervous chuckle*) I feel like you all lookin at me. You all be lookin at me? Did I say something wrong? I hurt anybody's feelings? Mr. Lum? Mr. Lum, I hurt your feelings?

LEE: Who're you? Everyone's so polite around here.

POPCORN: It's me, Charley Popcorn.

LEE: Oh, I've been hearing about you, you're...

POPCORN: No, I ain't no father of no Ovaltine Jack Dancer. I'm just a small businessman minding his own dirty movies.

LEE: Oh, I'm sorry to hear that.

POPCORN: I'm not. Maybe Mr. Lum is though, but he shouldn't be. It's Ovaltine that did him wrong, not me.

TAM: Would you say you're not the Dancer's father on camera, Mr. Popcorn? Hold it! You know what that would do to him?

POPCORN: ... for one lousy dollar?

TAM: It's my movie, my worry not yours. Be a good movie though, wouldn't it? Make up some hokey connection between faking up a father, not knowing your past, and the killer instinct. But he's an old man now. Trusts me. I've failed all the old men that ever trusted me. Sold 'em out, watched 'em die, lost their names and been... been what, Kenji? What've I been for that?

KENJI: Don't ask me.

TAM: ... You used to be like me, Tom? You've never been like me.You never knew better. I knew better. I must've known better. My whiteness runneth over and blackness… but people still send me back to the kitchen, you know what I mean?

TOM: You're oversensitive. You can't be oversensitive.

TAM: You're right. I can't be oversensitive. It's like havin too much taste. But that's me oversensitive. And I like it. I'm not going to dig up the Dancer, mock his birth, make a fool of him just to make a name for myself. That's the way it is with us Chinaman cooks! Dat's the code of the kitchen, children. Anybody hungry? (*Rises to go to kitchen*)

POPCORN: What about the movie, Mr. Lum?

TAM: There won't be a word of fathers in it, Mr. Popcorn. You'll be part of a straight, professional, fight film. I won't need your money, Kenji.

KENJI: Okay.

Donald Duk

17

(Excerpt)

Mr. Meanwright's classroom is dark for the slide show illustrating his lecture. The old photos out of his dreams, out of the library books, warm up the screen hanging over the chalkboard.

"Unlike other immigrant groups, the Chinese came to America with no intention of staying, settling or pioneering. They were called *sojourners*." Mr. Meanwright drones and buzzes in the dark. Donald Duk hears this from all his teachers and is surprised he's flashing hot blood and angry now at what he hears all the time.

That picture of the Chinese tearing out the crosstie that replaced theirs is bright light and dark shadow on the wall. "These Chinese who worked on the Central Pacific were called *Crocker's Pets*." There is a face that might be Donald Duk's. Donald Duk sees and looks harder as Mr. Meanwright recites on, "Their passive philosophy and noncompetitive nature rendered them ripe for exploitation and victimization. As the historian McLoed says, the Chinese failed in the gold fields and were driven by poverty and timidity to help build the Central Pacific leg of the transcontinental railroad." He changes the slide. The photo of the meeting of the engines at Promontory appears.

"Excuse me, Mr. Meanwright. You are incorrect, sir," Donald Duk says louder than he expects.

"Lights, please," Mr. Meanwight says. "Let us see who belongs to this voice out of the dark."

"Mr. Meanwright, what you just said about the Chinese is not true."

"And you are offended, Mr. Duk. How many of you saw Mr. Duk on the news this morning? Freeing an innocent, though what some might regard as an unsavory man is a very noble act, Mr. Duk." Mr. Meanwright leads the class in applause. Arnold cheers. "Now what offends you, Mr. Duk?"

"Yessir, I am offended," Donald Duk says in an agreeable way. A nervous buzz and hush dries the air and shrinks the wet people dry.

"Well, I never said I was perfect, did I, Mr. Duk. Please, enlighten me."

"You are … sir, Mr. Meanwright, not correct about us being passive, noncompetitive. We did the blasting through Summit Tunnel. We worked through two hard winters in the high Sierras. We went on strike for back pay and Chinese foremen for Chinese gangs, and won. We set the world's record for miles of track laid in one day. We set our last crosstie at Promontory. And it is badly informed people like you who keep us out of that picture there." Donald Duk jerks his chin up to look down his face with killer eyes at the slide of the Last Spike ceremony, still easy to see, like a faded painting projected on the wall. Everyone in the room avoids Donald Duk's eyes but follows his gesture to the screen. The slide changes back to an old grainy shot of the Chinese in the Sierra Nevadas, in the first year, working above the snowline. The white foreman standing to the side of work on the right of way is lost behind his beard, fur hat and puffy bearskin coat. The Chinese with picks and shovels in their hands work in *minop* jackets, like everyone in class has on. Everyone in class looks straight into the eyes of a young Chinese boy in the midground, turning toward the camera and smiling. His hat is pushed back off above his forehead. The face is Donald Duk's. No one asks to snap off the lights to see the face clearly.

"I have the books right here," Arnold Azalea says, pulling books out of his briefcase and piling them on his desk.

"We didn't do all of that being passive and noncompetitive, sir."

"The world's tracklaying record was set …" Mr. Meanwright ponders.

"April 29, 1869," Donald Duk says. "A Thursday, as I remember."

"As you remember, Mr. Duk?" the teacher says.

"Chinese set the record—1200 of us—and the history books don't have one of our names down. But the eight Irishmen who lifted rail off the flatcars with us, their names are the only names…"

"That's right. Mr. Duk is correct, Mr. Meanwright. We checked the books out of the library, and here they are."

"Gentlemen, boys, you have caught me completely unprepared for …" The lights go out. There's big thump on the door and it flies out of its casing and falls flat inside the classroom. Kwan Kung, red-faced, black-bearded, hairy arching eyebrows, green and blazing gold robe and armor, stands on one leg in the doorway. He brings his leg down and strikes another pose.

"Ha ha ha! I smell a room full of paaaaassivity! Arrrggghhh!" Kwan Kung says. Drums and gongs beat and crash in the hallway. Characters out of Cantonese opera are kicking down classroom doors all over the school. Kwan Kung charges around the room lit by the light streaming through the door and the slats of the Venetian blinds. Up and down the aisles between the desks he brandishes his Black Dragon Doh, never acknowledging, never touching any of the students so close they can touch him. He returns to the doorway and strikes another pose and with a grand gesture grabs the tips of the long pheasant feathers arching out of his helmet.

Out in the hall a voice—Dad's voice? —booms behind Kwan Kung. "This free demonstration of the fine art of Cantonese opera courtesy of Duk Lau Opera. Now appearing at the Sun Sing Theater in the heart of Chinatown."

Kwan Kung twirls his weapon and strikes another pose. A kid from the opera company runs in and holds his hand out to Mr. Meanwright. "Here are the hinge pins to your door," the kid says, drops the steel pins clinking into Mr. Meanwright's hand, and leaves.

"Happy New Year!" the voice in the hall calls, and a pack of firecrackers snickering a burning fuse drops at the doorway of every room. Everyone in the class yells and dives for cover. Mr. Meanwright stands with his eyes on replay. Donald Duk grins at him. "*Goong hay fot choy*," Donald Duk says.

8
(Maxine Hong Kingston, 1940—)
汤亭亭

作者简介

汤亭亭（Maxine Hong Kingston, 1940—），出生于美国加利福尼亚州斯托克顿。1958年进入加州大学柏克莱分校读工程学，后转读英语文学；1962年毕业后与演员厄尔·金斯顿结婚。曾在夏威夷大学教授英语，在加州大学柏克莱分校教授创意写作。作品入选多种文学选集或教材。主要作品有《女勇士》（*The Woman Warrior*, 1976）、《中国佬》（*China Men*, 1980）、《孙行者：他的即兴曲》（*Tripmaster Monkey: His Fake Book*, 1989）、《第五部和平之书》（*The Fifth Book of Peace*, 2003），编辑出版《战争老兵，和平老兵》（*Veterans of War, Veterans of Peace*, 2006）。处女作《女勇士》使她一举成名，获得1976年美国国家书评人协会奖（纪实文学类）。《中国佬》获得1981年美国国家图书奖（纪实文学类）（National Book Award for Nonfiction）。她荣获有美国艺术文学院文学奖、国家人文勋章、国家艺术勋章、美国文学杰出贡献奖等。

汤亭亭的作品题材相当广泛，如彰显女权主义、反抗性别歧视与种族歧视、构建族裔文化属性、倡导世界和平等。《女勇士》探讨了种族冲突与文化差异、性别政治、家族历史和自我身份等主题。全书展示了叙述者少女时代追求独立自我的精神，作为美国华裔女孩，她要克服来自移民群体的性别歧视与来自主流社会的性别歧视和种族歧视。《第五部和平之书》贯穿着反战、和平的主题，作者将此书献给“战争的老兵，和平的老兵”。小说书稿焚毁于火灾，给作者造成沉重打击，也让她体会到他人遭受的痛苦；她与战争老兵一样，经历着创伤后应激障碍。作者创建了退伍军人写作坊，与退伍老兵一起用文字书写和静心修行来治愈这种应激障碍，共同缔造和平。

《羌笛野曲》（“A Song for a Barbarian Reed Pipe”）选自《女勇士》第5部分。主人公憎恨一位在学校始终沉默不语的华裔女孩。拧她、扯她头发、哀求她，用尽各种办法让她开口说话，但都失败了。在受她折磨的沉默华裔女孩身上，叙述者看到了如果不开口讲话就有失去自己声音和身份的危险。《地》（“Earth”）选自《第五部和平之书》第4部分，描写了作者在西部柏克莱举办的一期写作坊。老兵们聚在一起讲述、书写他们在越战中的行为和遭遇。战争的血腥与残酷给退伍老兵造成了严重的心理阴影，而书写能起到治疗作用。

作品选读

The Woman Warrior

A Song for a Barbarian Reed Pipe
(Excerpt)

I ran back into the girls' yard, and there was the quiet sister all by herself. I ran past her, and she followed me into the girls' lavatory. My footsteps rang hard against cement and tile because of the taps I had nailed into my shoes. Her footsteps were soft, padding after me. There was no one in the lavatory but the two of us. I ran all around the rows of twenty-five open stalls to make sure of that. No sisters. I think we must have been playing hide-and-go-seek. She was not good at hiding by herself and usually followed her sister; they'd hide in the same place. They must have gotten separated. In this growing twilight, a child could hide and never be found.

I stopped abruptly in front of the sinks, and she came running toward me before she could stop herself, so that she almost collided with me. I walked closer. She backed away, puzzlement, then alarm in her eyes.

"You're going to talk," I said, my voice steady and normal, as it is when talking to the familiar, the weak, and the small. "I am going to make you talk, you sissy-girl." She stopped backing away and stood fixed.

I looked into her face so I could hate it close up. She wore black bangs, and her cheeks were pink and white. She was baby soft. I thought that I could put my thumb on her nose and push it bonelessly in, indent her face. I could poke dimples into her cheeks. I could work her face around like dough. She stood still, and I did not want to look at her face anymore; I hated fragility. I walked around her, looked her up and down the way the Mexican and Negro girls did when they fought, so tough. I hated her weak neck, the way it did not support her head but let it droop; her head would fall backward. I stared at the curve of her nape. I wished I was able to see what my own neck looked like from the back and sides. I hoped it did not look like hers; I wanted a stout neck. I grew my hair long to hide it in case it was a flower-stem neck. I walked around to the front of her to hate her face some more.

I reached up and took the fatty part of her cheek, not dough, but meat, between my thumb and finger. This close, and I saw no pores. "Talk," I said. "Are you going to talk?" Her skin was fleshy, like squid out of which the glassy blades of bones had been pulled. I wanted tough skin, hard brown skin. I had callused my hands; I had scratched dirt to blacken the nails, which I cut straight across to make stubby fingers. I gave her face a squeeze. "Talk." When I let go, the pink rushed back into my white thumbprint on her skin. I walked around to her side. "Talk!" I shouted into the side of her head. Her straight hair hung, the same all these years, no ringlets or braids or permanents. I squeezed her other cheek. "Are you? Huh? Are you going to talk?" She tried to shake her head, but I had hold of her face. She had no muscles to jerk away. Her skin seemed to stretch. I let go in horror. What if it came away in my hand? "No, huh?" I said, rubbing the touch of her off my fingers. "Say 'No, ' then," I said. I gave her another pinch and a twist, "Say 'No.'" She shook her head, her straight hair turning with her head, not swinging side to side like the pretty girls'. She was so neat. Her neatness bothered me. I hated the way she folded the wax paper from her lunch; she did not wad her brown paper bag and her school papers. I hated her clothes—the blue pastel cardigan, the white blouse with the collar that lay flat over the cardigan, the homemade flat, cotton skirt she wore when everybody else was wearing flared skirts. I hated pastels; I would wear black always. I squeezed again, harder, even though her cheek had a weak rubbery feeling I did not like. I squeezed one cheek, then the other, back and forth until the tears ran out of her eyes as if I had pulled them out. "Stop crying," I said, but although she habitually followed me around, she did not obey. Her eyes dripped; her nose dripped. She wiped her eyes with her papery fingers.The skin on her hands and arms seemed powdery-dry, like tracing paper, onion skin. I hated her fingers. I could snap them like breadsticks. I pushed her hands down. "Say 'Hi,'" I said. "'Hi.' Like that. Say your name. Go ahead. Say it. Or are you stupid? You're so stupid, you don't know your own name, is that it? When I say, 'What's your name?' you just blurt it out, o.k.? What's your name?" Last year the whole class had laughed at a boy who couldn't fill out a form because he didn't know his father's name. The teacher sighed, exasperated, and was very sarcastic, "Don't you notice things? What does your mother call him?" she said. The class laughed at how dumb he was not to notice things. "She calls him father of me," he said. Even we laughed, although we knew that his mother did not call his father by name, and a son does not know his father's name. We laughed and were relieved that our parents had had the foresight to tell us some names we could give the teachers. "If you're not stupid," I said to the quiet girl, "what's your name?" She shook her head, and some hair caught in the tears; wet black hair stuck to the side of the pink and white face. I reached up (she was taller than I) and took a strand of hair. I pulled it. "Well, then, let's honk your hair," I said. "Honk. Honk." Then I pulled the other side— "ho-o-n-nk"— a long pull; "ho-o-n-n-nk"—a longer pull. I could see her little white ears, like white cutworms curled underneath the hair. "Talk!" I yelled into each cutworm.

I looked right at her. "I know you talk," I said. "I've heard you." Her eyebrows flew up. Something in those black eyes was startled, and I pursued it. "I was walking past your house when you didn't know I was there. I heard you yell in English and in Chinese. You weren't just talking. You were shouting. I heard you shout. You were saying, 'Where are you?' Say that again. Go ahead, just the way you did at home." I yanked harder on the hair, but steadily, not jerking. I did not want to pull it out. "Go ahead. Say, 'Where are you?' Say it loud enough for your sister to come. Call her. Make her come help you. Call her name. I'll stop if she comes. So call. Go ahead."

She shook her head, her mouth curved down, crying. I could see her tiny white teeth, baby teeth. I wanted to grow big strong yellow teeth. "You do have a tongue," I said. "So use it." I pulled the hair at her temples, pulled the tears out of her eyes. "Say, 'Ow,'" I said. "Just 'Ow.' Say, 'Let go.' Go ahead. Say it. I'll honk you again if you don't say, 'Let me alone.' Say, 'Leave me alone,' and I'll let you go. I will. I'll let go if you say it. You can stop this anytime you want to, you know. All you have to do is tell me to stop. Just say, 'Stop.' You're just asking for it, aren't you? You're just asking for another honk. Well then, I'll have to give you another honk. Say, 'Stop.'" But she didn't. I had to pull again and again.

Sounds did come out of her mouth, sobs, chokes, noises that were almost words. Snot ran out of her nose. She tried to wipe it on her hands, but there was too much of it. She used her sleeve. "You're disgusting," I told her. "Look at you, snot streaming down your nose, and you won't say a word to stop it. You're such a nothing." I moved behind her and pulled the hair growing out of her weak neck. I let go. I stood silent for a long time. Then I screamed, "Talk!" I would scare the words out of her. If she had had little bound feet, the toes twisted under the balls, I would have jumped up and landed on them—crunch!—stomped on them with my iron shoes. She cried hard, sobbing aloud. "Cry, 'Mama,'" I said. "Come on. Cry, 'Mama.' Say, 'Stop it.'"

I put my finger on her pointed chin. "I don't like you. I don't like the weak little toots you make on your flute. Wheeze. Wheeze. I don't like the way you don't swing at the ball. I don't like the way you're the last one chosen. I don't like the way you can't make a fist for tetherball. Why don't you make a fist? Come on. Get tough. Come on. Throw fists." I pushed at her long hands; they swung limply at her sides. Her fingers were so long, I thought maybe they had an extra joint. They couldn't possibly make fists like other people's. "Make a fist," I said. "Come on. Just fold those fingers up; fingers on the inside, thumbs on the outside. Say something. Honk me back. You're so tall, and you let me pick on you.

"Would you like a hanky? I can't get you one with embroidery on it or crocheting along the edges, but I'll get you some toilet paper if you tell me to. Go ahead. Ask me. I'll get it for you if you ask." She did not stop crying. "Why don't you scream, 'Help'?" I suggested. "Say, 'Help.' Go ahead." She cried on. "O.K. O.K. Don't talk. Just scream, and I'll let you go. Won't that feel good? Go ahead. Like this." I screamed, not too loudly. My voice hit the tile and rang it as if I had thrown a rock at it. The stalls opened wider and the toilets wider and darker. Shadows leaned at angles I had not seen before. It was very late. Maybe a janitor had locked me in with this girl for the night. Her black eyes blinked and stared, blinked and stared. I felt dizzy from hunger. We had been in this lavatory together forever. My mother would call the police again if I didn't bring my sister home soon. "I'll let you go if you say just one word," I said. "You can even say, 'a' or 'the,' and I'll let you go. Come on. Please." She didn't shake her head anymore, only cried steadily, so much water coming out of her. I could see the two duct holes where the tears welled out. Quarts of tears but no words. I grabbed her by the shoulder. I could feel bones. The light was coming in queerly through the frosted glass with the chicken wire embedded in it. Her crying was like an animal's—a seal's—and it echoed around the basement. "Do you want to stay here all night?" I asked. "Your mother is wondering what happened to her baby. You wouldn't want to have her mad at you. You'd better say something." I shook her shoulder. I pulled her hair again. I squeezed her face. "Come on! Talk! Talk! Talk!" She didn't seem to feel it anymore when I pulled her hair. "There's nobody here but you and me. This isn't a classroom or a playground or a crowd. I'm just one person. You can talk in front of one person. Don't make me pull harder and harder until you talk." But her hair seemed to stretch; she did not say a word. "I'm going to pull harder. Don't make me pull anymore, or your hair will come out and you're going to be bald. Do you want to be bald? You don't want to be bald, do you?"

Far away, coming from the edge of town, I heard whistles blow. The cannery was changing shifts, letting out the afternoon people, and still we were here at school. It was a sad sound—work done. The air was lonelier after the sound died.

"Why won't you talk?" I started to cry. What if I couldn't stop, and everyone would want to know what happened? "Now look what you've done," I scolded. "You're going to pay for this. I want to know why. And you're going to tell me why. You don't see I'm trying to help you out, do you? Do you want to be like this, dumb (do you know what dumb means?), your whole life? Don't you ever want to be a cheerleader? Or a pompon girl? What are you going to do for a living? Yeah, you're going to have to work because you can't be a housewife. Somebody has to marry you before you can be a housewife. And you, you are a plant. Do you know that? That's all you are if you don't talk. If you don't talk, you can't have a personality. You'll have no personality and no hair. You've got to let people know you have a personality and a brain. You think somebody is going to take care of you all your stupid life? You think you'll always have your big sister? You think somebody's going to marry you, is that it? Well, you're not the type that gets dates, let alone gets married. Nobody's going to notice you. And you have to talk for interviews, speak right up in front of the boss. Don't you know that? You're so dumb. Why do I waste my time on you?" Sniffling and snorting, I couldn't stop crying and talking at the same time. I kept wiping my nose on my arm, my sweater lost somewhere (probably not worn because my mother said to wear a sweater). It seemed as if I had spent my life in that basement, doing the worst thing I had yet done to another person. "I'm doing this for your own good," I said. "Don't you dare tell anyone I've been bad to you. Talk. Please talk."

I was getting dizzy from the air I was gulping. Her sobs and my sobs were bouncing wildly off the tile, sometimes together, sometimes alternating. "I don't understand why you won't say just one word," I cried, clenching my teeth. My knees were shaking, and I hung on to her hair to stand up. Another time I'd stayed too late, I had had to walk around two Negro kids who were bonking each other's head on the concrete. I went back later to see if the concrete had cracks in it. "Look. I'll give you something if you talk. I'll give you my pencil box. I'll buy you some candy. O.K.? What do you want? Tell me. Just say it, and I'll give it to you. Just say, 'yes,' or, 'O.K.,' or, 'Baby Ruth.'" But she didn't want anything.

I had stopped pinching her cheek because I did not like the feel of her skin. I would go crazy if it came away in my hands. "I skinned her," I would have to confess.

Suddenly I heard footsteps hurrying through the basement, and her sister ran into the lavatory calling her name. "Oh, there you are," I said. "We've been waiting for you. I was only trying to teach her to talk. She wouldn't cooperate, though." Her sister went into one of the stalls and got handfuls of toilet paper and wiped her off. Then we found my sister, and we walked home together. "Your family really ought to force her to speak." I advised all the way home. "You mustn't pamper her."

The Fifth Book of Peace

Earth

(Excerpt)

Larry Heinemann, hero writer, Viet Nam veteran, sixth cousin of Abe Lincoln, is here to speak on writing the Viet Nam truth. So he tells them: Be honest. Tell the truth. Write it all. Don't spare your reader. He quotes Cochise, Chiricahua Apache: "You must speak straight, so your words may go like sunlight to our hearts." He himself speaks direct and sure. "Everything has texture, the air of this room, the air outside. Even what we can't see has texture. What is its feel on your skin, inside of your body? Get physicality—your physicality, its physicality, Viet Nam's physicality—on the page. Use your body's senses—write the truth. The worst day of my life … we killed five hundred people … nothing left of them but human meat. Human meat all over the goddamned place. We brought in a bulldozer." His arms thrust out and scoop out a huge field. "We dug a trench forty or fifty feet wide, and head deep, five, six feet deep"—his hands on his head—"and shoveled the meat into it, and then a layer of quicklime, then another layer of meat. We made a human-meat lasagna." I am so horrified, my ears keep shutting. "We weren't burying the bodies because they were soldiers to be honored. It was for sanitation. We lived next to the human-meat lasagna. The smell was in our hair, in our eyes, in the food we ate.

"Tell the truth. Tell the truth with your whole body. Don't spare the reader. You tell it. We killed plenty of people. I mean me. Me. Me. Tell the terror and horror of it. The total waste of it. Put the truth in your reader's hands. Write a letter. Write *her* a letter. Write *him* a letter. Write to me. Tell the truth to a real person here in front of you. She wants to hear your story. Tell it to her. I want to hear your story. Tell it to me."

He warns, "When you write the pain of war, you will relive it. You're going to live through the pain again. You *do* relive the war, the emotions, the smells. But this time, you have a method for handling it—writing. You can control it, put it down, pick it up. Writing is a craft of the hand."

I'd invited Larry Heinemann to help me teach because he had talked to my son and other sons about war. We were on a boat on the Yangtze, the closest he'd been to Viet Nam in twenty years. The weather was hot like Viet Nam, and the trees and flowers were the same. Chinese passengers pressed against the windows, and watched us eat. Earll and I and three draft-age young men were listening to Larry Heinemann talk story. Larry has three brothers. He and his younger brother were drafted at the same time. He tried to talk their youngest brother into not enlisting, even asked their family lawyer to keep him out. That brother has not forgiven him for interfering. Their mother pushed all of her sons to join the military. She *wanted* them to go to Viet Nam. Youngest Brother finished his tour of duty, and re-enlisted, a "two-time marine." He was sent home wounded. Larry doesn't know how he's doing now. Youngest Brother doesn't talk to or write to him.

As he told this, he looked at each of the quiet, listening boys, pinned them with the blue eyes with the black dot in the center. Husky dogs have eyes like that. People with dog eyes can see ghosts. Larry said to my son, and to the other sons, "Guys, no way is war good for you. It's harmful—to *you*. It's stupid. We were a bunch of dumb kids. The Vietnamese too, a bunch of dumb kids. Don't you be dumb kids." Larry, a veteran of Viet Nam, can say such things, which I want to say but do not have the authority to say.

Ted Sexauer tells Larry he re-upped in Viet Nam to save his younger brother from having to go. "I did the paperwork, took advantage of a little-known loophole, a legacy after the death of the five Sullivan brothers."

Edie Heinemann—"the real writer in the family," Larry says—speaks about writing letters to her husband every day when he was in Viet Nam. She is a red presence beside me, red hair, red cheeks. She wrote him the details of life back home, the daily events, the ordinary activities of family and friends, school. "Nothing important, not about the war." She wrote him safe; she wrote him home.

Addressing us women, Edie says, "It's easy for the support person to lose herself. You have to care for yourself, and not expend all your strength on someone else. Don't forget yourself." Edie met Larry at a mixer that her school gave for the servicemen stationed nearby. From there, he went to Viet Nam, and he returned there. ("I came back, I wasn't good for anything. The nuns at this weird Kentucky girls' school took me in. They saved my life.") Edie has spent two decades as support person for her husband, and for the kids, daughter and son. "I saved boxes and boxes of his letters, and he saved my letters. I'm thinking of bringing them out, reading them, and making a book. I'm getting ready to do my own writing."

Edie has visited Viet Nam. "I want to give you one important image from Viet Nam. The traffic is very fast, very busy with cars and bicycles and motorscooters. Our guide showed us how to cross the street. 'Don't look back.' Just scan one hundred and eighty degrees ahead of you, and don't stop moving." The way the Vietnamese cross the street is to pick out a goal—the place where they want to get to—and look only at it, not at the traffic. They walk steadily toward their spot, letting the cars and trucks and cyclos and bikes flow around them.

Larry says, "The news from Viet Nam is: The war is over over there. They went home, went to bed, and had lots of babies, who are playing all over the streets. They have wonderful trains. There's no sign of the war except for a little plaque in an out-of-the-way corner of Saigon. Now we need to get rid of the war here, and in here—in ourselves and in our memories."

I need Edie and Larry to be an example to us, show that it is possible for a veteran to come home and be married, and stay married. I wonder, but can't ask, How can you read Larry on being "fucking horny" on R&R? How can you bear to know that? That men go to war to fuck the enemy girls and women. American boys went to Viet Nam to lose their virginity. Earll was in Viet Nam—twice. Go ahead—kill, get killed, but don't be sexually unfaithful. But Larry writes fiction. He calls fiction "bullshit." "Bullshitting fiction." "You need to tell it. Tell it all. Tell it whether it happened or not. Don't leave anything out."

My turn, I tell about my brothers. I'm eldest sister to three of them. (I have the nerve to teach veterans because of being eldest sister to brothers.) Two of my brothers were in the Viet Nam War, one of them in-country. I admit that one motive for starting these workshops is, I want to give my brothers some ways to get over Viet Nam. "I sent them invitations the same as you." Neither one of them answered, and they aren't here. "Thank you for being my brothers."

Larry says, "Now I understand why you're having these get-togethers."

The Bell of Mindfulness sends all those who hear it off to write. The rings reverberate outward and define the silence, encircled momentarily by sounds. In the universe, there is much more silence than there are voices. Being quiet, we become like the great silence, and unite with it. Actually, the most that happens at these workshops is silence.

Loving to watch writers in the act of creation, I snoop out their writing places—a window seat, a winged armchair, an inglenook, a landing. I check Edie and Larry into their room upstairs; they can retire anytime. But they stay amidst everyone, write with everyone. We write all day, outside too, in the summer sun and in the shade under the redwoods beside the stream.

In the late afternoon, we bid one another good night. I suggest that tonight they have lucid dreams. "And remember what you dream, to tell us in the morning. Write those dreams down. We'll influence one another's dreaming."

The next morning, Hiroshima Day, I am rushing across Faculty Glade when the Campanile rings nine o'clock. I slow to walking-meditation pace, and spy Tom Currie on a bench next to the sculpture *The Last Dryad*. "Hi, Tom!" "Hi, Maxine!" Ever afterward, Tom marvels that I recognized and remembered him.

Sherdyl brings muffins he made from one bi-i-i-ig zucchini.

Eager Tom reads first. It's a letter to me. "Dear Maxine, I'm a blue shirt, a fireman, dreaming in my rack. The ship sails north into the beautiful Arctic Circle on top of the world." He trips out again into the cosmos. Time zooms, waves, turns, stops at the present moment. On a bench in Faculty Glade, a young man and a young woman are talking about *Star Trek*. Tom records their dialogue verbatim, then flies back to the Arctic Circle. A plane zooms out, then in; the tailhook catches it. A torpedo comes in, goes off, exploding colors, noise, death. "My first confrontation with death. Only death is damn final and certain. Death. Death. Death."

I want to reel Tom in. I'd rather hear about his down-to-earthly life in the streets. Is it true that he has a camp in the hills, and crashes receptions at Berkeley and Stanford for food? Long ago? Still? He grabs listeners, and tells whatever. The Ancient Mariner. He halts his reading at "Death," and says, "I don't know how to make sense of it."

Howard Lapin, our World War Ⅱ elder, writes a letter to Captain Willie, "a fuck-up, who because of macho daring-do crashed his plane with twenty people aboard." "Out of false bravery, you gave orders that caused an accident that killed our own men." (Larry says, "Captain Willie is the kind they fragged.") "Fuck you, Willie, and your stupid ground-pounder ways." World War Ⅱ, the good war, language same-same Viet Nam. Good that Howard's here. The Viet Nam vets can get straight with Father and with that generation's war. Someone uses the term "World War Ⅱ mentality," meaning jingoism. Howard goes quiet, and shakes his head. "No, that's not right. It wasn't like that." He asks the professional writers at the table, "Is it right to speak ill of the dead?"

Ted Sexauer has rewritten and continued the poem that began with the medic having to be cool, to keep down the "panic factor," and not "fail in the eyes of his unit." "I feared failing at my job more than my own death." He has lost his feelings, and can't make decisions. Ted *is* cool; he has the style that everyone wants. The others admire it, and seek his opinion of them and their writing. The instant he says the title, "Ambush of the Silver Cross," I see the Vietnamese medic's scissors open into a crucifix. (My mother's sewing scissors burned in the fire; she'd brought them from China, and must have used them for surgery in war.) The medic poet thinks about the enemy medic who was killed. "Today, peacetime more or less, 1993, holding the scissors, I can, at least, begin to wonder who he was."

Sherdyl continues a story about watching a "floating tree" on the infrared nightseeing scope. "It's moving straight across the river against an eleven-knot monsoon current. ... Porpoise twenty-four, this is Porpoise twenty-six. Follow us! Flank speed! That goddamn tree is crossing at Point Yale Alfa. ... We got to within two hundred meters of the tree and all of a sudden the damn thing opened fire at us!...VC palm trees. ... Outsmarted by a fucking palm tree ... After that, every tree we encountered in the river was treated to a liberal dose of grenades and small-arms fire." A tree flies by and explodes. "A tree sprouted arms and rifles, and shot at us. Suspicious palm trees. It took a long time for me to trust trees."

Then Sherdyl reads another scene, the Black River Rats on night patrol at Yale Bravo on the Soirop River in the Mekong Delta. A SEAL team, "real bad hombres," slid into the water to lay tricks and traps for VC. Sudden screams out of the dark. "There in the middle of the little river mouth was a large cypress tree, and both big, bad SEALs were up in the tree, yelling and waving frantically for us to come and get them. Our patrol boat bumped up against the cypress tree, and they both dropped down onto the deck with a sprawling thump. 'What the hell happened?' 'Crocogators!'" "Crocogators!" makes Larry Heinemann laugh his unstoppable laugh. All day, he'll think "Crocogators!" and start up again.

John Swensson, graduate of West Point, officer, writes about his last moments in Viet Nam, whose coordinates are: "East of Eden. Dau Tieng. Cu Chi." He caught the chopper, and took off amid ground-fire shelling. "Outta here! Goodbye, Dau Tieng! Goodbye, Viet Nam!" ("Outta here!" still current slang; Americans want out of wherever.) He reached down for the November *Playboy* on the floor of the chopper. Slithering out from under his seat—a cobra. He couldn't shoot it; he couldn't run out the door. Cobra wanted outta here too:

> "Snake! Snake!"
>
> I look down to my left and here's a cobra, head down, trying to crawl out. I look to my right and

here's the middle of the same cobra coming out from between the seats. I hadn't noticed her 'cause I was scrunched down; the vibrations from the rotor must have waked her up and now I am sitting on top of her as she heads back for the Garden.

So—they fought crocogators, cobras, trees, elephants. Vietnamese soldiers rode elephants; rifles stuck out on all four sides of the howdah. Our city boys were in the wilderness. Viet Nam was alive with jungle and animals. Even the woods moved, and were the enemy.

9

(Wing Tek Lum, 1946—)

林永得

作者简介

林永得（Wing Tek Lum, 1946—），出生于美国夏威夷檀香山，1969年从布朗大学（Brown University）毕业，取得工程学士学位。1973年从纽约协和神学院（Union Theological Seminary）毕业，取得神学硕士学位。林永得在从商之余，主要从事诗歌创作。

林永得的主要诗集有《疑义相与析》（*Expounding the Doubtful Points*, 1987）和《南京大屠杀诗歌》（*The Nanjing Massacre: Poems*, 2013）。作为诗人，林永得获得了美国图书奖、艾略特卡德文学奖等奖项。

受张纯如（Iris Chiang, 1968—2004）的代表作《南京大屠杀》（*The Rape of Nanking*, 1997）启发创作的《南京大屠杀诗歌》是林永得的最新诗集。在诗集中，林永得借助强烈的视觉意象对历史事件进行了反思观照，特别是通过诸多触目惊心的意象反思了人类遭受的战争之殇，寄托了对和平的无限憧憬。

诗歌《裸体》（"Naked"）、《逃离战争》（"Escaping the War"）、《乡村葬礼》（"A Village Burial"）均选自诗集《南京大屠杀诗歌》。《裸体》从"鱼"的意象视角呈现了被俘者的无助和遭受的凌辱。《逃离战争》从"泪桶"和"怀表"的意象视角呈现了民众逃难的艰辛和永恒的战争创伤记忆。《乡村葬礼》则通过对四具不完整尸首葬礼凄惨景象的描绘，表达了对战争以及侵略者的深刻谴责与控诉。

作品选读

The Nanjing Massacre: Poems

NAKED

is all I wear
second nature now

stripped of shame
served raw

like their fish
translucent

a sheen of gold
this lure

of musk
and surrender

my brazen veil
to hide

from sight
the daily panic.

ESCAPING THE WAR

My mother's tears filled a small barrel.
It was all I could carry
when we fled the capital.

Some people found passage down the river,
while others followed
our soldiers along the road west.

We took to the hills
wending our way through steep gullies
full of dry leaves.

The barrel grew heavy.

I feared I could not keep up
and hugged it with all my might.

At night we rested near the edge of a clearing.
As I dreamed, the moon burned through the barrel
turning the tears into molten gold.

I could hear the sounds
of shouts and weeping from within.
Our keening echoed throughout the night.

In the early dawn I tried to lift the barrel.
But it had sunk into the hard winter earth,
much heavier than before.

I pried open the top
scooping up whatever fistfuls
I could manage, and quickly slipped away.

We passed through abandoned farms, hid in forests,
but avoided ridgelines
where we might be spotted by airplanes.

We reached a camp and then another.
Later, we scattered,
disappearing into towns and small cities.

Throughout the rest of my life
I have held on to the pocket watch
that was made from the gold.

It has kept its shine all these years.
Every day I open its cover;
I am filled with sorrow's scent.

It tells me the same time
no matter what
—December 13, 1937, Nanjing, China.

A VILLAGE BURIAL

Four bodies lie slumped over
at the pond's edge,

one prone, the others on their sides curled up.
They are wearing soldier's uniforms,
ragged and caked with mud,
shorn of their belts, one without shoes.
They have been decapitated,
the spaces above their necks
where their heads should have been now empty,
the feeling of something missing,
unnerving like a small pin boring through
to prick the heart.
The heads are soon discovered,
floating, half submerged, in shallow waters
—no doubt dumped or kicked in.
They are waterlogged, rapidly decomposing,
one still with spectacles.
Each body is laid out on the bank,
turned over onto its back,
and heads are pressed on top of the necks
to see which fits.
It is hard to determine
which matches are correct
—the long, thin face perhaps
goes with the one with slender fingers,
or maybe another set can be paired
because of the same darker complexion.
They look like they belong, and yet do not.
Together they are loaded onto a two-wheeled cart
and pulled up to the mountains
to a burial pit dug in the hard earth
for all the recent dead.
But it does not seem right
to cast these four so haphazardly
among the other corpses,
though some are also maimed, with severed arms,
their bellies blown out.
So one last attempt is made
to set them down gently,

to rejoin each head to its rightful body.
Hopefully then one of them at least
might be reborn whole,
to re-enter this desecrated world again,
to seek revenge for himself and his comrades,
rending apart these invaders,
hacking limbs, ripping out entrails,
crushing bone, and shredding flesh,
splattering every drop of their blood
across this wide, perverted face of hell.

10

(Laurence Yep, 1948—)
叶祥添

作者简介

叶祥添（Laurence Yep, 1948—），出生于美国加利福尼亚州旧金山。儿童文学作家、剧作家。1970 年毕业于加州大学圣克鲁兹分校；1975 年获得纽约州立大学布法罗分校英语文学博士学位。主要作品有《魔笔》（*The Magic Paintbrush*, 2000）、《地龙苏醒：旧金山大地震》（*The Earth Dragon Wakes: The San Francisco Earthquake*, 2005）、"金山纪事系列"（Golden Mountain Chronicles）、"唐人街悬疑系列"（Chinatown Mysteries）、"匿海之龙奇幻系列"（Dragon of the Lost Sea Fantasies）、"虎学徒三部曲"（The Tiger's Apprentice）等。《龙翼》（*Dragonwings*, 1975）出版后广受欢迎，赢得国际阅读协会儿童图书奖、美国纽伯瑞儿童文学奖银奖、儿童文学协会凤凰奖等多种奖项。

叶祥添的作品主要探讨文化外来者的困境，关注文化内部与文化之间的冲突与复杂性。《龙翼》是儿童类历史小说，"金山纪事系列"的第一部作品，但在叙事顺序上是第五部，该系列目前已出版 10 部作品。《龙翼》常用作美国学校课堂教材，还改编成同名剧本。它是作者受到有关中国飞行事业先驱冯如（Fung Joe Guey, 1884—1912）的新闻报道启发而写成的，透过一位刚来美国的华人少年之双眼，展现了父亲为追求梦想而拼搏斗争的经历，描述了 20 世纪初期华人在美国旧金山的生活，探讨了种族和谐共处的可能性。作者意在驳斥媒体中呈现的华裔刻板形象，向世人表明华人也是有血有肉、有情有义、有理想、有抱负的群体。

《龙翼》(“Dragonwings”)选自《龙翼》第12章。“大伯”带着洗衣店所有人赶着马车帮忙把“龙翼”(飞机)拉上山顶，威特罗小姐和她侄女罗宾也赶来观看飞机试飞。父亲驾驶自己制造的飞机“龙翼”飞离地面升上了天空，人群欢呼起来。后来飞机坠落和父亲受伤让父亲明白鱼和熊掌不可兼得，家庭对他来说比飞行更重要。父亲在“大伯”的要求下又搬回洗衣店，疗养身体，并入股成为洗衣店合伙人。父亲又多方努力办妥相关文书，于次年回国将母亲接到美国。

作品选读

Dragonwings

12 Dragonwings

(September, 1909–June, 1910)

(Excerpt)

“Now help Red Rabbit,” Uncle called.

We strained at the ropes. I stumbled and got up. I stamped at the ground this time, getting better footing. Slowly, ever so slowly the wagon began to creep up the hill. The ropes burned at my hands so that the rope fibers seemed to brand my skin. And Dragonwings, its wings waving over either side of the wagon, lurched forward. Foot by foot, we pushed and pulled the wagon with Dragonwings up the hill, its wings dipping and bobbing as if it were tensing itself.

“Easy, easy,” Father called anxiously from the side. He was afraid of the wings breaking.

And for one moment I hated Dragonwings, for as light as we had tried to make it, it was still very heavy for only one old horse and several men and a boy. And I hated Dragonwings, not for what it had cost both my parents and me, but just for being so fat and heavy. I was beginning to be afraid for Father when he tried to fly in it.

Uncle began a chant that the Tang men had used nearly forty years ago when they were building the paths for the demons' trains. And the rest of us, hauling in rhythm to his chant, began to find it was easier. I would say, too, that Uncle pulled the hardest of any of us. And all of a sudden I saw that if life seems awfully petty most of the time, every now and then there is something noble and beautiful and almost pure that lifts us suddenly out of the pettiness and lets us share in it a little. It did not matter whether Father flew or not. It was enough that the Company had come.

I do not know how, but we managed to get Dragonwings to the top of the hill. For a long time, nobody said anything. We were all too busy trying to get back our wind. It was a good time, too, just to admire the view, each man with his own thoughts as he looked out at the great sweep of bay. The winds began rising from the bay waters, racing over Oakland and sweeping low over the hissing weeds, which nodded back and forth in great shimmering waves of gold. Father buttoned up his coat against the chill.

"The horoscope book said this is a most auspicious day," he told Uncle. "I looked it up before we left. I think the book was right. Just feel those winds."

"The book better be," Uncle said, "or the only one who will enjoy this day will be the mortician."

Lefty had sat off a ways on top of his coat, which he had spread over a rock. He shaded his eyes. "Someone is coming," he called.

We saw the heavily clothed figures tromp up the hill. Miss Whitlaw's face lit up when she saw all of us gathered on the top. "*Thank goodness*," she puffed. "*I thought we were going to be late*." Beside her, helping to support her arm, was Robin, also coated, scarfed, and booted against the cold damp of the morning. I suppose they figured to shed everything when it got hot later.

Father came down the road and took Miss Whitlaw's other arm. "*How you know we flying?*"

"*Oh*," Miss Whitlaw said gaily, and glanced at Uncle, "*a little birdie told me*."

"Did you tell them?" Father demanded of me.

"No, sir. I kept my promise. I don't know how they found out, but what does that matter? Your flying is as much theirs now as it is yours."

Father stood for a moment with his hand on Miss Whitlaw's elbow, but finally he grunted. "I guess it is."

Miss Whitlaw had not understood our conversation, but she could get the meaning of it just from Father's angry tone. "*Now you just blame a snoopy old lady, Mr.* Lee. *I just had to know what was wrong, so I had my employer, who knows your landlord, call him and find out what was the matter. And then I got hold of your friend, Mr.* Deerfoot, *over in the City, and he gave a message to your Uncle for him to call me up.* "

"You actually used an electric talker?" Father asked Uncle in disbelief.

"I'll admit that they can be convenient." Uncle shrugged.

"*And so we worked out everything between us*," Miss Whitlaw said.

Father grinned down at Robin. "*It good thing you got here. I wonder how we going to fly without one of my helpers here*."

We untied Dragonwings then and eased it down the ramp by sheer muscle power. Then, lifting, pulling, and pushing, we rolled it to the crest of the hill.

Robin tapped one big, bulging coat pocket. "*We brought a cordial to warm you*." She slid a large bottle out of her pocket.

"*That very, very thoughtful*," Father said. He uncorked the bottle and took a sip. "Now that's a righteous wine." He passed it to Uncle. "Here, old man, this should drive the chill out of your bones."

Uncle sipped the cordial. "I'll race you round the hill and back again."

He handed the bottle on to the rest of the Company. Even Robin and I got a sip. Then Father clapped his hands together nervously. "*Well, it time to start*." With a nod to Robin and me, he headed for Dragonwings.

Father had left about thirty feet between Dragonwings and the crest of the hill where it sloped sharply for some hundred feet before opening on the ruin of the *Esperanza* estate and our barn. And then the hill dipped sharply again until it came to rest in the flatlands below. We all marched around in the area in front of Dragonwings, tramping the weeds down so the ground would be fairly level. Then Father coiled up his queue into a tight bun behind his head and pinned it there.

Robin took her place before the left propeller with her hands resting on the blade. I took my place beside the right propeller. Father himself lay belly-down on the bottom wing. With his left hand he grabbed hold of the frame. With his right, he took the front rudder controls. He pulled back on the controls and the front rudders tilted upward. He pushed forward and they tilted downward. Then Father shifted his hips to the left. The rear vertical rudders twisted to the left and the wings curled slightly, as if they were alive. Father shifted his hips suddenly to the right and the rudders shifted to the right and the wings warped again. Father straightened the front and rear rudders and the wings again. The wind drummed at the canvas over the wings. The sky seemed alive and waiting.

"*All right*, Moon Shadow, *Robin*," Father said. We both pulled down at the propellers and backed away. The motor beside Father coughed into life, turned over, and caught. The bicycle chains clinked musically as they turned the propellers. The wings began to vibrate, and you could feel the life begin to course through Dragonwings. Robin stepped back and I ran around behind Dragonwings to join her. We were both exhilarated in the wind from the propellers, which rippled across the grass. Suddenly the wind had competition here on the hilltop. The flags on the front rudders stiffened, and we could now see the eyes painted on the flags. It was as if Dragonwings had finally woken.

Dragonwings lurched forward, bumped, stopped, and lurched forward again, like some great lumbering beast coughing to itself as it got up out of bed. Father gripped the frame of the wing tightly with his left hand and pulled back sharply with his right, so that the front rudders angled skyward. Dragonwings rolled toward the steeply slanting hillside. The wooden wheels made crisp, crunching sounds as they crushed the weeds. Dragonwings seemed to teeter for a moment, balancing on the very edge of the hillside. I wondered if Dragonwings were simply going to roll down the hill. Robin crossed her fingers. Silently, I asked Grandfather to help us.

Suddenly the wind blew even harder up the hillside. The grass all over the hill hissed even louder, like one giant snake. The nose of Dragonwings suddenly tilted up like some bird scenting the wind that would carry it home. The wind roared over the hilltop, seeming to gather beneath the wings. The canvas of the wings bellied upward, taut and swollen and eager. Dragonwings seemed to leap into the air about five feet and hang suspended. I held my breath. I saw Father twist his hips to the right, and the wings began to curl and the rear rudder curved to the right. Slowly, ever so slowly, Father began to *bank* in that direction. He had controlled his flight! He was free in the sky.

Everyone cheered spontaneously. Father turned in a leisurely circle over the hilltop, coming back toward us. In his traces, Red Rabbit stamped and snorted, so that Hand Clap had to run over and quiet him down. I raced along beside Dragonwings for a moment, my legs pumping, my head dizzy, my heart filled with pride. "Father, you did it. You did it."

Father turned his head. There were a few strands of hair that had slipped down over his eyes, but the wind of his passage blew them away from his face again. He grinned and winked. And then he passed me. His wings brushed the grasstops and then the left side of his wings dipped dangerously toward the ground, but he steadied Dragonwings with a shove of his hips. Dragonwings rose into the air as Father completed his circle and headed down the hillside toward the bay.

I plunged down the slope after him. I could hear the others pounding behind me. Robin shouted for me to wait, but I ignored her. My momentum carried me recklessly forward. Once I nearly fell, but I caught myself with my hands and scrambled on. By the time we had reached the bottom, where the garden stood along with our stable, Father had already reached the road that marked the end of the *Esperanza* property; he began to turn back over the orchards toward the garden. He was flying as high as twenty feet now, and the sun, gleaming through the painted canvas, made the wings seem like living flesh. It was as if he were no longer a man, but truly a dragon again.

We watched him fly for perhaps four minutes around the *Esperanza* estate while we stood knee-deep among the flowers.

"Look at him," Uncle shouted. He was as excited as a little boy. "Look at him. Just look."

"But how is he to come down?" Lefty asked.

Uncle laughed, "Tell this man how he is to come down."

"He'll land back on the hilltop." I added, "More or less."

"More or less?" Uncle asked, puzzled.

"We hope without cracking up the flying machine."

"Oh," was all that Uncle said. He began scratching anxiously at the back of his neck. "Whom do you ask to help an aeronaut? The winds? The dragons?"

"All of them," White Deer said.

But we never did get to see whether Father would land all right or not.

Father had just completed another circuit of the estate and was banking to the left over the fences, so his nose at the time was pointed toward the hillside. I heard a shrill, high, singing sound as the bolt that held the right propeller to the frame snapped. Horrified, I saw the propeller spinning away from Dragonwings in a lazy arc. The right side dipped dangerously. Father cut the motor and twisted the rear rudder hard to the left, tilting the front rudders upward so that the wind lifted the right side even more. Dragonwings straightened itself. It was deadly silent now in the garden. Father told me later that he had hoped to glide to a landing. But by now he had come too close to the hillside. I saw him twist violently to the left in his hip cradle, trying to turn even farther to the left, away from the hill. Too late.

The next moment seemed to take forever. I watched helplessly as Dragonwings started to turn, but the right side of its wings brushed the hillside. The wooden frame of the right wings snapped in a dozen places. Broken wooden poles ripped through the canvas as it flapped upward. The left wings rose leisurely until they were almost straight up, and then Dragonwings leaned forward and burrowed nose first into the hillside. The body of Dragonwings swung back and forth drunkenly and then hung at an odd angle.

I raced toward Dragonwings, feeling as if I had been betrayed. Somehow, after we had lavished so much time and effort and money on it, it should never have let one of its bolts snap and destroy itself and maybe kill Father. Father had been thrown clear of Dragonwings and lay on his back. I took his wrist. He still had a pulse.

Puffing, Uncle joined me. It was surprising that he could run at all, let alone outdistance the others. It must have been as Uncle always said: There was a lot of life still left in his old beat-up body. Uncle dropped to his knees beside me and, with delicate hands, felt Father's bones. The others gathered around, catching their breaths. Finally Uncle straightened and looked around, relieved. "I think his right leg is broken and maybe two of his right ribs. That's all."

"You mean he'll live?" I asked.

"For now, yes, until he tries his next flying machine." Uncle shook his head.

"*What did he say? What did he say*?" Robin demanded.

"*Father's all right*," I said.

We cannibalized Dragonwings to make a stretcher for Father out of the wooden poles and canvas. Uncle and White Deer set his leg—there was plenty of wood for that—and we bound up his sides tight with some old lengths of cloth. Miss Whitlaw sent Robin after a demon doctor. By the time she got back with one, Hand Clap had gotten the wagon down from the top of the hill and driven it into the meadow. We had lifted Father onto the wagon and taken him straight into the stable. Uncle had also sent the Company back to the hillside to clean up the wreckage, so it was all piled into the wagon. That way there would be no embarrassing questions to have to answer.

After the doctor left, we waited for Father to wake up. To occupy ourselves we made pots and pots of tea. "*I wish*," Miss Whitlaw said as she sipped her tea, "*that I had never had my employer begin making inquiries*."

"*I don't think Father would have wanted it any other way*." I added, "*Neither do I. It... it just had to be*."

Father stirred then and groaned and sat up, leaning on his elbows. He winced and looked at his sides. "What's broken?"

"Only a leg and some ribs, no thanks to you," Uncle snapped. "It could have been your head or your back, you know."

"Yes."

I got some tea for Father. "Dragonwings is a wreck. We'll have to build another one."

Father sipped his tea and set the cup down carefully on the dirt floor. "Would you be disappointed if we didn't?"

"Sir?"

"I'm not going to build another Dragonwings. When I was up there on it, I found myself wishing you were up there, and your mother with you. And I realized I couldn't have the two of them together: my family and flying. And just as I saw the hill coming at me, I realized that my family meant more to me than flying. It's enough for me now to know that I can fly."

11

(Shawn Hsu Wong, 1949—)

徐忠雄

作者简介

徐忠雄（Shawn Hsu Wong, 1949—），出生于美国加利福尼亚州奥克兰。1971年毕业于加州大学柏克莱分校；1974年获得旧金山州立大学创意写作硕士学位。曾在米尔斯女子学院、加州大学圣克鲁兹分校和旧金山州立大学讲授美国亚裔文学与历史课程。1997年至2002年任华盛顿大学（西雅图）英语系主任。他是界定美国亚裔文学传统并向美国读者介绍亚裔文学的先驱者之一。与陈耀光、赵健秀和稻田房雄合编《哎咿！》和《大哎咿！》两本美国亚裔文学选集。主要作品有《家园》(*Homebase*, 1979)、《美国膝》(*American Knees*, 1995)。《家园》1981年获得美国太平洋西北书商奖和华盛顿州长作家节奖。

《家园》的主人公兼叙述者雷恩斯福德·陈是成长于1950年代的第四代美国华裔青年。父母去世之后，他踏上了在美国大陆追寻祖先足迹的旅程，同时也揭开了陈姓家族男性被抹去、被遗忘的过往历史，了解到祖辈以及整个华裔在美国的奋斗史和对美国历史做出的贡献。小说叙述虚实相间，将不同时代、地方和人们的信件、散文、诗歌、对话、日记和虚构的场景编织在一起。《美国膝》讲述一位美国华裔在族裔关系方面的两难困境，涉及当代美国社会中的两性关系、族裔身份、种族刻板形象、个人偏见等问题，并试图表明，族裔身份不是一出生就确定下来的类别，不是一种稳定的本质，而是一个不断发展的创造过程。

第一篇选自《家园》第1章第2节。叙述者追忆了祖辈在内华达山脉修筑铁路的艰苦生活与恶劣的工作条件以及他们所遭受的精神痛苦。第二篇选文《忠诚、背叛与报复》（"loyalty, betrayal, & revenge"）选自《美国膝》第1章。主人公雷蒙·丁与华裔妻子达琳的七年婚姻走向了尽头。在家庭与工作中，他感到窒息、束缚、拘谨，整日像机器一样生活，终止了与妻子的沟通与交流，变成了一个沉默者，竟被视为理所应当。他开始出轨，达琳不久就发现了他的不忠。离婚时达琳通过她精明的律师把雷蒙搜刮得一干二净，这倒让他获得了解脱。

作品选读

Homebase

Chapter One

Ⅱ

(Excerpt)

I am the son of my father, my grandfathers, and I have a story to tell about my history, about a moment in the Pacific when I heard myself saying "ever yours." "Ever" is a word that moves like a song, exposing the heart in its tone, never hiding, never patronizing. The word speaks directly, creates form, and has its own voice.

Great-Grandfather built the railroad through the Sierra Nevada in difficult seasons. Night was a time of peace. On warm nights Great-Grandfather would move away from camp to sleep, away from the night workers. There was a river nearby the camp, and farther upstream, the falls. He always walked beside the moonlit river at night, the cascading water glowing white with the reflection made his footsteps visible. And in the windless night he crossed warm pockets of night air, then cool dark spots, but as he moved closer to the sound of the falls, the night air became moist and only cool. His skin tasted the air. It was an uphill hike to the base of the falls and a steeper climb to the top, where he rested, looking down on the fires of camp. He climbed on large granite stones to reach the top of the falls. He began to sweat. The mist from the crashing falls soaked him and mixed with his sweat. The noise was relief from the railroad iron noise of the day. He rested for a moment, looking down into the river's valley. The water appeared vague, uncertain, it became the sound of moonlight, rather than the sound of water rushing through the valley. The moonlit mist carved valleys out of the granite, not the river. The moon made sounds in Great-Grandfather's eyes, made the mist from the falls look like gray smoke floating down the valley, washing out all the details of the canyon walls, losing its night walker in its movement, cooling his exhaustion, and leaving him dreaming a moan out of all his years of living. But he always woke from that easy rest, and demanded that the tradition he passed on be more than a dream and moan of breath. It was his own voice.

Great-Grandfather heard the last anger of his body in late summer, he craved for the violence of bare lighted rooms, that yellow glow to calm himself, that congestion of men without lovers, without families. He knew he was stuck here. In Wyoming, the thunderstorms moved in every day to bring afternoon showers. The raindrops made the dust rise from the ground, filled his nostrils with the smell of moist earth, he felt the ache in his body rise as the dust rises in the wide meadows. His giving in to America, here, was the violence of his soul and he felt it, chased it, and let it overcome him. After the rains, the humidity rose and moist air mixed with the dust the rain had raised. It was a good smell and he bared his chest to that air.

We do not have our women here. My wife is coming to live here. We are staying. Nothing was sweet about those days I lived alone in the city, unless you can find sweetness in that kind of loneliness. I slept in the back of a kitchen by a grimy window where the light and noises of the wet city streets were ground in and out of me like the cold. The bed was so small I could hardly move away from my dreams. And when I awakened with the blue light of the moon shining in, there would be no dreams. That one moment when I wake, losing my dreams, my arms and heart imagining that she was near me moving closer and I float in her movements and light touch. But the blue light and the noise were always there and I would have nothing in my hands.

"I left for San Francisco one month before my brother. In those days, ships were bringing us in illegally. They usually dropped a lifeboat outside the Golden Gate with the Chinese in it. Then the ship steamed in and at night the lifeboat came in quietly to unload. If they were about to be caught, my people were thrown overboard. But, you see, they couldn't swim because they were chained together. My brother died on that night and now his bones are chained to the bottom of the ocean. Now I am fighting to find a place in this country."

My father and I used to drive down a dusty road on that tropical island singing "Home on the Range," the dust pouring through the windows, collecting on the big furry seats of our Buick Super Eight. I followed him on his rounds, checking building sites, riding shotgun, wearing my Superman shirt and a white starched sailor's hat, and carrying a replica of a long-barreled Colt that made my arm ache whenever I lifted it to take aim. And when my father got sick and we had to fly home, I thought of all those jeep rides we went on, running down a dusty road, holding yourself on with both hands, and when we stopped, the dust would catch us and get in my hair and the corners of my mouth. And instead of making you feel dirty, it dried your back. Before we left, mother pulled the Buick into the garage, scraping the side, pinning us in. I crawled out of the window and went for help.

Great-Grandfather's wife was a delicate, yet a strong and energetic lady, insisting in her letters to Great-Grandfather to let her come and join him. The loneliness was overpowering him, yet he resisted her pleas, telling her that life was too dangerous for a woman. "The people and the work move like hawks around me, I feel chained to the ground, unable even to cry for help. The sun blisters my skin, the winters leave me sick, the cold drains us. I look into the eyes of my friends and there is nothing, not even fear."

Upon receiving his letter, Great-Grandmother told her friends that she was leaving to join her husband, saying that his fight to survive was too much for a single man to bear. And so she came and was happy and the hawks had retreated.

She lived in the city and gave birth to a son while Great-Grandfather was still working in the Sierras building the railroad. He wrote to her, saying that the railroad would be finished in six months and he would return to the city and they would live together again as a family.

During the six months, the hawks came back into his vision. "The hawks had people faces laughing as they pulled me apart with their sharp talons, they had no voices, just their mouths flapping open in a yellow hysteria of teeth." He knew that this was the beginning of sickness for his lover, he sensed her trouble and moments of pain, no word from her was necessary. "Your wounds are my wounds," he said in the night. "The hawks that tear our flesh are disturbed by the perfect day, the pure sun that warms the wounds, I am singing and they cannot tear us apart."

She saw the sun as she woke that morning, after waking all night long in moments of pain. The sun was so pure. She thought that this could not be the city, its stench, its noise replaced by this sweet air. She knew that this air, this breath, was her husband's voice. The ground was steaming dry, the humus became her soul, alive and vital with the moving and pushing of growth. She breathed deeply, the air was like sleep uninterrupted by pain, there was no more home to travel to, this moment was everything that loving could give and that was enough. She was complete and whole with that one breath, like the security of her childhood nights, sleeping with mother, wrapping her arms around her, each giving the other the peace of touch. There was a rush of every happiness in her life that she could feel and touch and as she let go, she thought of their son, and the joy of his birth jarred her and she tried desperately to reach out to wake, to hold on to that final fear, to grasp his childhood trust, but the smell of the humus, the moist decaying leaves struck by sunlight and steaming in her dreams was too much, and she was moving too fast into sleep.

Great-Grandfather had dreams and made vows to his son. "I shall take my son away from these hawks who cause me to mourn. My tears leave scars on my face. There is no strength in self-pity. I will take my son away and move deeper into this country."

For Great-Grandfather it was not enough anymore to say he was *longtime Californ'*. He had lost his faith in the land. He fell into deeper depressions, not from mourning his wife's death, but from his loss of faith in the country. He had been defeated when he vowed not to lose ground to the harsh land and cruel people.

The country that accepted Great-Grandfather and his son now rejected them. He sent his son, my grandfather, back to China. The railroad was finished and the Chinese were chased out of the mines. They were allowed to live, but not to marry. The law was designed so that the Chinese would gradually die out, leaving no sons or daughters.

Great-Grandfather stayed in Wyoming. After the transcontinental railroad was finished, the men in the work teams were cut loose to wander through the West. Thousands of Chinese men had no jobs. Some moved to other parts of the country to build the railroad networks, others became migrant farm workers until the unemployed white laborers forced the passage of laws prohibiting the Chinese from working at certain jobs, in certain areas, and finally with the Exclusion Acts, restricting them from entering the country. The Chinese laborers were rounded up and taken back to Chinatown, San Francisco. And if they couldn't be taken back to Chinatown to stay, they were buried where they stood their ground. Great-Grandfather was standing at the eastern edge of the mountains he had worked in, in every season and temperature, and he left a trail of friends lying in the mountains. Wyoming land was different from the Sierra, where he had started.

For Great-Grandfather and the other Chinese who worked through the Sierra seasons on the Central Pacific Railroad, the one conqueror, the one element they feared the most was the wind. The wind did not bring death, but the dread of it in any season was even more powerful than the freezing nights of winter that stiffened the limbs of the sleeping workers, or the summer heat that caused men to pass out, or the fury of the lightning and thunderstorms. After a few hours, the wind makes them deaf, and after a few days of the strong wind, they begin to lose their senses. Hearing goes first, so they talk to themselves while they work, listening to their own voices, just to listen to something that is not the wind, they wrap cloth around their ears. But the wind never lets up. And at night the men can't talk to themselves all night long, can't sing in their sleep. So the wind interrupts their only peace with the loud noise of trees. Their eyes are swollen from the blood pushed into the aching veins of their sight.

American Knees

1 loyalty, betrayal, & revenge

(Excerpt)

DARLEEN'S FIRST WORDS to him had been "Say, Ray." When he looked back on that moment, he wanted to offer others this advice: "Never marry your first Chinese girlfriend." Raymond, at thirty, had just finished his graduate degree in public administration at Berkeley. Darleen, at twenty-six, had an M.B.A. degree and was working for a bank while she studied for the CPA exam. Her roommate was a classmate of Raymond's and had convinced Darleen that the Asian guys in the public administration program were less nerdy than the ones in the business school. After a meeting of a minority students' coalition, the three of them went to a Chinese restaurant, where Darleen ordered in Cantonese. The owner of the restaurant knew her father and didn't charge them. Darleen insisted on paying and left a twenty-dollar bill on the table, but the owner ran after her and gave her a bag of lichee candy, in which Darleen later discovered her twenty-dollar bill. The food, the money, the family honor, were played out to perfection in a classic Chinese morality play.

Raymond recognized all the right cultural signals. Darleen and her family would give him the large Chinese American family he'd never had. Her two older brothers and sisters had already married, in order of birth. He and Darleen would be the next. They would fall in love, get married, and have children—preferably male children—who would be given fabulous red-egg parties on their one-month birthdays. Raymond moved to West Covina, a suburb east of Los Angeles, to join the family and be Chinese. He felt lucky. Believing in luck and fate was very Chinese.

DARLEEN'S FATHER OWNED two upscale Chinese restaurants that catered to a white clientele. While Raymond was looking for a job in public administration, Darleen's father offered to let him be the night manager at General Chan's Palace restaurant. After all, Raymond had real college training in administration, employee relations, and management. Raymond tried to explain that his training was more in the public sector, specifically in issues relating to affirmative action and human rights. Darleen's father puffed on his cigar. "Perfect! We serve the public." Raymond thought managing a small minority-owned business right out of graduate school couldn't hurt his résumé. Things fell into place.

Raymond had left the restaurant a couple of times, once to become an affirmative action officer at a community college, then later to work as an investigator for Orange County's Department of Human Rights, but he lost both jobs to budget cut-backs. Each time he came back to the restaurant, and each time Darleen's father matched his salary in the "outside" world.

It was as if at the exact moment he married Darleen, whoever oversaw good Chinese boys had tapped him on the shoulder and said, "Son, your time has come. Follow me. Your dead mother would have wanted it this way." Ancestors for seventy-five generations back had nodded in agreement. "Good boy, good boy, good boy," they had chanted as he was led away.

Away. That was the key to the whole matter: away from what? Raymond knew exactly what he had given up and what he had been led away from. For Darleen, the marriage had been something she was directed to, a destination, the beginning of a life branching out in all directions from the common root of their union. But Raymond was already perched on the tip of one of the branches, and the ancestors were sawing it off and planting it in the ground, saying, "Good boy. Grow new roots and we'll forget about your girlfriends who weren't Chinese. You didn't know what you were doing. You were young. Too much rock and roll."

"Too moochie moobies," as Grandma would say about the grandson who strayed too far.

Loretta Young was the only white woman Grandma approved of. She watched *The Loretta Young Show* every week on television, and she never forgot that earlier in her career, Loretta Young had saved Chinese orphans and fought Japs with Alan Ladd in the movie *China*. In *The Hatchet Man*, Loretta Young *was* a Chinese daughter, her eyes taped and latexed into an "Oriental" slant. Edward G. Robinson was the tong hatchet man who was ordered to kill her father—who happened to be Edward G. Robinson's good friend—because he betrayed the tong. Friendship was one thing, but betrayal was a whole other thing. Before chopping his friend's head off, Edward G. Robinson promised to raise Loretta Young as if she were his daughter. Business was business, and a promise was a promise. In the end, all Chinese stories came down to loyalty, betrayal, and revenge.

Things fell into place until Darleen's father became Burl Ives and Darleen became Elizabeth Taylor and Raymond became Paul Newman in *Cat on a Hot Tin Roof.* Raymond realized what Darleen's brothers had known all their lives—in a family business, there is no free will. The only freedom Darleen's father offered her brothers was to give them their own restaurant to manage. They were destined to work in the restaurant business whether they wanted to or not. One of them once said to Raymond, "If I weren't paying myself such a high salary, I'd quit." But you couldn't quit family.

The freedom Raymond's father had given him as an only child hadn't prepared him for working within the patriarchy of a large Chinese family business. Neither had his studies in public administration prepared him; the courses he would have needed were all in the psychology department. In Darleen's family Raymond became just another son, another brother. He had no other social life.

His life at the restaurant became separate from Darleen's life and from their life together. At work under bright lights, his life was on constant display, surrounded by background music, the constant chatter bouncing off the walls as he moved between tables, and the metallic and ceramic noise of the kitchen. He came home after closing, craving a darkened and silent anonymity, and moved about the house without turning on the lights. Sometimes he pretended he was alone and unmarried. He stopped cooking for himself and Darleen, stopped eating meals at home, stopped listening to music, and watched television with the sound off. He never answered the phone; any call at home was for Darleen.

She was comfortable with Raymond's silence, which was just like her brothers'. Her brothers never spoke of work because it seemed they had been working and living in the restaurant for their entire lives, Darleen had an M.B.A. degree and a CPA license and had written a master's thesis on minority businesswomen who had received loans from the Small Business Administration, yet there was no place for her in the family business. She worked for a bank, in the commercial loan division. She understood that the power in the family rested on the shoulders of the men. This wasn't the legendary and oppressive Chinese patriarchy at work; it was freedom and the luxury of choice for Darleen.

In order to prevent arguments, Raymond avoided discussing work at home, because any dissatisfaction with work meant a dissatisfaction with the family. To express dissatisfaction meant he was an ungrateful Chinese son-in-law.

"The cooks don't listen to me, Darleen."

"You don't speak Cantonese."

"They understand English when your father speaks to them in English."

"He's the boss."

"What am I?"

"The son-in-law."

"Worse. The boss's youngest daughter's husband."

"You should be grateful Daddy pays you the same as you get on the outside."

"On the outside," Raymond thought, had a familiar ring to it: *Stalag 17*, perhaps, or *What Ever Happened to Baby Jane?*

His past was equally dangerous conversation, because everything he had done in his adult life, he had done with another woman. All his postpuberty experiences in Los Angeles were tainted with the company of former girlfriends. Darleen wanted him separated from them. At first her jealousy was amusing. Then it was not amusing. If he admitted to having been to UCLA or Newport Beach, or mentioned a couple of nice restaurants in Venice Beach, an interrogation would follow, or stony silence. He learned to control the urge to participate in conversations that required him to relate experiences other than childhood ones. A casual listener might have surmised that as an adult he had seen no movies, taken no vacations, had no girlfriends before Darleen. He would have admitted to going to Disneyland as a child, but no one in Los Angeles ever asked about that.

12

(Russell Leong, 1950—)

梁志英

作者简介

梁志英（Russell Leong, 1950—），出生于美国加利福尼亚州旧金山，先后毕业于旧金山州立大学（San Francisco State University）和加州大学洛杉矶分校（University of California, Los Angeles），取得艺术硕士学位。梁志英具有“多栖”身份，不仅是诗人、小说家、散文家，而且是资深评论家、纪录片制作人、文学编辑。他曾长期担任《亚美学刊》（*Amerasia Journal*）主编，其间提携了诸多作家、评论家和艺术家，对美国华裔文学研究的发展做出了不可磨灭的贡献。

梁志英的主要作品有诗集《梦想与尘埃之乡》（*The Country of Dreams and Dusts*, 1993）、短篇小说集《凤眼及其他故事集》（*Phoenix Eyes and Other Stories*, 2000）、诗歌《你的“同志”之身》（“Your Tongzhi Body”, 2001）、诗歌《别有洞天》（“Bie You Dong Tian: Another World Lies Beyond”, 2011）、长诗《飞蛾诗学》（“Mothsutra: for bicycle delivery men New York”, 2015）等。梁志英的这些作品 主要以悲悯的情怀对性别边缘群体、种族边缘群体、经济边缘群体、社会边缘群体、文化边缘群体等边缘人物进行了关注。

作为最能体现梁志英深刻关切边缘群体的作品，诗歌《你的“同志”之身》通过对“同志”生活、感情和梦想的描绘，为其生存发展发出了时代强音。在作品中，梁志英先从视觉、触觉和听觉三个层面描述了“同志”群体在世界范围共存的客观现实，进而呼吁要对艾滋病毒携带者的“同志”进行关爱，因为爱情没有对错之分，每个人都可以爱与被爱。

作品选读

Your Tongzhi Body

I see a brown *tongzhi* body—
Neither Female nor Male
Eyes from Beijing
Lips from Hong Kong
Spleen from Guizhou
Belly from Guangzhou
Feet from Singapore.

I touch a smooth *tongzhi* body—
Without day, month, or year of birth
Whose fingertips
Reach to Canada and America
Whose thighs and calves stretch to Malaysia
Whose toes touch Thailand and Vietnam
Whose body travels from Italy to Australia.

I hear a *tongzhi* body
Speak out—
A Voice sings, cries, and prays
As she/he tells stories
Of love and lust
Of homelessness and loneliness.

I know a *tongzhi* body like yours
Who is HIV positive
And HIV negative
But I will kiss you on the lips anyway
And on every part of your body
For everyone's love
And nobody's fault.

For I possess this brown *tongzhi* body—
And so do you and you and you.
For we are one, or are we not?

13
(Amy Tan, 1952—)
谭恩美

作者简介

谭恩美（Amy Tan, 1952—），出生于美国加利福尼亚州奥克兰，曾就读于林菲尔德学院（Linfield College）、圣何塞城市学院（San Jose City College）、圣何塞州立大学（San Jose State University）等多所大学，取得语言学硕士学位，现主要居住于加州和纽约，专门从事文学创作。

谭恩美的主要作品有《喜福会》（*The Joy Luck Club*, 1989）、《灶神之妻》（*The Kitchen God's Wife*, 1991）、《通灵女孩》（*The Hundred Secret Senses*, 1995）、《接骨师之女》（*The Bonesetter's Daughter*, 2001）、《我的缪斯》（*The Opposite of Fate: A Book of Musings*, 2003）、《沉没之鱼》（*Saving Fish from Drowning*, 2005）、《惊奇山谷》（*The Valley of Amazement*, 2013）、《往昔之始：作家回忆录》（*Where the Past Begins: A Writer's Memoir*, 2017）等。她的作品不仅长期占据《纽约时报》等多个媒体畅销书排行榜，而且荣获英联邦金奖（Commonwealth Gold Award）等图书大奖。

《惊奇山谷》是谭恩美蛰伏八年创作的最新一部小说。小说虽然延续了作者一贯的"母女关系"书写传统，但却从独特的场景设置、人物身份设定、情爱刻画等视角，对人类存在、爱情、家庭关系与文化身份等问题进行了全新思考。《往昔之始：作家回忆录》是谭恩美截止到目前最为详尽的一部回忆录作品。该作品从想象力、情感记忆、时空变迁、灰暗时刻、阅读创作、语言兴趣等层面全面呈现了谭恩美的创作心路历程。

《海那边的城市》（"The City at the End of the Sea"）节选自《惊奇山谷》第十五章，主

要讲述了三代母女历经磨难后终于在上海聚首、分别的故事，隐约表达了对上海、对中国的依恋和不舍之情。《有裂缝的想象力》（“A Leaky Imagination”）节选自《往昔之始：作家回忆录》第一章，主要呈现了谭恩美文学创作“想象力”的生发机制，阐明了《喜福会》中一些意象的诞生过程，传递出作家特有的想象观：神奇的比喻意象不受逻辑思维控制，而只是作为一种真实的感性认识而存在。

作品选读

The Valley of Amazement

15. The City at the End of the Sea
(Excerpt)

FLORA AND I took walks in the early morning and we watched everyday life pour out of doorways and onto the widest boulevards and narrowest alleys. She wanted to understand my life in Shanghai and what her father had experienced. What was it like to be Chinese? What was it like for a Westerner? Whose morals were more severe? Who did I think I would have become if my mother had not left?

I used to ask that last question all the time. Who would I have become? If I had lived in San Francisco, would my mind have been different? Would I have had different thoughts? Would I have been happier? “I wanted to live somewhere else,” I told Flora. “But I didn’t want to become anyone different. I wanted to be who I had always been. And I was and still am.”

We went to the house on Bubbling Well Road, where Edward and I had lived. It was now a middle school for the children of foreigners.

“Foreigners,” Flora said. “I’m a foreigner.”

The big tree was still in the courtyard garden. We stood in its shade, as we had just before she was taken away. The stone bench was there, and it bore a plaque with Edward’s name. Beneath were violets. Mother and I had placed the plaque there a week ago and replanted the flowers. She had given the school a nice contribution and also paid for a gardener to tend it.

“Is he really buried here?” Flora asked.

I nodded. I remembered watching the dirt falling on the cabinet that had served as Edward's coffin. The old sorrow came back: Edward, how could you be leaving me?

Flora brushed her fingers over the violets and closed her eyes. "I want to feel he's holding me in his arms."

I pictured Edward rocking Little Flora, looking at her with a wondrous face, soothing her, telling her she was pure and unharmed.

FLORA AND MY mother stayed for a month. A few days before they would leave, I felt she was again being pulled from me.

"You should come to visit us in San Francisco," Mother said. "You have a birth certificate under the name of Danner that says you're an American citizen. I can help you get it. Although maybe you'd be too wary to let me try that again."

"We wouldn't be able to get a visa for Loyalty. Thousands of Chinese citizens want to leave, and the consulate knows they wouldn't return. I can't leave Loyalty by himself," I said. "He wouldn't know how to take care of himself." I did not tell her that Loyalty had already made me promise that I would not leave without him. He was afraid I would be pulled to America, now that I had found both my mother and my daughter. When people go to America, he had said, they don't come back for a long time. "After the war, Loyalty and I will both come," I told Mother. "Or you come back here and bring Flora. We can go to the mountain that Edward and I climbed, or to Hong Kong and Canton, places I've never been. We can see them together. "

Mother gave me a sympathetic look. She knew I wanted to see Flora again. "I'll see what I can do. " She squeezed my hand.

Three days later, Loyalty, Magic Gourd, and I stood on the dock with Flora and Mother. How long would it be before we could see each other again? How long would the war last? What other terrible things could happen between now and when I would next see them? What if I did not see Flora again for ten or fifteen years? What if Mother died in the middle of writing a letter to me? They were leaving me again. It was too soon.

Magic Gourd shoved a large sack of candied walnuts into Flora's arms. She had been cooking them for the past two days. "She looks like you when you were that age," Magic Gourd said. She had said that nearly every day since Flora arrived. "I used to wonder what would happen if someone saved you and you left and I was all alone. I wanted you to be saved, but then …" She put her fist against her mouth to keep from crying. "Watching her leave is like watching you go." Flora embraced her and thanked her in Chinese for her good care when she was little.

"She has a good heart," Loyalty said to me in Chinese. "She got that from you. Three and a half years was enough time to give that to her. She's the daughter we might have had. I'll miss our daughter." He made Flora promise to send a cable as soon as she arrived so that we would know she was safe.

And then it was time. Flora came to me and said in an oddly stiff voice, "I know we'll see each other soon. And we'll write often."

I thought she had warmed to me and was stricken to realize it wasn't true. She couldn't leave now. I needed more time with her. I was panicking, shaking.

She took my hands. "It's not as hard this time, is it? I'm leaving, but I'll be back." She threw her arms around my neck, hugged me close, and whispered, "What did I call you when I was little and they were taking me away? Was it Mama? It was, wasn't it? I found you, Mama. I'll never lose you again. My mama came back from a memory, and Little Flora came back, too."

I whispered back that I loved her. And then that was all I could say.

"No more heartbreak," she said. She kissed my cheek and pulled away. "There's that face on your chin." She poked my chin and rubbed it until I laughed. "We don't need to be scared anymore," she said. She kissed my cheek again. "I love you, Mama."

She and Mother walked toward the gangplank. She turned back three times to wave, and we waved as well. I watched them ascend, and at the top of the gangplank, she and Mother waved again. We waved furiously until Flora put her arm down. She stood still and looked at me. And then she and Mother went inside and were gone.

I remembered the day when I was supposed to leave Shanghai for San Francisco. My mother should have waited for me. She did not. She should have returned. She did not. The American life that should have been mine sailed away without me, and that day I no longer knew who I was.

On sleepless nights, when I could not bear my life, I thought of that ship and imagined I was aboard. I had been saved! I was its only passenger, standing at the back of the ship, watching Shanghai recede—an American girl in my sailor dress, a virgin courtesan in a high-necked silk jacket, an American widow with streaming tears, a Chinese wife with a black eye. A hundred of me over the years were crowded on the deck, looking back at Shanghai. But the ship never left, and I would have to disembark, and begin my life again each morning.

Once again, I imagined myself as that girl in the sailor dress. I was on the ship, standing at the back of the boat. I was going to America, where I would be raised by a mother who took me to San Francisco. I would grow up in a beautiful house and sleep in a bedroom with sunny yellow walls and a window next to an oak tree, and another that looked out upon the sea. From that window, I would be able to see all the way across to a city at the end of the sea, to a dock by the Huangpu River, where I was standing with Magic Gourd, Edward, Loyalty, Mother, and Little Flora, waving to the girl in the sailor dress as the ship receded, waving until it disappeared.

Where the Past Begins: A Writer's Memoir

Chapter One A Leaky Imagination

(Excerpt)

When I write, I'm certain my frontal lobes are very much in active mode. The self-censors are busy. The wellspring of doubt and worry are overflowing. The standards of perfection are polished and on display. I imagine a look of deep concern on my editor's face when he reads the manuscript. I think I have a brain disease. I suspect the gray matter in my precuneus is becoming a bit threadbare. My need to avoid complacency has trapped me. It has had an ill effect on my writing. It is time to put away the imagined critics, the ones who said, "Lacks imagination or drive, which are necessary to a deeper creative level."

Like those jazz pianists, I, too, have also had nonstop improvisational flights. I know exactly what they feel like. They have occurred at least once with every work of fiction, both in short stories and novels. They come as unexpected openings in portals that enable me to step into the scene I am writing. I am fully there, the observer, the narrator, the other characters, and the reader. I am clearly doing the writing, yet I do not know exactly what will happen in the story. I am not planning the next move. I am writing without hesitation and it feels magical, not logical. But logic later tells me that my writing was freed because I had already set up the conditions that allowed my frontal lobes to idle in neutral. Most of the logistics of time, place, and narrative structure had been established. There was less to decide, because there was less to eliminate. What was left was for me to say what happens next, letting emotions and tension become the momentum driving the story forward. If I can push out my inhibitions, I will have access to intuitions, and with that come the autobiographical metaphors I have garnered over a lifetime. The imagery arrives without my consciously choosing it. The narrative knows intuitively where to go.

I cannot tell you the exact mechanics of how this happens. That would be tantamount to trying to deconstruct the arrival and contents of any stream of thought or emotions. But I do sense that the mind has an algorithm of sorts for detecting possible interactions of visual imagery, language, and emotion that can form autobiographic metaphors. Those combinations are not haphazard. There are patterns and parameters. It may be similar to chemistry. The brain is, after all, a busy hive of chemical interactions of oxygen, metals, hormones, and the like. Maybe each image has a valence—a potential for bonding with intuitions and emotions to form metaphoric compounds. Perhaps narrative tension is the electrically charged state that attracts pairings of words to thought, words to emotions, molecules of meaning.

I do know that the more tension I feel in the story, the further I am pulled forward—once close to fifty continuous pages in a twelve-hour period. That run occurred during the writing of my third novel, the same one I had been trying to write the year before at the artists' colony. By then I knew what was at stake for the narrator—the disappearance of a woman who may or may not have been her sister. I felt the same urgency and tension in thinking about the impending disappearance of my mother, who had just been diagnosed with Alzheimer's disease. The stakes were doubled when my editor Faith Sale was diagnosed a month later with Stage Ⅳ cancer. She was like a sister to me. I had no excuse to delay the book and keep it from her. I rented an apartment in New York City, near where Faith lived. Like the room at the artists' colony, the apartment was too sunny, the desk was not aligned according to the dimensions of the room. I put a plastic table and chair inside a lightless butler's pantry, and I started writing at 6:00 P.M. My mind was clear. There was no hesitation, no puzzling over plot points. I wrote in a state of elation, not knowing how much time was passing. When I finished, I opened the door and gasped to find the sun rising at dawn. Twelve hours had gone by. That day I gave the completed manuscript to Faith. The words I wrote that night were the ones that were published.

Looking back, those fifty pages seem like a miracle to me. I have never been in a similar fugue state since, neither in length nor intensity. In writing about this now, I realize what can free the mind of self-consciousness: uncertainty and urgency, and in the case of my third novel, the urgency was the combination of terror and love. Uncertainty and urgency moved the story forward in other novels. These days, those uninterrupted passages last for only a few paragraphs or at most, a few pages. They almost always arrive as the ending of a chapter or the novel—when the narrator and I reach a point where we recognize what this confluence of thought, emotion, and events has led to. As I continue to write, I don't know what will happen, and yet I do. It is inevitable, like déjà vu moments, experienced as familiar as soon as I write them, the revelation of my spiritual twin—the intuitive part of me made conscious.

That was what I sensed while writing *The Joy Luck Club*. When the metaphoric understanding came, I felt astonishment similar to what I experienced when I emerged from my spell in a lightless room to find the sun rising at dawn. In the story "Scar," I had not anticipated that imagery that was both violent and painful would also be emotionally freeing.

Even though I was young. I could see the pain of the flesh and the worth of the pain.

This is how a daughter honors her mother. It is *shou* so deep it is in your bones. The pain of the flesh is nothing. The pain you must forget. Because sometimes that is the only way to remember what is in your bones. You must peel off your skin, and that of your mother, and her mother before her. Until there is nothing. No scar, no skin, no flesh.

This was unexpected understanding from a place in the brain where metaphoric imagery is not governed by logic but exists as a sensation of truth steeped in memory, the twin to intuition.

Spontaneous epiphanies always leave me convinced once again that there is no greater meaning to my life than what happens when I write. It gives me awareness so sharp it punctures old layers of thought so that I can ascend—that's what it feels like, a weightless rising to a view high enough to survey the moments of the past that led to this one. Too soon, that feeling dissipates, and I am hanging on to contrails as I come back down to a normal state of mind—the one that requires me to write in the more laborious, conscious, preplanned way, all the while hoping I will soon have another intuitive run in which the pieces join, lose their seams, and become whole.

Has my imagination worked this way since birth? What enables me to draw a bird that looks like a bird? When did I start noticing that one thing is emotionally like another? When did emotion and imagery start colluding with velvety sharks?

Whatever imagination is, I am grateful for its elasticity and willingness to accommodate whatever comes along, for giving me flotillas of imagery circumnavigating a brain that finds emotional resonance in almost anything. I just have to let go of self-consciousness for it to spill out freely, as if all I am doing is listening to music.

14
(Qiu Xiaolong, 1953—)
裘小龙

作者简介

裘小龙（Qiu Xiaolong, 1953—），出生于上海。1988 年获得美国福特基金资助前往密苏里州圣路易斯的华盛顿大学研究现代主义诗歌；1995 年在华盛顿大学获得比较文学博士学位。他以“陈超探案系列”侦探小说闻名于世。主要作品有《红英之死》（*Death of a Red Heroine*, 2000）、《外滩花园》（*A Loyal Character Dancer*, 2002）、《石库门骊歌》（*When Red Is Black*, 2004）、《双城案》（*A Case of Two Cities*, 2006）、《红旗袍》（*Red Mandarin Dress*, 2007）、《别哭，太湖》（*Don't Cry, Tai Lake*, 2012）、《中国结》（*Enigma of China*, 2013）、《上海救赎》（*Shanghai Redemption*, 2015）等。《红英之死》是裘小龙的首部长篇推理小说，获得安东尼小说奖，他成为第一位获得此项世界推理小说大奖的华人。

裘小龙的作品是以侦探小说这种形式展现当代中国的风貌，反映中国改革开放后发生的巨大变化。《红英之死》作为悬疑推理小说，探讨的不仅仅是谁是罪犯、如何犯罪的问题，而是把关注点放在了为什么犯罪上。小说近一半处嫌疑人已经锁定，鉴于嫌犯的强大政治背景，陈超在查案过程中遇到了刁难与阻挠，因此他的重点是要找出嫌犯的作案动机。小说思考了政治与个人生活的关系、自然欲望与社会面具的冲突。《双城案》讲述刑侦队长陈超受命调查一起震惊全国的腐败大案，展现了中国政府严厉打击腐败的决心。主犯及其家人早已逃往美国，但罪恶的贪腐网络仍然丝毫未损。陈超利用到美国出访的机会与美国司法部执法官凯瑟琳·罗恩再度联合，终于将罪魁祸首引渡回国。

第一篇选自《红英之死》第 36 章。陈超再次来到关红英的宿舍进行搜索，终于在相框后面发现了她隐藏起来的吴晓明拍的那些色情照片，从而也找出了嫌犯的犯罪动机。第二篇选自《双城案》第 17 章。在美国洛杉矶，老同学帮忙打听到嫌犯邢行要陪母亲去寺庙上香拜佛，陈超便扮作寺院师父为香客解签，占卜吉凶。通过测字算命，机智巧妙地从邢行口中探知到一些与案件有关的重要信息和证据。

作品选读

Death of a Red Heroine

Chapter 36
(Excerpt)

The stick of sugar haw was as yet unfinished when the taxi pulled up at Qinghe Lane.

Chief Inspector Chen threw the stick into a trash bin. A few feet away, an idiot stood tittering all by himself, holding a plastic bag above his head like a hood. He did not see anybody else near Guan's dorm building. The Internal Security people were probably stationed under his own window.

On his way up to Guan's room he met nobody. It was a Friday night. People were watching a popular, sentimental Japanese soap opera that showed a young girl losing a battle to cancer. His mother had told him about it; everybody was enthralled.

Not Guan.

At her door, the lock remained unchanged. He still had the key. Once inside, he locked the door behind him. He did not turn on the light; instead, he took out a flashlight. He stood in the middle of the room. There was something he wanted to find. Something crucial to the conclusion of the case. If it had ever been there, it might have vanished by now. Wu might have been to the room, found it, and made away with it—hadn't one of the neighbors mentioned a man who might have come from Guan's room? Perhaps he should have searched more thoroughly, should have borrowed a forensic expert. But they were so understaffed, and it had not seemed worthwhile. The small room could not conceal much.

If Guan had intended to hide something from Wu, where would she have put it?

Any searcher would have looked in the desk, and the drawers, tapped on the walls, turned over the bed, combed through every book and magazine … Chief Inspector Chen had already checked these obvious places.

He let his flashlight sweep around the room without consciously directing it: An effortless effort, as advocated in *Tao Te Ching*. The light finally came to a stop at the framed portrait of Comrade Deng Xiaoping hanging on the wall.

He did not know why the light had stopped there. He stared at the now illuminated portrait. It was a huge picture for the room, but such a size was not uncommon for a national leader's portrait. In fact, it was the standard size. He had a similar one in his own tiny office.

He had thought highly of Comrade Deng Xiaoping. Whatever might be said against the old man, it was undeniable that China had made great progress under Deng's guidance in economic reform and, to some extent, in political reform as well. The last decade had witnessed tremendous changes—in various aspects of people's lives.

Chen moved a chair against the wall and climbed onto it. He removed the framed portrait from the wall, laid it on the floor, and turned it over. Several clips secured the frame to the board. They were easily bent. He removed the board cautiously.

A stack of pictures wrapped in tissue paper was revealed. He unwrapped them and spread them out on the table.

He stared at them, or they stared up at him.

The first few showed Guan in intricate poses, nude or seminude, her body cleverly composed to heighten various effects—her long hair covering her breasts, or her body partially wrapped in a towel, or even more shockingly, in the newspaper showing her picture as she was awarded the title of national model worker. There was one of Guan lying naked on a brown rug in front of a fireplace. The crackling fire illuminated the curves of her body, her hands handcuffed behind her back, her mouth gagged, and her legs spread wide apart. He recognized the fireplace. It was the one in Wu's living room, the green marble fireplace.

The next few were of Guan with Wu, both stark naked. The pictures must have been taken with some time-delay device. One showed Guan in Wu's lap, smiling nervously at the camera. Her arms were around his neck, and his hands on her nipples.…

To Chen's astonishment, there was also a picture of Guan with a different man on top of her, posing in a gesture of studied obscenity. This man's face was partially obscured, but it was not Wu. Guan lay spread-eagled on her back, her eyes closed, as if in ecstasy.

Then came some pictures of Wu with other women—on the bed, on the rug, in front of the fireplace, or on the floor, in various poses ranging from the erotic to the obscene. One showed Wu having sex with three women.

Chen thought he recognized one of them, a movie star who had played a talented courtesan of the Ming dynasty.

The last picture was of Guan again: wearing a mask, manacled to the wall, but otherwise stark naked, staring into the camera with a mixed expression of uneasiness and wantonness.

There was a feeling of unreality about the whole thing. Chief Inspector Chen had finally found what he had been trying so hard to find. The motive.

Now everything was coming into perspective. Toward the end of their relationship, Guan had got hold of the pictures, which Wu had used against her, but which she had later used to threaten him. She was aware of how destructive the pictures could have been to him, especially at the moment of his potential promotion. She suspected Wu would try to get them back. That was why she had hidden them.

What she had not anticipated, however, was Wu's desperation. It cost her her life. Wu's political career was at a critical moment. With his father lying so ill, this might be his last chance to advance. A scandalous affair or a divorce, either would have damaged his chances. There was no choice left for him. To silence Guan forever would have been his only way out. Now he knew why Wu Xiaoming had committed the crime.

Chief Inspector Chen put the pictures in his pocket, hung Deng's portrait back on the wall, and turned off the flashlight.

At the beginning of his investigation, Chen had cherished a vision of Guan as a poor victim. An alabaster statue smashed by a violent blow. Guan was a victim. On May 11, 1990, she had been murdered by Wu, but even before that, she had long been victimized—by politics. And she was not an innocent, passive statue either. She was in part responsible for her own destruction.

To make no choice is, in existentialist terms, in itself to make a choice.

Guan could have married Engineer Lai, or somebody else. An ordinary housewife, bargaining over a handful of green onions in the food market, searching through her husband's pockets in the morning, fighting for stove space in the common kitchen area … But alive, like everybody else, not too good, and not too bad. But politics had made such a personal life impossible. With all the honors heaped on her, an ordinary man was out of the question for her, not enough for her status or ambition. There was no way she could step down from the stage to pick up a man at a bus stop, or to flirt with a stranger in a café. On the other hand, what man would really desire a Party member wife delivering political lectures at home—even in bed?

And then she had came across Wu Xiaoming. In Wu, she believed she saw her answer. She also glimpsed the hope of holding on to the power through her connection with him. In politics, such a union could have worked out: A model couple in the tradition of orthodox socialist propaganda. Love based on common communist ideals. So her union with Wu appeared to be her last chance both for personal happiness—and for political ambition.

The only problem was that Wu was married, and that Wu did not want to divorce his wife to marry her.

She must have been stung by Wu's decision, the pain in proportion to her passion. She had given everything to him, at least that was what she must have felt. When everything else failed she resorted to blackmail, turning his own weapon against him. In a crisis, some people will fight back by any means, fair or foul. Chief Inspector Chen could well understand that.

Or was it possible, he wondered, that Guan finally awoke to a passion she had never known before? And surrendered to it because she had never learned how to cope with it. Having been used to wearing a mask, she had come to take the mask as her true identity. She knew how politically incorrect it was to become enamored of a married man, but that was what she had become, a helpless woman groaning behind the mask, her hands and feet bound. Had she felt for the first time an overwhelming passion that gave her life a new meaning, which she had to keep at any cost?

Chief Inspector Chen was more inclined to the second scenario: Guan Hongying, the national model worker, had been carried away by passion.

What the truth was he might never discover.

A Case of Two Cities

17

(Excerpt)

Xing might not necessarily be a man of high intelligence, but he was definitely not a gullible one. Chen had to risk being seen as a quack—or worse, as a disguised cop. It would then no longer be a matter of facing the possibly armed bodyguard standing in the background. The exposure of Chen's secret police activity here—under the cover of the government delegation—could lead to diplomatic troubles. But so far he had succeeded in tricking the old woman, and he might be able to do so with Xing. He could always try to give Xing's reading in metaphysically ambiguous sentences. A fortune-teller didn't have to be responsible for his superstitious claptrap. What really mattered was fishing something crucial out of Xing. For this to work, he had to include the old woman in the talk too.

"As madam has demonstrated, a character arising from the heart of her hearts will tell. The choice of the character is simply made by you, but more by the divine power of the universe, so it contains the *qi* from you, as well as from everything else, including this great temple, including your great mother."

"That's right. The temple makes a difference too," the old woman said, nodding vigorously. "Write your character. It's too good an opportunity for you to miss."

"Well, the same character then." Xing wrote it on the paper. *"Xing."*

"Now, is it about yourself?" Chen said, studying the character anew.

"Yes, it's about myself."

"The same character, but with all the different *qi* from your heart," Chen said. "Let me say one thing first. Your handwriting is bold and powerful. The shape of the character bears a certain resemblance to dragon. Very impressive, like in a proverb often used to describe Chinese calligraphy, *'like a dragon moving and like a tiger walking.'* It's in line with the meaning of the character *xing* too. So I would say there is something of a dragon in you."

Chen knew Xing had been born in the dragon year. A dragon was generally considered a lucky, masculine symbol in traditional Chinese culture, with the connotation of great power. It was a compliment Xing would snatch up, Chen supposed, and Xing nodded approvingly.

"You are no ordinary man," Chen pushed on. "In your case, the double person radical may not be just about two. Your movement concerns a lot more. It's difficult to see the direction for the moment. Also, the character *xing* for you means, among other things, a sort of business center, possibly with a great deal of money at your disposal, as in *yinghang*."

Chen watched Xing's reaction. He had to convince Xing of his authenticity by throwing out information unavailable to an ordinary quack, but at the same time he should not go so far as to arouse Xing's suspicions. His interpretation had to remain open, ambiguous, yet specific enough for Xing to think in the way Chen had planned. Only through that could Xing let out some information, unwittingly, in his anxiousness to obtain "divine" advice.

"More and more interesting!" Xing said composedly. "What else can you read in the same character?"

"What time period do you want to know about?"

"The near future, I think."

"If it's about traveling, the people with water element in them may not be good for you."

"What do you mean by water element?"

"*Wuxing*—five elements, as you know. For instance, those with their names containing water radical in them, like Jiang."

"Names containing water radical in them, like Jiang," Xing repeated without making an immediate response.

"Yes. Don't you remember the man in charge of land development in Shanghai, Xing?" the old woman said, growing pale. "His name is Jiang—river, water radical, no mistake. Both you and Ming have met him a number of times. He's in trouble now, you have told me."

"Mom, you don't have to believe too much in those things," Xing said, frowning. "What else, Master Chen?"

Chen restudied the character for another two or three minutes, resting his forehead on his hand, with his eyes half closed, before he resumed, "There's something strange. It is a very complicated situation."

"A man asks about misfortune, not about fortune," Xing said, "Don't worry. Go on with your interpretation."

"I'll be frank. There's another character: *xing* plus the plant radical. Also pronounced *xing*, but means floating without a root. Now it's unusual for somebody of your weight. In a flight of association, with the plant radical plus the character *zhong*, or weight, it brings in somebody surnamed Dong into the picture. He may not be helpful to your movement."

"Dong, anybody surnamed Dong, Xing?" the old woman asked anxiously. "Dong?"

"That's weird," Xing said, visibly shaken. "Dong Deping. He's in charge of the State Industry Reform Committee in Shanghai. He also helped with that land deal for our little brother."

"Is he also in trouble?" The old woman was growing hysterical, grasping at Xing's sleeve.

"I don't know, but he took a big red envelope from us," Xing said to her. "So did Jiang. The amount was large enough to lock them up for life. Their days may not be easy with the investigation going on."

"Then my little son is really in trouble. Master Chen knows everything," she said, sobbing. "If anything happened to him, how could I live?"

"Don't worry too much, Mother. I don't think they know anything about our little brother's whereabouts."

"Oh Buddha, protect my little son, and I'll gild all the images in the hall." She turned to Chen with the string of beads trembling in her hands. "Master Chen, you know everything. Please tell us what to do."

"Again, we are talking about movement," Chen said, facing Xing. "For a mighty man like you, your movement means something. As in the proverb, it's like the movement of a dragon and a tiger. However, I wonder if you are associated with someone named 'tiger'. Someone close or staying close to you. A neighbor or something like that. Now be careful. A dragon and a tiger may eventually not go together. Needless to say, the tiger in question could come from the top."

"Now what are you talking about?" Xing took a step back, glaring at Chen in spite of himself.

"I'm talking about what I read from the character, sir. Still, things might have a turn in the near future. Both good and bad involved."

"Can you be more specific?" the old woman cut in again.

"You may believe you have someone powerful behind you." He paused significantly before looking at Xing. "Believe it or not, what will help you comes from your heart."

"How? I'm totally confused."

"The fact that both you and your mother have chosen the same character speaks for itself. The Way of Heaven is mysterious, but filial piety always comes first. *Who says that the splendor / a grass blade can prove / enough to return / the generous warmth / of the ever-returning spring sunlight?*"

It was not really advice, but he'd better not push things too far. All this might sound compelling to the old woman, but after the initial shock, Xing would come back to himself. As in those stories he had read, a mediocre fortune-teller usually ended up by giving some sort of "do good things" advice.

But Xing decided it was time to leave. Perhaps he was too shaken to stay on. It was just as well. Xing would probably not reveal any more.

"You have spent a long while with us. Here is your fee," Xing said, putting another hundred-dollar bill on the table. "Don't say to anybody what you have said to us today."

"Of course not."

As the Xings walked quickly out of sight, Chen turned to Master Illusionless with a smile.

"I don't know who you are," Master Illusionless said, scratching his clean-shaven scalp, "but you are no ordinary man."

"I don't know who I am. As the scriptures say, identity is an illusion too," Chen said. "At this moment, I am your apprentice. Now I have to go, like a tumbleweed turning and turning around the distraction of humdrum vanities."

15

(David Wong Louie, 1954—)

雷祖威

作者简介

雷祖威（David Wong Louie, 1954—），出生于美国纽约长岛，先后毕业于美国瓦萨学院（Vassar College）和爱荷华大学（University of Iowa），取得创意写作硕士学位。雷祖威现今居住在美国加利福尼亚，在加州大学洛杉矶分校英语系任教。

雷祖威的作品虽然不多，但几乎个个精品。他的处女作是短篇小说集《爱的痛苦》（*Pangs of Love*, 1991），这也是使其一举成名的扛鼎之作。雷祖威截止到目前的唯一一部长篇小说是《野蛮人来了》（*The Barbarians Are Coming*, 2000）。由于身体原因很少诉诸笔端的雷祖威于 2017 年 8 月在美国《哈珀杂志》（*Haper's Magazine*）上发表了一篇回忆录《吃饭、回忆：难以进食的生活》（"Eat, Memory: A Life without Food"）。

短篇小说集《爱的痛苦》主要以黑色幽默的手法刻画出华裔身处美国边缘文化地位的种种心态。在作品中，雷祖威通过观察强势文化和弱势文化的冲撞，呈现出华裔青年内化强势文化（白人文化）后与仍然坚守弱势文化（中国文化）的老一代之间难以调和的矛盾。回忆录《吃饭、回忆：难以进食的生活》是描述雷祖威自身状况的一篇新作。这篇回忆录讲述了身患重疾六年来雷祖威与病魔抗争的励志心酸故事。除了分享手术治疗细节外，雷祖威还刻画出妻子对其悉心照顾、相濡以沫的感人形象。

《爱的痛苦》选自同名小说集《爱的痛苦》。在《爱的痛苦》中，雷祖威通过对华裔母子生活的细微描绘，营造出"带笑的眼泪"的心酸氛围，深入细致地反映了人与人之间的隔阂。《吃饭、回忆：难以进食的生活》选自同名回忆录。在回忆录选段中，雷祖威不仅向读者展示了治疗过程中的痛苦，而且展示了一种乐观向上的精神。

作品选读

Pangs of Love

(Excerpt)

Each night, like most Americans. my mother watches hours of TV. She loves Lucy and Carol Burnett, then switches to cable for the Chinese channel, but always concludes the broadcast day with the local news and Johnny Carson. She doesn't understand what Johnny says, but when the studio audience laughs, she laughs too, as if invisible wires run between her and the set.

My mother has lived in this country for forty years and, through what must be a monumental act of will, has managed not to learn English. This does no one any good, though I suppose when it comes to TV her linguistic shortcoming can't be anything but a positive evolutionary adaptation; dumb to the prattle that fills the airwaves, maybe her brain will wither proportionately less than the average American's.

I am thirty-five years old, and for the past months have lived with mother in a federally subsidized high-rise in the lower reaches of Chinatown. After my father died, my siblings convened a secret meeting during which they unanimously elected me our mother's new apartment mate. They moved her things from Long Island, carpeted her floors, bought prints for the walls, imported me for company, then returned to their lives. I work for a midsize corporation that manufactures synthetic flavors and fragrance. We are the soul of hundreds of household products: the tobacco tastes in low-tar cigarettes, the pine forests in aerosol cans, the minty pizzazz of toothpastes. We have sprays that simulate the smell of new cars; in fact, we have honed the olfactory an to a level of sophistication that enables us to distinguish between makes and models. Our mission is to make the chemical world, an otherwise noxious, foul-tasting, polysyllabic ocean of consumer dread, a cozier place for the deserving noses and tastebuds of American.

My mother's in her pajamas, her hair in a net that seems to scar her forehead. I'm sitting up with her, putting in time. I flip through the day's paper, Johnny in the background carrying on a three-way with Ed and Doc, when my mother's laugh starts reviving like a siren. I shoot her a look—fatlipped, pellet-eyed—that says, What business do you have laughing, Mrs. Pang? My mother's a sweet, blockish woman whom people generally like. She's chatty with her friends in her loud Cantonese voice and keeps her cabinets and refrigerator jammed tight with food, turning her kitchen into a mini grocery store—she's prepared for a long famine or a state of siege. Now, feeling the stab of my glare, she holds in her laughter, hand over mouth schoolgirl-style, hiding those gold caps that liven up her smiles, eyes moist and shifty dancing.

I roll my eyes the way Johnny does and return to the paper. The world's going through its usual contortions: bigger wars, emptier stomachs, more roofless lives; so many unhappy, complicated acres. As a responsible citizen of the planet, I slip into my doom swoon, a mild but satisfying funk over the state of the world. But then she starts again. Fist on cheek blocking my view of her gold mine. Her round shoulders quivering with joy. I click my tongue to let her know she has spoiled my dark mood. She turns toward me, sees the sour expression hanging on my face like dough, points at the screen where Johnny's in a turban the size of a prize pumpkin, then waves me off, swatting at files. Ed's "ho-ho-ho" erupts from the box, the siren in her throat winds up, and all I see is the dark cave of her mouth.

What I need is a spray that smells of mankind's worst fears, something on the order of canned Hiroshima, a mist of organic putrefaction, that I'll spritz whenever the audience laughs. That'll teach her.

I stumble over my own meanness. Some son I am. What does she know about such things anyway? It's fair to say she's as innocent as a child. Her mind isn't cluttered with worries that extend beyond food and family. When she talks about the Japanese raids on her village back home, for instance, it's as a personal matter, the larger geopolitical landscape escapes her. She blinks her weary eyes. She's fighting sleep, hanging on to Johnny for one more guest before turning in. Suddenly, I have the urge to wrap my arms around her solid bulk and protect her, only she'd think I'm crazy, as I would if she did the same to me. "Go to bed," I say. "I'm not tired yet," she says. I cup my hands over my face, my fingers stinking of toilet-tissue lilacs and roses, and think things that should never enter a son's mind: a bomb explodes over the Empire State, forty blocks due north on a straight line from where we are seated, and glass shatters, and she's thrown back, the net on her hair, her pajamas, her headed slippers on fire, and she hasn't a clue how such a thing can happen in this world. And I imagine I'll never see her again.

I fetch the newspaper, go to the couch where my mother's seated, and splash-land down beside her. I'll all set to translate the headlines, to wake her up to the world, when I stop, my tongue suddenly lead. I don't have the words for this task. Once I went to school, my Chinese vocabulary stopped growing: in conversation with my mother I'm a linguistic dwarf. When I talk Chinese, I'm at best a precocious five-year-old, and what five-year-old chats about the military budget? Still I'm determined and gather my courage. "What's that?" I ask, pointing at the dim photo on the front page. An Afghan guerrilla, eye to sky, on the lookout for planes, crouches near the twisted body of a government solider; in the desolate background there's a tank, busted up in pieces. My mother pulls on the glasses she bought at the drugstore and takes a closer look. "A monkey?" she says. I finger the body. She gives up. "That's a dead person," I say, pulling the paper away. "People are dying everywhere."

"You think I don't know. Your father just died." Her voice is quivering, but combative.

I realize I'm on shaky ground. "This man's killed by another man," I say. I'm supposed to talk about freedom, about self-determination, but with my vocabulary that's a task equal to digging a grave without a shovel. "People are killing people and all you worry about is your next bowl of rice."

"You don't need to eat?" she snaps. "Fine, don't eat. It costs money to put food on the table."

She keeps talking this way, but I tune her out, giving my all to Johnny. That guy from the San Diego Zoo's on, and with him is the fleshy pink offspring of an endangered species of wild boar. It knocks over Johnny's coffee, and Johnny jumps. The audience roars; I laugh too, but it's forced, a forgery; my mother's still sore and just sits there, holding herself in like a bronze Buddha.

Eat, Memory: A Life without Food
(Excerpt)

Four years ago, after living crisis to crisis for so long after the surgery, it finally seemed safe to exhale and dig out of the chaos. It was time to reclaim a measure of normalcy. I was going to surprise my wife with a dinner out with our daughter. We were celebrating our wedding anniversary, after letting the past few slip by virtually without notice. I made a reservation at Connie and Ted's, a New England seafood shack in West Hollywood. The menu was right up my culinary alley—raw bar, steamers, chowder—but I would go as a bystander.

It hadn't occurred to me that people would stare until I walked into the restaurant. I hadn't been out in public except for doctor's appointments and walks in the neighborhood. While I was getting dressed, my wife had asked if I planned to wear a scarf to hide the tracheostomy tube that poked from my throat. As we were seated, I wondered if she had asked for my comfort or hers.

At the table, though, we were back to the old normal, studying the menu in forensic detail. "They have Fanny Bays," my wife said, reading off the oyster list. "And Malpeques. Or is it Malaspinas that you like?" Our dinner out came crashing down around me. What did it matter which bivalve I preferred? I was here only to window-shop.

My wife was undeterred. She ordered enough food for three adult eaters. Nothing says festive like a crowded table, and she was determined that I not withdraw to the fringes of the party. She would eat the oysters, and I would sip the liquor from the shells. For my entrée she ordered Rhode Island clam chowder. It was undeniably briny and clammy, easily the most delicious thing I'd tasted since I stopped eating. But I didn't take a second spoonful. We were out in public now. I couldn't take in liquid without dribbling on my shirt. I wouldn't embarrass us here.

My wife couldn't maintain her good cheer. By the time the entrées arrived, she was overwhelmed by the accumulation of food — lobster roll for her, squid for the kid—joining the *we're still working* dishes that remained on the table.

In the photos of that night my daughter looks wretched. She was nine, and had entered the stage in which smiles for the camera are self-conscious, betraying little of what is going on inside. Even with a just-delivered plate of fried clams and French fries in front of her, her eyes mirrored how the rest of the table felt: We wished we were far away.

We faked it, played at dining out. We pretended that cancer was behind us, throwing a scarf over it. Whenever we remember that dinner, my wife says, "Never again," and I flash the thumbs-up: *I'll drink to that.*

People dine. We eat consciously, looking, tasting, smelling, gauging texture and temperature. We share. We talk. My wife and I seemed to talk differently when there was food between us. We loved restaurants, loved to go out and indulge in the rituals of a shared meal: settling in at our table, scanning the room, dissecting the menu, faking our knowledge of wine. After our orders arrived, we dug in, tasted each other's dishes, critiqued the kitchen's hits and misses. For hours we sipped and chewed.

Do I miss it?

I can tell you that eating nice food and drinking good wine with my wife was the best thing ever. In my memories of dinner together we are enveloped in gilded light that seems to emanate from the table's 720 square inches and the plates of food and glasses of red wine between us. "Communion," "spiritual," "intimacy," come to mind as words to describe these moments.

I can also tell you that chewing was glorious. Swallowing was king. I can remember specific dishes and name the ingredients, but I can no longer tell you what it felt like with a platter of Dungeness crab on the table, what the sight of the orange carapace, the aroma of garlic, ginger, scallion, aroused in me. I can't relate to the old, eater version of me. I don't remember how it feels to be in the presence of food and crave it, want to own it, or how it feels to know its pleasure and anticipate having that pleasure again. I can't relate to that kind of beauty anymore.

I am told that cancer has not changed the essential me. "You're still David," my wife says, tactfully omitting the rest of the sentence: *despite physical damage and eroded quality of life*. As much as I love her for saying that she sees me past the wreckage, I think she's lying, at least a little, because from in here things have changed. Five years without a morsel of food passing between my lips has made me a stranger. Seeing food now doesn't make me hungry; neither does reading about it or thinking about it. Drop a steak in front of me and what am I going to do? Will my mouth water or my blood pressure rise, my pleasure centers spark in my brain? None of this happens, because it can't. A plate of rib eye might as well be behind the glass of a Hall of Mammals diorama.

At home, in my kitchen, I watch the dog eat. She puts her head down and doesn't come up for air until she's emptied the bowl. All day she wants food, and as soon as food arrives, it's gone. She has all that mouth, all those teeth, all that jaw, and she doesn't chew, just mindlessly inhales the premium kibble. It's textbook carnivore behavior, I know, brutal at its core, tear and swallow, take in the largest hunks that won't choke you. All the dog does is ingest a substance for the sole purpose of loading up the gastrointestinal tract: the same joyless thing that I do. Breathe, I would tell her, if I could. Sniff. Relish the chicken-and-liver recipe. Chew.

16

(Marilyn Chin, 1955—)

陈美玲

作者简介

陈美玲（Marilyn Chin, 1955—），出生于香港，随后举家移民美国俄勒冈州波特兰市，先后毕业于马萨诸塞大学（University of Massachusetts）和爱荷华大学（University of Iowa），取得艺术硕士学位。陈美玲身份多重，除了是杰出的诗人之外，还是翻译家、编辑、教授、社会活动家和女权主义者。

陈美玲的主要作品有诗集《矮竹》（*Dwarf Bamboo,* 1987）、《凤去台空》（*The Phoenix Gone, the Terrace Empty*, 1994）、《纯黄色狂想曲》（*Rhapsody in Plain Yellow*, 2002）、《情天恨海》（*Hard Love Province*, 2014），故事集《雌狐月饼复仇记》（*Revenge of the Mooncake Vixen*, 2009）。凭借诗歌创作，陈美玲荣获海湾地区书评奖（Bay Area Book Review Award）、加州图书奖（California Book Award）等重要奖项。

陈美玲的诗歌通过对东方诗歌的深度借鉴，在形式和内容上，开创出一个明显不同于西方的模式，不仅映射出女权主义模型和族裔身份的命题，而且彰显了继承中国传统文化和重构美国华裔文化的诉求。散文诗《忧伤吉他之歌》（"Song of the Sad Guitar"）选自诗集《凤去台空》，通过对中国唐宋诗词的巧妙植入，以20世纪80年代的加州为背景，讲述了美玲与一个悲伤吉他弹奏女邂逅交往的动情故事，透射出浓郁的女性关怀气息。诗歌《摆脱X》（"Get Rid of the X"）选自诗集《纯黄色狂想曲》，以"影子"和"月亮"为主要意象，映射出族裔群体在美国经历的酸甜苦辣。诗歌《台湾挽歌：致查理》（"Formosan Elegy: For Charles"）选自诗集《情天恨海》，以悖论抒写的形式，清晰再现了人类生活的精神困境。

作品选读

Song of the Sad Guitar

In the bitter year of 1988 I was banished to San Diego, California, to become a wife there. It was summer. I was buying groceries under the Yin and Yang sign of Safeway. In the parking lot, the puppies were howling to a familiar tune on a guitar plucked with the zest and angst of the sixties. I asked the player her name.

She answered:

"Stone Orchid, but if you call me that, I'll kill you."

I said:

"Yes, perhaps stone is too harsh for one with a voice so pure."

She said:

"It's the 'orchid' I detest; it's prissy, cliché and forever pink."

From my shopping bag I handed her a Tsing Tao and urged her to play on.

She sang about hitchhiking around the country, moons and lakes, home-ward-honking geese, scholars who failed the examination. Men leaving for war; women climbing the watchtower. There were courts, more courts and inner-most courts, and scions who pillaged the country.

Suddenly, I began to feel deeply about my own banishment. The singer I could have been, what the world looked like in spring, that Motown collection I lost. I urged her to play on:

Trickle, trickle, the falling rain.
Ming, ming, a deer lost in the forest
Surru, surru, a secret conversation
Hung, hung, a dog in the yard.

Then, she changed her mood, to a slower lament, trilled a song macabre, about death, about a guitar case that opened like a coffin. Each string vibrant, each note a thought. Tell me, Orchid, where are we going? "The book of changes does not signify change. The laws are immutable. Our fates are sealed." Said Orchid—the song is a dirge and an awakening

Two years after our meeting, I became deranged. I couldn't cook, couldn't clean. My house turned into a pigsty. My children became delinquents. My husband began a long lusty affair with another woman. The house burned during a feverish Santa Ana as I sat in a pink cranny above the garage singing, "At twenty, I marry you. At thirty, I begin hating everything that you do."

One day while I was driving down Mulberry Lane, a voice came over the radio. It was Stone Orchid. She said, "This is a song for an old friend of mine. Her name is Mei Ling. She's a warm and sensitive housewife now living in Hell's Creek, California. I've dedicated this special song for her, 'The Song of the Sad Guitar.'"

I am now beginning to understand the song within the song, the weeping within the willow. And you, out there, walking, talking, seemingly alive—may truly be dead and waiting to be summoned by the sound of the sad guitar.

for Maxine Hong Kingston

Get Rid of the X

My shadow followed me to San Diego
 silently, she never complained.
No green card, no identity pass,
 she is wedded to my fate.

The moon is a drunk and anorectic,
 constantly reeling, changing weight.
My shadow dances grotesquely,
 resentful she can't leave me.

The moon mourns his unwritten novels,
 cries naked into the trees and fades.
Tomorrow, he'll return to beat me
 blue—again, again and again.

Goodbye Moon, goodbye Shadow.
 My husband, my lover, I'm late.
The sun will plunge through the window.
 I must take my leap of faith.

Formosan Elegy
For Charles

You have lived six decades   and you have lived none
You have loved many   and you have loved no one
You wedded three wives   but you lie in your cold bed alone
You sired four children   but they cannot forgive you

Knock at emptiness   a house   without your love
Strike the pine box   no answer   all hollow
You planted plums near the gate   but they bear no fruit
You raised herbs in the veranda   fresh and savory

I cry for you   but no sound wells up in my throat
I sing for you   but my tears have dried in my gullet
Walk the old dog   give the budgies a cool bath
Cut a tender melon   let it bleed into memory

The robe you washed   hangs like a carcass flayed
The mug you loved   is stained with old coffee
Your toothbrush is silent   grease mums your comb
Something's lost   something's made strong

Around the corner   a new prince yearns to be loved
A fresh turn of phrase   a had strophe erased
A random image   crafts itself into a poem
A sleepless Taipei night   a mosquito's symphony

Who will cry for you   me and your sister Colette
Who will cry for you   me and your Algerian sister
You were a rich man   but you held on to your poverty
You were a poor man   who loved gold over dignity

I sit near your body bag   and sing you a last song
I sit near your body bag   and chant your final sutra
What's our place on earth?   nada   nada   nada
What's our destiny?   war   grief   maggots   nada

Arm   cheeks   cock   femur   eyelids   nada
Cowl   ox   lamb   vellum   marrow   nada
Vulva   nada   semen   nada   ovum   nada

Eternity   nada   heaven   nada   void   nada

Birth and death   the same blackened womb
Birth and death   the same white body bag
Detach   detach   we enter the world alone
Detach   detach   we leave the world bone lonely

If we can't believe in god   we must believe in love
We must believe in love   we must believe in love
And they zip you up   in your white body bag
White body bag   white   white   body   bag

17

(Lisa See, 1955—)
邝丽莎

作者简介

邝丽莎（Lisa See, 1955—），拥有八分之一的中国血统，出生于法国巴黎，主要成长于美国洛杉矶唐人街，毕业于美国西海岸最大的天主教大学——洛约拉马里蒙特大学（Loyola Marymount University），获得学士学位。邝丽莎目前居住在洛杉矶，主要从事文学创作。

邝丽莎的作品主要有回忆录《百年金山——我的美籍华人家族奋斗史》（*On Gold Mountain: The One-Hundred-Year Odyssey of My Chinese-American Family*, 1995），长篇小说《花网》（*Flower Net*, 1997）、《内地》（*The Interior*, 1999）、《龙骨》（*Dragon Bones*, 2003）、《雪花与秘扇》（*Snow Flower and the Secret Fan*, 2005）、《恋爱中的牡丹》（*Peony in Love*, 2007）、《上海女孩》（*Shanghai Girls*, 2009）、《乔伊的梦想》（*Dreams of Joy*, 2011）、《中国娃娃》（*China Dolls*, 2014）、《蜂鸟巷的茶女》（*The Tea Girl of Hummingbird Lane*, 2017）。邝丽莎的多部小说获得美国亚太文学奖（Asian/Pacific American Awards for Literature）等奖项。

作为邝丽莎首部获得美国亚太文学奖的小说，《雪花与秘扇》以中国19世纪闭塞落后的瑶族村落为背景，讲述了雪花与百合两个老同之间曲折动人的情感故事，渲染了深刻的东方女性主题。作为《纽约时报》最佳小说销售排行榜的冠军，《乔伊的梦想》以细腻的笔触再现了特殊民族灾难史中的伦理混乱和秩序重构过程。

邝丽莎的作品充满了浓郁的中国情怀，中国文化在她笔下有种抚慰人心、弥合裂缝的力量。《静坐》（“Sitting Quietly”）选自小说《雪花与秘扇》，讲述了已为老妪的百合在“静坐”中忆往昔的故事，其中特别以睹“扇”思人的方式简单分享了她与“老同”雪花的情感故事。《虎跃》（“The Tiger Leaps”）选自小说《乔伊的梦想》，讲述了赵珠重返中国寻找女儿乔伊，却发现女儿与生父可能一同陷入政治纠葛的故事。

作品选读

Snow Flower and the Secret Fan

Sitting Quietly

(Excerpt)

I AM WHAT THEY CALL IN OUR VILLAGE “ONE WHO HAS NOT yet died”—a widow, eighty years old. Without my husband, the days are long. I no longer care for the special foods that Peony and the others prepare for me. I no longer look forward to the happy events that settle under our roof so easily. Only the past interests me now. After all this time, I can finally say the things I couldn’t when I had to depend on my natal family to raise me or rely on my husband’s family to feed me. I have a whole life to tell; I have nothing left to lose and few to offend.

I am old enough to know only too well my good and bad qualities, which were often one and the same. For my entire life I longed for love. I knew it was not right for me—as a girl and later as a woman—to want or expect it, but I did, and this unjustified desire has been at the root of every problem I have experienced in my life. I dreamed that my mother would notice me and that she and the rest of my family would grow to love me. To win their affection, I was obedient—the ideal characteristic for someone of my sex—but I was too willing to do what they told me to do. Hoping they would show me even the most simple kindness, I tried to fulfill their expectations for me—to attain the smallest bound feet in the county—so I let my bones be broken and molded into a better shape.

When I knew I couldn’t suffer another moment of pain, and tears fell on my bloody bindings, my mother spoke softly into my ear, encouraging me to go one more hour, one more day, one more week, reminding me of the rewards I would have if I carried on a little longer. In this way, she taught me how to endure—not just the physical trials of footbinding and childbearing but the more torturous pain of the heart, mind, and soul. She was also pointing out my defects and teaching me how to use them to my benefit. In our country, we call this type of mother love *teng ai*. My son has told me that in men's writing it is composed of two characters. The first means *pain*; the second means *love*. That is a mother's love.

The binding altered not only my feet but my whole character, and in a strange way I feel as though that process continued throughout my life, changing me from a yielding child to a determined girl, then from a young woman who would follow without question whatever her in-laws demanded of her to the highest-ranked woman in the county who enforced strict village rules and customs. By the time I was forty, the rigidity of my footbinding had moved from my golden lilies to my heart, which held on to injustices and grievances so strongly that I could no longer forgive those I loved and who loved me.

My only rebellion came in the form of *nu shu*, our women's secret writing. My first break with tradition came when Snow Flower—my *laotong*, my "old same," my secret-writing partner—sent me the fan that sits here on my table, and then again after I met her. But apart from who I was with Snow Flower, I was resolved to be an honorable wife, a praiseworthy daughter-in-law, and a scrupulous mother. In bad times my heart was as strong as jade. I had the hidden might to withstand tragedies and sorrows. But here I am—a widow, sitting quietly as tradition dictates—and I understand that I was blind for too many years.

Except for three terrible months in the fifth year of Emperor Xianfeng's reign, I have spent my life in upstairs women's rooms. Yes, I have gone to the temple, traveled back to my natal home, even visited with Snow Flower, but I know little about the outer realm. I have heard men speak of taxes, drought, and uprisings, but these subjects are far removed from my life. What I know is embroidery, weaving, cooking, my husband's family, my children, my grandchildren, my great-grandchildren, and *nu shu*. My life course has been a normal one—daughter days, hair-pinning days, rice-and-salt days, and now sitting quietly.

So here I am alone with my thoughts and this fan before me. When I pick it up, it's strange how light it feels in my hands, for it records so much joy and so much grief. I open it quickly, and the sound each fold makes as it spreads reminds me of a fluttering heart. Memories tear across my eyes. These last forty years, I have read it so many times that it is memorized like a childhood song.

I remember the day the intermediary handed it to me. My fingers trembled as I opened the folds. Back then a simple garland of leaves adorned the upper edge and only one message trickled down the first fold. At that time I didn't know many characters in *nu shu*, so my aunt read the words. "*I understand there is a girl of good character and women's learning in your home. You and I are of the same year and the same day. Could we not be sames together*?" I look now at the gentle wisps that compose those lines and see not only the girl that Snow Flower was but the woman she would become—persevering, straightforward, outward-looking.

My eyes graze along the other folds and I see our optimism, our joy, our mutual admiration, our promises to each other. I see how that simple garland grew to be an elaborate design of interwoven snow blossoms and lilies to symbolize our two lives together as a pair of *laotong*, old sames. I see the moon in the upper right-hand corner shining down on us. We were to be like long vines with entwined roots, like trees that stand a thousand years, like a pair of mandarin ducks mated for life. On one fold, Snow Flower wrote, *We of good affection shall never sever our bond*. But on another fold I see the misunderstandings, the broken trust, and the final shutting of the door. For me, love was such a precious possession that I couldn't share it with anyone else, and it eventually cut me away from the one person who was my same.

I am still learning about love. I thought I understood it—not just mother love but the love for one's parents, for one's husband, and for one's *laotong*. I've experienced the other types of love—pity love, respectful love, and gratitude love. But looking at our secret fan with its messages written between Snow Flower and me over many years, I see that I didn't value the most important love—deep-heart love.

These last years I have copied down many autobiographies for women who never learned *nu shu*. I have listened to every sadness and complaint, every injustice and tragedy. I have chronicled the miserable lives of the poorly fated. I have heard it all and written it all down. But if I know much about women's stories, then I know almost nothing about men's, except that they usually involve a farmer fighting against the elements, a soldier in battle, or a lone man on an interior quest. Looking at my own life, I see it draws from the stories of women and men. I am a lowly woman with the usual complaints, but inside I also waged something like a man's battle between my true nature and the person I should have been.

I am writing these pages for those who reside in the afterworld. Peony, my grandson's wife, has promised to make sure that they are burned at my death, so my story will reach them before my spirit does. Let my words explain my actions to my ancestors, to my husband, but most of all to Snow Flower, before I greet them again.

Dreams of Joy

Part One The Tiger Leaps

Pearl: Forever Beautiful

(Excerpt)

"How much do you want?"

We negotiate until we reach a fair price—balancing the hazards against the value of American dollars—which May will send to him each month. Then it's back to Canton. I'm driven to the docks, where I find a ship to take me to Shanghai, which will be faster than taking a train and cheaper than flying. I tell myself I've bought Louie Yun's loyalty, but I have no way of knowing.

FOUR MORNINGS LATER, I'm on the deck watching Shanghai come into view. A week ago, I stepped off a plane in Hong Kong and was enveloped by odors I hadn't smelled in that particular combination in years. Now, as I wait to disembark, I breathe in the scents of home—the oil- and sewage-infused water, rice being cooked on a passing sampan, rotting fish moldering on the dock, vegetables grown upriver wilting in the heat and humidity. But what I see ahead of me looks like a badly rendered drawing of Shanghai. The buildings along the Bund—the Hong Kong and Shanghai Bank, the Shanghai Club, the Cathay Hotel, and the Custom House—look gray, neglected, and shabby. It doesn't help that nets hang like trampolines from the facades. I don't expect to see coolies. Isn't this supposed to be the New China? But here they are on the wharf: barely dressed, scurrying back and forth, heavy loads on their backs.

This initial impression doesn't dampen my mood. I'm home! I can't wait to get off the boat and onto the streets. For a moment, I wish May were here with me. How many times have we sat together, talking about this or that café or shop, always wanting things to be as they were in our beautiful-girl days?

I, along with the other passengers, am herded into a processing shed, I hand my Certificate of Identity to an inspector, who looks it and then me over. I wear a cotton skirt and a pink blouse, because I can't imagine entering Shanghai looking like a country bumpkin. Still, I definitely look different from everyone else. This seems to single me out for extra attention. One inspector searches my luggage, while another questions me about my reasons for returning to China, if I'm committed to giving up my capitalist ways, and if I'm here to serve the people. This is short compared with the border stop. Maybe they hear my Wu dialect and recognize me as the Shanghainese I am. Once their interrogation is finished—and I've lied repeatedly—one of the men pulls out a camera.

"We like to take photos of returning patriots," he says, motioning to the framed pictures on the wall.

I hurry to the wall and search the photos, hoping to find my daughter. There she is! My daughter's alive and she's here! In the photograph, she stands in the middle of a group of men wearing green uniforms and green hats with red stars. A lovely smile lights her face. I ask the men about her. They remember her. How could they not? It's not as though pretty young girls from America pass through their building every day.

"Where did she go?" I ask.

"Her father is a cultural worker," an inspector offers helpfully. "We sent her to the Artists' Association to find him."

I smile for the camera. It isn't hard. I'm happy. Joy found Z.G., which means I ought to be able to find the two of them very quickly. This is going to be much less complicated than I thought.

I pay a nominal fee to leave my bags in the shed and then hurry across the Bund and rush along the boulevards, paying no attention to the sights around me. In the Artists' Association lobby, I approach a woman sitting behind a desk.

"Can you tell me how to find Li Zhi-ge?"

"He's not here!" she snaps.

Bureaucrats are the same all over the world.

"Can you tell me where he lives?" I ask.

She eyes my suspiciously. "What do you want with him? You should not try to see Li Zhi-ge. This man has a black mark against him."

That's alarming. It seems like the inspector would have mentioned this.

"What did he do?"

"Who are you?" Her voice rises. "What do you want with him?"

"It's personal business."

"There's nothing personal in China. Who are you?" she asks again. "Are you a troublemaker too?"

A troublemaker? What has Z.G. done? And please, God, tell me he hasn't dragged my daughter into it.

"Have you seen a girl—"

"If you keep asking questions, I'm going to call the police," she warns.

For a moment, I'd thought this was going to be easy, but nothing in life is easy, not one single thing. And I'm not myself. This is my hometown, but I feel clumsy and inadequate in the new Shanghai. Still, I have to try one more time.

"Have you seen a girl? She's my daughter—"

The woman slaps her palm flat on her desk and glares at me. Then she picks up the phone and dials.

"Never mind," I say, slowly backing away. "I'll come back another time."

I walk out the door, down the steps, and keep going for another two blocks before I stop. I sweat from the heat, humidity, and terror. I lean against a wall, fold my arms over my stomach, and take several deep breaths, trying to bring my fear under control. Despite the effortlessness of my disembarkation, I need to remember the problems I had at the border. I must be careful. I can't end my search before it's even begun.

I have another idea of where to go. I start to walk toward the French Concession. This used to be a lively area—with brothels, nightclubs, and Russian bakeries—but somehow it all looks grim and depressed. Many street names have changed too, but even after all these years I remember the way to Z.G.'s old apartment, where May and I used to model. His landlady is still there, and she's as mean and cantankerous as she always was.

"You!" she exclaims when she sees me. "What do you want this time?"

This, after not having seen me for twenty years.

"I'm looking for Z.G."

"You're *still* looking for him? He doesn't want you. Haven't you figured that out yet? Only your sister, see?"

The words she speaks are like needles jabbing into my eyes. Why would she say this now, when she never said it back then?

"Just tell me where he is."

"Not here. Even if he were, you're too old now. Look in the mirror. You'll see."

All the while she's staring at my clothes, my face, my hands, my haircut. She's probably been taking in my smell too, since years of a Western diet of beef and milk come out in my sweat. She may be a cruel old woman, but she's not stupid. It's not hard for her to deduce I'm a foreigner.

"He returned to Shanghai after Liberation," she recounts. "He paid the rent he owed me and gave me more money for the items I'd stored for him—his paints, brushes, clothes, and the rest of it. He paid my grandson to deliver everything to his new home. Then he paid me even more—"

She's hinting pretty strongly. Maybe some of the old China ways still work.

"How much for his address?"

She probably thinks she's proposing an astronomical sum, but it's little more than one U.S. dollar.

Z.G. lives not far from here on a pretty pedestrian lane lined with graceful Western style houses built in the twenties. I stop to put on lipstick and run a comb through my hair. Then I smooth my hands over my hips to make sure all my seams are straight and my skirt hangs perfectly. I can't help it. I want to look beautiful.

"He's not here," the pretty servant girl who answers the door tells me.

"May I come in? I'm an old friend."

The servant girl stares at me curiously, but she lets me in, which is surprising until I step inside. My breath catches, and I'm frozen in place by what I see. Old posters of my sister and me are on the walls. They've been hidden from public view and protected from the grimness of the streets. They are for Z.G.'s eyes only. None of this is what I expected—not the posters, wealth, sophistication, or the three servant girls, who line up before me nervously and stare down into their folded hands.

I motion to the posters on the walls. "You can see your"—what would be the right word in the New China?—"employer and I knew each other well many years ago. Please tell me where he is."

The girls shift their feet, refusing either to meet my eyes or to respond to my request. It's been a long time since I've had to deal with servants. I do what I did with Z.G.'s former landlady. I open my purse and bring out my wallet.

"Where is he?" I ask.

"He was sent to the countryside," the girl I assume to be in charge answers. She appears to be the oldest, although I doubt she's more than twenty-five. The other two girls continue to fidget.

I don't remember Z.G. having ties to the countryside. I've also read that being sent to the countryside is a common punishment in the New China.

"Is it because he lives like this? Or ..." I look again at the young faces before me. Has there been a problem with him living with these three women? All kinds of improprieties used to happen in the past. I'm calculating how to broach that subject when the servant with a short bob volunteers new information.

"Guns always shoot the leading bird," she says in a low voice. "Master Li is in trouble."

"Things always change to the opposite," the third servant pipes in.

"Dog today, cat tomorrow," the girl with the bob adds. "They could have sent him to a labor camp."

"Or killed him," the third servant says, raising anxious eyes to mine.

"Has he been arrested?" I ask. When the girls don't respond, I say, "I want the truth. All of it."

"He's gone of his own choice to the countryside to redeem himself, learn from the peasants to be more humble, and remember the goals of socialist art," the head girl quickly recites before the other servants can start in again with their gibberish.

"When will he come home?" I ask.

"Don't you mean, *will* he come home?" the girl with the bob asks. "A big tree catches the wind, after all."

The one in charge pinches her subordinate to get her to stop talking, apparently not liking the lesser servants stepping out of their places.

"I remain hopeful," the head servant says. "Otherwise, he wouldn't have left money for me to take care of the house."

"And to feed us too," the quiet one mutters.

I glance from girl to girl. They're all about Joy's age. What kind of man is Z.G.? Is he still falling for any pretty face?

"Have you had any visitors?" I ask. "A young woman perhaps."

"We get those all the time," chirps the girl with the bob.

My jaw clenches. For so long, I felt I lived like a servant, but I wasn't a servant. I wasn't impudent...

"I'm looking for my daughter," I say sternly. I start to put my wallet away.

"We know the one!"

"Yes! We do!"

"Tell me," I say.

"She came the day Master Li was leaving. We heard her say she was his daughter. She came from a different place ..."

"Like you."

"Where is she now?" I ask.

"She went with him to the countryside."

It's not the worst thing I could hear, but it's not the best either.

"Do you know where they went? To which village?"

They shake their heads. Even when I offer more money, they can't help me.

After they let me out, I stand in the lane for some time. I've run up against a blank wall, and I'm unsure what to do next. I'm desperate and terrified for my daughter, who is with someone in such trouble that he appears to have chosen banishment over arrest. In my hopelessness, I find myself speaking to May, as though she could hear me so far away in Los Angeles. *I haven't found our girl yet. She's with Z.G., and he could cause problems for her—things we haven't even thought of.*

18

(Gish Jen，1955—)
任璧莲

作者简介

任璧莲（Gish Jen, 1955—），出生于美国纽约长岛。1977 年毕业于哈佛大学；1983 年获得爱荷华大学作家坊小说创作艺术硕士学位。她被公认为当代美国文学界的重要声音。主要作品有长篇小说《典型的美国佬》（*Typical American*, 1991）、《蒙娜在希望之乡》（*Mona in the Promised Land*, 1996）、《爱妻》（*The Love Wife*, 2004）、《世界与小镇》（*World and Town*, 2010）和短篇小说集《谁是爱尔兰人？》（*Who's Irish?*, 1999）。短篇小说多次收录于年度《美国最佳短篇小说选》（*The Best American Short Stories*）。《典型的美国佬》曾入围美国国家书评人协会奖（小说类）。《世界与小镇》荣获 2011 年马萨诸塞州图书奖（小说类）。

任璧莲的作品阐释了美国经验中共有的主题，如移民、同化、个人主义、选择人生道路的自由等，并试图表明族裔性不是固定的、封闭的，而是浮动的、多重的。《典型的美国佬》以轻快、幽默、反讽的笔触，表现了中国移民追求美国梦的奋斗历程，探讨了美国华裔双重文化身份的转换与建构、双重价值标准的冲突与调和，颠覆了美国主流社会对少数族裔本质论式的偏见。《世界与小镇》采用全知叙事方式讲述了中学退休教师海蒂·孔移居新英格兰小镇里弗雷克两年后发生的故事。里弗雷克受到全球化、现代科技、城市文明和商业文明的冲击，是美国小镇生活的缩影。当宗教信仰、迷信思想与科学思维发生冲突时，尊重、宽容、妥协才是我们应有的态度。

《魔力商标，千真万确》(“A Brand of Alchemy, Indeed”)选自《典型的美国佬》第4部分《结构松动》(“Structural Weakening”)。拉尔夫刚刚获得终身教职，受到格罗弗的蛊惑，休假经营起炸鸡店。他的办公室里到处都是励志书，墙上也贴满了追求财富的语录，他完全成了个人主义和拜金主义的俘虏。《海蒂2: 起而再战》(“Hattie II: Rising to Fight Again”)选自《世界与小镇》第3部分。柬埔寨移民清洪的女儿索皮受到基督教宗教激进主义教派的影响，为了追求精神重生，认为哥哥沙伦是家中的罪恶之源，便纵火焚烧了一座在建的小型超市，试图嫁祸于他。在海蒂的帮助下，索皮认识到宗教信仰并不是要人们远离家庭，而是要维护家庭的团结与完整。

作品选读

Typical American

PART IV Structural Weakening

A Brand of Alchemy, Indeed

(Excerpt)

But he just got tenure! In fact, Ralph did have misgivings about switching careers. Teaching might be the tip of a bull’s horn, his father’s idea, and nothing he was good at, but he sporadically recalled what it was like not to have any degree, and that gave him pause. Sometimes he saw himself hunched over his rooming house desk, working on his master’s thesis; he remembered the lonely desperation with which he’d worried the equations. And with what might he had striven for tenure! For how many years he had oriented his very being toward it, like a Muslim toward Mecca! Now, finally, he was truly Professor Chang; he wasn’t sure he was ready to return to plain Ralph, or, worse yet, Yifeng.

Still, this was only a leave of absence he was taking; and in winning over Helen (which took a few days), he also won over himself. He became the most fervent sort of convert. There was nothing he didn’t know; his former life, that dark age, could not recede fast enough. Handshakes, phone calls. Negotiations. What passed in between was nothing. A president came in, an invasion failed—both in meaningless suspension. It was as if the Changs had run flat life through a fancy new sewing machine, and seen it emerge smocked. Papers were signed; the art of seasoning was revealed to Ralph, the key to crispiness.

And the next thing anyone knew, Grover was dropping in to say hello all the time. It was because of the woods behind their house. Ralph had tipped Grover off about the developer being in over his head; Grover was thinking to buy him out. This necessitated visits to the property. And wouldn't it be rude of him not to stop by while he was in the neighborhood? "Coming!" Helen would warn, if Theresa was home, so that she would know to shut herself up in her room. Sometimes Theresa plugged her ears so she wouldn't have to hear Grover's booming voice. "*These walls are like paper*," she began to complain. "*These walls are no walls*."

Variations: "*Anyone who wanted to could kick this door in.*" "*We should get stronger locks.*"

But what door, what lock, could keep out of a house what someone inside hankered for? Just as Theresa had found a way to an affair, and Helen a way to her split-level, Ralph had found his way to Grover; and as Theresa and Helen had been changed for the finding, so had Ralph, in inalienable ways. The sorts of things Ralph talked about had begun to change; his voice had taken on a new boldness; and with other small changes of manner, it became suddenly striking that he and Grover were both five four, more or less, with haircuts they sometimes slicked down, sometimes let reach for the sky like wiry versions of the Kennedys' lawn. Their faces remained very different. But from the back it was noticeable that they moved more and more alike. Both strode rather than walked; both stood very straight when they stopped; and when they ate, both tended to stick their elbows in the air as though they were sitting at an unusually high table, that came to their chins.

"Who knows? Maybe we're long-lost cousins," Grover joked once—to which Theresa exclaimed when she heard, "Impossible!" And of course, as she said, she ought to know. But one day, Ralph told Mona and Callie a long story that began with their great-grandmother's father, who was, he said, a rich guy.

"That guy has lotta, lotta money."

Mona and Callie nodded; they'd heard this before.

"And because he has so much money, that guy is not have one wife, like here. That guy is have five, ten wives."

"Ten wives!" Mona and Callie were amazed.

"Sure." Ralph shrugged. "Chinese guys, those rich guys, they have as many wives they like. I'm talking about those guys, really rich.

"So my grandmother's father, he has ten, twenty wives. And so he has lotta children. Mister! Lotta children. Some boys, some girls. And most of those children, they are good ones. But so happen, one little boy not so good. This boy is something the matter with his head." Ralph pointed to his own head. "I don't know what's happen. Maybe one day he fall down, hit his head on one piece rock. Anyhow, this boy does all kind of crazy thing. One day he is play with knife, you know? Big cutting knife. Another day he is throw everything into the lake. And nighttime, he is not sleep in regular bed. Everyone else sleeps regular bed, he sleeps in some kind of strange bed. You know what that bed is? That bed is a big box he is built by himself, make out of one piece wood. And inside the box is not the regular blanket. Inside is all those paper money."

"Money!"

"That's right. Inside is all those paper money, big pile, and when nighttime comes, that's where he's sleeping. Instead of use the regular blanket, he's hide himself inside there.

"Of course, his father, mother, everybody, thinks he is crazy. But what can they do? Father blames mother, mother blames grandmother. Everybody crazy now. Then one day, the boy say he's like to leave the family. So father talks to grandmother, mother talks to grandmother, and finally grandmother says okay."

"So then what?"

"So then the boy leaving."

"And then?"

"And then nobody knows what's happen to him." Ralph nodded thoughtfully. "But I think maybe that boy go somewhere, have children. And then those children maybe come to United States, and then maybe one of them has a son who come to New York, become manager of grease factory and so forth." He winked.

"How could it be! That's not true. He's making it up!" Theresa's voice pulsed when she heard. "Your father is talking nonsense. I've never heard such a story!"

Still Ralph laughed and insisted, "Sure is true," until finally she confronted him. *"You're just joking,"* she said, *"but the girls believe you."*

Ralph gave her a look. *"You have nothing to say,"* he said—what he always said now. There was uncertainty in his voice, though, and later Theresa hearkened to this. Grover might be rubbing off on Ralph, but Ralph was still Ralph. Or was he? One day she happened into his office, only to discover an entire wall of it papered with inspirational quotes.

ALL RICHES BEGIN IN AN IDEA.

WHAT YOU CAN CONCEIVE, YOU CAN ACHIEVE.
DON'T WAIT FOR YOUR SHIP TO COME IN, SWIM OUT TO IT.
FOLLOW THE HERD, YOU END UP A COW.

She sank into the desk chair, thinking *cheng yu*—idiomatic sayings, the Chinese had a lot of them too. But no, these were different. She stood back up; the quotes fluttered with her motion, a flock of starlings.

YOU CAN NEVER HAVE RICHES IN GREAT QUANTITY UNLESS YOU WORK YOURSELF INTO A WHITE HEAT OF DESIRE FOR MONEY.

There were books everywhere. *Making Money. Be Your Own Boss! Ninety Days to Power and Success*. Theresa pictured her brother, feet up on the desk like Pete the super, thumbing through these. Where was the Ph.D. he'd worked so hard for? Helen had taken it to a special place to have it framed, Theresa recalled. Now it languished on a high shelf, under a box full of cash register tapes.

World and Town

Hattie II: Rising to Fight Again

(Excerpt)

Hattie puts on her turn signal. "I'm an old retired lady with a dead husband and a faraway son and no sisters. I've got Reveille and Annie, as you know. And I've got friends. But first Joe died two years ago and then my best friend went, right after him. Her name was Lee." She stops. "And now Cato."

"That sounds hard." Sophy hits an adult note even as she flicks her zipper toggle up and down.

"It is. Joe was a good man. And Lee was wonderful. Funny." Hattie makes her turn. "For a long time, I wished that I'd died, too."

"You should go to church more."

"I go every week, just about," says Hattie. "And I go to the library. There are always warm bodies there. And my walking group is great."

"Except for Ginny."

"She's not my favorite," admits Hattie. "And you know, there's no getting around the fact that I need other people more than they need me. I'm just not an integral part of anyone's picture, if you know what I mean."

She makes her turn, expecting Sophy to ask her what "integral" means, but instead Sophy says, "You mean you're old."

"Yes. In a way." Hattie nods. "Though you'd have to say I was always old, then. Or that I've been old longer than most people. Or that coming to America made me old."

Sophy doesn't ask Hattie what she means by any of that, either. Instead, she plays with her cross. "Sarun didn't steal any plywood, you know," she says suddenly.

And Hattie is just as suddenly grateful that she is in such a concertedly even frame of mind. "That was Ginny's idea, wasn't it?" she asks, coolly. "To blame him."

"It was. But he didn't do it."

"Don't I turn left up here?"

"At the light."

The wipers squeak on their downward stroke.

"She wanted to blame him because whoever got blamed for the plywood might just get blamed for the fire, too," guesses Hattie. "And she wanted to burn down the mini-mall to get Everett. Is that it?"

Sophy nods, more open now than Hattie has ever seen her. "How do you know everything? I told Sopheap and Sophan that, and they said you were just smart."

Hattie shakes her head. "I don't think so." She frowns.

" You keep going straight."

"Are you sure?"

"Oh, wait, you see? You know everything. Go right, kind of around that island."

Hattie steers. "I have a question about all that, though."

"You mean about the fire and everything?"

"Yes." Hattie glances sideways; Sophy's face is open and friendly. "Did you really think that would work—that people would link the fire and the stealing in the end? Without evidence? Did you really think Sarun and his friends would be convicted when they were innocent? Just because they were strangers and made people nervous?"

Sophy slumps a little, her hands back in her hoodie pocket. "I don't know. I mean, sure. I mean it was, like, Jesus's plan, so..." She shrugs. "Ginny said we were like Esther, put where we were put for a reason, we just had to look at what we were given and, like, try to figure out what it was. Like it was a puzzle."

"And you let her try to pin it on Sarun because he was ruining things for your family. Is that it?"

"I guess. Straight."

"Because here your family was, starting over, and he was driving your dad crazy. Messing things up with his gang. Disturbing things."

"He was no good."

"And this was a chance to stop him."

"The Lord gave us this chance—I believe that. I mean, why else would He have sent the white van, right? Why else would He drive it right up to our trailer and put it right under our noses? Why else would He have terrorists attack America so people would believe anything?"

Why else would He have terrorists attack America.

"You mean, spooking people so they would believe almost anything about that scary van," says Hattie, slowly.

Sophy nods. "I mean, the terrorists were probably sent to help a lot of people with a lot of things, not just us," she says.

"The Lord God acting with divine efficiency."

Sophy nods again.

"His plan," says Hattie, "just happening to accord with your hopes."

Sophy nods a third time.

"Because your father didn't want Sarun anymore, and you didn't, either."

"I told my sisters the whole thing was my fault, but they said I was too sensitive. Like how could it be my fault, they said, just like they didn't think they ended up in foster homes because of me, they said they just did stupid things themselves. Like the time Sopheap stole that car with her boyfriend. She said that was her own stupid decision, she just wishes somebody had told her she'd end up in a foster home for it. And Sophan said she was stupid to break into people's houses and, like, try on their clothes and listen to their stereos and shit. She didn't even steal stuff, but it was break and entry anyway, and they definitely should not have snorted any of the people's coke. Like that was just so stupid. And when I said didn't they feel that people looked down on them because of me, they said that was no excuse. They said they made bad choices and didn't think about the consequences. And now they're making, like, different choices. Like Sopheap says she's going to be an independent woman and not get married or have children or anything. She says in ancient Cambodia women were more powerful than men, and that she's going to go back to that and be like a she-man." She makes a muscle.

Hattie laughs. "Wonderful. But this thing with Sarun really is your fault, you're saying."

"It is." Sophy's eyes suddenly fill. "I'm no good, Hattie. I'm not even a real older sister. Like when I was talking to my sisters, they sounded so much smarter than me—like they sounded older than me, instead of my being older than them. And look at the mess I made. I should never have been born."

"Oh, Sophy." Hattie pulls into a parking spot and turns her engine off. "You know, part of this may be your fault, but what about Ginny?" She digs some tissues out from the between-seat storage compartment. "Hasn't Ginny sinned, too? I mean, who set the fire, right?"

"I set it." Sophy blows her nose.

Hattie shuts the compartment lid.

"I did. I set it," Sophy says again. "Do you see what I mean? How wack I am? Do you see?"

"Did Ginny help?"

"She showed me how to strike a match."

"Was she there when you did it?"

"No."

"Did she drive you there?"

"No."

"Sophy." Hattie speaks slowly, clearly, as if she is talking to Mum. "Did you know what you were doing? Did you know it was wrong?"

"I thought it was Christ's plan."

"You were like Esther, and Sarun was like Haman."

"He was, he was like Haman—like he didn't like anyone doing things different than him, or following different laws. He couldn't tolerate difference."

He couldn't tolerate difference.

"He couldn't tolerate holiness," Sophy goes on. "He wanted to kill it because he knew he was doing bad things."

"Was it drugs?"

"Bear stuff. Bear paws and bear—what do you call it—gallbladders. You know, like people use for traditional medicine. I guess the paws are for soup or something. The gang got them from the hunters and brought them up to some guy in Canada—it was all Sarun's idea. I mean, some of the *puak maak* knew guys who did it in Cambodia, I guess in Cambodia there were guys who, like, sold stuff to Hong Kong and Korea, places like that. But it was Sarun who realized they could do the same thing here." Sophy blows her nose again.

"He was the mastermind."

Sophy nods with energy—as if despite herself she's a little proud of Sarun. "The *puak maak* liked it because it was a new gig. Like they didn't have to compete with a zillion other gangs, it was theirs."

"Is it illegal?"

"I don't know. Probably."

"So why didn't you turn him in for that? Why try to get him for plywood the gang didn't even steal? Or did they."

Sophy folds up her tissue so she can wipe her nose on a fresh part. "I don't think so."

"Was it because you'd have to act by yourself on the bear parts? Whereas this way you had company?"

"I don't know." Sophy looks genuinely confused. "I mean, it just didn't seem like that was what Jesus wanted, I guess. Like Jesus sent me Ginny, and that wasn't what Ginny wanted, so it didn't seem like that's what He wanted. It didn't seem like the reason we were given what we were given."

"I see. But let me ask you—did Ginny make you help her? This is important, Sophy. Did she make you?"

"No." Another flash of pride. "I wanted to, I wanted to be like Esther. I knew Jesus would give us victory, I knew that He'd protect us." Sophy's face is blank, but her voice is strong. "I knew He'd be with us when we passed through the water and the fire. I knew He'd make sure we wouldn't get, like, drowned or burned."

"Or caught?"

Sophy slumps. "Anyway, that guy was building on the wrong foundation."

"You mean Everett?"

Sophy nods.

" 'For other foundation can no man lay than that is laid, which is Jesus Christ,' " quotes Hattie. "Is that it?"

Sophy unfastens her seat belt.

"How does it go after that?" Hattie looks up, undoing her belt, too. " 'Every man's work shall be made manifest; for it shall be revealed by fire.' Something like that. First Corinthians."

"You know a lot of scripture."

"I can't always remember what happened yesterday, but I remember my scripture from when I was a girl. Oh, wait, I'm missing part of it. 'For the day shall declare it, because it shall be revealed by fire; and the fire shall try every man's work of what sort it is.' "

"I'll never be as good as you."

"Of course you will, if you want to be. But tell me—you've heard that verse before?"

Sophy hesitates but then nods.

"From Ginny," guesses Hattie.

"She said Everett was meddling with God and should know better!" Sophy says. "Like he should know that verse 'Forbear thee from meddling with God' something something—"

" 'Forbear thee from meddling with God, who is with me, that He destroy thee not.' "

Sophy plays with her toggle. "I just wish someone would destroy me," she says, in a small voice. "I do. I wish someone would put me in jail."

"What about a foster home again? Or a girls' group home? I don't think they're going to put you in jail, Sophy."

Sophy presses her tissue to her eyes. "I made a bad choice," she cries. "I made a bad choice." Her earrings swing.

Hattie puts a hand on her hoodied back; Sophy's whole body is shaking.

"I should have listened to you. Why didn't I listen to you? I loved Annie so much!"

"Annie loved you, too," says Hattie. "And still does, you know."

But Sophy does not hear her. "I am ashamed to have been born," she sobs. "I am. There's no reason for me to live. I'm sorry I was ever born."

"Don't say that," says Hattie, but there's no stopping Sophy. She cries even as the clouds start to part and thin and lift; she cries even as visiting hours end and Hattie starts up the car. There is nothing to do but fill up the gas tank and head home.

19

(Ha Jin, 1956—)

哈·金

作者简介

哈·金（Ha Jin, 1956—），本名金雪飞，出生于辽宁省。1985 年赴美留学，1992 年取得布兰迪斯大学博士学位。毕业后曾在爱默里大学讲授诗歌写作，2002 年以来在波士顿大学教授创意写作课程。2014 年当选美国艺术文学院院士。主要作品有长篇小说《等待》（*Waiting*, 1999）、《战废品》（*War Trash*, 2004）、《自由生活》（*A Free Life*, 2007）、《南京安魂曲》（*Nanjing Requiem*, 2011）、《折腾到底》（*The Boat Rocker*, 2016）等；短篇小说集《好兵》（*Ocean of Words: Army Stories*, 1996）、《新郎》（*The Bridegroom*, 2000）、《落地》（*A Good Fall*，2009）等；诗集《沉默之间》（*Between Silences: A Voice From China*, 1990）、《残骸》（*Wreckage*, 2001）等。荣获海明威基金会 / 笔会奖（《好兵》）、美国国家图书奖（《等待》）、美国笔会 / 福克纳奖（《等待》《战废品》）。

哈·金深受 19 世纪俄罗斯和英国现实主义文学大师的影响，坚持写实主义风格，文风简洁冷静，叙述语调平缓亲切。《等待》是一部悲凉而充满反讽的爱情小说，探询了人性的复杂与人类的生存困境。军医孔林等待十八年与妻子离婚后才得以与吴曼娜结婚，而婚后生活并非他想象的那样幸福美满，不禁反思自己多年来并不清楚真正想要什么。想着病入膏肓的妻子，他又盼望着将来能重回前妻身边过安宁的生活。《南京安魂曲》讲述了日本侵华期间南京陷落后明妮·魏特琳与国际安全区委员会一起竭力救助中国难民的感人故事，同时揭露了日军对中国人民犯下的滔天罪行。魏特琳把南京金陵女子文理学院改为难民营，勇敢保护了一万多名妇女儿童，使她们免遭日军蹂躏，她被南京市民尊称为“活菩萨”。

第一篇选自《等待》第3部第11章。一次琐碎的争吵迫使孔林深深质疑自己的婚姻。他的苦恼与矛盾淋漓尽致地展现了出来。他诘问自己是否懂得爱情、漫长地等待究竟在等待什么，醒悟了自己虚度十八年的青春时光。作为丈夫与父亲，他觉得自己要继续承担家庭的责任和义务。第二篇选自《南京安魂曲》第1部《首都沦陷》(“The Fall of the Capital”)第8章。日军在南京城中肆意抢劫、放火、抓捕男人、强奸妇女，其凶残恶毒令人发指。魏特琳把寻求避难的几百名乡下人带到南京大学难民营安置下来。

作品选读

Waiting

Part III

11

(Excerpt)

One Sunday morning in January, Lin was cooking rice for lunch. While the pot was boiling, he set out for the mess to buy a dish. The previous evening, he had seen a notice on the small blackboard at the entrance to the kitchen, saying there would be beef and fried potato for lunch, seventy fen a helping. On his way there he ran into Commissar Su. They talked for a while about initiating a crash program for training paramedics from the local counties the next spring. The prefecture's Department of Public Health had just asked the army hospital for help and was willing to finance the program. This meant the hospital's staff would receive a larger bonus at the end of next year.

Because of the talk, Lin forgot the rice boiling at home. When he got back with a bowl of potato and beef, the kitchen was white with smoke. He rushed to the cooking range, put the bowl down, and removed the pot. The second he opened the lid a wave of steam clouded his glasses and made him unable to see anything. After wiping the lenses with the end of his jacket and putting the glasses back on, he saw that the rice was already burned through. He picked up an iron scoop and was about to put a little water into the pot when Manna came into the kitchen, coughing and buttoning her jacket. "Put a scallion into the pot, quick!" she shouted.

Lin planted a scallion stalk into the rice to get rid of the burned smell, but it was too late, a good part of the rice was already brown. He pushed the transom open to let the smoke out.

Suddenly Manna yelled at him, "Why did you leave while the rice pot was boiling? You can't even cook such a simple thing, idiot."

"I—I went to buy a dish. You were home, why couldn't you keep an eye on it?"

"You didn't tell me, did you? Besides, I'm too sick to cook. Don't you know that?" With her fingertips holding the cuff of her sleeve, she swept the pot and the bowl off the cooking range; they crashed to the cement floor; beef and potato cubes and smoking rice were scattered about. The aluminum lid of the pot rolled away and hit the threshold, where it came to rest, leaning upright against two bricks piled together as a doorstop.

"Even pigs won't touch this," she added.

From inside the bedroom Lake broke out crying, then screamed at the top of his lungs. A few seconds later River started bawling too. Manna hurried back in to calm them. Without tending to the stove or cleaning up, Lin turned and stormed out. His green mittens, connected by a string, flapped wildly beside his flanks as he strode away. "I hate her! I hate her!" he said to himself.

He went to the hill behind the hospital grounds. It was a cold day. The orchard on the slope was deserted, the apple-pear trees thick and bulky, their frosty branches sprawling and looking feathery. For a while he couldn't think of anything, his skull numb and his temples tight. He climbed toward the hilltop, which was covered by snow except for two clusters of brownish rocks. Beyond the hill, on the riverbank, there was a village that had a deer farm and a boat house, which Lin for some reason wanted to watch from the crown of the hill. The scent of winter was clean and intense. It was windless, and the sun was glinting on the boulders here and there and on the tree trunks crusted with ice. In the distance a flock of rooks were circling and cawing hungrily.

As Lin calmed down, a voice rose in his head and said, Do you really hate her?

He made no reply.

The voice continued, You asked for this mess. Why did you marry her?

I love her, he answered.

You married her for love? You really loved her?

He thought a while, then managed to answer, I think so. We waited eighteen years for each other, didn't we? Doesn't such a long time prove we love each other?

No, time may prove nothing. Actually you never loved her. You just had a crush on her, which you didn't get a chance to outgrow or to develop into love.

What? A crush! He was taken aback and paused in his tracks. His sinuses became congested.

Yes, you mistook your crush for love. You didn't know what love was like. In fact you waited eighteen years just for the sake of waiting. You could have waited that long for another woman too, couldn't you?

I waited for Manna only. There wasn't another woman involved.

All right, there were only the two of you. Let's assume you and she loved each other. Were you sure that you both would enjoy living together as husband and wife?

We really loved each other, didn't we? Lin's temples were throbbing, and he took off his hat so that the cold air could cool his head.

Really? the voice resumed. What do you know about love? Did you know her well enough before you married her? Were you sure she was the woman you'd spend the rest of your life with? Be honest now, among all the women you've known, who are you most fond of? Isn't there someone else who is more suitable for you than Manna?

I can't tell. Besides her there's only Shuyu in my life. How could I compare Manna with someone else? I don't know much about women, although I wish I did.

Suddenly he felt his head expanding with a shooting pain. He was giddy with the intuition that this marriage might not be what he had wanted. He sat down on a rock to catch his breath and think more.

The voice went on, Yes, you waited so many years, but for what?

He found his mind blank and couldn't answer. The question frightened him, because it implied that all those years he had waited for something wrong.

Let me tell you what really happened, the voice said. All those years you waited torpidly, like a sleepwalker, pulled and pushed about by others' opinions, by external pressure, by your illusions, by the official rules you internalized. You were misled by your own frustration and passivity, believing that what you were not allowed to have was what your heart was destined to embrace.

Lin was stunned. For a moment he was at a loss for words. Then he began cursing himself. Fool, eighteen years you waited without knowing for what! Eighteen years, the prime of your life, gone, wasted, and they led you to this damn marriage. You're a model fool!

What's to be done now? the voice asked.

He heaved a deep sigh, not knowing what to do or whether he should try to do something. Tears were sliding down his cheeks and reached the corners of his mouth; time and again he raised his hand to wipe them off. His ears were freezing, so he put the fur hat back on and turned down its earflaps.

Then the image of Manna in her late twenties emerged in his mind. She had a vivacious face smiling radiantly; on her palm perched a tiny green frog, its mouth quivering. A few sky-blue dragonflies were flying around her, their wings issuing a whirring sound. As Lin stretched out his hand to touch the frog's back, it jumped and plopped into the limpid stream flowing along the edge of an eggplant field. She turned and looked at him, her eyes dim with affection and kindness, as though full of secrets that she was eager to share with him. The end of her loose hair was thrown up a little by the warm breeze, revealing the silky nape of her neck. How different she was now from then! He realized that the long waiting must have changed her profoundly—from a pleasant young woman into a hopeless spitfire. No matter how he felt about her now, he was certain she had always loved him. Perhaps it was the unrequited love that had dragged her down. Or perhaps it was the suffering and despondency she had experienced in the long waiting that had dissolved her gentle nature, worn away her hopes, ruined her health, poisoned her heart, and doomed her.

The voice interrupted his thoughts. Yes, she has loved you. But isn't it this marriage that has been debilitating her?

He tried to answer, She wanted a family and children, didn't she? She must have been starved for human warmth and affection, any bit of which she might have taken as love. Yes, she's been blind to the true situation, always believing I loved her. She doesn't know what a true lover is like.

His heart began aching. It dawned on him that he had never loved a woman wholeheartedly and that he had always been the loved one. This must have been the reason why he knew so little about love and women. In other words, emotionally he hadn't grown up. His instinct and ability to love passionately had withered away before they had had an opportunity to blossom. If only he had fallen in love soulfully just once in his life, even though it might have broken his heart, paralyzed his mind, made him live in a daze, bathed his face in tears, and drowned him in despair!

What are you going to do? the voice kept on.

He could not think of an answer. Being a husband and a father, he felt he ought to carry out the responsibilities imposed on him by his marriage. What else could he do to alleviate his sense of guilt and convince himself that he was a decent man? What else could he do other than to endure?

He sighed. If only he had had enough passion and energy left in him so that he could learn how to love devotedly and start his life afresh. If only Manna were healthy and not dying. He was too old to take any action now. His heart was weary. He only hoped that before his wife died their sons would be old enough for kindergarten.

Down below, along the brick wall behind the hospital, a man and a woman were strolling eastward despite the cold weather. Both of them wore uniforms; the man was a head taller than the woman, who looked rather small and delicate. Every once in a while she would run a few steps to catch up with him. They looked familiar to Lin. Lin strained his eyes to make out who they are, but his sight failed him. It occurred to him that the rule that prohibited two people of opposite sex from walking together outside the wall had been almost abandoned in the past year. Few leaders would now bother to criticize young men and women who walked in pairs outside the compound. He had heard that some nurses had even gone into the woods with their patients. Yet somehow to him and Manna, there still seemed to be a wall around them. They had never walked together outside the hospital since they were married, and Manna still could not ride a bicycle.

A moment later Lin stood up and whisked the snow off his lap with the mittens. Instead of going up to the summit, he turned back at the middle of the slope, coming down slowly, weak at the knees. A few goats were bleating from the birch woods on the left; a line of cow dung dotted the white road, still sending up curls of steam. Up on the slope a cart was climbing toward the hilltop, its iron-rimmed wheels rattling away on pebbles and ice. Down there, at the foot of the hill, a tiny whirlwind was hurling dried leaves along the bank of the frozen brook, swirling away toward the vast field studded with corn stubble.

He reached home twenty minutes later. On opening the door, he was suddenly nauseated by the smell of rice vinegar, which had been blown into the air to deactivate the flu virus and which, before now, had always been pleasant to his nose. Manna came and told him in a soft voice that lunch was in the bamboo steamer on the cooking range. She had made noodles and fried some soy paste. But he didn't go to the kitchen. Instead, he went into the bedroom, flopped down on the camp bed, and pulled a blanket over his face. The bedsprings under him creaked as he turned now and then.

Manna began sobbing. For a while he didn't want to comfort her, for fear that he might join her in weeping if he tried. But a moment later he pulled himself together, got out of bed, and went up to her. Sitting down beside her, he put his arm around her shoulders and said, "Come, stop now, dear. You've cried enough. It's bad for your health." For the first time he felt she was as fragile as though her bones might fall apart at any moment. His heart was again filled with sadness and compassion. He kissed her cheek.

She raised her eyes and said with shame, "I was nasty. Can you forgive me?"

"Forget about it, darling. I should have been more careful."

"Say you forgive me."

"It wasn't your fault."

"Just say it!"

"I forgive you."

"Please eat lunch."

"I'm not hungry."

"Please eat."

"All right, if you say so." He tried to smile, but the effort distorted his face, which he turned aside to avoid being noticed. He got up and went to the kitchen.

Nanjing Requiem

One The Fall of The Capital

8

(Excerpt)

IT WAS MILD and sunny the next morning. Watching the refugees in the quad, I was grateful for the warm weather, which felt like October. This would make the uprooted people less miserable on the road or in the wilderness, since they had nothing to protect themselves from the elements. Never had I imagined that our fortified capital could be smashed so easily, like a ceramic vat hit by a mallet. In the north, artillery fire surged and ebbed, rumbling amid smoky and blazing clouds. There was still fighting in the Hsia Gwan area, and the Japanese warships were shelling the remaining Chinese troops and sinking boats and rafts that attempted to cross the river. Around Jinling, rifles crackled from time to time.

Early in the afternoon Holly and I went out to the Drum Tower area, a short walk to the northeast. She had not returned home three nights in a row and was afraid that her house might have been plun-dered, though she had thumbtacked an American flag to the front door and sealed it with a poster from the U.S. embassy. As we walked along Shanghai Road, many Japanese flags were flying from the houses and buildings, flapping like laundry. A few banners made of white cloth even declared, LONG LIVE THE EMPEROR!

"Those people will do anything to save their skin," Holly grunted.

"They must be terrified," I said.

"I'm a Chinese citizen too, but I won't say a good word about the Japanese brutes."

"You have a foreign face, Holly. To tell the truth, I wouldn't dare to step off campus without your company."

We turned into the small alley alongside the eastern border of the Safety Zone. Seven or eight houses on the street had been razed, set on fire after being looted. Holly's home was among them, and her car was gone too. A young man, bayoneted twice in the chest, lay dead on his side below the brick wall of her yard, his back naked, his hair scorched, and the exposed side of his face eaten by dogs. He looked like a stranger to Holly. "Savages, worse than beasts!" she cursed the soldiers, and broke into tears, wiping her face with the end of her scarf.

"Holly, I'm sorry," I murmured, and wrapped my arm around her.

The neighborhood was very quiet; you couldn't hear any noise, not even the tiny chirps made by the sparrows that used to live in many of the roofs. Then a Siamese cat jumped out of a coal shack in the next-door neighbor's yard and meowed forlornly, as though starved. Brushing away her tears, Holly said, "I guess this is it. Now I have no place to go."

"You can always stay with us," I said. That was hardly an invitation, since she was already indispensable to our school. She wasn't just the only other foreigner on campus but was also, as a musician, needed for the chapel services. Besides, she'd been helping our nurse care for the sick and the women expecting or in labor.

When we returned to the campus, about four hundred men, women, and children were at the front gate, begging Luhai and Miss Lou to let them in. All the women wore white terry cloth over their hair; apparently they were from the countryside. A few old men were sucking on long pipes. I was somewhat surprised, because by now we were known as a camp for only women and children, and most men wouldn't come to seek refuge anymore.

Minnie said to the villagers, "We accept only women and kids."

"Please, we can't go elsewhere," a thirtyish man begged.

"Most of the other camps take in families. You should try them," I told him.

"We dare not walk anywhere, " an older man said, donning a skullcap, the type called a melon-rind cap. "If the Japanese devils see us, they'll kill us and grab our wives and daughters."

A girl in her mid-teens shuffled over, wearing a pair of bandages on her forehead like two miniature crosses standing together, one taller than the other. "Please let me in, Aunties," she wailed to Holly and me as we were still standing outside the gate. "I'm the only one left in my family." She burst into tears.

"What happened?" I asked.

"Some Japs broke into the deserted building where we stayed last night, and they cut down my dad and brothers. Then they stripped my mom and me and started torturing us. I screamed, so they punched me again and again until I lost my voice and blacked out. When I came to, I saw my mom's body in the room. She couldn't take it anymore and hit her head on the doorjamb and killed herself."

Minnie had come out of the gate by now. I realized that the girl had been raped and told her, "You must get treated. I'll get someone to take you to the University Hospital."

"I can't walk anymore. If not for these good-hearted folks, I couldn't have made it here."

"Then you can come in," I said.

After telling a staffer to take the girl to our infirmary, Minnie decided to lead the rest of them to the university camp. Holly offered to go along, but Minnie told her to stay because John Magee had just left and we needed at least one foreigner on campus to deter the soldiers.

Nanjing University was about a fifteen-minute walk from our college, and Minnie led the crowd away with a small U.S. flag in her hand, while I brought up the rear, bearing a Red Cross flag. Passing the closed American embassy, we saw two Japanese soldiers coming from the opposite direction and hee-hawing while prodding a reedy boy ahead of them with rifles. The teenager pushed a barrow that had a large wooden wheel ringed with steel. It was loaded with booty—a stack of dried salt fish, a bundle of potato noodles, a jar of duck eggs still in brine, a wall clock, and a trussed pregnant sheep, still bleating. The soldiers each had about a dozen silver bracelets, watches, and gold rings affixed to their belts. All the women in the procession lowered their heads until the soldiers passed.

When we arrived at the university, we found George Fitch, who had been managing the large camp there with Searle, squatting under a bulky linden, his head in both hands. "Hey, George, what's the matter?" Minnie asked.

He raised his bony face, his eyes watery and somewhat bloodshot. "The Japanese took away two hundred men just now, " he told her.

"Were they surrendered soldiers?"

"No, many of them were civilians."

"They just took whoever they wanted?"

"They ordered them to undress and checked their shoulders and hands. If there was a mark like something left by a knapsack or a rifle, they took the man. But most of the poor fellows were coolies who had to work with tools and carry stuff around, and of course they had marks on their shoulders and calluses on their hands. The Japanese arrested practically all the young men. There was no way to reason with them. Oh, Minnie, this is horrible, as if we still live in the Dark Ages."

"What are they going to do to them?"

"Finish them off, I'm sure."

"I guess they just want to kill to terrify the Chinese."

"Also to wipe out all the able-bodied males." He sniveled and blew his nose into a piece of straw paper.

Minnie said, "Maybe we shouldn't have offered protection to those Chinese soldiers in the first place. Some of them were reluctant to give us their weapons, but we were so foolish that we promised them more than we can deliver."

"I've thought about that too. With firearms they could at least have defended themselves."

As we were speaking, a group of Japanese soldiers emerged, two of them dragging a scrawny man onto the lawn. I recognized Chang, who used to be a librarian at the university and now worked in the refugee camp as a file clerk. They meant to take him away, but he refused to go with them.

We all stood up to watch. The leader of this group, a lieutenant, ordered a new recruit to stab Chang. The young soldier hesitated, but the officer barked out orders again. The man charged at Chang, whose cotton-padded overcoat was so thick that the bayonet didn't go through. Realizing they meant to kill him, Minnie and George hustled toward them to intervene. I followed, but the soldiers blocked us. Then, to our astonishment, Chang undid his buttons and dropped his coat on the ground, facing his attacker with just his thin jacket on, his sparse goatee wet with snot. The lieutenant again yelled at the young man, who rushed toward Chang with a wild shriek and stabbed him through. The clerk's legs buckled, but his eyes were still fixed on his killer. Then he fell, blood pooling around him.

We were so stunned that for a while nobody could move or say a word. Then the troops marched away, and people gathered around Chang, who was breathing his last. "Revenge, revenge," he mouthed.

He died within a few minutes. I had known this wispy moonfaced librarian by sight and heard he had a fiery temper, but I'd never thought much of him.

Having left the four hundred refugees with George Fitch, Minnie and I headed back. She panted a little as she walked, her gait ponderous but steady.

"I wonder why God let this happen to us Chinese," I said. "What did we do to deserve this? Why doesn't God punish those heartless men?" Just that morning I'd heard that a nephew of mine, my cousin's seventeen-year-old son, had been seized by the Japanese the night before. His parents were distraught but dared not go out and look for him.

"God works in his own ways, hard for us to fathom," Minnie said, but not convincingly.

Our ancient city, noted for its beauty and cultural splendor, had become hell overnight, as if forsaken by God. I couldn't stop wondering whether there'd be retribution in store for the ruthless soldiers and their families. No one could brutalize others like this with impunity in the long run, I was sure.

That night, Searle Bates and Plumer Mills slept in our main dormitory and the Arts Building, respectively, while Lewis Smythe kept Luhai company at our gatehouse. Before turning in, the husky Plumer wept and cursed again, his heavy-jawed face scrunched and his hair damp with sweat. He suffered from pain in his chest caused by being hit twice by the Japanese with rifle butts that morning when he had attempted in vain to prevent them from taking thirteen hundred Chinese soldiers out of the police headquarters. A group of American missionaries had disarmed those men and promised them personal safety, but all the poor fellows had been dragged away and executed in the afternoon. Fifty policemen guarding the Safety Zone were also rounded up and shot for letting the Chinese soldiers enter the neutral district. With the three American men in our camp we felt a little more secure. Minnie stayed with Miss Lou in the Practice Hall, which was more than two hundred yards away from the nearest building, tucked in the southeast corner of campus, while I was in charge of the main dormitory. The college's two policemen still patrolled, but in plainclothes. In addition, an old watchman, lantern in hand, would make rounds throughout the night.

20

(Siu Kam Wen, 1956—)

萧锦荣

作者简介

萧锦荣（Siu Kam Wen, 1956—），生于广东中山，20世纪50年代先后迁居中国香港、秘鲁利马，毕业于秘鲁国立圣马尔科斯大学（National University of San Marcos），1985年移居夏威夷获得美国国籍。

虽然是一位以西班牙语写作的美国华裔作家，萧锦荣却亲自几乎把其所有作品翻译成了英文，其主要作品有短篇小说集《末程》（*The Final Stretch*, 1985）和《天下第一剑》（*The First Sword of the Empire*，1988），自传体小说《伊萨卡之旅》（*A Journey to Ithaca*, 2004），长篇小说《花园中的雕像》（*The Statue in the Garden*, 2006）、《此生不易》（*This Sort of Life*, 2007）、《图与剑》（*The Map and the Sword*, 2015）等。萧锦荣的作品已荣获秘鲁最佳图书（the Book of the Year）等荣誉。

《伊萨卡之旅》以自传性质讲述了多重文化背景下的文化寻根之旅，凸显了异乡人在异域文化背景下的精神彷徨状态。《图与剑》则采用中国特有的“武侠小说”形式，遵循历史发展脉络，生动再现了秘鲁的被征历程。

《伊萨卡之旅》选段讲述了“我”的一段婚姻情感经历：已有心上人的“我”，迫于压力，被迫向未来岳父写出一封恭敬回信，答应与其女儿交往，而其心中隐藏了太多的无奈与不甘。《图与剑》选段讲述了在秘鲁殖民过程中，以皮萨罗为统治者的西班牙殖民者杀死胡安德拉达等前任守军、夺取城池的惊险故事。

作品选读

A Journey to Ithaca

One

(Excerpt)

I did not answer; I waited for the coffee to drip and fill the pot. My mother went on to ask me whether Father had told me.

"Told me what?" I asked, mystified.

"He did not? The old fool!" The "old fool" was sitting right in the living room, just a few steps away, but since he was turning stone deaf he was spared the indignity of having to take offense. "And of course he did not show you the letter!"

"What letter? When?"

"Your godfather's," my mother said. "He has it delivered especially through a mutual friend of ours, about this time the last year."

"Father's never told me anything about it," I said.

"He's a malicious man," my mother raved. "That's what he is; a wicked, obnoxious man. And he hates you so much that the last thing he wants is to see you happily married and with children of your own. Why, he couldn't possibly have forgotten to mention to you something of such importance that your godfather didn't trust the post office enough to deliver!"

Even if it was not hard for me to guess what was in the letter, my mother eventually spelled it out for me. She told me my godfather had written to my father to say that a betterment of bonds between the two families was long overdue, and that for that purpose he was willing to marry one of his daughters to me.

I asked, "Which of them?"

"Rosa, of course," my mother said. "The youngest."

I had spent almost a year living in my godfather's home, after I had sold off all the family possessions, including my flat, in the belief that the visa was forthcoming. It was a miscalculation; I did not get my visa until the next spring, after being turned down three times by the American consul in Lima. I had no other place to go, so for most of the lag I lived in my godfather's house, whiling the time away in anguish. I got to know my godfather's sons fairly well; but less so with Rosa and her older sister. They were two of a kind, these two girls. They were smart and wild; they never stayed fifteen minutes in the same place. And they were good looking in a petite way. The only reason why I didn't fall in love with any of them is that I was already in love with another girl, one with a hard body and an aquiline nose; and also because they had somehow managed, with their unflappable self-assurance and their direct, no- nonsense manners, to frighten me away.

"What do you think?" my mother wanted to know. "She's really not such a bad choice. And her parents are just so fond of you…"

She did not get right away an answer from me, but then she must have sensed that her words hadn't fallen completely on deaf ears, either. She went on scrubbing the aluminum sink.

It took me a whole week to make up my mind and sit down to write a few lines to my would-be father-in-law. The letter ran like this:

Dear Sir,

Only in recent days did I learn about the letter you have written my father last spring. Up until then I have been living in ignorance and knew nothing of the matter. I am planning to go back to Lima for a short visit in June, with on of my sisters, Will Rosa be around and not elsewhere?

I reread the letter a few times and thought it a masterpiece in subtlety and ambiguity. It meant nothing to a reader unless he shared also in the conspiracy; I was letting my godfather know that I had accepted his generous offer, but on the other hand I did not have to go through the embarrassment of spelling out the very word "yes"; and I could deny everything if I chose to. It was a piece of writing that Machiavelli would have approved for its spirit, and Henry James for its wording.

I put the letter in an envelope and then I sent it off the next morning on my way to work, knowing that if I delayed I would never mail it at all.

As the month slowly faded into another, I tried to keep my mind off the matter but found it impossible. Like tidal waves, my thoughts kept going back to the same beaches. This was especially frequent in the quiet of night, as I sauntered down the five blocks of solitary road that separated my house from the bus stop, beneath a black canopy decked with a myriad stars and, occasionally, with a full moon. Sometimes I was assailed by doubts and the feeling that I had knowingly subverted my own life. I imagined myself being weighed down by responsibilities, crushed by the constant need for money, enslaved by the drab routine of a drab existence; and I recoiled in horror. And then sometimes I would come home in a gloomy, unhappy mood; and while wading through the solitude of the road, I would find comfort in thinking that, before long, I would not have to wade though, always alone and unaccompanied, the thousand-fold more unnerving solitude of another road.

Every night the first thing I would do upon reaching home was to check the day's mail; and, depending on my particular mood in that moment, I would feel either relieved or disappointed, when I failed to find my godfather's answer waiting there for me. This would not happen until the month's end: unbeknown to me, my godfather and godmother had moved over to San Francisco, leaving the business in the care of their sons. My letter had to make an unexpected and time-consuming detour; I had almost given it for lost when I finally got a letter from the old man. My godfather was glad that his shot in the dark had somehow borne fruit. And, yes, my sister and I were welcome to spend our stay in his Limean home; he had already instructed his sons by phone to get the guest rooms ready.

Strange to say, I can't remember in what state of mind I went to bed that night; whether with elation or in a mental agony. But I'm sure I dreamed of no singing violins or lit candles.

The Map and the Sword

Part V The Gold of Ambaya

LXXVI

(Excerpt)

Let us now leave Cuzco and move to Lima, which was then known as the City of Kings.

Unlike Cuzco, Lima was not built on the foundations of an existing city, but upon desert land. Realizing that the geography of the coast was more favorable for the use of cavalry and artillery, Francisco Pizarro decided to move the capital of New Castille to the Rimac Valley. Another consideration was that he needed a port for the ships from Spain and Panama bringing men and weapons.

With the port of Callao nearby, Lima came to solve the problem. When Pizarro first laid out the city, it consisted of a small checkerboard of rudimentary adobe houses, and it took five years for it to start acquiring the appearance of a typical Spanish town. As such, the churches, palaces and important buildings clustered around the Main Square. Most of its inhabitants were Spaniards, with some Indians and blacks, either servants or slaves of the former, living in the city's outskirts.

A man called Juan de Rada was living on a side street off the Main Square, occupying a very modest house. He was already quite advanced in age. He had participated in the conquest of Mexico and of Honduras, which he followed up with similar adventures in Peru and in Chile. Before he was killed by Hernando Pizarro, Diego de Almagro had appointed him protector of his son Diego de Almagro the Younger.

One Saturday in June, a group of soldiers came to Juan de Rada's house with the message that the Governor wanted to see him. Not wanting to be looked down upon by Pizarro and his companions, Rada, who lived in wretched poverty, borrowed a cloak from one of the other eleven Almagristas who had taken refuge in his house.

He found Governor Pizarro in the orchard of his palace, looking at the orange trees. He had aged greatly in the last few years. His gray hair and beard had become white. He even stooped a little. Only when he put on his helmet with the great white plumes and his armor would his long figure acquire again its former aura of heroism.

Hearing the footsteps of the other, he turned.

"Who are you?"

He did not recall he had sent for the Sergeant Major of his former partner.

"I'm Juan de Rada, Your Excellency," the other replied. "What do you want to see me for?"

"I've been informed by some Indians that you and your companions intend to kill me," the Governor said sourly, "and that for this purpose you've acquired coats of mail and spears. What do you say to that?"

"I'd say those Indians were lying or very much misinformed," Juan de Rada said. "The truth is, we're the ones who'd been told that Your Excellency wanted to see us dead, and if we had bought coats of mail or spears it was because we did not want to die like lambs being led to the slaughterhouse."

"I don't need to resort to the dagger of an assassin," Pizarro said angrily, "if indeed I wanted to kill you."

"We can't afford to guess what Your Excellency wants or not wants to do, and proved to be wrong..."

Presently Pizarro's anger subsided. He turned his back to the other.

"I'll give you now the opportunity you and your accomplices so fervently want," he said, bending down to look at something on the ground. "My guards and secretaries are too far away to intervene, if you pull out now the dagger hidden in your boot and make good use of it."

Juan de Rada hesitated. Pizarro had suffered in recent days a series of incidents that had made him somewhat fatalistic. Returning from an inspection from Collao, he and his companions had been caught by a storm, and one of the porters had fallen off a cliff with a chest full of his personal effects and papers. As everyone was deploring the accident and looking at the mangled body of the unfortunate Indian, a condor, which was flying overhead, descended from the clouds and came to rest on the chest. The Spaniards felt it was a sign of luck, but the Indians were alarmed enough to beg the Governor not to return to Lima.

Disregarding the Indians' advice as superstition, Pizarro resumed his journey, but he had barely set his foot in Lima when he was met by the bells of the Cathedral, which were tolling for a neighbor who had recently passed away.

Of course, he did not tell any of this to Juan de Rada.

He asked about Almagro's son: How old was he? How was he being schooled? He expressed his desire to send him to Spain.

"Even though the country is nearly pacified," he said, his expression softening, "it's still not the right place to educate a young *hidalgo*... I've known him since he was still a child, back then in Panama, and if I do not exactly love him as a son, neither do I want him to be destroyed by the hatred that had divided me and his hapless father."

He again turned his back to the other. He walked up slowly to the tallest tree in the orchard, picked four oranges and, without uttering another word, handed them to Juan de Rada.

The Almagrista was moved in spite of himself, but he was unwilling to spare the other's life for all the oranges in the world.

When he came back from the palace to his modest dwelling, his co-conspirators surrounded him and peppered him with questions.

"Why did the fucking Old Man want to see you?"

"Is our plan still safe?"

"The Old Man and his friends have been warned. We must defer the matter..."

But Juan de Rada did not change his mind. "Quite the contrary," he said resolutely, "now we can't do anything but forge ahead... Before they have time to react, we must act without delay."

21

(Anchee Min, 1957—)
闵安琪

作者简介

闵安琪（Anchee Min, 1957—），出生于上海，1984 年移民美国，就读于芝加哥艺术学院（School of the Art Institute of Chicago），取得艺术硕士学位。她目前主要居住在加州旧金山湾区，全职从事写作。

闵安琪的主要作品有回忆录《红杜鹃》（*Red Azalea*, 1994）、小说《凯瑟琳》（*Katherine*, 1995）《成为毛夫人》（*Becoming Madam Mao*, 2000）、《狂热者》（*Wild Ginger*, 2004）、《兰贵人》（*Empress Orchid*, 2004）、《末代女皇》（*The Last Empress*, 2007）、《中国珍珠》（*Pearl of China*, 2010）、回忆录《煮熟的种子》（*The Cooked Seed*, 2013）等。

作为一个移民作家，闵安琪不仅以尖锐和启示性的笔触讲述了作为一个中国移民的辛酸复杂经历，而且以关注历史的口吻塑造了一系列强悍的女性人物形象。在她的笔下，女性可以忽略或超越来自国家、种族、文化和阶级的差异，在特定的历史阶段建立一种牢不可摧的联合阵线，来保护和捍卫女性之间的姐妹情。《中国珍珠》是闵安琪根据赛珍珠生平创作的一部小说。小说通过讲述珍珠与一个中国乡村女孩杨柳一起成长的经历，以温情的形式清晰展现了两个女人之间深厚的姐妹情谊，再现了当时中国对其一生的影响。本书选段出自小说《中国珍珠》第 36 章。该章节讲述了杨柳亲赴美国大地，来到珍珠墓前与之倾诉关于中国的一切，以弥补珍珠不能回到中国之缺憾的动情故事。

作品选读

Pearl of China

Chapter 36
(Excerpt)

If it hadn't been for the heavy bag I was carrying, I wouldn't have believed that I was walking on American soil. It was early evening. The tour was over and the other visitors were gone. The air was brisk and the sky was turning dark. The trees and earth were blending into one gray color like shadows. It was clear that Pearl had bought this house and the land around it because the place had reminded her of Chin-kiang. For the rest of her life, this was the China she lived with.

How many times had she walked the path where I stood?

Darkness had almost settled in when I exited the house. I went on looking for Pearl's grave, but it was getting hard to see. I moved like a ghost following the barely visible path. The side road led me back to the inn where I was staying.

The innkeeper, a middle-aged lady, asked if I'd had a pleasant visit.

"I missed seeing Pearl's grave," I told her.

"You must have walked right by it," she said. "It's easy to miss."

"There wasn't a sign, or did I miss that too?" Since arriving in the United States, I had learned that Americans were good with signs.

"Well, it was the way Pearl Buck wanted it." The lady took out her keys and led me to my room. "Would you like me to book you a cab for tomorrow morning? What time is your train or flight?"

"I won't leave until I see Pearl's grave," I said.

The lady looked at me and I could see the questions in her eyes.

"I have some business at the grave," I tried to explain, hoping that my English would make sense to her.

"What kind of business?" She sounded cautious, a little suspicious.

I unzipped my backpack and took out the incense and the bag of dirt. I made a gesture of sprinkling dirt and put my palms together under my chin.

She didn't seem to understand but said, "Here, let me draw you a map."

I had been awake for a long time waiting for the dawn. At first light, I got up. I followed the inn lady's map carefully. After turning off the main road, I went down a small dirt path.

The sun outlined the mountains and trees and coated the leaves gold. The view was unfamiliar yet I felt I had been here before. I could hear the sound of my feet moving through the sandy dirt. After a while, I thought I heard the sound of running water. Was it my imagination, because Chin-kiang was known for its creeks? I didn't expect myself to be missing home, not yet. But no, I wasn't imagining the sound of water. Here it was, in front of me, under my feet, a running creek.

I decided to inspect the creek and then continue my search for the grave.

The sunlight played across the water's surface. I followed a path along the creek as it curled into the hills. On the far side of the creek were giant pine trees.

A view opened up. In front of me was a stand of bamboo—the same kind of golden bamboo we had in Chin-kiang.

Then I saw it, my friend's grave, hidden among the bamboo.

My strength fled me. I dropped to my knees.

There was no English. The grave had three Chinese characters carved in the stone. 賽珍珠 meaning Pearl Sydenstricker.

My eyes filled with tears of happiness, and this time I did not fight them. I understood Pearl's intent. Her roots in China hadn't died. China was the final thing on her mind. China was what she took with her to eternity. It was impossible for her to remove her love, for she, in her own words, "had known the fullness of such love, which was absolute in height and depth." A Westerner wouldn't understand the meaning of these Chinese characters, but Pearl didn't care. No wonder the innkeeper had said that the grave was easy to miss.

I felt as if Pearl were greeting me. I could hear her voice. "How was your journey?"

The three Chinese characters were Pearl's signature stamp, given to her by her Chinese tutor, Mr. Kung. Pearl once explained her name to me when we were young. The first letter was pronounced *Sy*, as in Sydenstricker. Out of many same-tone-sounding characters, Mr. Kung chose the one with a "mansion, which has a grand roof," and a "baby" playing underneath.

"My last name in Chinese means 'a darling doll in the mansion.'"

Pearl was proud as she explained. "Do you like it?"

"I do," I remembered replying, although I couldn't read. I tried to hide this by examining the shape of the first character, 賽 ."Look," I said.

"This is not an ordinary mansion. It is the symbol of money."

"That's not money," my friend laughed. "That's the people shape."

"Four of them under the roof!"

"Four workers. My father said that we are all the Lord's workers."

"The baby is big-bellied," I cried.

"She loves food!" Pearl laughed.

The second Chinese character, 珍, was the picture of an oyster, but when combined with the third character, 珠, the meaning changed into *Pearl.*

My friend had chosen her final resting place beside the creek on purpose. The grave faced east, demonstrating that she had followed the rule of feng shui. The surrounding garden was walled in by pines and cypresses. Besides the bamboo, there were maples, evergreen bushes, and flowers. Wild lilies were scattered alongside the creek. There was a seemingly dead old tree that looked as if it had fallen across the creek. Its trunk was about two feet in diameter and it was rotten and hollow inside. What amazed me was that the tree had a lush green canopy. In the center of the rotten trunk, a young branch was healthy and robust. Pearl must have liked this tree. It fit a line from a Chinese poem, *"Spring shows its power in rotten wood and dying trees."*

I touched the cold stone and rested my cheek against it.

* * *

Dear Pearl,

Since you couldn't go to China, I have brought China to you.

It is not the reunion I wished for for so long, but I feel blessed to have the opportunity. Because my memory is failing, and because I didn't want to forget a thing, I have written six notes to be burned with the incense at your grave.

The first note regards the end of Madame Mao. When she denied you a visa, she was sure of her power. She believed that she would rule China after her husband. But she didn't last. After Mao died, she was arrested and sentenced to death. It was less than four years after Nixon's visit.

The second note regards your mother's grave. It almost didn't survive during the Cultural Revolution. Mao's teenage mobs came to destroy the grave. Lilac removed the stone tablet and fooled them. In other words, what the Red Guard destroyed was not your mother's grave. Today the town of Chin-kiang has reclaimed Carie's status. She is officially titled the founder of the Chin-kiang middle school. Her spirit is celebrated and honored at each Spring Memorial.

The third note regards you. The mansion where your mother last lived has been turned into the Pearl Buck Residence. I can hear you say, "But that wasn't my house!" True, however, it is important that the residence in your name be presentable. You should understand that to a Chinese, the place that houses your spirit has to be a temple. Copies of your photos, letters, and books are on permanent display. I was not happy about the display of your calligraphy, because the strokes were not yours. Your writing was touched up by a professor from Beijing College of Art and Calligraphy. It was part of the act of transforming you into a goddess so that people could worship you. I didn't bother to fight, because I thought that it was better than calling you an American Cultural Imperialist.

The fourth note regards the people who knew you, who, as long as they lived, wondered how you did in America. I'd like to begin with Dick because he knew you well and had the worst luck. He was too close to Mao and died a horrible death. Please forgive me for being unable to report more about him. Dick knew that Hsu Chih-mo loved you. Dick wanted to congratulate you in person when he learned that you won the Nobel Prize. We were not allowed to send a telegram to America. Dick said that Hsu Chih-mo would have been so proud. He would have danced on his head. You will be pleased to know that today Hsu Chih-mo's poems are extremely popular. Young people worship him as a poet whose voice speaks to their own generation. Newspapers continue to print stories of his affairs as if they took place yesterday, and, of course, they continue to miss the real target.

Papa kept the church going until he died. He became a fighting angel like Absalom except he fought guerrilla style. I am sure you missed Carpenter Chan and Lilac. You knew that Carpenter Chan became a Christian, converted by Absalom, but you might not have known that he joined the Communists after Mao took power. Later he went back to God and worked for Papa. I don't think Americans are able to comprehend such a life, but you would. You lived in China and knew how things can be.

Lilac missed you so much that she could never stop talking about you. She is the town's longevity star and is in her nineties. Her three sons inherited their father's trade. It was a pity that you couldn't see how they rebuilt Absalom's church, which is called the Chin-kiang Christian Church. Lilac still fights with Vanguard, the beggar lady Soo-ching's son, whose name used to be Confucius. This was the mother and son you found in your garden so long ago. He betrayed everyone to please Madame Mao. Soo-ching wanted to disown her son, but Papa convinced her that she'd better forgive or she wouldn't go to heaven.

You don't know my daughter, Rouge, but she knows everything about you. She is currently the mayor of Chin-kiang and is in charge of the Pearl Buck Scholarship and the Hsu Chih-

mo Scholarship. She gave birth to one girl and adopted two girls from her husband's previous marriage. All my granddaughters share the same middle name, Pearl. They are Pearl Delight, Pearl Bright, and Pearl Flight.

Remember Bumpkin Emperor, the warlord? He became an ardent Christian and the pastor of our church. You will be shocked. Who wouldn't be? Like your father, Bumpkin Emperor was obsessed with converting people. He tried to save them the way your father saved him. Bumpkin Emperor remembered you as the mean, straw-haired girl. He never got tired of telling people the story of how you fooled him with that bucket of ink. The People's Publishing House approached him with the idea of publishing a children's comic book based on the story.

My fifth note regards the dirt I brought here. It is from your mother's grave. I'll sprinkle it around. In the meantime, if I may, I will dig some soil here, a little, just enough to fill the bag. I'll carry it to your mother's grave as soon as I return and mix the soils. It pleases me to join your spirits.

The last note regards my own wish. If you don't mind, I'll collect some seeds from your trees here. I have no idea of the names of all the trees except that they are American trees. According to the shapes of the nuts, they are flowering trees. The importance of the trees is that they are from where you are buried. I wouldn't be surprised if you planted them yourself. I imagine you would have. You understood that spirits gather through nature. I hear your voice speaking through the creek, the pines, maples, bamboo, birds, and bees. I will plant the seeds where I will be buried when my time comes. We should then accompany each other forever. I have brought your favorite Tang dynasty poem, "The Tune of Posaman." "Yangtze River" ought to be changed to "Pacific Ocean," but I leave it the way it is. I know you always preferred the original.

I live by the Yangtze River near its source,
While you reside farthest down its course.
You and I drink water out of the same stream,
I haven't seen you though daily of you I dream.

When will this river water cease to run?
When shall I not love you, the way I do?
I only wish our two hearts would beat as one,
And you wouldn't disappoint me in my love for you.

Joy, gratitude, and sense of peace are what this moment means to me. I thank God for the fortune of having known you.

The creek is singing a happy song. The wind whispers like our old conversations through trembling leaves. The air is pure and the sun warm. Once again, I see you running toward me with sunshine in your face. You look like a jumping cloud in your indigo floral Chinese dress, your golden hair bouncing.

"Willow, " I hear you call, "hurry up, the popcorn man is here!"

22

(David Henry Hwang, 1957—)
黄哲伦

作者简介

黄哲伦（David Henry Hwang, 1957—），出生于美国加利福尼亚州洛杉矶。在斯坦福大学学习期间（1975—1979），对戏剧产生了浓厚兴趣，创作了第一部剧本《新移民》（*FOB*, 1979）。1980 至 1981 年间，进入耶鲁大学戏剧学院学习。主要剧本有《舞蹈与铁路》（*The Dance and the Road*, 1981）、《睡美人之家》（*The House of Sleeping Beauties,* 1983）、《蝴蝶君》（*M. Butterfly*, 1988）、《黄面孔》（*Yellow Face*, 2007）、《中式英语》（*Chinglish*, 2011）、《功夫》（*Kung Fu*, 2014）、《软实力》（*Soft Power*, 2018）等。《新移民》1980 年获得奥比奖。黄哲伦凭借《蝴蝶君》获得 1988 年度托尼奖最佳剧作奖（Tony Award for the Best Play）、外评奖、约翰·加斯纳年度杰出戏剧家新人奖等，成为百老汇历史上第一位获得美国戏剧最高奖托尼奖的亚裔剧作家。

黄哲伦的作品主题涉及少数族裔身份认同、东西文化冲突、对种族主义的批评以及对人类自身命运的探询。《新移民》描写了美国土生华裔（ABC）与新移民（FOB）之间的紧张关系，反映了华裔作为美国少数族裔如何确定自身属性的问题。故事围绕三个年轻人（史蒂夫、格蕾丝和戴尔）展开，他们各自的经历体现了华人在美国社会中不同的同化历程。《蝴蝶君》探讨身份与性别属性的社会建构、东西文化冲突等主题，尤其是对东方主义的批判。法国驻华外交官加利马尔因从事间谍活动被捕入狱。他与京剧演员宋莉龄生活了二十年，竟不知对方是位男性，还是潜伏在自己身边的间谍。该剧颠覆了意大利作曲家普契尼《蝴蝶夫人》的情节，也解构了亚洲人在西方人心目中的刻板形象。

第一篇《晚餐之后》(“after dinner”)选自《新移民》第2幕。戴尔对史蒂夫这样的新移民抱有很多偏见，格蕾丝提醒他现在的情况跟过去相比已发生了很大变化。许多家庭有经济实力将孩子送到美国上大学，新移民中好多已经西化，其行为表现并不像初来乍到者。第二篇选自《蝴蝶君》第3幕第1场。宋莉龄向法官讲自己能轻而易举操纵加利马尔是因为后者透过对亚洲和亚洲女性的种种偏见而很容易认为他确实遇到了自己“想象中的女人”。宋莉龄还暗示西方人把西方看成占据支配地位、具有男子汉气概而把东方看成百依百顺、有女人味儿的观念同样导致了西方帝国主义和军事行动的失败。

作品选读

FOB

ACT II: after dinner

(Excerpt)

DALE (*Taking the box*): Let’s see what’s inside, is that okay?

(*Steve shoves Dale to the ground and takes the box.*)

STEVE: IT IS NOT! (*With accent*) THIS IS MINE!

DALE: Well, what kind of shit is that?

STEVE: She gave this to me.

DALE: What kind of ... we’re not at your place. We’re not in Hong Kong, you know. Look—look all around you—you see shit on the sidewalks?

STEVE: This is mine!

DALE: You see armies of rice-bowl haircuts?

STEVE: She gave this to me!

DALE: People here have their flies zipped up—see?

STEVE: You should not look in it.

DALE: So you’re not in Hong Kong. And I’m not one of your servant boys that you can knock around—that you got by trading pornographic playing cards—that you probably deal out to your friends. You’re in America, understand?

STEVE: Quiet! Do you know who I am?

DALE: Yeah—you're a FOB. You're a rich FOB in the U.S. But you better watch yourself. 'Cause you can be sent back.

STEVE: Shut up! Do you know who I am?

DALE: You can be sent back, you know—just like that. 'Cause you're a guest here, understand?

STEVE (*To Grace*): Tell him who I am.

DALE: I know who he is—heir to a fortune in junk merchandise. Big deal. Like being heir to Captain Crunch.

STEVE: Tell him!

(*Silence.*)

GRACE: You know it's not like that.

STEVE: Tell him!

DALE: Huh?

GRACE: All the stuff about rice bowls and—zippers—have you ever been there, Dale?

DALE: Well, yeah. Once. When I was ten.

GRACE: Well, it's changed a lot.

DALE: Remember getting heat rashes.

GRACE: People are dressing really well now—and the whole place has become really stylish—well, certainly not everybody, but the people who are well-off enough to send their kids to American colleges—they're really kinda classy.

DALE: Yeah.

GRACE: Sort of.

DALE: You mean, like him. So what? It's easy to be classy when you're rich.

GRACE: All I'm saying is …

DALE: Hell, I could do that.

GRACE: Huh?

DALE: I could be classy, too, if I was rich.

GRACE: You *are* rich.

DALE: No. Just upper-middle. Maybe.

GRACE: Compared to us, you're rich.

DALE: No, not really. And especially not compared to him. Besides, when I was born we were still poor.

GRACE: Well, you're rich now.

DALE: Used to get one LifeSaver a day.

GRACE: That's all? One LifeSaver?

DALE: Well, I mean, that's not all I lived on. We got normal food, too.

GRACE: I know, but…

DALE: Not like we were living in cardboard boxes or anything.

GRACE: All I'm saying is that the people who are coming in now—a lot of them are different—they're already Westernized. They don't act like they're fresh off the boat.

DALE: Maybe. But they're still FOBs.

STEVE: Tell him who I am!

DALE: Anyway, real nice dinner, Grace. I really enjoyed it.

GRACE: Thank you.

STEVE: Okay! I will tell myself.

DALE: Go tell yourself—just don't bother us.

GRACE (*Standing, to Steve*): What would you like to do now?

STEVE: Huh?

GRACE: You wanted to go out after dinner?

STEVE: Yes, yes. We go out.

DALE: I'll drive. You sent the hearse home.

STEVE: I tell driver—return car after dinner.

DALE: How could you … ? What time did you … ? When did you tell him to return? What time?

STEVE (*Looks at his watch*): Seven-five.

DALE: No—not what time is it. What time you tell him to return?

STEVE: Seven-five. Go see.

(Dale exits through the kitchen.)

(*No accent*) Why wouldn't you tell him who I am?

GRACE: Can Gwan Gung die?

(*Pause.*)

STEVE: No warrior can defeat Gwan Gung.

GRACE: Does Gwan Gung fear ghosts?

STEVE: Gwan Gung fears no ghosts.

GRACE: Ghosts of warriors?

STEVE: No warrior ghosts.

GRACE: Ghosts that avenge?

STEVE: No avenging ghosts.

GRACE: Ghosts forced into exile?

STEVE: No exiled ghosts.

GRACE: Ghosts that wait?

(*Pause*.)

STEVE (*Quietly*): May I… take you out tonight? Maybe not tonight, but some other time? Another time? (*He strokes her hair*) What has happened?

DALE (*Entering*): I cannot believe it … (*He sees them*) What do you think you're doing? (*He grabs Steve's hand. To Steve*) What… I step out for one second and you just go and—hell, you FOBs are sneaky. No wonder they check you so close at Immigration.

GRACE: Dale, I can really take care of myself.

DALE: Yeah? What was his hand doing, then?

GRACE: Stroking my hair.

DALE: Well, yeah. I could see that. I mean, what was it doing stroking your hair? (*Pause*) Uh, never mind. All I'm saying is … (*He gropes*) Jesus! If you want to be alone, why don't you just say so, huh? If that's what you really want, just say it, okay? (*Pause*) Okay. Time's up.

GRACE: Was the car out there?

DALE: Huh? Yeah. Yeah, it was. I could not believe it. I go outside and—thank God—there's no limousine. Just as I'm about to come back, I hear this sound like the roar of death and this big black shadow scrapes up beside me. I could not believe it!

STEVE *(Speaking with accent again)*: Car return—seven-five.

DALE: And when I asked him—I asked the driver, what time he'd been told to return. And he just looks at me and says, "Now."

STEVE: We go out?

DALE: What's going on here? What is this?

STEVE: Time to go.

DALE: No! Not till you explain what's going on.

STEVE (*To Grace*): You now want to dance?

DALE (*To Grace*): Do you understand this? Was this coincidence?

STEVE (*To Grace*): I am told good things of American discos.

DALE (*To Grace*): You and him just wanna go off by yourselves?

STEVE: I hear of Dillon's.

DALE: It's okay, you know.

STEVE: In Westwood.

DALE; I don't mind.

STEVE: Three—four stories.

DALE: Really.

STEVE: Live band.

DALE: Cousin.

STEVE: We go. (*He takes Grace's hand*)

DALE: He's just out to snake you, you know.

(*Dale takes Grace's other hand. From this point on, almost unnoticeably, the lights begin to dim.*)

GRACE: Okay! That's enough! (*She pulls away*) That's enough! I have to make all the decisions around here, don't I? When I leave it up to you two, the only place we go is in circles.

DALE: Well…

STEVE: No, I am suggesting place to go.

GRACE: Look, Dale, when I asked you here, what did I say we were going to do?

DALE: Uh—dinner and a movie—or something. But it was a different "we," then.

GRACE: It doesn't matter. That's what we're going to do.

DALE: I'll drive.

STEVE: My car can take us to movie.

GRACE: I think we better not drive at all. We'll stay right here. (*She removes Steve's tie. To Steve*) Do you remember this?

DALE (*Assumes Grace is talking to him*): What—you think I borrow clothes or something? Hell, I don't even wear ties.

(*Grace takes the tie, wraps it around Dale's face like a blindfold.*)

M. Butterfly

act three

scene 1

(Excerpt)

A courthouse in Paris. 1986.

As he promised, Song has completed the bulk of his transformation, onstage by the time the houselights go down and the stagelights come up full. He removes his wig and kimono, leaving them on the floor. Underneath, he wears a well-cut suit.

SONG: So I'd done my job better than I had a right to expect. Well, give him some credit, too. He's right—I was in a fix when I arrived in Paris. I walked from the airport into town, then I located, by blind groping, the Chinatown district. Let me make one thing clear: whatever else may be said about the Chinese, they are stingy! I slept in doorways three days until I could find a tailor who would make me this kimono on credit. As it turns out, maybe I didn't even need it. Maybe he would've been happy to see me in a simple shift and mascara. But ... better safe than sorry.

That was 1970, when I arrived in Paris. For the next fifteen years, yes, I lived a very comfy life. Some relief, believe me, after four years on a fucking commune in No-wheresville, China. Rene supported the boy and me, and I did some demonstrations around the country as part of my "cultural exchange" cover. And then there was the spying.

SONG moves upstage, to a chair. Toulon enters as a judge, wearing the appropriate wig and robes. He sits near Song. It's 1986, and Song is testifying in a courtroom.

SONG: Not much at first. Rene had lost all his high-level contacts. Comrade Chin wasn't very interested in parking-ticket statistics. But finally, at my urging, Rene got a job as a courier, handling sensitive documents. He'd photograph them for me, and I'd pass them on to the Chinese embassy.

JUDGE: Did he understand the extent of his activity?

SONG: He didn't ask. He knew that I needed those documents, and that was enough.

JUDGE: But he must've known he was passing classified information.

SONG: I can't say.

JUDGE: He never asked what you were going to do with them?

SONG: Nope.

Pause.

JUDGE: There is one thing that the court—indeed, that all of France—would like to know.

SONG: Fire away.

JUDGE: Did Monsieur Gallimard know you were a man?

SONG: Well, he never saw me completely naked. Ever.

JUDGE: But surely, he must've … how can I put this?

SONG: Put it however you like. I'm not shy. He must've felt around?

JUDGE: Mmmmm.

SONG: Not really. I did all the work. He just laid back. Of course we did enjoy more … complete union, and I suppose he *might* have wondered why I was always on my stomach, but…. But what you're thinking is. "Of course a wrist must've brushed ... a hand hit … over twenty years!" Yeah. Well, Your Honor, it was my job to make him think I was a woman. And chew on this: it wasn't all that hard. See, my mother was a prostitute along the Bundt before the Revolution. And, uh, I think it's fair to say she learned a few things about Western men. So I borrowed her knowledge. In service to my country.

JUDGE: Would you care to enlighten the court with this secret knowledge? I'm sure we're all very curious.

SONG: I'm sure you are. (*Pause*) Okay, Rule One is: Men always believe what they want to hear. So a girl can tell the most obnoxious lies and the guys will believe them every time—"This is my first time"—"That's the biggest I've ever seen"—or *both*, which, if you really think about it, is not possible in a single lifetime. You've maybe heard those phrases a few times in your own life, yes, Your Honor?

JUDGE: It's not my life, Monsieur Song, which is on trial today.

SONG: Okay, okay, just trying to lighten up the proceedings. Tough room.

JUDGE: Go on.

SONG: Rule Two: As soon as a Western man comes into contact with the East—he's already confused. The West has sort of an international rape mentality towards the East. Do you know rape mentality?

JUDGE: Give us your definition, please.

SONG: Basically, "Her mouth says no, but her eyes say yes."

The West thinks of itself as masculine—big guns, big industry, big money—so the East is feminine—weak, delicate, poor … but good at art, and full of inscrutable wisdom—the feminine mystique.

Her mouth says no, but her eyes say yes. The West believes the East, deep down, *wants* to be dominated— because a woman can't think for herself.

JUDGE: What does this have to do with my question?

SONG: You expect Oriental countries to submit to your guns, and you expect Oriental women to be submissive to your men. That's why you say they make the best wives.

JUDGE: But why would that make it possible for you to fool Monsieur Gallimard? Please—get to the point.

SONG: One, because when he finally met his fantasy woman, he wanted more than anything to believe that she was, in fact, a woman. And second, I am an Oriental. And being an Oriental, I could never be completely a man.

Pause.

JUDGE: Your armchair political theory is tenuous, Monsieur Song.

SONG: You think so? That's why you'll lose in all your dealings with the East.

JUDGE: Just answer my question: did he know you were a man?

Pause.

SONG: You know, Your Honor, I never asked.

23

(Chay Yew, 1965—)

谢耀

作者简介

谢耀（Chay Yew, 1965—），出生于新加坡。1980年代在美国佩珀代因大学（Pepperdine University）学习戏剧，后来到波士顿大学攻读硕士学位。曾在伦敦的木兰剧团做驻团剧作家、洛杉矶的马克·泰珀剧坛亚裔戏剧工作坊担任导演；荣获2007年奥比导演奖；2011年开始担任胜利花园剧场（Victory Gardens Theater）艺术总监。主要剧作有《瓷》（*Porcelain*, 1992）、《他们自己的语言》（*A Language of Their Own*, 1995）、《红》（*Red*, 1998）、《美丽国家》（*A Beautiful Country*, 1998）、《仙境》（*Wonderland*, 1999）、《漫长季节》（*The Long Season*, 2005）、《问题27，问题28》（*Question 27, Question 28*, 2006）、《看得见的城市》（*Visible Cities*, 2011）等。主编《3.0版本：当代美国亚裔戏剧选集》（*Version 3.0: Contemporary Asian American Plays*, 2011）。

《仙境》讲述一家三口——男人、女人和儿子——追求美国梦而最后幻灭的故事，探讨了少数族裔所处的边缘地位、他们攀登社会阶梯时遭遇的无形障碍（玻璃天花板效应）、父母与子女的关系、青少年同性恋问题等主题。通过一系列诗意的独白，人物的梦想与抱负、他们在美国日益加剧的生活压力下为求生存所做的努力呈现在读者面前。男人是建筑师，他设计的购物中心“仙境”发生火灾导致人员伤亡。经过调查，男人对建筑质量负有主要责任，被吊销设计执照。失业后，男人因无力继续支付房屋抵押贷款，房子被房产公司强行收回，便投海溺亡。“仙境”一词寓意深刻，具有反讽效果。主人公对自己设计的“仙境”购物中心十分自豪，似乎象征着如梦似幻的美国梦变成了现实，然而最终这梦境像肥皂泡一样破灭了。

下面选文选自《仙境》第一部分。男人悠闲的生活被突然打断，正在酒吧消磨时光的他从电视上看到新闻，他所设计的“仙境”购物中心屋顶坍塌，伤亡惨重，有人抱怨建筑结构有漏洞、工程粗制滥造。他疯一样驱车前往事故现场，那里围满了消防车、救护车。他僵直而沉默地站在那里，感到十分挫败。后来他接受电视采访，竭力否认渎职的指控，否认自己是杀人犯。

作品选读

Wonderland

(Excerpt)

Sound of bar chatter and noise.

YOUNG MAN Welcome to La Cucaracha
You know the bar
tucked away
in some quiet street corner
musty dark and dank
the clack clack crack
of billiard balls
strained guitar riffs
classic Springsteen on the wailing jukebox
Moldy stench of
Cheap cigarettes and booze

(*Young Man assumes role of a bartender.*)

Regulars
they cluster at the bar
nursing the wounds of life
Late afternoon
and someone is being a naughty boy—

MAN I play hooky from work
some afternoons
Head across the street to a bar
where I'd sit
with another double scotch on the rocks
Eating stale peanuts
Watching a droning baseball game
on a beat-up TV set overhead

My mind invariably drifts
I wonder why I'm doing what I'm doing?
And should I?
since the glass ceiling is only so high?

Suddenly
a news bulletin
it pulls me back to the real world
A middle-aged woman with a bad permanent
She says
there is a disaster
a tragedy
Armageddon
The governor
the mayor
every elected public official
all appear on the screen
Speaking in an election voice
"State of emergency, disaster area, crisis"
they say
"Our hearts, our sympathies, our thoughts"
they say
"Terrorist attacks, bombs, Arabs"
they say
I stop hearing what they say

I stand
like everyone else in the bar
transfixed
intoxicated
An image of destruction
a building
its roof punctured
crumpled
fallen

The woman with a bad permanent
she interrupts
Roof collapse
Structural failure
Shoddy construction
Death toll high
still climbing

The woman with a bad permanent
she says
the building
is
the Wonderland mall
My mall
I don't hear anymore

Man runs off.

Sound of pandemonium, sirens and people yelling.

YOUNG MAN A car lunging
hurtling on Interstate 5
The Man
he drives
like a maniac
at breakneck speed
to the mall—

In another corner of the stage, Woman looks at Man.

WOMAN I come home
Look at him
Nothing to say
What to say?—

MAN When I arrive
the pungent smell
of burning wood metal brick greets me—

YOUNG MAN The Man
he stands small
against the looming mall
The devastated part of the building
the food court
is surrounded
by wailing ambulances
fire engines
cranes—

MAN I stand there
paralyzed
not knowing where to run
where to turn
right or left
I just stand there
Staring—

WOMAN He stand there
Silent
Defeated—

YOUNG MAN Like a site of a ravenous war
in defeat
retreat

In the distance
raging amber flames
consume the food market
Walls stained black by soot and fire—

MAN I notice
the rest of the mall remains standing
as if in defiance—

WOMAN You do what wife supposed to do
Be understanding
Listen
Hold him
But he push you away
Don't tell you a thing—

YOUNG MAN Pandemonium
Thick in the bilious smoke
A towering babble
Howling sirens
People running standing
People screaming crying—

MAN I want to rush forward
to help them
but I don't
I can't
Instead
I just keep staring
at the mall
my beautiful mall—

YOUNG MAN Outside the mall
People fearful
hopeful
for their loved ones

trapped deep in the rubble—

SON The day it happened
I got home from school
I saw on TV
Body bags on the streets
Like it's Beirut or Bosnia
Bombed-out buildings and stuff
Wild

YOUNG MAN Rescue workers and their dogs
rummage through
twisted steel
fractured concrete
for signs of life
any life—

WOMAN Outside
He just stand in balcony
Don't look at me
Ignore me
Looking at ocean—

MAN The rescue workers
they say
they hear voices—
voices praying for God
But a few hours later
their prayers
stop—

Son enters.

SON When I saw him
Dad on TV
A middle-aged woman with a bad permanent

She says it's his mistake
his fault
the roof collapsed
For a moment
I want to speak to him
Say something
But what's there really to say?
Especially when everything's being
said on TV?

He has my father's voice
His face his posture his size
But yet it isn't him
He's someone else

WOMAN Inside
I see him
My husband
on TV
A middle-aged woman with bad permanent
She say it's his mistake
his fault
the roof collapse

For a moment
I want to speak to him
say something
But what to say?
Especially when everything's being said on TV?—

YOUNG MAN Television newspaper reporters
they aim
point in Dad's direction
They make a run towards him
Armed with cameras lights sound

They blind him—

Man shields his eyes from the lights.
Young Man and Woman surround Man. They batter him with an endless barrage of questions.

SON (*Overlapping*) Are you accountable for the
collapse of the roof?—
MAN (*Overlapping*) No—no—
WOMAN (*Overlapping*) Did you know—?
Were you—?
MAN (*Overlapping*) No—no charges of negligence
have been filed against me—
YOUNG MAN (*Overlapping*) Did you know the civil engineer
has corroborated with federal
authorities?—
WOMAN (*Overlapping*) Are you—?
Why did you—?
SON (*Overlapping*) Was it a bad judgement call?
MAN (*Overlapping*) No—no—
I don't intend to sell my story
to *60 Minutes*—
No interviews—
YOUNG MAN (*Overlapping*) A fatal miscalculation?—
WOMAN (*Overlapping*) Are you—?
Why could you—?
Why did you—?
YOUNG MAN (*Overlapping*) Are you a murderer?—
Charges of manslaughter—
MAN (*Overlapping*) No—no—
I'm not a murderer—
SON (*Overlapping*) Do you know you are subpoenaed?
Your architectural license has been—
MAN (*Overlapping*) Not a murderer—

YOUNG MAN (*Overlapping*)   Sixteen lives have been lost—

SON (*Overlapping*)   Men—women—children—

WOMAN (*Overlapping*)   Why didn't you—?
How can you—?
Look at you—

MAN   Not a murderer!
not a murderer!
not a murderer!

Silence.

24

(Ted Chiang, 1967—)
姜峯楠

作者简介

姜峯楠（Ted Chiang, 1967—），出生于美国纽约杰斐逊港，毕业于布朗大学（Brown University），取得计算机科学学位，曾参加旨在培养科幻作家的写作坊“克莱里恩工作坊（Clarion Writers Workshop）”。姜峯楠目前主要从事短篇和中短篇小说创作。

姜峯楠的主要小说作品有《巴比伦塔》（*Tower of Babylon*, 1990）、《领悟》（*Understand*, 1991）、《除以零》（*Division by Zero*, 1991）、《你一生的故事》（*Story of Your Life*, 1998）、《七十二个字母》（*Seventy-Two Letters*, 2000）、《人类科学之演变》（*The Evolution of Human Science*, 2000）、《地狱是上帝不在的地方》（*Hell Is the Absence of God*, 2001）、《赏心悦目》（*Liking What You See: A Documentary*, 2002）、《前路迢迢》（*What's Expected of Us*, 2005）、《商人和炼金术士之门》（*The Merchant and the Alchemist's Gate*, 2007）、《呼吸》（*Exhalation*, 2008）、《软件体的生命周期》（*The Lifecycle of Software Objects*, 2010）、《达西的新型自动机器保姆》（*Dacey's Patent Automatic Nanny*, 2011）、《双面真相》（*The Truth of Fact, the Truth of Feeling*, 2013）、《大寂静》（*The Great Silence*, 2015）等。他的作品不仅被改编成影视作品，而且多次荣获星云奖（Nebula Award）、雨果奖（Hugo Award）等科幻文学大奖。

《巴比伦塔》是姜峯楠的处女作，也是其首次获得星云奖的作品。在作品中，作者借助瑰丽无比的想象，通过一连串令人惊叹的细节，把一个原本神圣虚幻的通天塔以别样形式呈现出来。《你一生的故事》是2016年电影《降临》（*Arrival*）的改编原著。该小说通过对科学、欲望、认知、世界，甚至对语言本身的多角度思考，构建了一个我、你、他、环境之间的反思结构。

《巴比伦塔》选段讲述了矿工希拉勒姆登塔达到一定高度后见到的奇特世界以及遇到的不适和些许恐慌，而同时发现塔上的居民在异样的空间里却无比安逸自在。《你一生的故事》选段通过一条线索讲述了女儿已死的事实，而通过另外一条线索讲述了人类尝试用自身语言体系与"七肢桶"沟通交流的无效性。

作品选读

Tower of Babylon

(Excerpt)

As the miners ascended, in the course of time there came the day when the tower appeared to be the same when one looked upward or downward from the ramp's edge. Below, the tower's shaft shrank to nothing long before it seemed to reach the plain below. Likewise, the miners were still far from being able to see the top. All that was visible was a length of the tower. To look up or down was frightening, for the reassurance of continuity was not provided; they were no longer part of the ground. The tower might have been a thread suspended in the air, unattached to either earth or heaven.

There were moments during this section of the climb when Hillalum despaired, feeling displaced and estranged from the world; it was as if the earth had rejected him for his faithlessness, while heaven disdained to accept him. He wished Yahweh would give a sign, to let men know that their venture was approved; otherwise how could they stay in a place that offered so little welcome to the spirit?

The tower dwellers at this altitude felt no unease with their station; they always greeted the miners warmly and wished them luck with their task at the vault. They lived inside the damp mists of clouds, they saw storms from below and from above, they harvested crops from the air, and they never feared that this was an improper place for men to be. There were no divine assurances or encouragements to be had, but the people never knew a moment's doubt.

With the passage of the weeks, the sun and moon peaked lower and lower in their daily journeys. The moon flooded the south side of the tower with its silver radiance, glowing like the eye of Yahweh peering at them. Before long, they were at precisely the same level as the moon when it passed; they had reached the height of the first of the celestial bodies. They squinted at the moon's pitted face, marveled at its stately motion that scorned any support.

Then they approached the sun. It was the summer season, when the sun appears nearly overhead from Babylon, making it pass close by the tower at this height. No families lived in this section of the tower, nor were there any balconies, since the heat was enough to roast barley. The mortar between the tower's bricks was no longer bitumen, which would have softened and flowed, but clay, which had been virtually baked by the heat. As protection against the day temperatures, the pillars had been widened until they formed a nearly continuous wall, enclosing the ramp into a tunnel with only narrow slots admitting the whistling wind and blades of golden light.

The crews of pullers had been spaced very regularly up to this point, but here an adjustment was necessary. They started out earlier and earlier each morning, to gain more darkness for when they pulled. When they were at the level of the sun, they traveled entirely at night. During the day, they tried to sleep, naked and sweating in the hot breeze. The miners worried that if they did manage to sleep, they would be baked to death before they awoke. But the pullers had made the journey many times, and never lost a man, and eventually they passed above the sun's level, where things were as they had been below.

Now the light of day shone *upward*, which seemed unnatural to the utmost. The balconies had planks removed from them so that the sunlight could shine through, with soil on the walkways that remained; the plants grew sideways and downward, bending down to catch the sun's rays.

Then they drew near the level of the stars, small fiery spheres spread on all sides. Hillalum had expected them to be spread more thickly, but even with the tiny stars invisible from the ground, they seemed to be thinly scattered. They were not all set at the same height, but instead occupied the next few leagues above. It was difficult to tell how far away they were, since there was no indication of their size, but occasionally one would make a close approach, evidencing its astonishing speed. Hillalum realized that all the objects in the sky hurtled by with similar speed, in order to travel the world from edge to edge in a day's time.

Story of Your Life
(Excerpt)

The request for that meeting was perhaps the second most momentous phone call in my life. The first, of course, will be the one from Mountain Rescue. At that point your dad and I will be speaking to each other maybe once a year, tops. After I get that phone call, though, the first thing I'll do will be to call your father.

He and I will drive out together to perform the identification, a long silent car ride. I remember the morgue, all tile and stainless steel, the hum of refrigeration and smell of antiseptic. An orderly will pull the sheet back to reveal your face. Your face will look wrong somehow, but I'll know it's you.

"Yes, that's her," I'll say. "She's mine."

You'll be twenty-five then.

The MP checked my badge, made a notation on his clipboard, and opened the gate; I drove the off-road vehicle into the encampment, a small village of tents pitched by the Army in a farmer's sun-scorched pasture. At the center of the encampment was one of the alien devices, nicknamed "looking glasses."

According to the briefings I'd attended, there were nine of these in the United States, one hundred and twelve in the world. The looking glasses acted as twoway communication devices, presumably with the ships in orbit. No one knew why the aliens wouldn't talk to us in person; fear of cooties, maybe. A team of scientists, including a physicist and a linguist, was assigned to each looking glass; Gary Donnelly and I were on this one.

Gary was waiting for me in the parking area. We navigated a circular maze of concrete barricades until we reached the large tent that covered the looking glass itself. In front of the tent was an equipment cart loaded with goodies borrowed from the school's phonology lab; I had sent it ahead for inspection by the Army.

Also outside the tent were three tripod-mounted video cameras whose lenses peered, through windows in the fabric wall, into the main room. Everything Gary and I did would be reviewed by countless others, including military intelligence. In addition we would each send daily reports, of which mine had to include estimates on how much English I thought the aliens could understand.

Gary held open the tent flap and gestured for me to enter. "Step right up," he said, circus-barker-style. "Marvel at creatures the likes of which have never been seen on God's green earth."

"And all for one slim dime," I murmured, walking through the door. At the moment the looking glass was inactive, resembling a semicircular mirror over ten feet high and twenty feet across. On the brown grass in front of the looking glass, an arc of white spray paint outlined the activation area. Currently the area contained only a table, two folding chairs, and a power strip with a cord leading to a generator outside. The buzz of fluorescent lamps, hung from poles along the edge of the room, commingled with the buzz of flies in the sweltering heat.

Gary and I looked at each other, and then began pushing the cart of equipment up to the table. As we crossed the paint line, the looking glass appeared to grow transparent; it was as if someone was slowly raising the illumination behind tinted glass. The illusion of depth was uncanny; I felt I could walk right into it. Once the looking glass was fully lit it resembled a life-sized diorama of a semicircular room. The room contained a few large objects that might have been furniture, but no aliens. There was a door in the curved rear wall.

We busied ourselves connecting everything together: microphone, sound spectrograph, portable computer, and speaker. As we worked, I frequently glanced at the looking glass, anticipating the aliens' arrival. Even so I jumped when one of them entered.

It looked like a barrel suspended at the intersection of seven limbs. It was radially symmetric, and any of its limbs could serve as an arm or a leg. The one in front of me was walking around on four legs, three non-adjacent arms curled up at its sides. Gary called them "heptapods."

I'd been shown videotapes, but I still gawked. Its limbs had no distinct joints; anatomists guessed they might be supported by vertebral columns. Whatever their underlying structure, the heptapod's limbs conspired to move it in a disconcertingly fluid manner. Its "torso" rode atop the rippling limbs as smoothly as a hovercraft.

Seven lidless eyes ringed the top of the heptapod's body. It walked back to the doorway from which it entered, made a brief sputtering sound, and returned to the center of the room followed by another heptapod; at no point did it ever turn around. Eerie, but logical; with eyes on all sides, any direction might as well be "forward."

Gary had been watching my reaction. "Ready?" he asked.

I took a deep breath. "Ready enough." I'd done plenty of fieldwork before, in the Amazon, but it had always been a bilingual procedure: either my informants knew some Portuguese, which I could use, or I'd previously gotten an introduction to their language from the local missionaries. This would be my first attempt at conducting a true monolingual discovery procedure. It was straightforward enough in theory, though.

I walked up to the looking glass and a heptapod on the other side did the same. The image was so real that my skin crawled. I could see the texture of its gray skin, like corduroy ridges arranged in whorls and loops. There was no smell at all from the looking glass, which somehow made the situation stranger.

I pointed to myself and said slowly, "Human." Then I pointed to Gary. "Human." Then I pointed at each heptapod and said, "What are you?"

No reaction. I tried again, and then again.

One of the heptapods pointed to itself with one limb, the four terminal digits pressed together. That was lucky. In some cultures a person pointed with his chin; if the heptapod hadn't used one of its limbs, I wouldn't have known what gesture to look for. I heard a brief fluttering sound, and saw a puckered orifice at the top of its body vibrate; it was talking. Then it pointed to its companion and fluttered again.

I went back to my computer; on its screen were two virtually identical spectrographs reprenting the fluttering sounds. I marked a sample for playback. I pointed to myself and said "Human" again, and did the same with Gary. Then I pointed to the heptapod, and played back the flutter on the speaker.

The heptapod fluttered some more. The second half of the spectrograph for this utterance looked like a repetition: call the previous utterances [flutter1], then this one was [flutter2flutter1].

I pointed at something that might have been a heptapod chair. "What is that?"

The heptapod paused, and then pointed at the "chair" and talked some more. The spectrograph for this differed distinctly from that of the earlier sounds: [flutter3]. Once again, I pointed to the "chair" while playing back [flutter3].

The heptapod replied; judging by the spectrograph, it looked like [flutter3flutter2]. Optimistic interpretation: the heptapod was confirming my utterances as correct, which implied compatibility between heptapod and human patterns of discourse. Pessimistic interpretation: it had a nagging cough.

At my computer I delimited certain sections of the spectrograph and typed in a tentative gloss for each: "heptapod" for [flutter1], "yes" for [flutter2], and "chair" for [flutter3]. Then I typed "Language: Heptapod A" as a heading for all the utterances.

Gary watched what I was typing. "What's the 'A' for?"

"It just distinguishes this language from any other ones the heptapods might use," I said. He nodded.

"Now let's try something, just for laughs." I pointed at each heptapod and tried to mimic the sound of [flutterl], "heptapod." After a long pause, the first heptapod said something and then the second one said something else, neither of whose spectrographs resembled anything said before. I couldn't tell if they were speaking to each other or to me since they had no faces to turn. I tried pronouncing [flutterl] again, but there was no reaction.

25

(Iris Chang, 1968—2004)
张纯如

作者简介

张纯如（Iris Chang, 1968—2004），出生于美国新泽西州普林斯顿。1989 年毕业于伊利诺伊大学厄巴纳–香槟分校；1991 年获得约翰·霍普金斯大学写作硕士学位。曾为《纽约时报》《新闻周刊》等撰写新闻稿件。获得麦克阿瑟基金会和平与国际合作项目奖、美国华人团体年度女性奖等多项荣誉。2004 年 11 月 9 日，张纯如在加利福尼亚州自己的车内开枪自杀。主要纪实作品有《南京大屠杀：被遗忘的二战浩劫》（*The Rape of Nanking: The Forgotten Holocaust of World War II*, 1997）、《蚕丝：钱学森传》（*Thread of the Silkworm*, 1995）和《美国华人》（*The Chinese in America: A Narrative History*, 2003）。去世前，她正为第四本书《巴丹死亡行军》（*Bataan Death March*）的写作进行研究工作。

《南京大屠杀》于 1997 年 11 月“南京大屠杀”60 周年之际出版，很快登上《纽约时报》纪实文学类畅销书排行榜。它是第一部用英语全面研究南京惨剧的专著，果敢而极富感染力地讲述了第二次世界大战时期日军对中国人民犯下的恐怖暴行。作者在收集材料过程中发现的《拉贝日记》和《魏特琳日记》，与《南京大屠杀》一道，成为向世人昭示侵华日军南京暴行的铁证。该书不仅翔实地记录了日军惨绝人寰的屠杀行动，而且分析了在军国主义背景下成长起来的士兵对人类生命的漠视，深刻揭示了日军的凶残本性。作者还生动记述了南京国际安全区里德国商人约翰·拉贝、美国外科医生罗伯特·威尔逊、“南京活菩萨”明妮·魏特琳帮助和拯救中国人民的英雄壮举。南京大屠杀留给世人很多重要教训：人类文明的脆弱、权力在种族灭绝中所起的作用以及人类面对暴行时的无动于衷。

下面选文选自《南京大屠杀》第 1 部分第 4 章《恐怖的六星期》(“Six Weeks of Horror”)。日本兵以杀人为乐，完全灭绝人性。在一场惨无人道的杀人比赛中，数百名中国人失去了生命；日军对南京当地居民施加的严酷折磨也超出了人类所能理解的极限。

作品选读

The Rape of Nanking

Part I

4 Six Weeks of Horror

(Excerpt)

THE KILLING CONTESTS

Unlike thousands of hapless civilians who were bombed out of their homes and stranded on the streets of Nanking, Tang had actually secured a haven during the massacre. Then a twenty-five-year-old shoemaker's apprentice, Tang hid in the home of two fellow apprentices on Xiaomenkou, a tiny street in the northern part of the city. His friends (known to Tang as “Big Monk” and “Little Monk”) had camouflaged the doorway of their house by removing the door and filling the open space with bricks so that it resembled, from the outside, a smooth, unbroken wall. For hours they sat on the dirt floor of the house, listening to the screams and gunshots outside.

Tang's problem began when he experienced a sudden urge to see a Japanese soldier with his own eyes. All his life he had heard that the Japanese looked like the Chinese, but never having been to Japan, he had been unable to verify this. Here was a golden opportunity to see for himself. Tang tried to suppress his curiosity but finally succumbed to it. He asked his friends to remove the bricks from the doorway to let him out.

Not surprisingly, his friends pleaded with Tang not to go, warning him that the Japanese would kill him if they caught him wandering around outdoors. But Tang was not so easily dissuaded. Big Monk and Little Monk argued with him at length but finally gave up trying to change his mind. Risking their own safety, they removed the bricks from the door and let Tang out.

As soon as Tang stepped outside, he began to regret it. A scene of almost surreal horror gripped him. He saw the bodies of men and women—even the bodies of small children and the elderly—crumpled before him in the streets. Most had been stabbed or bayoneted to death. "Blood was splattered everywhere," Tang recalled of that horrible afternoon, "as if the heavens had been raining blood."

Then Tang saw another Chinese person in the street and, behind him, a group of eight or nine Japanese approaching in the distance. Instinctively, Tang and the stranger jumped into a nearby rubbish bin, heaping straw and paper over their heads. They shivered from cold and fear, causing the sides of the bin to shiver with them.

Suddenly the straw was knocked away. A Japanese soldier hovered overhead, glaring at them, and before Tang quite knew what was happening the soldier had decapitated the person next to him with his sword. Blood gushed from the victim's neck as the soldier reached down and seized the head as a trophy. "I was too frightened to even move or think," Tang remembered. "I thought of my family and knew that if I died here, they would never know what happened to me."

Then a Chinese voice ordered Tang out. "*Gun chu lai!* (Roll out!)," exclaimed a Chinese man whom Tang suspected was a traitor for the Japanese. "*Gun chu lai,* or I'll kill you!"

Tang crawled out of the trash bin. Seeing a ditch by the road, he wondered whether he should fling himself into it and attempt an escape but found that he was too frightened even to move his legs. Then he saw a group of Japanese soldiers herding hundreds of Chinese people down the street. Tang was ordered to join them. As he marched next to the other prisoners, he saw corpses sprawled on both sides of the streets, something that made him feel so wretched he almost welcomed death.

Before long Tang found himself standing near a pond and a freshly dug, rectangular pit filled with some sixty Chinese corpses. "As soon as I saw the newly dug pit, I thought they might either bury us alive or kill us on the spot. I was too frightened to move so I stood there motionless. It suddenly occurred to me to jump into the pit but then I saw two Japanese military wolf dogs eating the corpses."

The Japanese ordered Tang and the other prisoners to line up in rows on each side of the mass grave. He stood in one closest to the edge. Nine Japanese soldiers waited nearby, soldiers who presented an imposing sight to Tang with their yellow uniforms, star-studded caps, and shiny bayonets and rifles. At such proximity, Tang could see that Japanese men really did resemble Chinese men, although at this point he was too frightened to care.

Then, to Tang's horror, a competition began among the soldiers—a competition to determine who could kill the fastest. As one soldier stood sentinel with a machine gun, ready to mow down anyone who tried to bolt, the eight other soldiers split up into pairs to form four separate teams. In each team, one soldier beheaded prisoners with a sword while the other picked up heads and tossed them aside in a pile. The prisoners stood frozen in silence and terror as their countrymen dropped, one by one. "Kill and count! Kill and count!" Tang said, remembering the speed of the slaughter. The Japanese were laughing; one even took photographs. "There was no sign of remorse at all."

A deep sorrow filled Tang. "There was no place to run. I was prepared to die." It saddened him to think that his family and loved ones would never find out what happened to him.

Lost in such thoughts, Tang snapped back to reality when the commotion started. Two rows up from him a pregnant woman began to fight for her life, clawing desperately at a soldier who tried to drag her away from the group to rape her. Nobody helped her, and in the end the soldier killed her, ripping open her belly with his bayonet and jerking out not only her intestines but a squirming fetus. That, Tang believes, should have been the moment for them all to rebel, to do *something*, to fight back and try to kill the soldiers even if they all died in the process. But even though the Chinese prisoners greatly outnumbered their Japanese tormentors and might have been able to overwhelm them, no one moved. Everyone remained eerily docile. Sad to say, of all the people around the pit, Tang remembers only the pregnant woman showing the slightest bit of courage.

Soon a sword-wielding Japanese soldier worked his way closer to Tang, until he was only one row up from him. Then Tang had a stroke of luck, which was nothing short of a miracle. When the soldier decapitated the man directly in front of Tang, the victim's body fell against Tang's shoulder. In keeping with the corpse's momentum, Tang also toppled backwards and dropped, together with the body, into the pit. No one noticed.

Tang ducked his head under the corpse's clothing. His ploy would have never worked had the Japanese stuck with their original game of decapitation. In the beginning the soldiers used the heads of their victims to keep score. But later, to save time, they killed prisoners not by lopping off heads but by slashing throats. That is what saved Tang—the fact that dozens of bodies were piling up in the pit with their heads intact.

The killing spree lasted for about an hour. While Tang lay still, feigning death, the Japanese pushed the rest of the bodies on top of him. Then, as Tang recalls, most of the soldiers left the scene except for one who thrust his bayonet into the mass grave repeatedly to make sure everyone was dead. Tang suffered five bayonet wounds without a scream, and then fainted.

Later that afternoon, at about 5:00 P.M., Tang's fellow apprentices Big Monk and Small Monk came to the pit, hoping to retrieve his corpse. Through a crack in the brick wall of their house, they had seen the Japanese herd Tang and the others away and assumed that he was now dead with all the others. But when they found Tang moving under the heap of bodies, they pulled him out immediately and ushered him back to the house.

Out of the hundreds of people killed that day during the competition, Tang was the only survivor.

TORTURE

The torture that the Japanese inflicted upon the native population at Nanking almost surpasses the limits of human comprehension. Here are only a few examples:

—*Live burials*: The Japanese directed burial operations with the precision and efficiency of an assembly line. Soldiers would force one group of Chinese captives to dig a grave, a second group to bury the first, and then a third group to bury the second and so on. Some victims were partially buried to their chests or necks so that they would endure further agony, such as being hacked to pieces by swords or run over by horses and tanks.

—*Mutilation*: The Japanese not only disemboweled, decapitated, and dismembered victims but performed more excruciating varieties of torture. Throughout the city they nailed prisoners to wooden boards and ran over them with tanks, crucified them to trees and electrical posts, carved long strips of flesh from them, and used them for bayonet practice. At least one hundred men reportedly had their eyes gouged out and their noses and ears hacked off before being set on fire. Another group of two hundred Chinese soldiers and civilians were stripped naked, tied to columns and doors of a school, and then stabbed by *zhuizi*—special needles with handles on them—in hundreds of points along their bodies, including their mouths, throats, and eyes.

—*Death by fire:* The Japanese subjected large crowds of victims to mass incineration. In Hsiakwan a Japanese soldier bound Chinese captives together, ten at a time, and pushed them into a pit, where they were sprayed with gasoline and ignited. On Taiping Road, the Japanese ordered a large number of shop clerks to extinguish a fire, then bound them together with rope and threw them into the blaze. Japanese soldiers even devised games with fire. One method of entertainment was to drive mobs of Chinese to the top stories or roofs of buildings, tear down the stairs, and set the bottom floors on fire. Many such victims committed suicide by jumping out windows or off rooftops. Another form of amusement involved dousing victims with fuel, shooting them, and watching them explode into flame. In one infamous incident, Japanese soldiers forced hundreds of men, women, and children into a square, soaked them with gasoline, and then fired on them with machine guns.

—*Death by ice*: Thousands of victims were intentionally frozen to death during the Rape of Nanking. For instance, Japanese soldiers forced hundreds of Chinese prisoners to march to the edge of a frozen pond, where they were ordered to strip naked, break the ice, and plunge into the water to go "fishing." Their bodies hardened into floating targets that were immediately riddled with Japanese bullets. In another incident, the Japanese tied up a group of refugees, flung them into a shallow pond, and bombarded them with hand grenades, causing "an explosive shower of blood and flesh."

—*Death by dogs*: One diabolical means of torture was to bury victims to their waist and watch them get ripped apart by German shepherds. Witnesses saw Japanese soldiers strip a victim naked and direct German shepherds to bite the sensitive areas of his body. The dogs not only ripped open his belly but jerked out his intestines along the ground for a distance.

The incidents mentioned above are only a fraction of the methods that the Japanese used to torment their victims. The Japanese saturated victims in acid, impaled babies with bayonets, hung people by their tongues. One Japanese reporter who later investigated the Rape of Nanking learned that at least one Japanese soldier tore the heart and liver out of a Chinese victim to eat them. Even genitals, apparently, were consumed: a Chinese soldier who escaped from Japanese custody saw several dead people in the streets with their penises cut off. He was later told that the penises were sold to Japanese customers who believed that eating them would increase virility.

26

(Yiyun Li, 1972—)
李翊云

作者简介

李翊云（Yiyun Li, 1972—），出生于中国北京，1996 年在北京大学取得生物系学士学位后留学美国，在爱荷华大学（The University of Iowa）取得免疫专业硕士和艺术创作硕士学位。目前,李翊云除了是兰登书屋的签约作家外,也在加州大学戴维斯分校（University of California, Davis）任教。

李翊云的主要作品有短篇小说集《千年敬祈》(*A Thousand Years of Good Prayers*, 2005)、《金童玉女》(*Gold Boy, Emerald Girl*, 2010)，长篇小说《漂泊者》(*The Vagrants*, 2011)、《比孤独更温暖》(*Kinder Than Solitude*, 2014)，短篇小说《仁慈》(*Kindness*, 2012)，回忆录《亲爱的朋友，从我的生活写向你的生活》(*Dear Friend, from My Life I Write to You in Your Life*, 2017)等。她的作品不仅被改编成影视作品，而且荣获弗兰克·奥康纳国际短篇小说奖（Frank O'Connor International Short Story Award）、海明威基金会 / 笔会奖（PEN/Hemingway Award）等多个奖项。

短篇小说集《千年敬祈》中的作品，大多以改革开放后的中国和当代美国为背景，通过对退休教师、知青、清洁工等人物形象的刻画，再现了小人物的悲欢离合和内心世界。短篇小说集《金童玉女》主要以中国为背景，通过对单身、独身、相亲、婚外情、同性恋、代孕等题材的关注，塑造出普通人物真实的失落悲伤情绪。

《千年敬祈》选自同名小说集，通过描绘一对父女所经历的心理困境，道出了现代人内心的孤独与寂寞，从而把海外华人家庭关系主题提高到了一个新的高度。《像他一样的男人》（“A Man Like Him”）选自短篇小说集《金童玉女》。在小说中，一个退休教师通过登录女孩网站劝阻她不要控告自己父亲出轨，但是他的言语不但被人删除而且自己也遭到谩骂。无奈之下退休老师只能放弃这边的努力转而去联系女孩的父亲，希望能从道义上给他以支持。

作品选读

A Thousand Years of Good Prayers

(Excerpt)

A ROCKET SCIENTIST, MR. SHI TELLS PEOPLE when they ask about his profession in China. Retired, he then adds, out of modesty, when people marvel. Mr. Shi learned the phrase from a woman during a layover at Detroit, when he tried to explain to her his work, drawing pictures when his English failed to help. “A rocket scientist!” the woman exclaimed, laughing out loud.

People he meets in America, already friendly, seem more so when they learn his profession, so he likes to repeat the words whenever possible. Five days into his visit at his daughter’s place, in this Midwest town, Mr. Shi has made quite a few acquaintances. Mothers with babies in strollers wave at him. An old couple, the husband in suit and the wife in skirt, show up in the park every morning at nine o’clock, her hand on his arm; they stop and greet him, the husband always the one speaking, the wife smiling. A woman living in the retirement home a block away comes to talk to him. She is seventy-seven, two years his senior, and was originally from Iran. Despite the fact they both speak little English, they have no problem understanding each other, and in no time they become friends.

“America good country,” she says often. “Sons make rich money.”

America is indeed a good country. Mr. She’s daughter works as a librarian in the East Asian department in the college library and earns more in a year than he made in twenty.

“My daughter, she make lots of money, too.”

“I love America. Good country for everybody.”

“Yes, yes. A rocket scientist I am in China. But very poor. Rocket Rocket scientist, you know?”

Mr. Shi says, his hands making a peak.

"I love China. China a good country, very old," the woman says.

"America is young country, like young people."

"America a happy country."

"Young people are more happy than old people," Mr. Shi says, and then realizes that it is too abrupt a conclusion. He himself feels happier at this moment than he remembers he ever did in his life. The woman in front of him, who loves everything with or without a good reason, seems happy, too.

Sometimes they run out of English. She switches to Persian, mixed with a few English words. Mr. Shi finds it hard to speak Chinese to her. It is she who carries the conversation alone then, for ten or twenty minutes. He nods and smiles effusively. He does not understand much of what she is saying, but he feels her joy in talking to him, the same joy he feels listening to her.

Mr. Shi starts to look forward to the mornings when he sits in the park and waits for her. "Madam" is what he uses to address her, as he has never asked her name. Madam wears colors that he does not imagine a woman of her age, or where she came from, would wear, red and orange and purple and yellow. She has a pair of metal barrettes, a white elephant and a blue-and-green peacock. They clasp on her thin hair a wobbly way that reminds him of his daughter when she was a small child—before her hair was fully grown, with a plastic butterfly hanging loose on her forehead. Mr. Shi, for a brief moment, wants to tell Madam how much he misses the days when his daughter was small and life was hopeful. But he is sure, even before he starts, that his English would fail him. Besides, it is never his habit to talk about the past.

IN THE EVENINGS, when his daughter comes home, Mr. Shi has the supper ready. He took a cooking class after his wife died, a few years ago. and ever since has studied the culinary art with the same fervor with which he studied mathematics and physics when he was a college student. "Every man is born with more talents than he knows how to use," he says at dinner. "I would've never imagined taking up cooking, but here I am, better than I imagined."

"Yes, very impressive," his daughter says.

"And likewise"—Mr. Shi takes a quick glance at his daughter—"life provides more happiness than we ever know. We have to train ourselves to look for it."

His daughter does not reply. Despite the pride he takes in his cooking and her praises for it, she eats little and eats out of duty. It worries him that she is not putting enough enthusiasm into life as she should be. Of course, she has her reasons, newly divorced after seven years of marriage.

His ex-son-in-law went back to Beijing permanently after the divorce. Mr. Shi does not know what led the boat of their marriage to run into a hidden rock, but whatever the reason is, it must not be her fault. She is made for a good wife, soft-voiced and kindhearted, dutiful and beautiful, a younger version of her mother. When his daughter called to inform him of the divorce, Mr. Shi imagined her in inconsolable pain, and asked to come to America, to help her recover. She refused, and he started calling daily and pleading, spending a good solid month of his pension on the long-distance bill. She finally agreed when he announced that his wish for his seventy-fifth birthday was to take a look at America. A lie it was, but the lie turned out to be a good reason. America is worth taking a look at; more than that. America makes him a new person, a rocket scientist, a good conversationalist, a loving father, a happy man.

After dinner. Mr. Shi's daughter either retreats to her bedroom to read or drives away and comes home at late hours. Mr. Shi asks to go out with her, to accompany her to the movies he imagines that she watches alone, but she refuses in a polite but firm manner. It is certainly not healthy for a woman, especially a contemplative woman like his daughter, to spend too much time alone. He starts to talk more to tackle her solitude, asking questions about the part of her life he is not witnessing. How was her work of the day? he asks. Fine, she says tiredly. Not discouraged, he asks about her colleagues, whether there are more females than males, how old they are, and, if they are married, whether they have children. He asks what she eats for lunch and whether she eats alone, what kind of computer she uses, and what books she reads. He asks about her old school friends, people he believes she is out of contact with because of the shame of the divorce. He asks about her plan for the future, hoping she understands the urgency of her situation. Women in their marriageable twenties and early thirties are like lychees that have been picked from the tree; each passing day makes them less fresh and less desirable, and only too soon will they lose their value, and have to be gotten rid of at a sale price.

Mr. Shi knows enough not to mention the sale price. Still, he cannot help but lecture on the fruitfulness of life. The more he talks, the more he is moved by his own patience. His daughter, however, does not improve, She eats less and becomes quieter each day. When he finally points out that she is not enjoying her life as she should, she says, "How do you get this conclusion? I'm enjoying my life all right."

"But that's a lie. A happy person will never be so quiet!"

She looks up from the bowl of rice. "Baba, you used to be very quiet, remember? Were you unhappy then?"

Mr. Shi, not prepared for such directness from his daughter, is unable to reply. He waits for her to apologize and change the topic, as people with good manners do when they realize they are embarrassing others with their questions, but she does not let him go. Her eyes behind her glasses, wide open and unrelenting, remind him of her in her younger years. When she was four or five, she went after him every possible moment, asking questions and demanding answers. The eyes remind him of her mother too; at one time in their marriage, she gazed at him with this questioning look, waiting for an answer he did not have for her.

He sighs. "Of course I've always been happy."

"There you go, Baba. We can be quiet *and* happy, can't we?"

"Why not talk about your happiness with me?" Mr. Shi says. "Tell me more about your work."

"You didn't talk much about your work either, remember? Even when I asked."

"A rocket scientist, you know how it was. My work was confidential."

"You didn't talk much about anything," his daughter says.

Mr. Shi opens his mouth but finds no words coming. After a long moment, he says, "I talk more now. I'm improving, no?"

"Sure," his daughter says.

"That's what you need to do. Talk more," Mr. Shi says. "And start now."

His daughter, however, is less enthusiastic. She finishes her meal quickly in her usual silence and leaves the apartment before he finishes his.

A Man Like Him

(Excerpt)

IT WAS A few minutes after five when Teacher Fei arrived at the institute, betting that the girl's father was not the type to leave work early, since there would be little reason for him to hurry home. While Teacher Fei waited for a guard to inform the man of his arrival, he studied the plaque at the entrance to the institute. THE ASSOCIATION OF MARXIST DIALECTICAL MATERIALISM, it said, and it occurred to Teacher Fei that had his father been alive he would have said that it was the parasites in these institutes who had ended hope for Chinese philosophers.

"Please don't get me wrong. I am a serious man," Teacher Fei said to the girl's father when he appeared. "A man most sympathetic to your situation."

"I don't know you," the man said. Had Teacher Fei not known his age, he would have guessed him to be older than sixty; his hair was more gray than black, and his back was stooped with timidity. A man closer to death than most men his age, Teacher Fei thought. But perhaps he would have more peace to look forward to in death.

A stranger could be one's best friend just as one's wife and daughter could be one's deadly enemies, Teacher Fei replied, and he suggested that they go out for tea or a quick drink. A small group of workers, on their way from the institute to the bus stop across the street, passed the pair of men; two women looked back at them and then talked in whispers to the group. The girl's father recoiled, and Teacher Fei wondered if the daughter knew that her father already lived in a prison cell, its bars invisible to the people in the street.

They could go to the man's office for a chat, Teacher Fei offered, knowing that this was the last thing he would want. The father hurriedly agreed to go to a nearby diner instead. He was the kind of man who was easily bullied by the world, Teacher Fei thought, realizing with satisfaction that he had not sought out the wrong person.

At the diner the girl's father chose a table in the corner farthest from the entrance, and in the dim light he squinted at the bench, wiping off some grease before he sat down. When the waitress came, Teacher Fei asked for a bottle of rice liquor and a plate of assorted cold cuts. He was not a drinker, nor had he ever touched marinated pig liver or tongue, but he imagined that a friendship between two men should start over harsh liquor and variety meats.

Neither spoke for a moment. When their order arrived, Teacher Fei poured some liquor for the girl's father. A good drink wipes out all pain for a man, Teacher Fei said, and then poured a glass for himself, but it soon became clear that neither of them would touch the drink or the meat, the man apparently feeling as out of place in the dingy diner as Teacher Fei did.

"What are you going to do?" Teacher Fei asked when the silence between them began to attract prying glances from the diner's middle-aged proprietress, who sat behind the counter and studied the few occupied tables.

The man shook his head. "I don't understand the question," he said.

"I think you should sue your daughter," Teacher Fei said, and immediately saw the man freeze with hostility. Perhaps someone had approached him with a similar proposition already. Or perhaps that was why the young girl had sued her father in the first place, egged on by an attorney, a manipulative man using her rage for his own gain.

Not that he could offer any legal help, Teacher Fei explained. He had been an art teacher in an elementary school before his retirement. He was in no position to do anything to hurt the girl's father, nor did he have the power to help him in his situation. It was only that he had followed his daughter's story in the media, and when he had seen the family picture he had known that he needed to do something for the girl's father. "'How many people in this world would understand this man's pain?' I asked myself when I saw your picture."

The girl's father flinched. "I am not the kind of man you think I am," he said.

"What?" Teacher Fei asked, failing to understand his meaning. He was not into other men, the girl's father said, so could Teacher Fei please stop this talk of friendship? The proprietress, who had been loitering around the nearby tables checking on the soy sauce bottles, perked up despite the man's hushed voice.

It took Teacher Fei a moment to grasp what the man was hinting at. Nor am I who you think I am, he thought of protesting, but why should he, when he had long ago made the decision not to defend himself against this ridiculous world?

27

(Ken Liu, 1976—)

刘宇昆

作者简介

刘宇昆（Ken Liu, 1976—），出生于甘肃兰州，11 岁时随父母移民美国。先后在哈佛大学主修英国文学和法学专业。做过企业税法律师、知识产权诉讼顾问等，业余创作科幻小说。他的作品发表于美国各大幻想文学杂志和网站，如《奇幻与科幻小说》（*F&SF*）、《阿西莫夫科幻杂志》（*Asimov's*）、《光速》（*Lightspeed*）等。已出版《蒲公英王朝：七王之战》（*The Grace of Kings*, 2015）、《暴风雨屏障》（*The Wall of Storms*, 2016）、《星球大战：天行者卢克传奇》（*Star Wars: The Legends of Luke Skywalker*, 2017）和短篇小说集《折纸动物园和其他故事》（*The Paper Menagerie and Other Stories*, 2016）等。《手中纸，心中爱》（"The Paper Menagerie", 2011）是第一部荣获星云奖、雨果奖和世界科幻奖的短篇小说。《蒲公英王朝：七王之战》获得 2016 年轨迹奖。他还将中国科幻作品译成英文在国外发表，主编第一部中国当代科幻小说英文选集《看不见的星球》（*Invisible Planets*, 2016）。

刘宇昆善于运用东西方的双重视角观察世界，在描写技术进步影响社会的同时抒写人性的思考与关怀，作品贯穿着深邃的思想。《蒲公英王朝：七王之战》以奇幻小说的形式演绎了秦末汉初群王并起、楚汉相争的历史。作者在这部科幻史诗中融合了东方古典美学与西方科学精神，创造了"丝绸朋克"（silkpunk）这一概念；为了避免东西方交流中存在的东方主义偏见，虚构了一个由众多岛屿构成的神秘国度——达拉群岛。《手中纸，心中爱》是讲述移民家庭情感隔阂的魔幻现实主义短篇小说，探讨了每个人年少时曾经的懵懂无知，表达了情感是根植于语言之上的深刻哲理。

《刺客》(“An Assassin”)选自《蒲公英王朝：七王之战》第1部分《天下》(“All Under Heaven”)第1章。达拉群岛上乍国皇帝征服六国之后巡游诸岛，场面极为壮观。有刺客乘鸟形风筝向皇帝行刺，导致一片混乱。故事开始就暴露了表面太平的帝国其实面临着严重危机。《手中纸，心中爱》选自同名短篇小说。杰克为了融入美国朋友当中，要求家中应吃美式饭菜，还要求玩像样的玩具并收起母亲做的折纸动物，要求母亲讲英语。母亲没有任何怨言，尽力满足儿子的愿望。母亲患癌症去世后，杰克在折纸动物中发现了一封母亲用中文写给他的信，经别人念给他听才得以了解母亲的过去，了解母亲对他深深的爱。

作品选读

The Grace of Kings

All Under Heaven

Chapter One An Assassin

Zudi: The Seventh Month In The Fourteenth Year of The Reign of One Bright Heaven

(Excerpt)

The crowd's cheers rose to a crescendo.

On top of the Throne Pagoda, the emperor was seated with his legs stretched out in front of him in the position of *thakrido*, cushioned by soft silk pillows. Only the emperor would be able to sit like this publicly, as everyone was his social inferior.

The Throne Pagoda was a five-story bamboo-and-silk structure erected on a platform formed from twenty thick bamboo poles—ten across, ten perpendicular—carried on the shoulders of a hundred men, their chests and arms bare, oiled to glisten in the sunlight.

The four lower stories of the Throne Pagoda were filled with intricate, jewel-like clockwork models whose movements illustrated the Four Realms of the Universe: the World of Fire down below—filled with demons who mined diamond and gold; then, the World of Water—full of fish and serpents and pulsing jellyfish; next, the World of Earth, in which men lived—islands floating over the four seas; and finally the World of Air above all—the domain of birds and spirits.

Wrapped in a robe of shimmering silk, his crown a splendid creation of gold and glittering gems topped by the statuette of a cruben, the scaled whale and lord of the Four Placid Seas, whose single horn was made from the purest ivory at the heart of a young elephant's tusk and whose eyes were formed by a pair of heavy black diamonds—the largest diamonds in all of Dara, taken from the treasury of Cocru when it had fallen to Xana fifteen years earlier—Emperor Mapidéré shaded his eyes with one hand and squinted at the approaching form of the great bird.

"What *is* that?" he wondered aloud.

At the foot of the slow-moving Throne Pagoda, the Imperial scout informed the Captain of the Imperial Guards that the officials in Zudi all claimed to have never seen anything like the strange bird. The captain whispered some orders, and the Imperial Guards, the most elite troops in all of Dara, tightened their formation around the Pagoda-bearers.

The emperor continued to stare at the giant bird, which slowly and steadily drifted closer. It flapped its wings once, and the emperor, straining to listen through the noise of the clamoring, fervent crowd, thought he heard it cry out in a startlingly human manner.

The Imperial tour of the Islands had already gone on for more than eight months. Emperor Mapidéré understood well the necessity of visibly reminding the conquered population of Xana's might and authority, but he was tired. He longed to be back in Pan, the Immaculate City, his new capital, where he could enjoy his zoo and aquarium, filled with animals from all over Dara—including a few exotic ones that had been given as tribute by pirates who sailed far beyond the horizon. He wished he could eat meals prepared by his favorite chef instead of the strange offerings in each place he visited—they might be the best delicacies that the gentry of each town could scrounge up and proffer, but it was tedious to have to wait for tasters to sample each one for poison, and inevitably the dishes were too fatty or too spicy and upset his stomach.

Above all, he was bored. The hundreds of evening receptions hosted by local officials and dignitaries merged into one endless morass. No matter where he went, the pledges of fealty and declarations of submission all sounded the same. Often, he felt as though he were sitting alone in the middle of a theater while the same performance was put on every night around him, with different actors saying the same lines in various settings.

The emperor leaned forward: this strange bird was the most exciting thing that had happened in days.

Now that it was closer, he could pick out more details. It was . . . not a bird at all.

It was a great kite made of paper, silk, and bamboo, except that no string tethered it to the ground. Beneath the kite—could it be?—hung the figure of a man.

"Interesting," the emperor said.

The Captain of the Imperial Guards rushed up the delicate spiral stairs inside the Pagoda, taking the rungs two or three at a time. "*Rénga*, we should take precautions."

The emperor nodded.

The bearers lowered the Throne Pagoda to the ground. The Imperial Guards halted their march. Archers took up positions around the Pagoda, and shieldmen gathered at the foot of the structure to create a temporary bunker walled and roofed by their great interlocking pavises, like the shell of a tortoise. The emperor pounded his legs to get circulation back into his stiff muscles so that he could get up.

The crowd sensed that this was not a planned part of the Procession. They craned their necks and followed the aim of the archers' nocked arrows.

The strange gliding contraption was now only a few hundred yards away.

The man hanging from the kite pulled on a few ropes dangling near him. The kite-bird suddenly folded its wings and dove at the Throne Pagoda, covering the remaining distance in a few heartbeats. The man ululated, a long, piercing cry that made the crowd below shiver despite the heat.

"Death to Xana and Mapidéré! Long live the Great Haan!"

Before anyone could react, the kite rider launched a ball of fire at the Throne Pagoda. The emperor stared at the impending missile, too stunned to move.

"*Rénga!*" The Captain of the Imperial Guards was next to the emperor in a second; with one hand, he pushed the old man off the throne and then, with a grunt, he lifted the throne—a heavy ironwood sitting-board covered in gold—with his other hand like a giant pavise. The missile exploded against it in a fiery blast, and the resulting pieces bounced off and fell to the ground, throwing hissing, burning globs of oily tar in all directions in secondary explosions, setting everything they touched aflame. Unfortunate dancers and soldiers screamed as the sticky burning liquid adhered to their bodies and faces, and flaming tongues instantly engulfed them.

Although the heavy throne had shielded the Captain of the Imperial Guards and the emperor from much of the initial explosion, a few stray fiery tongues had singed off much of the hair on the captain and left the right side of his face and his right arm badly burned. But the emperor, though shocked, was unharmed.

The captain dropped the throne, and, wincing with pain, he leaned over the side of the Pagoda and shouted down at the shocked archers. "Fire at will!"

He cursed himself at the emphasis on absolute discipline he had instilled in the guards so that they focused more on obeying orders than reacting on their own initiative. But it had been so long since the last attempt on the emperor's life that everyone had been lulled into a false sense of security. He would have to look into improvements in training—assuming he got to keep his own head after this failure.

The archers launched their arrows in a volley. The assassin pulled on the strings of the kite, folded the wings, and banked in a tight arc to get out of the way. The spent bolts fell like black rain from the sky.

Thousands of dancers and spectators merged into the panicked chaos of a screaming and jostling mob.

The Paper Menagerie

(Excerpt)

My fight with Mark didn't end there. Mark was popular at school. I never want to think again about the two weeks that followed.

I came home that Friday at the end of the two weeks. *"Xuexiao hao ma*?" Mom asked. I said nothing and went to the bathroom. I looked into the mirror. *I look nothing like her, nothing.*

At dinner I asked Dad, "Do I have a chink face?"

Dad put down his chopsticks. Even though I had never told him what happened in school, he seemed to understand. He closed his eyes and rubbed the bridge of his nose. "No, you don't."

Mom looked at Dad, not understanding. She looked back at me. *"Sha jiao* chink?"

"English," I said. "Speak English."

She tried. "What happen?"

I pushed the chopsticks and the bowl before me away: stir-fried green peppers with five-spice beef. "We should eat American food."

Dad tried to reason. "A lot of families cook Chinese sometimes."

"We are not other families." I looked at him. *Other families don't have moms who don't belong.*

He looked away. And then he put a hand on Mom's shoulder. "I'll get you a cookbook."

Mom turned to me. "*Bu haochi?*"

"English," I said, raising my voice. "Speak English. "

Mom reached out to touch my forehead, feeling for my temperature."*Fashao la?*"

I brushed her hand away. "I'm fine. Speak English!" I was shouting.

"Speak English to him," Dad said to Mom. "You knew this was going to happen someday. What did you expect?"

Mom dropped her hands to her side. She sat, looking from Dad to me, and back to Dad again. She tried to speak, stopped, and tried again, and stopped again.

"You have to," Dad said. "I've been too easy on you. Jack needs to fit in."

Mom looked at him. "If I say 'love,' I feel here." She pointed to her lips. "If I say '*ai*,' I feel here." She put her hand over her heart.

Dad shook his head. "You are in America."

Mom hunched down in her seat, looking like the water buffalo when Laohu used to pounce on him and squeeze the air of life out of him.

"And I want some real toys."

Dad bought me a full set of Star Wars action figures. I gave the Obi-Wan Kenobi to Mark.

I packed the paper menagerie in a large shoe box and put it under the bed.

The next morning, the animals had escaped and took over their old favorite spots in my room. I caught them all and put them back into the shoe box, taping the lid shut. But the animals made so much noise in the box that I finally shoved it into the corner of the attic as far away from my room as possible.

If Mom spoke to me in Chinese, I refused to answer her. After a while, she tried to use more English. But her accent and broken sentences embarrassed me. I tried to correct her. Eventually, she stopped speaking altogether if I was around.

Mom began to mime things if she needed to let me know something. She tried to hug me the way she saw American mothers did on TV. I thought her movements exaggerated, uncertain, ridiculous, graceless. She saw that I was annoyed, and stopped.

"You shouldn't treat your mother that way," Dad said. But he couldn't look me in the eyes as he said it. Deep in his heart, he must have realized that it was a mistake to have tried to take a Chinese peasant girl and expect her to fit in the suburbs of Connecticut.

Mom learned to cook American style. I played video games and studied French.

Every once in a while, I would see her at the kitchen table studying the plain side of a sheet of wrapping paper. Later a new paper animal would appear on my nightstand and try to cuddle up to me. I caught them, squeezed them until the air went out of them, and then stuffed them away in the box in the attic.

Mom finally stopped making the animals when I was in high school. By then her English was much better, but I was already at that age when I wasn't interested in what she had to say whatever language she used.

Sometimes, when I came home and saw her tiny body busily moving about in the kitchen, singing a song in Chinese to herself, it was hard for me to believe that she gave birth to me. We had nothing in common. She might as well be from the moon. I would hurry on to my room, where I could continue my all-American pursuit of happiness.

Dad and I stood, one on each side of Mom lying in her hospital bed. She was not yet even forty, but she looked much older.

For years she had refused to go to the doctor for the pain inside her that she said was no big deal. By the time an ambulance finally carried her in, the cancer had spread far beyond the limits of surgery.

My mind was not in the room. It was the middle of the on-campus recruiting season, and I was focused on résumés, transcripts, and strategically constructed interview schedules. I schemed about how to lie to the corporate recruiters most effectively so that they'd offer to buy me. I understood intellectually that it was terrible to think about this while your mother lay dying. But that understanding didn't mean I could change how I felt.

She was conscious. Dad held her left hand with both of his own. He leaned down to kiss her forehead. He seemed weak and old in a way that startled me. I realized that I knew almost as little about Dad as I did about Mom.

Mom smiled at him. "I'm fine."

She turned to me, still smiling. "I know you have to go back to school." Her voice was very weak, and it was difficult to hear her over the hum of the machines hooked up to her. "Go. Don't worry about me. This is not a big deal. Just do well in school."

I reached out to touch her hand, because I thought that was what I was supposed to do. I was relieved. I was already thinking about the flight back, and the bright California sunshine.

She whispered something to Dad. He nodded and left the room.

"Jack, if—" She was caught up in a fit of coughing, and could not speak for some time. "If I don't make it, don't be too sad and hurt your health. Focus on your life. Just keep that box you have in the attic with you, and every year, at *Qingming*, just take it out and think about me. I'll be with you always."

Qingming was the Chinese Festival for the Dead. When I was very young, Mom used to write a letter on *Qingming* to her dead parents back in China, telling them the good news about the past year of her life in America. She would read the letter out loud to me, and if I made a comment about something, she would write it down in the letter too. Then she would fold the letter into a paper crane and release it, facing west. We would then watch as the crane flapped its crisp wings on its long journey west, toward the Pacific, toward China, toward the graves of Mom's family.

It had been many years since I last did that with her.

"I don't know anything about the Chinese calendar," I said. "Just rest, Mom."

"Just keep the box with you and open it once in a while. Just open—" She began to cough again.

"It's okay, Mom." I stroked her arm awkwardly.

"*Haizi, mama ai ni*—" Her cough took over again. An image from years ago flashed into my memory: Mom saying *ai* and then putting her hand over her heart.

"All right, Mom. Stop talking."

Dad came back, and I said that I needed to get to the airport early because I didn't want to miss my flight.

She died when my plane was somewhere over Nevada.

Dad aged rapidly after Mom died. The house was too big for him and had to be sold. My girlfriend, Susan, and I went to help him pack and clean the place.

Susan found the shoe box in the attic. The paper menagerie, hidden in the uninsulated darkness of the attic for so long, had become brittle, and the bright wrapping paper patterns had faded.

"I've never seen origami like this," Susan said. "Your mom was an amazing artist."

The paper animals did not move. Perhaps whatever magic had animated them stopped when Mom died. Or perhaps I had only imagined that these paper constructions were once alive. The memory of children could not be trusted.

It was the first weekend in April, two years after Mom's death. Susan was out of town on one of her endless trips as a management consultant, and I was home, lazily flipping through the TV channels.

I paused at a documentary about sharks. Suddenly I saw, in my mind, Mom's hands, as they folded and refolded tinfoil to make a shark for me while Laohu and I watched.

A rustle. I looked up and saw that a ball of wrapping paper and torn tape was on the floor next to the bookshelf. I walked over to pick it up for the trash.

The ball of paper shifted, unfurled itself, and I saw that it was Laohu, who I hadn't thought about in a very long time. "*Rawrr-sa*." Mom must have put him back together after I had given up.

He was smaller than I remembered. Or maybe it was just that back then my fists were smaller.

Susan had put the paper animals around our apartment as decoration. She probably left Laohu in a pretty hidden corner because he looked so shabby.

I sat down on the floor and reached out a finger. Laohu's tail twitched, and he pounced playfully. I laughed, stroking his back. Laohu purred under my hand.

"How've you been, old buddy?"

Laohu stopped playing. He got up, jumped with feline grace into my lap, and proceeded to unfold himself.

In my lap was a square of creased wrapping paper, the plain side up. It was filled with dense Chinese characters. I had never learned to read Chinese, but I knew the characters for "son", and they were at the top, where you'd expect them in a letter addressed to you, written in Mom's awkward, childish handwriting.

I went to the computer to check the Internet. Today was *Qingming*.

I took the letter with me downtown, where I knew the Chinese tour buses stopped. I stopped every tourist, asking, "*Nin hui du zhongwen ma?*" *Can you read Chinese?* I hadn't spoken Chinese in so long that I wasn't sure if they understood.

A young woman agreed to help. We sat down on a bench together, and she read the letter to me aloud. The language that I had tried to forget for years came back, and I felt the words sinking into me, through my skin, through my bones, until they squeezed tight around my heart.

28
(Celeste Ng, 1980—)
伍绮诗

作者简介

伍绮诗（Celeste Ng, 1980—），出生于宾夕法尼亚州匹兹堡。2002年毕业于哈佛大学；接着到密歇根大学攻读创意写作课程，获得艺术硕士学位。主要作品有长篇小说《无声告白》（*Everything I Never Told You,* 2014）、《小小小小的火》（*Little Fires Everywhere*, 2017）。处女作《无声告白》被评为美国亚马逊2014年度最佳图书，在其他数十家媒体及网站的评选中也名列前茅，荣获2015年马萨诸塞图书奖、美国图书馆协会2015年埃里克斯奖（ALA's Alex Award）等。《小小小小的火》不仅被评为美国亚马逊2017年度最佳小说，还被二十多家媒体评为年度最佳图书。

《无声告白》将华裔在美国面临的种族和文化冲突集中到一个失衡的跨族裔家庭：一心希望融入主流社会的华裔父亲詹姆斯、为追求与众不同而嫁给华人的白人母亲玛丽琳，以及父母间的理念矛盾给三个混血孩子带来的困惑和无所适从。莉迪亚在三兄妹中遗传了母亲的蓝眼睛和父亲的黑头发，被父母视为掌上明珠，同时也承载了父母最多的期望与关爱，正是这些期望与关爱逐渐变成她肩头的负担与枷锁，最终酿成悲剧。《小小小小的火》探讨了身份认同和人生选择、秘密带来的重压、母性的强烈影响以及信奉遵守规则能避免灾祸而存在的风险；同时也让我们相信艺术与善良具有变革性力量，相信即使一切遭到摧毁、变成灰烬，但仍然有新生的希望。一对夫妇收养美国华裔女婴事件引起的监护权之争打破了夏克·海茨小镇宁静的田园生活，把小镇居民分为敌对的两派。作者以敏锐的眼光揭示了家庭生活中的裂痕和居住在美国中西部亚裔的抗争。

第一篇选自《无声告白》第11章。杰克的一番话让莉迪亚夜不能寐、开始审视自己的人生：她原来一直生活在父母的期望之中，生活在恐惧之中。她决心向父母吐露自己的缺点与压力，找回真正的自我。她决定与过去做个了断，重新开始自己的人生。第二篇选自《小小小小的火》第19章。理查森家的房客米娅与她女儿珀尔的出现打破了伊奇身上的种种束缚，伊奇发现自己再也回不到过去的生活了。米娅母女的离开让伊奇明白自己的哥哥姐姐们都以某种方式利用了珀尔，不禁对他们十分生气。于是她在他们的房间里泼上汽油点起了火。

作品选读

Everything I Never Told You

eleven

(Excerpt)

Later, when they look back on this last evening, the family will remember almost nothing. So many things will be pared away by the sadness to come. Nath, flushed with excitement, chattered through dinner, but none of them—including him—will remember this unusual volubility, or a single word he said. They will not remember the early-evening sunlight splashing across the tablecloth like melted butter, or Marilyn saying, *The lilacs are starting to bloom*. They will not remember James smiling at the mention of Charlie's Kitchen, thinking of long-ago lunches with Marilyn, or Hannah asking, *Do they have the same stars in Boston?* and Nath answering, *Yes, of course they do*. All of that will be gone by morning. Instead, they will dissect this last evening for years to come. What had they missed that they should have seen? What small gesture, forgotten, might have changed everything? They will pick it down to the bones, wondering how this had all gone so wrong, and they will never be sure.

As for Lydia: all evening, she asked herself the same question. She did not notice her father's nostalgia, or her brother's illuminated face. All through dinner, and after dinner, after she had said goodnight, that one question churned through her mind. How had this all gone so wrong? Alone, record player humming in the lamplight, she dug back through her memory: Before Jack's face that afternoon, defiant and tender and hunted all at once. Before Jack. Before the failed physics test, before biology, before the ribbons and books and the real stethoscope. Where had things gone askew?

As her clock flipped from 1:59 to 2:00 with a gentle click, it came to her, falling into place with the same tiny sound. The record had long since spun to a halt, and the darkness outside made the silence deeper, like the muffled hush of a library. She knew at last where everything had gone wrong. And she knew where she had to go.

The wood of the dock was just as smooth as she remembered it. Lydia sat down at the end, as she had so long ago, feet dangling over the edge, where the rowboat knocked softly against the pier. All this time, she had never dared come so close again. Tonight, in the dark, she felt no fear, and she noted this with a calm sense of wonder.

Jack was right: she had been afraid so long, she had forgotten what it was like not to be—afraid that, one day, her mother would disappear again, that her father would crumble, that their whole family would collapse once more. Ever since that summer without her mother, their family had felt precarious, as if they were teetering on a cliff. Before that she hadn't realized how fragile happiness was, how if you were careless, you could knock it over and shatter it. Anything her mother wanted, she had promised. As long as she would stay. She had been so afraid.

So every time her mother said *Do you want—?* she had said yes. She knew what her parents had longed for, without them saying a word, and she had wanted them happy. She had kept her promise. And her mother had stayed. Read this book. *Yes*. Want this. Love this. *Yes*. Once, at the college museum, while Nath had pouted about missing the star show, she had spotted a nugget of amber with a fly trapped inside. "That's four million years old," Marilyn whispered, wrapping her arms around her daughter from behind. Lydia had stared until Nath, at last, had dragged them both away. Now she thought of the fly landing daintily in the pool of resin. Perhaps it had mistaken it for honey. Perhaps it hadn't seen the puddle at all. By the time it had realized its mistake, it was too late. It had flailed, and then it had sunk, and then it had drowned.

Ever since that summer, she had been so afraid—of losing her mother, of losing her father. And, after a while, the biggest fear of all: of losing Nath, the only one who understood the strange and brittle balance in their family. Who knew all that had happened. Who had always kept her afloat.

That long-ago day, sitting in this very spot on the dock, she had already begun to feel it: how hard it would be to inherit their parents' dreams. How suffocating to be so loved. She had felt

Nath's hands on her shoulders and been almost grateful to fall forward, to let herself sink. Then, when her head had plunged beneath the surface, the water was like a slap. She had tried to scream and coldness slid down her throat, choking her. She'd stretched out her toes looking for ground and there wasn't any. Nothing when she reached out her arms. Only wetness and cold.

Then: warmth. Nath's fingers, Nath's hand, Nath's arm, Nath pulling her back up and her head coming up out of the lake, water dripping out of her hair into her eyes and her eyes stinging. Kick, Nath had told her. His hands held her up, surprising her with their strength, their sureness, and she had felt warm all over. His fingers caught hers and right then she had stopped being afraid.

Kick your legs. I've got you. *Kick*.

It had been the same ever since. Don't let me sink, she had thought as she reached for his hand, and he had promised not to when he took it. This moment, Lydia thought. This is where it all went wrong.

It was not too late. There on the dock, Lydia made a new set of promises, this time to herself. She will begin again. She will tell her mother: enough. She will take down the posters and put away the books. If she fails physics, if she never becomes a doctor, it will be all right. She will tell her mother that. And she will tell her mother, too: it's not too late. For anything. She will give her father back his necklace and his book. She will stop holding the silent phone to her ear; she will stop pretending to be someone she is not. From now on, she will do what *she* wants. Feet planted firmly on nothing, Lydia—so long enthralled by the dreams of others—could not yet imagine what that might be, but suddenly the universe glittered with possibilities. She will change everything. She will tell Jack she's sorry, that she'll never tell his secret. If he can be brave, so sure of who he is and what he wants, perhaps she can, too. She'll tell him that she understands.

And Nath. She will tell him that it's all right for him to leave. That she will be fine. That he's not responsible for her anymore, that he doesn't need to worry. And then she will let him go.

And as she made this last promise, Lydia understood what to do. How to start everything over again, from the beginning, so she would never again be afraid to be alone. What she must do to seal her promises, to make them real. Gently she lowered herself into the rowboat and loosed the rope. As she pushed away from the dock, she expected a surge of panic. It didn't come. Even once she had rowed, stroke by clumsy stroke, out onto the lake—far enough that the lamppost was just a dot, too small to contaminate the darkness around her—she felt strangely calm and confident. Above her the moon was coin-round, sharp and perfect. Beneath her the boat rocked so gently that she could hardly feel its motion. Looking up at the sky, she felt as if she were floating in space, completely untethered. She could not believe that anything was impossible.

In the distance, the light from the dock shone like a star. If she squinted, she could just make out the dim shape of the dock itself, the pale line of boards against the darker night. When she got a little closer, she thought, she would be able to see it perfectly: the boards worn smooth by generations of bare feet, the posts that held them up just above the surface of the water. Carefully, she got to her feet, spreading her arms as the boat swayed. It was not so far. She could do this, she was certain. All she had to do was kick. She would kick her way to the dock and reach up to the planks and pull herself up out of the water. Tomorrow morning, she would ask Nath about Harvard. What it was like there. She would ask him about the people he met, the classes he would take. She would tell him he'd have a wonderful time.

She looked down at the lake, which in the dark looked like nothing, just blackness, a great void spreading beneath her. It will be all right, she told herself, and she stepped out of the boat into the water.

Little Fires Everywhere

19

(Excerpt)

Serena's house was on Shaker Boulevard, by the middle school, nearly two miles away. Forty minutes later, Serena answered the doorbell to find Izzy, breathless, on the front steps.

"What are you doing here, freak?" Lexie said, coming down the stairs behind Serena.

"I need to ask you something," Izzy said.

"Ever heard of the telephone?"

"Shut up. It's important." Izzy pulled her sister by the arm into the living room and Serena, familiar with Richardson family dynamics, retreated to the kitchen to give them some privacy.

"What," Lexie said when they were alone.

"Did you have an abortion?" Izzy said.

"What?" Lexie's voice dropped to a whisper.

"When Mom was out of town. Did you?"

"It's none of your fucking business." Lexie turned to go, but Izzy barreled ahead.

"You did, didn't you. That time you said you slept over at Pearl's."

"It's not a crime, Izzy. Tons of people do it."

"Did Pearl go with you?"

Lexie sighed. "She drove me. And before you start getting all moralistic and self-righteous—"

"I don't care about your morals, Lex." Izzy flicked her hair out of her face impatiently. "Mom thinks Pearl's the one who had it."

"Pearl?" Lexie laughed. "Sorry, that's just funny. Virginal, innocent little Pearl."

"She must think that for a reason."

"I made the appointment under Pearl's name," Lexie said. "Whatever. She didn't mind." She turned to go, then wheeled around again. "Don't you dare tell anyone about this. Not Moody, not Mom, not anyone. Got it?"

"You are so fucking selfish," Izzy said. Without saying good-bye, she pushed past Lexie into the front hallway, where she nearly knocked Serena over on her way out the door.

It took her another forty minutes on foot to reach the little house on Winslow, and by the time she got there she knew something was wrong. All the lights upstairs were off and there was no sign of the Rabbit in the driveway. She hesitated for a moment on the front walk, poking at the peach tree, where the blossoms were shriveling and turning brown. Then she went around to the side of the house and rang the doorbell until Mr. Yang answered.

"Is Mia here?" she said. "Or Pearl?"

Mr. Yang shook his head. "They leave maybe five, ten minutes ago."

Izzy's heart went leaden and cold. "Did they happen to say where they were going?" she asked, though she already knew the truth: she had missed them, and they were gone.

Mr. Yang shook his head again. "They don't tell me." He had peeked out from behind the curtains just in time to see Mia and Pearl backing carefully out of the driveway, the Rabbit piled high with bags and boxes, and driving off into the growing darkness. They had been good people, he thought sadly, and he wished them a safe journey, wherever they were headed.

A note, Izzy thought wildly; there must be a note. Mia would not have left without a good-bye. "Can I go up and check their apartment for something?" she said. "I promise, I won't bother anything."

"You have a key?" Mr. Yang opened the door and let Izzy clomp up the stairs. "Maybe the door locked?" It was, in fact, and Izzy knocked several times and rattled the doorknob before giving up and coming back down.

"I don't have key," Mr. Yang said. He held the storm door open as Izzy rushed outside. "You ask your mommy, she have the key."

It took Izzy twenty-five minutes to walk home, where—although she would never know it—Mia and Pearl had dropped off their keys just a short time earlier. It took her another half an hour to find her mother's spare keys to the Winslow house in the catchall drawer in the kitchen. She was quiet, ignoring the half-eaten carton of lo mein and orange chicken left on the counter for her, careful not to disturb her brothers or her parents, who by then had dispersed to their various corners of the house. By the time she returned to Winslow Road, it was nine thirty, and Mr. Yang—who on weekdays rose at 4:15 in order to drive his school bus route, and liked to keep a regular schedule—had already gone to bed. So no one heard Izzy come in through the side door, unlock the door to Mia and Pearl's apartment, and step inside at last, knowing deep down that she was too late, that they were gone for good.

By nine the next morning, the Richardson house was nearly empty as well. Mr. Richardson had gone in to the office to catch up, as he often did on Saturday mornings; the recent developments in the McCullough case had set him behind in everything else. Lexie was asleep across town in Serena's queen-size bed. Trip and Moody had both gone out: Trip to distract himself with a pickup game at the community center, Moody on his bike to Pearl's house, where he intended to apologize but instead—to his consternation—found a locked door and no Volkswagen. And on Saturday mornings, Izzy knew, Mrs. Richardson always went to the rec center pool to swim laps. Her mother was such a creature of habit that Izzy didn't even bother to peek into her bedroom. She was certain she had the house to herself.

It was unfair, all of it, deeply unfair: that was the one thought that had pulsed through Izzy's mind all night. That Mia and Pearl had had to leave, that they'd finally made a home and now they had been driven away. The kindest people she knew, the most caring, the most sincere, and they'd been chased away by her family. In her mind she cataloged the many betrayals. Lexie had lied; she'd used Pearl. Trip had taken advantage of her. Moody had betrayed her, on purpose. Her father was a baby stealer. And her mother: well, her mother had been at the root of it all.

She thought of Mia's house, glowing golden and warm. All her life she'd felt hard and angry; her mother always criticizing her, Lexie and Trip always mocking her. Mia hadn't been like that. With Mia she'd been different, in a way she hadn't known she could be: in Mia's accepting presence she'd become curious and kind and open, as if under a magic spell. She had felt, finally, as if she could speak without immediately bumping into the hard shell of her sheltered life, as if she suddenly saw that the solid walls penning her in were actually bars, with spaces between them wide enough to slip through. Now Izzy tried to imagine going back to life as it had been before: life in their beautiful, perfectly ordered, abundantly furnished house, where the grass was always cut and the leaves were always raked and there was never, ever any garbage in sight; in their beautiful, perfectly ordered neighborhood where every lawn had a tree and the streets curved so that no one went too fast and every house harmonized with the next; in their beautiful, perfectly ordered city, where everyone got along and everyone followed the rules and everything had to be beautiful and perfect on the outside, no matter what mess lay within. She could not pretend that nothing had happened. Mia had opened a door in her that could not be shut again.

And then she thought about the first day she'd met Mia, what Mia had asked her: *What are you going to do about it?* It was the first time Izzy had ever felt there *was* something she could do about anything. Now she remembered what Mia had said to her the last time they'd seen each other, the words that had been echoing through her head ever since: how sometimes you needed to start over from scratch. Scorched earth, she had said, and at that moment Izzy decided what she was going to do.

She had spent the night planning and now that it was time, she hardly thought at all. It was as if she were standing outside herself, watching someone else do these things. Their father always kept a can of gasoline in the garage, to fill the snow blower, and to power the generator if the power went out during a storm. With the jerry can Izzy made a neat circle on her sister's bed, then her brothers'. The gasoline made a dark, oily blotch on Lexie's flowered comforter, on Trip's pillow, on Moody's plaid sheets. By the time she'd finished in Moody's room the can was empty, so she contented herself with setting it outside the closed door of her parents' bedroom. Then she replaced the keys to the Winslow house in the catchall drawer and removed the box of matches.

Remember, Mia had said: *Sometimes you need to scorch everything to the ground and start over. After the burning the soil is richer, and new things can grow. People are like that, too. They start over. They find a way*. She thought of Mia now and her eyes began to burn and she scraped the first match against the side of the box. On her shoulder she had her bookbag stuffed with a change of clothes, all the money she owned. They couldn't be far ahead, she thought. There was still time to find them. The sandpaper grated under the match head like nails on a chalkboard and there was a whiff of sulfur and the tip flared bright, and Izzy dropped it onto her sister's flowered comforter and ran out the door.

29
(Eddie Huang, 1982—)
黄颐铭

作者简介

黄颐铭（Eddie Huang, 1982—），出生于美国华盛顿特区，就读于匹兹堡大学（University of Pittsburgh）、罗林斯学院（Rollins College）、叶史瓦大学本杰明·卡多佐法学院（Benjamin Cardozo Law School, Yeshiva University），取得法学博士学位。黄颐铭职业身份多重，除了作家之外，也是成功的厨师、美食家、律师和餐馆老板。主要作品有回忆录《初来乍到》（*Fresh off the Boat: A Memoir*, 2013）和《双杯爱：在中国追寻家庭、美食和悲伤》（*Double Cup Love: On the Trail of Family, Food, and Broken Hearts in China*, 2016）。

黄颐铭虽然像诸多早期华裔作家一样继续探究华裔题材，但他却立足一个更具广阔的当代社会视角，不仅让作品焕发出犀利的幽默感，而且借助作品直击“族裔融合”社会的痛处。本书节选的《初来乍到》就以美国当下社会为空间背景，描绘了华裔遭受的种种歧视以及华裔的自我深思历程。

作品选读

Fresh off the Boat: A Memoir

Part Two

13. Royal Huang

(Excerpt)

When I came back from Taiwan, I was on a mission. Somehow everything was coming clear, like juices dripping from a turkey timer. I saw that my interests in hip-hop, basketball, food, comedy, and writing were symptoms of a larger interest: finding a place for myself in the world or making one. School helped me give that larger interest more precise names—racial identity, social justice—and I was determined to figure it all out.

I finally felt free. For years, I knew what I wanted to do but felt guilty because I knew my parents wouldn't approve. They wanted me to be a business major, but I knew it wasn't for me. I fought them, I argued, and hated them because so much of my life was stunted due to their wants and desires. Once I understood why, I stopped reacting with anger. They were so cute and delusional trying to come up in the world using the master's tools. Luckily, I got my Audre Lorde on and realized you can't tear down the master's house with the master's tools.

Instead of living my life trying to please them, I started to jux them.

Sometimes being honest isn't good for anyone. I knew I wasn't going to give in to my parents, but I also knew they'd never understand, so I had to be a trickster. I did what I wanted to do, made a plan for myself, and kept them in the dark. I said the things I needed to say so they could sleep at night. Every semester, I'd sign up for one class that I could show them a textbook for, like marketing or business administration. On my own time, I took a ton of classes in different departments: anthropology, sociology, English, Asian studies, film, women's studies, African-American studies, and even theater. I ate the shit up. All of a sudden, I loved school. I didn't even want to get fucked-up anymore. I started to read every book I could get my hands on and joined the school paper to practice writing. I couldn't believe how long I had been kept in the dark but as I opened each book I saw there were other people like me who saw the things I saw. I gave up trying to find friends at college and befriended dead people between the margins. For years, I just didn't know how to express it but reading things like Teresa de Lauretis, Audre Lorde, Booker T. Washington, W.E.B. Du Bois, and Toni Morrison, I got it.

The most important professor in my entire life was Dr. Jennifer Henton. She was a strong black woman from Philly with a voice like Marge Simpson. All the kids at Rollins hated her. No one recommended her classes, everyone said she was difficult, and no one really got good grades in her class. But I looked at the syllabuses for her classes and thought to myself, These are all hit records! Syllabuses became like playlists for me those days. I was just into school and got mad excited thinking about all the new shit I'd learn every semester. The first class I took with her was a film criticism class with a feminist angle. At first I had no idea how I was going to relate since I still called bitches hos and hos bitches, but I signed up anyway. The class was housed in a cottage on campus with a round table in the center of the room. Dr. Henton looked like a cat lady holding an Alcoholics Anonymous session. I knew because I was taking anger management and alcohol/drug abuse classes every week as part of probation.

She was fragile and soft-spoken, but once we got into the course work, I'd never seen a woman go so hard. She changed my entire view of women. Where she saw bias, misogyny, racism, classism, and the like, she pointed it out, and never felt like she needed to curb her opinion for people when she was right. She reinforced a lesson my pops tried to teach me with his hands: NEVER EVER EVER back down if you're right. If you have evaluated all the perspectives, gone around the round table, and come back around with the same opinion, then walk right up to the offending party and tell 'em why you mad. I realized that as wild as I'd been up to that point, I still curbed my opinion ever so slightly because I was surrounded by conservative white people at Rollins.

ONCE WE HAD a debate about emasculated Asian men in Hollywood. Dr. Henton busted out a book called *Screening the Asian Male* and it made total sense, but the idea of the emasculated Asian wasn't new to me. My cousin Allen was the first to point it out to me one day when we were still kids:

"Yo, you notice Asian people never get any pussy in movies? Jet Li rescued Aliyah, no pussy! Chow Yun-Fat saves Mira Sorvino, no pussy. Chris Tucker gets mushu, but Jackie Chan? No pussy!"

"Damn, son, you right! Even Long Duk Dong has to ride that stationary bicycle instead of fucking!"

"You see!"

I never thought a professor would back me up, but Dr. Henton literally put the topic onto the syllabus! We talked for hours about how Asian men should be getting pussy in movies and I couldn't have agreed more.

THEN THERE WAS Dr. Maurice O'Sullivan. He was the longtime English chair and if not the most respected, clearly the most pugnacious. He went by "Socky," short for Socrates, and he was definitely the gadfly of Orlando Hall. You see, most professors don't engage. They start conversations, let the kids play, and referee. Dr. O'Sullivan was a different animal. He's the old dude at the YMCA that will dunk on twelve-year-olds just 'cause he can. Every class, this dude knocked me out in the first round. No matter how prepared I was, he tore me apart. If I tried to use something from Shakespeare, he would undercut me by having an equal and opposite quote from another Big Bill work. He always got me because he had a deeper well to draw from. He also had a wit and sense of humor. He was my kryptonite. Bird and Magic, Hakeem and Shaq, Yao and Dwight Mo, and Me. But I went home, thought about what Dr. O'Sullivan said, and came back every day to get my ass kicked. I remember I turned in a satire as a book report once and he said to me, "Eddie, nice try. Tragedy is easy, comedy is hard, you're not funny." I laughed and went back to the lab.

Prof O was from an immigrant family like me. He told me that back in the day, Rollins charged him with teaching African-American literature because he was black Irish. All my arguments, strategies, and opinions were old news to him. Every work I referenced was available to him. I was twenty and he was sixty-plus. He had kids, a lifetime of memories and experiences, how the fuck was I going to beat this dude? Not only was he smart like the other professors, but he had logos, ethos, and pathos. Most professors got the logos and ethos but been in the ivory tower too long to have a handle on pathos. Then I realized ... I gotta hit this motherfucker the one place he's weak and play his strength against him: age.

One of the most influential texts I read was Emerson's "American Scholar." The one passage that really stuck with me was his line about young men in libraries:

> Meek young men grow up in libraries, believing it their duty to accept the views, which Cicero, which Locke, which Bacon, have given, forgetful that Cicero, Locke, and Bacon were only young men in libraries, when they wrote these books.

That was the answer. You can't idolize and emulate forever. At some point, you gotta cut the cord and go for dolo. I thought of Locke and his idea of tabula rasa. I realized that I needed to build arguments, philosophies, and a style grounded in my era and experiences.

Dr. Henton taught me to fight without hesitation, but Prof O taught me to box. He gave me a lesson on discipline. I remember he called me a shotgun: "You have all this energy and it's unruly, but like a shotgun, you need the barrel to direct the buckshot just enough."

Those professors changed my life. I went from a punk kid that fought without a true understanding of the who, what, when, where, and why to a contrarian with a cause. I'm probably the only student on felony probation that won college awards for women's, African-American, and English studies. I won the Zora Neale Hurston and Barbara Lawrence Alfond Award in 2004. By all accounts, it was the year of the Rotten Banana. I had all them cats quoting Biggie, Lao Tzu, and Nas by the time I was gone.

Finally, after three years of learning, I got my degree but not without a hitch. The last lesson came from Professor Papay. At first, I hated Professor Papay. She kept picking on my grammar. I always had a voice, heart, and now a mind to my writing, but no grammar. Up until my last year in college, I didn't know what semicolons were for so I just didn't use them. Whether it's cooking, basketball, or writing, I was like Latrell Sprewell. If I couldn't go left, I just got really good at going right until someone stopped me. That person was Professor Papay. No matter what I did, I couldn't get passing grades on my papers in her class because my grammar was so bad. If Prof O was my first title fight, Prof Papay was my first title defense, and she came southpaw.

I basically wrote in slang and had all kinds of fucked-up syntax, subject-verb agreement, and run-on sentence issues. While the other professors overlooked my grammar and credited me for my content and perspective, Papay focused on my weaknesses. She made me a deal. I could pass her class and graduate if I went to the writing workshop. It was worse than probation 'cause I cared about my writing, yet here I was walking with my head down into the writing center. I never wanted to admit I didn't know how to speak or write English properly, so I avoided it. For years I figured it was like video games. Some characters don't have any defense or hit points, but they compensate by being really ill in other categories. Luckily, Professor Papay didn't let me slide.

The kids at the center were really cool. My tutor was this girl Emily. She didn't judge me, she liked my writing, and I could ask her anything without being laughed at. We literally had to start with capitalization because I didn't understand what was supposed to be capitalized and what wasn't. Even to this day, I can't spit out the rules, but intuitively I can "feel" what is proper grammar. I remember asking her shit like:

"Yo, so, if semicolons break up complete sentences, why don't we just use periods?"

"Because they are complete sentences, but not separate thoughts."

"Oh, like 'My Melody'?"

"Huh?"

"You know, Rakim: 'I say one rhyme and I order a longer rhyme shorter; a pause, but don't stop the tape recorder.' "

"I guess that's it ..."

"Word! I get it. Use a semicolon when you want people to think about the shit together, right?"

"Ha, ha, yeah, exactly."

That was my thing. I learned enough from class and books that I wanted to see their thoughts, rules, and concepts at play in the modern art that I related to. No matter how much Shakespeare I read, it wasn't my era. The classics gave me a foundation and skill set, but now it was my turn to write some new shit.

I started applying to English or film schools. I figured, with good grades and two major awards from Rollins, that schools might overlook my felony but it wasn't so. There wasn't one grad school that I got into.

About six months later, I was chillin' at home with my family watching the Pacers play the Pistons at the Palace. With less than a minute left in the fourth quarter, Ben Wallace drove to the bucket and Ron Artest took a hack at him. Wallace wasn't feeling it so he came back hard at Ron and threw him back a good twelve to fifteen feet. As Ron fought to keep his balance, both benches cleared, mayhem ensued, and it was Reggie Miller in a two-piece jawn fencing off Ron Artest from the Pistons. Behind Reggie, Artest lay down on the scorer's table and even put on headphones at one point just to stunt on Wallace. Things started to calm down and you figured the dust would settle, but some fan threw a large soda from right field meant for Artest. Luckily, Reggie was able to keep Artest at the scorer's table, but then more fans threw drinks at the Pacers. Within seconds, Artest ran into the stands with Stephen Jackson and started whompin' the fan that threw the drink. Or at least someone close to the fan that threw the drink.

As Artest and Jackson started walking out of the stands, another Pistons fan ran up on them and took a swing. Artest sidestepped, dodged the punch, and then stuck the dude right in the face. Meanwhile, down on the floor a fan rushed Jermaine O'Neal and he had to defend himself, too. As the whole scene unfolded, my brothers and I got mad hyped. I was always an Artest fan from his St. John's days but I couldn't stand the Pacers. After watching the Pacers dismantle these punk-ass Pistons fans, I was a fan. For years, we've seen fans in Cleveland, Philly, and now Detroit throw shit at players from the stands. Who the fuck else goes to someone's work and thinks it's OK to just make it rain with fountain sodas and beer bottles?

You hear people spit that backward logic, "Athletes make tons of money, we bought tickets and have a right to throw shit!" Bankers make money, too, but I'm not running up into Chase and throwing milk shakes at the homie selling subprime mortgages. If anyone did that and then got the shit beat out of them, there would be no question whose fault it was. But here people threw shit at the Pacers and expected them to just take it. Typical American hypocrisy in action. The incident went a good eight minutes before the first semblance of security showed up.

The next day, David Stern suspended nine Pacers without pay for 146 games and a total of $11 million in lost wages. I understood why the Pacers were suspended, but Stern not only didn't protect his players, he took no responsibility for what ensued and buried his players. It was one of the most disloyal moves I've ever seen in my life. I always hated Stern. From changing the hand-check rules to his legislation of culture to his failure handling Malice at the Palace, Stern has proven to be one of the coldest, most heartless individuals I've ever seen.

I always listened to 740 AM Sports Talk Radio in Orlando. Everyone calling into the station placed blame on Artest, Jackson, and O'Neal, but as you listened to them you could literally hear the racism oozing out of their comments. Using code like "animals," "gorillas," "punks," "no class," "ghetto," "un-American," etc., people tried to tie the incident to a deeper cultural chasm. It was 100 percent horseshit. Look, if it's "hood" to hit someone for throwing a drink in your face, move me to the projects because that's me. I wasn't raised to take a shot in the face and curl up in a ball. I wrote a letter to the *Orlando Sentinel*, making that point.

IT WASN'T ONE of my best works, but what was meant as a letter to the editor became an article on page two of the sports section on November 28, 2004. My dad freaked out. "That's my son! Eddie! You're in the paper!"

Two minutes later he came back with the newspaper and asked, "Eh! Did you get paid for this?"

"Naw, it was just a letter to the editor."

"Ohhh, so you're still not professional?"

Typical. I didn't care, though. Later that day, I got a call from the *Sentinel*. After years of writing my own mock drafts and goofy pick 'em articles in the college newspaper, the editor of the sports section wanted to offer me a job as a beat writer. I couldn't believe it. Six months after college, still on felony probation, I was about to be a beat writer for the local paper. I put on my only suit, got a haircut, did push-ups, and got into my car as fast as I could.

You opened the doors to the *Sentinel* and the first tiling you smelled was fresh ink. Huge machines thirty feet long, nine feet tall, with endless sheets of newspaper running in and out. Instantly, I could see how "newspapermen" fell in love with the life, worked over these desks for decades, getting next to nothing in return. Running around Orlando for years without a purpose, I felt like I finally found one. For the last eleven years of my life, my dad and I had read the *Sentinel* every morning despite its conservative bent. He was addicted to the sports section and here I was. It wasn't just me that arrived, it was my father, too.

I was interviewing for a lowly beat writer position covering high school basketball, but we didn't care. The whole family bugged out and it was the most important interview I'd ever have. They led me to a conference room with a contract on the table. It was a standard contract for writers that I scanned quickly and signed. About fifteen minutes later, a big white guy standing six one and roughly 230 pounds came walking in with glasses on. I'll never forget the first words he said.

"Oh, wow, that face ..."

"My face?"

"I mean ... your face. You know ... you look young, that's all."

"Yeah, I know, but you don't put the beat writers' photos in the newspaper, do you?"

"No, but no one is going to talk to you with that face. I'll try to get you some work, but I just don't know how we can make this work."

Just like that, it was over. All because of "that face."

That face ... What the fuck did he mean by "that face"? I could go on for pages trying to unpack everything he meant by that, but I won't give this cracker the satisfaction. I knew what he meant, my family knew what he meant, and you know what he meant. That was it for me. I wanted power, I wanted respect, and I never ever ever wanted anyone to tell me about my face again.

30

(Tao Lin, 1983—)
林韬

作者简介

林韬（Tao Lin, 1983—），出生于美国弗吉尼亚，毕业于纽约大学，取得新闻专业学士学位。除了为媒体撰稿之外，林韬精于多种文学体裁创作。主要作品有诗集《你就是比我快乐一点儿》（*you are a little bit happier than i am*, 2006）、《认知行为疗法》（*cognitive-behavioral therapy*, 2008），小说《咿咿咿》（*Eeeee Eee Eeee*, 2007）、《美国窃贼日记》（*Shoplifting from American Apparel*, 2009）、《理查德·叶茨》（*Richard Yates*, 2010）、《台北》（*Taipei*, 2013），小说集《床》（*Bed*, 2007），散文集《旅行：致幻剂、异化和改变》（*Trip: Psychedelics, Alienation, and Change*, 2018）等。

小说集《床》以广阔开放的视角和冷峻幽默的语言，勾勒出一幅残酷荒诞与温情真实兼具的21世纪社会风情画。长篇小说《台北》有机融合了写实、超现实主义和黑色幽默的手法，艺术再现了当代人的生活与精神状态。《爱，苍穹下的冷漠之神》（"Love is the Indifferent God of the Religion in which Universe is Church"）选自小说集《床》，塑造了一个典型的现代"宅男"形象——肖恩。经常夜晚无聊、渴望爱情的肖恩，喜欢冥思发呆，对这个世界似乎没有激情，但对某种不明爱情的期待却使他继续存活。本书节选的《台北》通过对保罗和艾琳这一对情侣日常生活的描述，反映了现代都市青年的虚无，特别表现了其对死亡问题的莫名焦虑。

作品选读

Love is the Indifferent God of the Religion in which Universe is Church

(Excerpt)

Sean had been spending his nights leisurely, with much intuition and very little actual engagement with the real world—the real world outside that was really happening. He was twenty-one. He lived with his older brother, Chris, in Manhattan, and dreamt mostly of love. These were terrible, cloying dreams. They involved prolonged moments of passion, vague and painted colors, and people sitting around in a sort of curtained and euphoric gloom, which was what love, in Sean's dreams, seemed to be. He slept in the daytime, on the sofa, and would wake, sometimes, with such an awful, spongy feeling of love—the soggy cake of it pressed against his heart like another heart—that he would then move through the apartment, the one long room of it, like a hallway gone wrong, in an unenlightened sort of searching (where was the beloved?), not touching anything, but just moving, between things (piles of clothes, the TV, the low white raft of his brother's bed), feeling husked and ancient and—sitting, then, back on the sofa—thankless, as what was there, in this cheap and witless world, to he thankful for? Not much, Sean knew. He didn't like the world, and the world had perhaps grown weary of him.

The world was weary of him!

Though probably it was not even love that Sean dreamed of, but some sleight of love, some trick of crush or inwardly thwarted desire, like a chemical seed; or else some boldly fraudulent expectation—an expectation that leads a fantasy out into the real world, gets it an apartment and, illegally, a job—as Sean had probably never been in love. He'd once told a girlfriend that he loved her, but had then felt suddenly vanquished, as if in swift and arrow-y battle, on some nighttime field; as if the world, in that moment, had thought of him, and mastered him; memorized and set him aside, like a learned thing. The world was maybe finished with Sean. And yet—he remained. Alive, doing things (eating, writing a novel, moving to Manhattan), as there was still, and always, the feeling—the suspicion— that the world knew him, and loved him, that the world was trying hard to convey this, was forming itself a language, progressing gradually, thoughtwardly, and slowly, along. Which was, perhaps, the sensation of being alive—the reason why Sean existed, kept going—the waiting of that, the faith in it, that there was a big thing of love out there, a mansion of it, and that the world, however incompetent, was trying every day to get Sean there, was thinking of where he should go, and how.

Taipei

Chapter 6
(Excerpt)

In Paul's room around 3:30 a.m., after ordering a lot of food at Lodge but eating only a little and talking calmly, then working on things a few hours on Adderall, they decided to eat psilocybin mushrooms Paul had bought a few weeks ago from Peanut. The light was off and they were on Paul's mattress, forty minutes later, when Paul began asking what Erin, who seemed reluctant to answer, was thinking. She stood and turned on the light and asked where the "bag" of mushrooms was and, because she thought she was feeling it more than Paul, fed him the remaining amount and turned off the light.

"We're choosing to not talk, which itself is a communication, which seems good," thought Paul holding Erin. "I'll continue communicating in this manner, by not." His steady, controlled petting of one of Erin's vertebra with the cuticle of his right index finger gradually felt like his only method of remaining in concrete reality, where he and Erin, and other people, shared a world. Sometimes, forgetting what he was doing, his finger would slow or stop and he would become aware of a drifting sensation and realize he was being absorbed—from an indiscernible distance, beyond which he wouldn't know how to return—and, with some urgency, move his body or open his eyes, seeing grid-like overlays on the walls and holograms of graph paper in the air, to interrupt his being taken. The effort became gradually smaller and more unconscious and, as if for something to do, in place of what was now automatic, Paul began to discern his rhythmic petting as a continuous striving to elicit certain information from Erin by responding or not responding to her rhythms, in a cycle whose goal was to produce momentary equilibriums. He felt increasingly attuned to the speed and quality of her breathing and heart rate, until he felt able to instantly discern changes in her physiology, which in entirety began to seem like an inconstant unit of unique, irreducible information (an ever-changing display of only prime numbers) that was continuously expressed and that bypassed the parts of them that allowed for deliberation or perception or intuition, beginning and ending in the only place where they were exactly together, undifferentiated and unknowable, but couldn't, in their present form, ever reach, like a tiling communicating directly with itself, rendering them both irrelevant.

Paul began to sometimes laugh uncontrollably, with his face at the back of Erin's neck, unsure what was funny. When he saw her frowning, a few minutes later, she burrowed her head against his chest and he said "what are you thinking about?" and she didn't answer and, in an increasingly incredulous voice, like he mostly wanted to express how amazingly difficult it was to know—sometimes pausing after each word for emphasis—he repeatedly stated the question. "This isn't what I expected at all," he heard himself say, at some point, without knowing what he was referencing. He'd obviously wanted something good to happen, but what was happening wasn't expected, based on what he'd said, therefore it must be bad. He was yawning, so was factually bored of Erin. "I feel like I can't breathe," he said, and suddenly stood and felt confused and unreal. He repeatedly fell onto his mattress, which every time seemed much less substantial than expected, dropping his body with increasing force and desperation, then lay on his back, unsatisfied and worried. "Sleeping, waking," he said frustratedly. "Is there a difference? Am I dead?"

"You're not dead," said Erin.

"I think I'm dead," said Paul distractedly, and covered his face with a blanket. He was thinking of how people say that when you die you experience your last moments for an eternity, when Erin yanked away the blanket and began tickling him and pulling him from the mattress as he giggled and intensely struggled, with confusion and frustration, to hide beneath the blanket. After succeeding, facedown with Erin sitting on his back, he seemed, while hidden, to not be thinking anything, then when he absently shifted to expose his face, to breathe, he believed he was insane. He asked if he was and Erin said no, which proved he was, because if he were he would ask and Erin would say he was not. He would never be sane, now that he was insane, he knew, then moved directly past that conclusion—unable to stop there, or anywhere—and believed again that he was dead and remembered hearing the word "bag" and thought of heroin and said "did we overdose?" He realized he would be alone if he was dead, even if Erin had also died—death would seal them into their own private afterlives—and, in idle correction quietly said "did I overdose?"

"I just have to deal with it," he said in reference to being permanently alone, with only his weak projections of Erin and his room—requiring an amount of effort to sustain that was immense and debilitating, which was probably why, he realized, he couldn't sate his breath, feel comfortable, think coherently—to occupy himself forever. "It's okay," he said, to begin some process of consolation, but felt only more despair and a panicked suspicion that he'd barely comprehended the terribleness of his situation. "This will go on for twenty years," he said vaguely, and stood and slapped his thighs with both hands, then held the bathroom door's frame with his arms in a V and his head hung down and repeatedly said "oh my god" while thinking "I can't believe I OD'd" and failing to view his death—the horrible, inexcusable mistake of it—as interestingly absurd or blackly comic or anything except profoundly troubling. He fell facedown on a mound of blankets and pillows and rolled onto his back, suddenly contemplative. "I don't remember that at all," he said of the months, or years, when their drug use increased and they began injecting heroin, crudely visualizing a stereotypical montage of downward-spiraling drug use. "I don't remember … that. But it must have happened … I just can't believe I overdosed."

"You can't overdose on mushrooms," said Erin meekly.

"I forgot we used mushrooms," said Paul in a curious voice, but didn't consider the information and immediately forgot again. "I think I am where you were twenty minutes ago, so you need to console me," he said while thinking "that's exactly what I would tell a projection to do if I were dead." He tried to fondly recall a memory of his life, of life generally—he would need to learn to be satisfied with his memories, which was all he had now—and said "kissing is good" and "remember Las Vegas?" He said "Taiwan was good" knowing it hadn't been, aware he was openly trying to deceive himself, then thought of tracing back his life to determine what caused the sequence of events leading to his overdose. "The book tour . . . after the summer. Two trips to Taiwan. Remember Arby's? In Florida?" He heard Erin say they never went to Florida and realized he was talking to himself while sustaining an imaginary companion and that he wasn't saying what he was thinking. "Why do I keep thinking about RBIs, runs batted in? And something about Hank Aaron?" Paul believed again, at some point, that he was in the prolonged seconds before death, in which he had the opportunity to return to life—by discerning some code or pattern of connections in his memory, or remembering some of what had happened with a degree of chronology sufficient to re-enter the shape of his life, or sustaining a certain variety of memories in his consciousness long enough to be noticed as living and relocated accordingly. Lying on his back, on his mattress, he uncertainly thought he'd written books to tell people how to reach him, to describe the particular geography of the area of otherworld in which he'd been secluded.

Paul was on his back on his mattress thinking "faces are circles," and of cutting a face into four parts, as his room slowly brightened with indirect sunlight. Erin held his hand and he stood and went with her to the window and focused on the metaphysical area where he anticipated hearing her voice, wanting to be surprised, or to hear something consoling—apportioned from himself to his projection, to ventriloquize back to himself—about death. Erin was pointing at the sky, asking if Paul saw "that tiling"—a pale, logo-like silhouette of antennae, or leafless plant, rising from a sixth-floor roof's corner, foregrounding a pink sky. Paul said he did, and that it looked pretty, he felt like a sleepy child willingly distracted from worries about a lost pet by a mother pointing at a star saying "everything will be okay, just focus on the twinkling—that's where we came from and where we'll be again, no matter what happens here, yes, I promise."

He held Erin's hand and wandered somewhat aimlessly into the bathroom and picked up a tongue scraper. "You bought me this," he said with dull, unfocused eyes. "I never used it. But I really appreciated it. I liked getting it. I never told you." He put it down and disinterestedly thought "it's not going to work," as his hand idly turned a knob, and was surprised by the rupture and crackling of water, its instantaneous column of binary variations. He moved his hand into the water and was surprised again. "I didn't expect that... to feel like that," he said with a serious expression. "That's really weird." Realizing he had no concept of what water felt like until he touched it—cold, grasping, meticulous, aware—he felt self-conscious and said he wanted to pee alone. Sitting on the toilet, with the door closed, Paul realized he felt less discomfort and could breathe easier and that the surface of things was shinier and more dimensional from greater pixilation, all of which he viewed as evidence he was successfully convincing himself—through an increasingly elaborate, skillful, unconscious projection of a reality he would eventually believe he was exploring—that he wasn't dead. With an eternity to practice, he realized, he would forget everything he had thought or felt while dead, including his current thoughts and feelings; he would only believe, as he once had. that he was alive.

He was startled, entering his room, to see Erin already moving, as if independent of his perception. He briefly discerned her movement as incremental—not continuous, but in frames per second—and, like with insects or large predators, unpredictable and dangerous. He wanted to move backward and close the door and be alone again, in the bathroom, but Erin had already noticed him and, after a pause, distracted by her attention, he reciprocated her approach. They hugged a little, near the center of the room, then he turned around and moved toward the kitchen—dimly aware of the existence of other places, on Earth, where he could go—and was surprised when he heard himself, looking at his feet stepping into black sandals, say that he felt "grateful to be alive."

图书在版编目（CIP）数据

美国华裔文学作品选：英文 / 郭英剑，付军岭，刘向辉主编．—北京：中国人民大学出版社，2018. 9
（美国亚裔文学研究丛书）
ISBN 978-7-300-26117-1

Ⅰ. ①美… Ⅱ. ①郭… ②付… ③刘… Ⅲ. ①文学–作品综合集–美国–英文 Ⅳ. ①I712.11

中国版本图书馆 CIP 数据核字（2018）第 187707 号

美国亚裔文学研究丛书
美国华裔文学作品选
总主编 郭英剑
主 编 郭英剑 付军岭 刘向辉
Meiguo Huayi Wenxue Zuopinxuan

出版发行	中国人民大学出版社		
社 址	北京中关村大街 31 号	邮政编码	100080
电 话	010-62511242（总编室）		010-62511770（质管部）
	010-82501766（邮购部）		010-62514148（门市部）
	010-62515195（发行公司）		010-62515275（盗版举报）
网 址	http://www.crup.com.cn		
	http://www.ttrnet.com（人大教研网）		
经 销	新华书店		
印 刷	北京东君印刷有限公司		
规 格	185 mm × 230 mm 16 开本	版 次	2018 年 9 月第 1 版
印 张	15.25	印 次	2018 年 9 月第 1 次印刷
字 数	304 000	定 价	58.00 元

中国人民大学出版社外语出版分社读者信息反馈表

尊敬的读者：

感谢您购买和使用中国人民大学出版社外语出版分社的 ____________ 一书，我们希望通过这张小小的反馈卡来获得您更多的建议和意见，以改进我们的工作，加强我们双方的沟通和联系。我们期待着能为更多的读者提供更多的好书。

请您填妥下表后，寄回或传真回复我们，对您的支持我们不胜感激！

1. 您是从何种途径得知本书的：

□书店　□网上　□报纸杂志　□朋友推荐

2. 您为什么决定购买本书：

□工作需要　□学习参考　□对本书主题感兴趣　□随便翻翻

3. 您对本书内容的评价是：

□很好　□好　□一般　□差　□很差

4. 您在阅读本书的过程中有没有发现明显的专业及编校错误，如果有，它们是：

____

____

____

5. 您对哪些专业的图书信息比较感兴趣：

____

____

____

6. 如果方便，请提供您的个人信息，以便于我们和您联系（您的个人资料我们将严格保密）：

您供职的单位：______________________________

您教授的课程（教师填写）：______________________________

您的通信地址：______________________________

您的电子邮箱：______________________________

请联系我们：贾乐凯　黄婷　程子殊　鞠方安

电话：010-62515580，62512737，62513265，62515576

传真：010-62514961

E-mail：jialk@crup.com.cn　huangt@crup.com.cn　chengzsh@crup.com.cn

jufa@crup.com.cn

通信地址：北京市海淀区中关村大街甲 59 号文化大厦 15 层　邮编：100872

中国人民大学出版社外语出版分社